AUBERGINE
and
THE SEVEN SISTERS

JOHN HUNTER

© John Hunter 2021

All Rights Reserved

ISBN 978-0-578-96673-1

Library of Congress Cataloging-in-Publication Data

African-American Women; Families, African-Americans; Race; Detroit; Architecture

Printed in the United States of America

Cover Photograph: Martin K. Magid, Detroit Edison Conners Creek Power Plant, Burton Historical Collection, Detroit Public Library, bh018214

My eternal gratitude for all of the women in my family and the many women who have befriended and taught me to love and explore life.

Contents

	Note	vii
I	The End is the Beginning	1
II	Leona Bevin Moore	5
III	Obra-Jean Moore	67
IV	Estyllene Baker Moore	131
V	Patricia Tobias Moore	175
VI	Augusta Post	229
VII	Clemenza Bevin Post	301
VIII	Brothers	325
IX	Ondine Dash-Mahmoud	339
X	Sisters and Brothers — The Moore Family	391
XI	Sisters and Brothers — The Post Family	429
XII	Aubergine Perry Curtis	455
XIII	Aubergine and The Seven Sisters	507
	Thanks	567

Note

In the first days of 2020, I had a vague idea for a story but couldn't begin exploring its possibilities until March when the novel coronavirus (COVID-19) world pandemic struck New York City with killing force. Hundreds of thousands New Yorkers infected with the virus sought medical treatment; tens of thousands died within a few months. To prevent additional deaths and continued spread of the virus, our governor mandated a quarantine and lockdown of all New Yorkers. The governor's edict brought most economic activity in the city and state to a halt, furloughing millions of people from their jobs and livelihood and causing permanent loss of employment and income to many more. The resulting economic shutdown created an economic collapse on a personal and public scale not seen since the Great Depression. New York City became an eerily quiet place without pedestrian or automobile traffic. To protect themselves and loved ones, family, friends, and neighbors self-isolated from one another remaining in contact only by phone or internet. Like everyone else we knew in New York City, my husband, Dr. Harold Kooden, and I stayed in our apartment week after week, month after month until June when the quarantine and lockdown were lifted.

In the midst of the pandemic and economic crisis, a bystander's video recorded the deliberate murder of a black man, George Floyd, by a white Minneapolis police officer in daylight on a busy street and witnessed by many anguished passersby. The broadcast of the video sparked public outrage across the country, including New York City. Under the banner of the Black Lives Matter movement, marches and demonstrations expressed a national revulsion to systemic racism and white supremacy in America. Only those folks in complete denial of racism and white privilege—including, sadly, the then sitting president of the United States —willfully missed these messages of protest. The president's unwillingness to address the pandemic, the economic collapse, and evidence of racism contrasted with his unilateral decision to send military-garbed federal personal to quell peaceful protests in cities whose public officials had not, in fact, requested such force. The president also exhorted citizens to ignore what was so devastatingly obvious to them in the rising death toll and economic privation. Activists perceived his actions as a cynical strategy in his own failing re-election campaign. By the time the governor's mandate brought the pandemic under control in New York allowing lifting of the quarantine and lockdown in June, the virus was spreading quickly across the rest of the country to millions of people. By autumn, hundreds of thousands had died. Commentators noted parallels of this health crisis with previous plagues, particularly the Black Death of the fourteenth century, smallpox pandemics of the eighteenth and nineteenth centuries, the Spanish Flu of the early twentieth century, and the AIDS epidemic of the late twentieth century. Much of the human devastation in the USA from COVID could have been avoided with an early and thoughtful federal, as well as local, response to the pandemic.

As these several public crises continued to unfold, the 2020 presidential election in November loomed as a decisive event in the history of the American people. The outcome, that changed administrations but continued to divide public opinion, has not yet revealed where this country is likely headed. Unlike the virus—for which there are now vaccines that may end the pandemic and permit resumption of normal life and economic activity—optimism for the future is not spreading rapidly across this country. However, with the conviction of the former police office who callously killed George Floyd, there is a sense that, for once, injustice was properly handled. In this environment and under these conditions of death, quarantine, isolation, protest, and uncertainty but also of hope and renewal, this story took shape. Leslie Martin Brown read my first draft and made several astute criticisms that helped me to re-think every aspect of this text. My husband, Harold Kooden, read a revised draft and, during several intense discussions, he expressed many profound insights that helped me to better understand my characters, their lives, and both their familial and physical environments. Needless to say, despite the observations of Leslie and Harold, any deficiencies remaining in the story fall on me not them.

After the manuscript was essentially complete, I read Isabel Wilkerson's recent book, *Caste*. Its central thesis is that caste established and reinforces the racial hierarchy of the USA. Although I could never state her ideas as clearly or eloquently, I had already woven the idea of caste through my story of black women who, with intelligence, wit, and perseverance, faced the imposition of caste upon their lives. These are the kind of women who nurtured and influenced me.

New York City, 2021

x

I

The End is the Beginning

Baby, I am here . . .

And I'll always be here with you . . .

As long as you want or need me, I'll be here.

You're never out of my thoughts or distant from my love.

After all of these years, I know you love me . . . and that's all I ever wanted.

I know now why you want me here with you, and I think you know as well. You really understand a mother's love because you're also a mother, and you know my love for you fills a place that no other love can. I've always loved you from the moment I knew you were in my body. You were not my first child but you were special to me even before you announced your presence to the world with a sharp gasp for air and a soft, trailing cry. You were beautiful—dark brown like a roasted pecan, with black, curly wisps of hair on your big round head. Your tiny fingers were perfect as were your toes. I wanted to hold you forever just as you were. I sustained your life when you sucked my warm milk. You needed me and I needed you. My milk made you grow and, as you grew, you became a lovely being that I loved completely. You came from my body but you were very different from me. I watched you grow and change, at first slowly, imperceptibly, and then more rapidly and distinctly. You were always beautiful but you soon became something more, someone I didn't understand. I think I expected you would behave like the child you appeared to be but I was mistaken. You were hard like a pecan's shell, self-contained within it, and difficult to know. When you stopped nursing, you turned to the world around you. I wanted to help you learn about the world and you humored me while ignoring me. You explored your surroundings on your own. You walked and talked very early, much earlier than your sister or brother. You became very certain of yourself and stubborn. You wanted no one's help—especially mine—in learning all that a child needs to learn. I couldn't hold you or touch you. I became frightened for you and of you. I tried many ways to regain a bond I had with you when you were born. I failed. I could only set rules for you and try to control and direct your impulses. The more I tried, the more I felt you turning away from me, resisting me. I so loved you and I only wanted to feel your love. Everything I did for you was because of my love. It has always been difficult for you to understand this about me because you never really understood me. Maybe, I didn't understand myself because, if I had, I might have loved you in a way that could have made you love me in return. I had opportunities to try but my own life's demands always beat my intentions to the finish line.

You knew me but you didn't know me. You knew me as your mother but you didn't know me as me, not the me who had a life before you, or who even lived a life with, but separate, from you. You saw me and you didn't see me. You saw a person who intruded upon your life without ever knowing who or what I was or how I became your mother. You weren't interested in me, certainly not in the way I was interested in you. By the time you reached an age when you could appreciate me as a person, not just your mother, your attention was singularly focused on yourself. That's not a criticism of you; it's only a statement of fact. You entered your teens as the main character in your own drama. Members of your family were walk-ons in that drama unfolding as your life. I wanted a bigger and more central role. I tried as best I could but I had my own drama in which I had multiple roles, none of which I could focus on exclusively. This is not an excuse; it is a fact. Each of us in our family lived our own story even as we played a role in everyone else's script. I want you to know my story and the story of every other member of our family because our stories are also your story; our dramas are your drama. We are all players in a bigger drama that has many beginnings and endings. I will tell you our stories to help you understand me but especially to help you understand yourself.

Her mother continued talking—that is, Aubergine Curtis could hear her mother's voice as she drove her car to a restaurant for her aunt's birthday celebration. The chatter of her female passengers didn't distract her from her mother's voice because Aubergine knew that what she heard her mother say was only in her mind. Her mother, Leona Bevin Moore, had been dead for several years and, when she was alive, she never spoke or said anything similar to what Aubergine now heard in her head. Aubergine knew this as fact and yet she felt this was the authentic voice of her mother. She listened carefully because her mother had a lot she wanted to say. Leona told her there were many stories to tell, some of which her daughter already knew because they were her own stories. However, there were other stories about several different women—the sisters—who were mostly members of her extended family. There were also stories of men—the brothers—also members of her extended family but their stories were secondary in importance to Aubergine. It was the women who mattered. Aubergine hoped to understand how all of these stories wove themselves into one and how her life interwove with theirs.

Although Aubergine knew she was imagining all that she heard, she couldn't explain to herself how she was hearing things she hadn't previously known. In the days, weeks, months, and years that followed the first time she heard her mother's voice—the day she was driving to the restaurant—Aubergine would occasionally find a quiet place in her house, smoke a joint, and review the stories in her mind to better understand herself and her family. Her reverie inevitably began with an early spring morning when she was fourteen years old.

II

Leona Bevin Moore

— Morning —
Spring 1957

In their modest two-story home on the east-side of Detroit, six members of the Moore family slept as the first light of dawn gradually and imperceptibly dispelled the darkness of night. A light rain pelted their house. Husband and wife and their three children slept in complete stillness in their second floor bedrooms. The breaking dawn and gentle rain awoke only one member of the family. She was the wife's mother who moved silently from her bed in a room behind the kitchen on the first floor. Her room was part of a one story addition at the rear of the two story house. Dressed in an old nightgown, terry cloth bathrobe, and wearing slippers, Clemenza Bevin Post walked slowly and carefully through the darkened kitchen, then the dining room and living room to the stair which she silently climbed to the second floor. There, in the dim hallway connecting the three bedrooms where the other family members slept, she opened the bathroom door and closed it behind her without a sound, turned on the bathroom light and attended to her morning toilet as quietly as possible so as not to wake anyone. When finished, she turned off the light, returned just as quietly down the stairs to the kitchen, turned on the overhead light, prepared coffee for the adults, toast for all, and set out boxes of cereal and a bowl of fruit for the family's breakfast. She sipped a cup of coffee with milk and sugar, ate a piece of buttered toast with strawberry jelly, then retired to her room to await indication that the rest of the family was awake and preparing themselves for their weekday routine. She was mildly alarmed that the family was sleeping late on a work and school day but dared not awaken her daughter or her daughter's family.

In the parent's bedroom, Leona Bevin Moore was dreaming of a violent summer storm. It gained intensity with terrible thunderclaps and brilliant flashes of lightning which she viewed through a window streaked with rain. She was hot and sweating as she moved away from the window in a low-ceilinged room of someone's house. She pushed her way through the room jammed with laughing young people dancing to loud jive records. As she moved through the writhing bodies, she choked on the room's smoky pungency of too many cigarettes and weed. A man reached out grasping her arm, pulling her to him, and slow-dancing close—sweaty close to her. The music and the crowd were intense. The man's hand pressed against her moist back, another massaged her butt as he ground his crotch into hers. She didn't like it. She didn't like him. He smelled foul and diseased, worse than cigarette smoke. She pushed him away but he came back and whispered in her ear—"five dollars." They were outside in back of the house under the eaves standing in a shallow, muddy puddle of water. Her shoes were soaked. It was still raining, but lightly. She could breath again. The air, though humid and hot, was refreshing. The man thrust his full weight on her, pinning her to a wall. His tongue bored into her mouth depositing a vile secretion. She gagged and coughed in his face. He gripped her crotch and pulled up her dress. She slapped him across his face and, as he pressed against her again— penetrating her. She dug her long fingernails into his back. "No," she said. "Stop." It was dark and raining lightly. There was a flash of lightning and a clap of thunder. The dog huddling nearby was watching. He didn't bark.

Leona became aware that she was dreaming but now she couldn't decide if she were fully awake or still dreaming. She thought her eyes were open but there was only darkness. She was conscious that she lay in bed, feeling heat from a man's body next to hers. She noticed a faint first light of dawn seeping in at the edges of drapes closed over a window. Naked except for his boxer shorts, the man next to her was asleep, facing away from her, breathing heavily. She stared towards the ceiling in the darkness of the room. She couldn't see a ceiling fan but she heard it whirring through the heavy, unseasonably humid air. She reassured herself that this was her own bedroom, that she was in bed with her husband, and that he was asleep. She must be awake now and not dreaming. It was raining heavily outside the house with lightning and thunder just as in the dream. She wondered if the storm had triggered that particular dream. But, as soon as she had that thought, another pressed more urgently on her mind: What time was it? She squinted at the luminescent hands of the clock on the nightstand and sat up in bed in shock and dismay.

This was a moment of reckoning for Leona. A dozen thoughts jammed her mind and prevented her momentarily from thinking clearly. She was confused. She was agitated. She tried to make calculations. She was pissed as hell. She had to make herself fully awake, fully in charge of her thoughts, and most importantly, in complete control of her still slumbering family. She had to awaken her husband and her children and speed them in readiness to begin their day. As she finally synched all of her thoughts, she set herself in motion by first admonishing herself for oversleeping. She hated to start the day like this. Shaking her husband hard to wake him, she feared the family's morning routine was already behind schedule and out of control. She called to her husband, Perry, to wake up. He barely stirred. She had to get Perry moving and out the door to his job. She had to wake their kids and send them to their schools, and she had to prepare herself to leave for work. All of this had to be done with a precious forty-five minutes lost to her oversleeping. She shook her husband again. He finally replied with annoyance, asking why was she was shoving him. Leona became annoyed as she tried to explain she had overslept and they were behind schedule. Perplexed and still drowsy, Perry wondered what time it was. Leona, growing more agitated by his sluggishness, told him it was six-fifteen. They were forty-five minutes late in starting their usual workday at five-thirty. Perry couldn't understand why the alarm didn't sound. Leona said it probably did sound but she must have turned it off and fallen into a deep sleep when she had her dream. She reminded him that, because of Henry Hatcher's birthday party which Perry had insisted on attending the previous evening, they went to bed late and didn't get a full night's sleep. Now, they were both feeling foggier than usual when they needed to move quickly to leave the house and arrive on time for their respective jobs. Leona planned her life to be orderly and punctual. She expected the same from her family. Now her carefully regimented morning was seriously behind schedule. She had much to do—too much before she could walk out the door and head downtown to her own job. Having roused her husband, her next task was to wake her kids. It was never easy to get three children moving but now haste was needed. Her first target was her son, E.J. She put on her bathrobe over her nightgown, slipped into her house shoes, and entered E.J.'s bedroom across the hallway from her own.

E.J. was sleeping lightly and responded quickly when Leona woke him. He was not surprised that it was time to get up but he didn't realize that they were late. Leona explained the situation. It was now almost six-thirty. The entire family was nearly an hour behind schedule and they all had to hurry their morning routine. Perry had to leave in less than a half hour. Everyone else had to get up, get ready, and leave shortly after him. She warned E.J. not to waste time. His father was in the bathroom. She suggested E.J. should ask his father if he could join him in the bathroom to make up time. When E.J. was finished in the bathroom, she wanted him to get dressed quickly in his school uniform and hurry downstairs for breakfast. Today, she also insisted that he not only walk his younger sister, Obra-Jean, to school but also from school home. She wanted him to get moving now and hurry because both of his sisters and Leona still had to use the bathroom after him and his father.

Leona left E.J.'s bedroom and walked next door to the bedroom her two daughters shared. She entered and approached the twin bed where her younger daughter was sleeping. Calling softly to Obra-Jean, she told her it was time to get up and get ready for school. Obra-Jean was already awake but feigned sleepiness. Barely audibly, she asked her mother if she could stay home and not attend school this day. Leona, who had leaned close to her daughter to hear her whisper, was surprised at the oddness of this request and inquired why Obra-Jean wanted to do something she never had done previously. Her daughter's reply completely confused an already preoccupied mother. Obra-Jean confessed she had not done her math homework the previous evening and had not studied for a test scheduled for this day. Leona was incredulous. Her daughter always did her homework and never failed to study for a test. Not receiving a convincing explanation, Leona told Obra-Jean the conversation was over because everyone was late getting up. There was no time for discussion. Her daughter would have to get ready for school immediately, homework or not. Her brother would escort her to school. She brushed Obra-Jean's forehead with a kiss as she ended the conversation, glanced at her elder daughter, Toby, who was still asleep in the other twin bed, and left the girls' bedroom making a note to herself to return to Toby after everyone else was on their way. She was startled to see E.J. still waiting outside the bathroom and questioned why he had not joined his father inside. E.J.

replied that his father had told him to wait in the hallway until he was finished. Frustrated by her husband's lack of cooperation and her younger daughter's strange behavior, Leona asked E.J. what he knew about Obra-Jean. E.J. said that Obra-Jean had told him she didn't do her homework or study for an exam but she didn't explain why and he didn't ask. Baffled, Leona wondered aloud why her daughter—a straight "A" student—would be so irresponsible about her schoolwork. Leona turned to the bathroom door and yelled at Perry to finish in a hurry because she needed to talk with him. The rest of the family was waiting their turn to wash up.

Perry, wearing a bathrobe over his boxer shorts, opened the door and stepped into the hallway. He glanced at his wife and son with a look of exasperated annoyance. As E.J. went into the bathroom, Leona reminded her son again not to waste time. She followed Perry into their bedroom where he proceeded to dress. As he was hurrying with fresh underwear, socks, work pants, and sport shirt, Leona wanted him to listen to what their daughter told her. Perry was not disturbed by the news but asked Leona if Obra-Jean had provided an explanation. She said that their daughter's excuse didn't make sense so Leona told her emphatically to get ready for school. Obra-Jean would have to explain to Sister Angelica what she had failed to do and hope Sister would allow her to make up her assignments. If Obra-Jean didn't maintain her grades, Leona wanted to take away all of their daughter's privileges. There would be no TV, no movies, and no visiting with her friends. While putting on his work shoes, Perry wanted to know what she wanted him to do. Leona replied that she wanted her husband to promise to back her up when their daughter inevitably came whining to him. She did not want Perry to give in to her. He promised to follow Leona's wishes. Now he had to run, get some coffee downstairs, and be on his way. He thought he could drive to work and arrive on time by seven-thirty if there were no traffic problems. Leona reminded him that her mother made lunches for the family last night and that he should get his lunch bag and not forget his umbrella because it was still raining. After work, she hoped he wouldn't waste time having beers with his buddy, Henry, because she wanted him to stop at the grocery store on his way home and get some milk, bread, and four cans of tuna fish. He agreed and kissed Leona on her cheek and left. Leona saw Obra-Jean entering the bathroom as E.J. exited. Leona waited outside of the door until her daughter was finished. She then went into the bathroom and closed the door behind her, relieved to have a few minutes to herself without her family.

As Obra-Jean dressed in her school uniform—a variation of her brother's with a white blouse and blue skirt instead of E.J.'s blue pants—she made no effort to keep quiet while her sister was sleeping. She hummed. She opened and slammed closed her dresser drawers. She dropped a shoe on the wooden floor. The noise had its intended effect. Her awakened and irritated sister, Toby, asked Obra-Jean what the hell she was doing. Obra-Jean replied with false innocence that she was simply getting dressed. Toby wondered why getting dressed required making so much noise to which Obra-Jean replied by asking why Toby was still in bed since everyone else was already up and rushing to leave. Realizing that her younger sister was provoking her, Toby said that, unlike her sister and brother, she didn't have to be at school at eight o'clock. Obra-Jean should get the hell out of their bedroom, go downstairs, and stop bothering her. Obra-Jean finished dressing, picked up her book bag, slammed the bedroom door behind her, and went downstairs to join her brother in the kitchen.

She noticed their father was gone. E.J. said their father was leaving when E.J. arrived in the kitchen. As Obra-Jean got her bowl of cereal and toast and sat at the kitchen table, she told E.J. their mother was making her go to school even after she told her mother she didn't want to go. E.J. mocked Obra-Jean because she knew their mother wouldn't let her skip school unless she had cut off a finger or poked out her eye. While Obra-Jean ate her cereal, she paused before the next spoonful, and looked at E.J. until he noticed that she was staring. "What now?" he asked. Obra-Jean spoke slowly and deliberately. She didn't like math and she didn't like her school anymore and she was going to do something about it. E.J. replied that he wasn't interested in her problems. She should stop talking and hurry up because they had to leave in five minutes or both would be late. The sisters at school did not like tardiness. Obra-Jean leaned back in her chair and said she didn't care about being late or about the sisters because she hated Catholic school and wanted to go to public school like Toby did. E.J. again stated that he wasn't interested in her problems. She was wasting time with a stupid conversation. Obra-Jean ignored him and wondered aloud how Toby managed to quit Catholic school and attend Cass Tech, a public high school. E.J. reminded her that Toby fought their mother who didn't think public schools were good enough for her kids. Their father supported Toby because, as he told his wife, Cass Tech was the best high school in the city. He said if Toby wanted to go there, she should because all of the smart kids in the city went to Cass. So, despite their mother's objections, their father gave his permission for Toby to leave Catholic school. Obra-Jean reminded E.J. that she had gotten "A's" in all of her classes so she was smart enough for Cass too. E.J. leaned forward and declared that grades weren't the issue. He and Toby also got all "A's." Their mother knew she had smart kids but she wanted them in Catholic school because they would learn discipline, order, and responsibility. More than anything, however, their mother believed in obedience. She hated that Toby rebelled with her father's consent and she was determined that Obra-Jean would not become another rebel. Obra-Jean didn't see herself as a rebel so she asked him what he meant. Growing more impatient with his sister, E.J. snapped that he never argued with their mother and always did what she asked. The thing about their mother was not to argue with her. If she said no, it was better not to fight and eventually she might agree to whatever you wanted if she thought you were obedient. Obra-Jean snapped back that their mother always let E.J. do what he wanted because he was a boy. It was unfair that their mother treated him differently from the girls. She insisted that their mother had always been more strict with the girls ever since Obra-Jean was little. E.J. ridiculed his sister by noting that she was still little. Growing angry with her brother, Obra-Jean declared that she was fourteen and would start high school next year. She was going to Cass because she didn't want to stay in Catholic school and she didn't want to be Catholic anymore. Raising her voice, she said their parents weren't even Catholic. They didn't go to any church. The only reason she could understand why their children were Catholic was because that's how they could stay in Catholic school. E.J. leaned closer to Obra-Jean and, and in a low voice, said their mother didn't care what Obra-Jean wanted because she had plans for her kids. She believed girls needed more supervision than boys, like at Catholic school, because girls could get themselves into trouble. Obra-Jean looked at him in disbelief and asked if he meant trouble, like getting pregnant. E.J. leaned back in his chair and replied he meant exactly that, and worse. Obra-Jean lowered her voice and observed that girls didn't get pregnant by themselves. She added it was not fair the way their mother treated the girls and, anyway, she knew how to take care of herself. E.J. whispered for her to shut up because their mother had just entered the kitchen.

Leona looked at the mess Perry and the children made with dishes, boxes, and bottles on the counters and table. She exploded and admonished them for not cleaning up after themselves. She accused them of being as bad as their father. The kitchen was another mess their grandmother would have to clean up. She added that the bathroom was bad enough but now the kitchen was in disarray. E.J. quickly noted that he cleaned up after himself in the bathroom. He blamed Obra-Jean because she was always the messy one in the bathroom. Obra-Jean retorted that she was always blamed even when she wasn't guilty of anything. Leona raised her hands to signal an end to the discussion. She wanted to know if Obra-Jean was ready for school and if she had her book bag and lunch. When Leona was assured daughter and son were ready, she reminded them to take their raincoats and boots so they wouldn't get wet and catch a cold. For her final instructions, she reminded E.J. not only to walk his sister to school but also to escort her home. She wanted both of them to stay in the house until their father arrived home from work. She would see them in the evening after she returned from work. Obra-Jean still had an unsettled matter on her mind and wanted to know why E.J. had to walk her both to and from school. Leona was running out of patience as well as time but decided to be blunt. She told Obra-Jean that her brother could provide for her safety and protection. Leona had heard that some hoodlums at the public middle school on the route to their school had beat up a Catholic school kid. She reminded Obra-Jean that she was a fourteen year old girl who couldn't protect herself from hoodlums. She didn't want anything to happen to her. She wanted, for now, to be on the safe side so Obra-Jean must go to and from school with her brother who was eighteen and bigger. Now, Leona wanted them to leave because she had to wake "Her Highness." Obra-Jean told her mother that Toby was already awake because she accidentally woke her when she was getting dressed. Leona accepted a kiss on her cheek from her daughter and son as they headed out of the kitchen.

After Obra-Jean and E.J. put on their rain gear and left the house, Leona climbed the stairs. When she reached the second floor, she stepped inside the girls' bedroom again. She spoke in a sharp, loud voice asking Toby if she were awake which she was. Leona announced that it was seven-twenty and past time for her to get up. Leona was late leaving for work and she wanted to be assured that the last of her children was getting ready for school. From her bed, Toby replied in a sullen tone that she heard what her mother said and that she had been awake for some time because her younger sister was extremely noisy this morning when getting dressed. Leona wanted to know why, if she was already awake, Toby was still in bed. What time was her first class at the university? Toby replied that she had Sociology at ten, Calculus at one, and Music Appreciation at three. That was her schedule for today and she had plenty of time to get ready and leave. There was no need for her mother to work herself up into a huff. She was getting up now. Looking at her sister's twin bed, she wondered why Obra-Jean didn't make it up. Leona replied that Obra-Jean didn't have time. Everyone was rushing to get ready, except for "Her Highness, the Queen of the Nile, Miss Toby." Leona mentioned Obra-Jean's inexplicable story about not doing her homework or studying for a test. In her "Mammy" voice, Toby smirked "That chile's prob'ly lyin'. She's always lyin', yuh noh." Leona was incredulous, replying that she never caught Obra-Jean in a lie. Toby muttered to herself that her mother's failure to catch her younger daughter in a lie was because her younger daughter was an expert liar. Toby then got out of bed, stretched, and tugged at her nightshirt. She started towards the door when Leona asked her if she was having breakfast before she left. Toby yawned and replied that she would pick up something on campus at the cafeteria. Leona questioned why she would buy something on campus when there was plenty of food at home; she thought that buying a cafeteria meal was wasting money. Her favorite retort was: "Money doesn't grow on trees you know." Toby replied that a cafeteria breakfast was only a dollar and fifty cents. Leona reminded her that a dollar and fifty cents was a waste of money that Toby didn't earn. Her parents were working the butts off for the money she was spending on breakfast at the cafeteria because Toby didn't earn a dime. Toby turned to her mother and replied that this was an old, tired argument. Leona retorted that Toby was damn right this the same argument because there was better food at Toby's home than the junk at the cafeteria, and her grandmother had made a sandwich for her lunch. Toby replied that she didn't need a sandwich, and that her grandmother could eat it.

Exasperated, Leona unloaded, accusing Toby of thinking she knew everything and of being "Miss Know-It-All." Toby, feeling that she had heard all of these accusations many times before and that this discussion would not resolve anything, commented that it was too early in the morning for her mother's sarcasm. She wondered if there was something important her mother wanted to say to her besides to complain and accuse. Leona declared that she was done talking. She was late and leaving for work. As Leona marched out of the bedroom, Toby told her mother in a completely insincere tone to "Have a nice day, Mother."

Leona left for work a half hour later than the usual seven-fifteen. She grabbed her raincoat and an umbrella on her way out of the front door. It was still raining lightly. She didn't want to get her hair wet which she had pressed at the beauty parlor the previous week. There were puddles of water on the sidewalk. Leona had to watch where she walked in her high heel pumps. All that had transpired that morning at home played over and over in her mind—her dream, her husband, her son, her younger and older daughters. However, Obra-Jean's behavior puzzled her most of all. She could not fathom why such a smart and good student would fail to do schoolwork that was so easy for her. Gradually, during her walk to her bus stop, she had to shift her thoughts from her family to how she would explain to her boss that matters at home delayed her usual punctual eight o'clock arrival time. She decided to mollify him by promising to make up the lost time working through her lunch break. It was three blocks to her bus stop where she caught a crowded bus headed downtown. She was lucky to find an empty seat next to another black woman. After a half hour ride, she got off at a downtown bus stop several blocks from the Cadillac Tower. That is where she worked for the Internal Revenue Service as a secretary to one of the chiefs of the Field Audit Division. She arrived at her desk at eight-thirty, a half hour late after the start of the office's business day. Her boss, a white man named Arthur Becellus, expected her to get his coffee with cream and sugar and place it on his desk which she did dutifully every work day. Today, his coffee was late, and he was irritable. He would then give her dictation, which she took in shorthand, for letters to be sent to businesses that were scheduled for tax audit. Then, she took dictation for letters that detailed results of recent audits. These two stacks of correspondence would keep Leona busy on her manual typewriter most of the day while she fielded phone calls from anxious administrators at companies that had recently received notices of an audit by the IRS. It was an endless round-robin of phone calls, dictation, and letters typed with carbon copies for various files. Leona was very good at all of this. She was a fast, accurate typist and earned her boss's praise as well as his consistently good job evaluations. At lunch time, she, like most of the secretaries and clerical staff, ate lunch at her desk. Today, as she promised her boss, she also continued working. Her mother had prepared for her a tuna fish salad sandwich with lettuce and tomato on white bread slathered with mayonnaise. Her husband had two similar sandwiches in his lunch bag; E.J. and Obra-Jean had one tuna fish salad sandwich each. Everyone also had an orange or an apple. Leona got a cup of coffee from the office coffee pot to have with her lunch; she drank it black never with cream or sugar. She seldom chatted with other clerical staff most of whom were middle-aged or younger black women like herself. It wasn't that she or the other women didn't have things to discuss; it was that they didn't want to discuss anything not pertaining to the IRS in front of their white bosses or their white co-workers. They would wait until they were leaving the building at five, the end of the workday, to hastily share news or gossip. On this particular day, Leona said goodbye to her boss and co-workers and retreated into her own thoughts as she took the elevator to the lobby and then passed through the exit to the street where she walked to her bus stop. She was relieved that the rain had finally stopped. The bus came within five minutes and was crowded. Leona stood in the aisle although a young black man offered her his seat. She politely refused out of habit of not encouraging the attention of male strangers. She was attractive—beautiful in fact—with dark skin like her mother and daughters. Although she had birthed three children, she had a trim figure sculpted by her girdle that accentuated her rounded hips and full behind. She was tastefully dressed in a black skirt-suit with a white silk, high-collared blouse, nylon stockings, and black high heels. She wore a paisley scarf—babushka-style—on her head and tied under her chin. It had protected her dark, pressed hair from the morning rain. After signaling to the man she did not want his seat, she looked off into space as if to suggest that he and everyone else on the bus were not part of her world. She had things to think about and they didn't include him or anyone else around her.

When her bus reached its stop in her neighborhood, she pushed her way through the standees to the rear exit and stepped onto the sidewalk. The May sun was still bright. She walked to the corner and turned right, passing neat rows of modest single family homes. The neighborhood was populated mostly with whites when Leona and Perry purchased their house four years previously. Now, the neighborhood was mostly black with far too many renters than homeowners for Leona's taste. The neighborhood was not quite as tidy as it had been when they first moved in. Some lawns were not meticulously tended. A few houses needed exterior repairs and a fresh coat of paint. She attributed these lapses to white absentee landlords with black tenants who either weren't invested in the neighborhood or didn't have the financial resources. When she reached the porch of her house and walked up several stairs to the front door, she could hear music inside her home—very loud music. She opened the door and a wave of sound hit her.

Damn it! Whoever has the music on, turn it off now. Do you hear me? After a moment, the house went silent.

I'm sorry, Momma. I was listening to a new song on the radio and I wanted E.J. to hear it.

Is E.J. deaf, Obra-Jean? I don't think so but I will be with that loud music.

I know he's not deaf, Momma, but he's upstairs in his room and he couldn't hear the radio unless I turned the music up loud.

Obra-Jean, don't be such a damn knucklehead. You know you can't play music that loud in this house. So, don't ever do it again. Do you hear me?

You don't have to shout, Momma. I said I was sorry.

I'm sorry too, Obra-Jean. Listen, it's been a busy day. I need some peace and quiet so why don't you just settle down and stay out of my way? Did your grandmother start dinner? Where's your father?

Dinner's almost ready and Daddy's in the backyard.

Tell him I'm home and set the table for dinner.

Is Grandma eating with us?

How in hell should I know? Ask her. Don't bother me about her.

Later that evening, everyone sat at the dining room table except Toby who had not returned from campus. Leona's mother, Clemenza, had prepared baked chicken with potatoes and green beans. Before they could eat, Perry said a blessing followed by a chorus of "Amen." Leona served everyone's plate so that the food could be properly portioned and plated. Obra-Jean asked that she not be given too much because she wasn't very hungry. Everyone ate heartily except Obra-Jean who barely touched her dinner. Although the food and conversation dominated dinner, Perry noticed Obra-Jean's uneaten food and asked her what was wrong.

Nothing, Daddy.

Nothing? Something is wrong, Sweetie. You've hardly eaten. Did something happen at school today?

Nothing happened, Daddy. What makes you think something happened?

I mean you weren't prepared for your math class today so maybe Sister said something to you. Is that right?

Yes.

Well, come on. Tell me what happened? What did Sister Angelica say to you?

She said if I do better on the next exam, she won't count today's exam.

I think that's pretty fair and generous of her. What about your math homework?

Oh, that. I finished yesterday's lesson already and today's homework too.

Then, what's the problem, Baby?

Daddy, I just don't like Catholic school anymore.

But, what does that have to do with your math class?

I don't like math. And why do I have to go to Catholic school, anyway? You and Momma aren't Catholic. Why do I have to be a Catholic?

Honey, you know we sent you, your sister, and your brother to Catholic school because we thought you'd get a better education than in public school.

But I'm the only colored kid in my class.

Honey, you've always been the only colored kid in your class for the last four years, ever since we moved to this neighborhood. Why is that a problem now?

Because, Daddy, I don't like being the only one anymore.

What's going on, Obra-Jean? Did someone say or do something to you?

No, but the other kids make me feel like I don't belong there.

When did that start? What do they say or do to you? This is the first time you've said anything about this.

The other kids have started doing things together after school and they never invite me. They don't like our music. They say bad things about colored people. They say we aren't smart or clean. They say we're lazy and make problems for everybody else. They say we don't take care of our neighborhood. They don't want to live next door to us. I don't like what they say because it means I'm not as good as they are. They don't want me in their group anyway.

Baby, you don't believe that crap, do you? You must be about the smartest kid in your class. All "A's." You live in a nice home in a nice neighborhood. Your momma and daddy both work hard. Your sister goes to college and, after your brother graduates from high school this month, he'll start college in the fall too.

Yeah, Daddy, I know they're talking about other colored people, not us. But I don't like it and I can't do anything about it. So, I don't want to be there anymore because it makes me feel bad.

Obra-Jean, Honey, you'll have to get used to people, especially white people, saying mean things to you. You're a very pretty and intelligent young girl. You'll go to college like your sister and brother and you'll have a family like ours. You'll probably have a good job someday and do even better than your momma and daddy. You're as good as any of those white kids, maybe better. There's nothing you can't do and do well. You can do anything you want in life. So, don't pay attention to those kids. You've got colored friends right here in your own neighborhood. You don't need those white kids for friends.

Wait a minute, Perry. I agree with you that Obra-Jean is as good as any of those white kids at her school. She doesn't need them as friends. But I've told you more than once, don't tell our kids they can do anything they want in life because that's just not true.

Oh, Leona. Are we really going to have this argument again? We both know things are changing for colored folks. Our kids will do things we could never dream of doing.

Perry, we don't know what gonna happen in the future. We only know what we know now. Everything else is just a dream and a dream is nothing but a dream. It's not real. Dreamers who don't understand this get hurt. I don't want my daughter hurt. I don't want any of my children hurt when other people stand in their way, and somebody will always stand in their way.

Leona, you're not hearing me. I know we grew up in a world that said colored folks couldn't have big dreams. But our kids' world will be different from ours. We can see it happening already. You read *Ebony* magazine. Our people are doing all kinds of things they never were able to do before. So, let's let our children dream. I really believe their world will be bigger and brighter for them than ours has been. The world for their kids will be even bigger and brighter. It's happening for some of us now.

Okay, Perry, you're a dreamer and always have been. Maybe because you got some breaks other colored men didn't get, you don't see the real hardness out there for most colored people. Some things may be changing for some colored people but life is still hard for most of us. It could be for our kids. Dreaming is not going to cut it for them. This world will beat them down if they dream too much or too big. Our kids have to be ready for a real world. It will tell them they are colored, and colored aren't good enough or smart enough. You just heard Obra-Jean. White kids at her school are already telling her that. So don't you say she can have everything she wants just because she's a good kid and smart. I want tough kids, especially my daughters. I want them to be ready for the real world. That means ready for the white folks' world. So, listen to me, Obra-Jean, and you too, E.J. You've got to get real about preparing yourself for the future. Momma and Daddy won't be around forever to make life easy for you. And, you can't go out in life expecting the world owes you something just because you're smart or pretty. Obra-Jean, you don't know yet what you might want in life but, whatever you decide, you must be realistic. Don't dream unrealistic dreams, Obra-Jean. They will crush you. Plan for what is real, for what we know now. Listen to your mother. I'm telling you things for your own good. Get to work on yourself because whatever you do, it's gonna be a rough road. Just don't make it rougher for yourself. Now, if you and E.J. are finished, you're excused from the table. I want to talk to your father.

Momma, since I've already finished my homework, I want to listen to music in my room. I won't play it too loud.

Okay, but first, help your grandmother to clear the table and wash the dishes. What about you, E.J.?

I've got more homework to do.

Okay. Go to your room and finish your schoolwork.

Clemenza, who sat quietly throughout the meal, began clearing the dining room table with Obra-Jean's help and removed the dishes to the kitchen. E.J. went upstairs to his room. Perry went into the den behind the dining room and sat down on the couch to read the *Detroit Free Press*. Leona joined him after seeing order restored to the dining room and kitchen. Perry put down his newspaper and turned to his wife.

Leona, is it a good idea to talk to Obra-Jean like that?

Do you mean getting real with her? Of course, it's a good idea. Somebody in this family has to know what's what. Look, we both know Obra-Jean is smart, maybe too smart. School work is easy for her and she could probably do any kind of work a white girl could do. But, she's not white. She's colored. If she sets herself too high for a colored girl, she's gonna have a mighty fall. And, if she pulls that stunt again of not doing her homework or studying for an exam, she's gonna end up cleaning white folks' houses, or worse.

Then, why did we go to all of the trouble and expense to send our kids to Catholic school for a better education? Now we're telling them don't dream of a better future?

Perry, we want them to have the best possible future for colored children which is different from dreaming they can do anything they want. A girl like Obra-Jean won't even have the chances her brother might have. As a colored girl—as smart as she is—she will never have the chances of a white girl. So, where does that leave her?

Baby, do you hear yourself? You're encouraging her to be the best. And, you're telling her she can't do everything she might want to do because she's a girl and colored. That's crazy.

It may sound crazy to you but it's the real world, Perry. You and me have never agreed on this and we never will. Maybe it's because I grew up so differently from you. I've seen how hard life can be. So let's drop it. Right now I'm more concerned about what's happening at her school. Of course, we sent her and E.J. to an all-white Catholic school because it's the best school in our neighborhood, better than those hoodlum-infested public schools.

Leona, you know damn well all of the public schools are not alike. There are good ones and bad ones. We didn't think the public schools in this neighborhood were good so we wanted to send our kids to the Catholic school. We tried not to worry how an all-white Catholic school might affect them.

E.J. has never complained.

E.J. can get along anywhere with anybody. But, Toby refused to go there. You and her fought about it for months but she wouldn't go. Do we know why?

Your daughter is hardheaded, obstinate, and disobedient because you allowed her to be that way. She decided she didn't want to do what we wanted her to do simply because I insisted she do it. You gave in to her and cut me down. I'll never forget that, Perry.

Honey, there was no point in fighting with Toby. She made up her mind. She's really like you, you know. In any case, Obra-Jean is upset and it seems like she's made up her mind as well.

Obra-Jean is just a child. What does she know? She's probably got mad at someone. I should talk with Sister Angelica and find out if she knows anything.

I'll bet Sister Angelica isn't even aware how Obra-Jean feels. Let's hold off a while and see what's going on. This might be a temporary thing.

Perry refreshed his rum and coke in the kitchen and returned to the den and his newspaper. Leona had turned on the black and white TV and, after changing the channels, couldn't find anything that interested her. She turned off the TV and picked up an *Ebony* magazine. At ten o'clock, Perry was asleep on the couch. Leona woke him to go upstairs to bed.

Perry, it's getting late. Toby never came home. Where do you suppose she is?

With her friends maybe?

What friends? Do you know her friends? Aren't you concerned when she comes home late? She doesn't tell us where she's been or what she's been doing. I don't like it. Don't you tell me again she's an adult and can take care of herself.

Leona, she's twenty and she is an adult. She can take care of herself. Why make a fuss and get yourself all upset? She's always been headstrong—just like you—and you two have been at each other for years ever since she was Obra-Jean's age. She hasn't changed and you haven't changed. What are you worried about anyway?

Perry, a young woman—especially an attractive young woman out at night—can get into trouble. What if she's someplace with someone who might force himself on her and hurt her or get her pregnant? Perry, you should know damn well men refuse to understand that when a woman tells them "no," it means "no."They think us women are always as hot for sex as they are. And, maybe, sometimes we are. But "no" is still "no." I've told Toby not to be stupid about men. If she won't be careful, I won't have her setting a bad example for her sister. I don't want her bringing me any babies to take care of. I won't do it.

Toby? Come on. She knows how to take care of herself.

What in hell makes you so damn sure? I have friends who have been raped, whose daughters have been raped, and they thought they were being careful. You can't plan for an attack; you have to be prepared and very cautious. Toby is not cautious. She thinks she can do anything anywhere at anytime. I can't convince her otherwise because you've convinced her she can. You've encouraged her to think like that just like you're encouraging Obra-Jean.

Baby, let it rest.

Hell no. Toby needs to hear from her parents—both of us.

Well, you've never been able to persuade her so I'll talk with her and let her know we're both concerned.

And when are you going to have this talk?

I promise you, I'll talk to her at the first chance I get.

Perry, if you only encourage her willfulness, you'll cause your daughter more harm than good. She must understand there are real dangers out there. Really, if you go all soft on her, she'll just be bolder because she'll think she's superwoman. And she isn't.

Leona, give Toby and me some credit. We aren't stupid, you know.

You aren't? Really? Sometimes, I wonder.

Leona, have you ever considered that men might not be a danger to our daughter because she might not be interested in men? She's never dated boys. All of her friends have been girls.

So what? There are probably other girls her age who aren't interested in boys yet.

What I mean is you may be worrying about nothing. Leona, she's twenty. If an attractive woman her age is not interested in men, I don't think she'll ever date or get married to a man.

Of course, she will. You'll see. You need to cut back on your rum and coke, Sweetheart. It's affecting your thinking.

And you need to stop denying the obvious. Toby is like your sister.

And what does that mean?

Has Augusta ever had a serious interest in men?

She's had several boyfriends.

My god, Baby, the woman is in her thirties. When was the last time she had a boyfriend?

I don't know. A few years ago.

How about ten years ago? And that doesn't suggest anything to you?

Perry, she hasn't found the right man.

I don't think she's looking for the right man.

You're wrong about my sister. I know her better than you do.

Just like you know your daughters better than me.

Leona dismissed Perry with a wave of her hand and headed upstairs to bed. Perry followed her a half hour later. Both were asleep by ten-thirty. Stillness embraced the Moore household except for Clemenza who sat on her bed and stared out the window into the darkness of the backyard. Moonlight illuminated the leaves on the trees. A dog barked. The moon disappeared behind clouds. All was dark. Clemenza lay back on her bed and brought her hand up to her face. She closed her eyes and finally fell asleep. The next morning, the household was up on schedule and their routine began anew.

Perry, it's time to get up.

It's five-thirty?

Yes, the alarm just sounded. Let's get moving. Go wash and dress. Clemenza will have some coffee and toast for you. I'll get the kids up. Last night, Clemenza made you a couple of ham and cheese sandwiches for lunch.

With mustard?

Of course.

Following her usual routine, Leona awakened E.J. first. He was sleeping soundly. Leona noted that his room had a funny odor. She made a note to herself to tell Clemenza to clean E.J.'s room and see if she could rid it of that odor.

Wake up, E.J. It's time to get up.

I was really having a good sleep.

Good for you, but it's time to get up and get going. As soon as your father finishes in the bathroom, it's your turn to go in and wash. Don't take all day.

Can I have hot oatmeal for breakfast?

You can if your grandmother will fix it. You'll have to tell her. Now get up.

Moving on to the girl's room, Leona sniffed to see if she could detect any odd odors. Noting none, she did see a lot of clutter—dirty clothes, magazines, papers, an empty bottle of soda pop. She must tell Clemenza to clean the girls' room as well. Leona walked over to Obra-Jean's bed and awakened her.

Obra-Jean, wake up, Honey. Time to get up and get ready for school.

Can't I sleep a little longer?

No. Get up now. Are you ready for school today?

Yes, Momma.

Well, get up. When your father and brother finish in the bathroom, you're next. Where's Toby? What the hell? She's not in her bed. Didn't she come home last night?

I didn't hear her come into the room.

Shit. Get up now. I have to talk to your father about his daughter. This family is getting out of control.

Leona went to bathroom to talk to Perry who was shaving. She entered without knocking. Perry stood before the bathroom mirror over the sink. He turned slightly to see Leona as she entered and waited for her to speak. Since she seldom interrupted him while he was in the bathroom, he prepared himself for some bad news.

27

Perry, I don't think Toby came home last night.

What?

She's not in her bed, and Obra-Jean says she didn't hear her come into the room last night.

She could have come home after we all went to sleep and left early this morning.

I don't think so. Toby? Are you kidding? Not this early. That doesn't sound like something she would do since she usually sleeps later than all of us.

Maybe, she decided to stay overnight with one of her college friends.

Who are these friends you keep mentioning? I've never met any of them. Have you?

I'm just guessing. I don't know who her friends are but I think she must have some.

Perry, this is exactly what I didn't want to happen—us not knowing what she's doing; if she's okay; if she's in some kind of trouble, or unable to contact us. I don't like this. I can't live with this kind of behavior. I don't want to constantly worry about her. She's irresponsible and inconsiderate of us. All of my friends who have adult daughters are having the same worries but I don't want to be one of them. As I've been saying, this new freedom for our daughters to do whatever they want is not good.

Calm down, Honey. We'll hear from her. She probably didn't think we would mind if she stayed with a friend overnight. She'll be home, and we'll hear what happened. Stay calm.

Perry, how can you be so damn blasé—so "Nothing's wrong; there's nothing to worry about." That's how someone thinks whose brain is full of booze.

Can you lay off my drinking, Leona? I work hard every day and need something to help me relax in the evening since you don't do anything anymore to help me relax.

Let's stick to the case.

Are you really concerned for Toby's safety or is it something else? You puzzle me, Leona. Frankly, Baby, in my opinion you want our daughters to follow your vision of life. That's how I see it. Toby hasn't made any really bad choices so far. Obra-Jean, on the other hand, still lives in a fourteen year-old's world. We have to be more concerned about her because of her age. But she's smart and I think she'll find her way. I say, her way; it might not be your way. Let the girls have as much freedom to make their own lives as we give our son.

Damn it, Perry, you know boys have a different life than girls. I've got to raise two girls and raise them so they'll survive in this world. They don't have the choices or advantages boys have. They won't be treated like boys. Their path is harder, much harder and much more limited. You only see things from a man's point of view. I know what women face in life. I want my daughters to know what they'll face and be prepared to deal with it. If you continue to treat them as if they're Princess Grace, they'll face certain ruin. This white world doesn't have a place for colored princesses.

I love our girls as much as you do, Leona, and I want them to have a good life. But, I'm willing to let them find out for themselves who they are and what they want. I don't want to box them in with my fears and disappointments. That's what I think you're doing.

Oh, now it's my fears and disappointments? And what would that be, Mister Psychiatrist?

You know as well as I do the biggest influence on your life has been Clemenza. Everything about you comes from her. Your life has been shaped by her. You're putting your experiences and insecurities on our girls because of the effect Clemenza's had on you. I've lived with you for over twenty years, Leona. I've made my peace with your fears but I don't want you to make these girls fearful like you.

Then, you're a bigger fool than I thought, Perry Moore. What you call my "fears and disappointments" are lessons I've learned the hard way. I don't want my children to have to learn those lessons. I can warn them. I can show them. I can prepare them. If I do that from my own fears and disappointments, then I believe it's a good thing for them.

And I don't.

Well, we'll just have to battle this one out.

Leona, I can't argue this now. I have to get dressed, grab some coffee, and leave for work. Call me if you hear anything.

So, you're leaving all of this for me? Well, isn't that typical? Well, go ahead. Go to work while I worry about "our" daughter. Don't forget to take your umbrella. It's raining again this morning.

Call me when you hear something. I'm finished in here. Excuse me.

Leona watched Perry as he exited the bathroom. Knowing she would be very late for work, Leona decided to call her office at eight o'clock when she knew her boss would be at his desk. She surveyed the mess Perry left in the bathroom and decided to tell Clemenza to clean the entire second floor. She then headed to the kitchen. Clemenza was setting out breakfast for the rest of the family. Leona issued her directive and dismissed her by telling her to go to her room. Leona would take care of breakfast and busied herself by making oatmeal and taking laundry to the basement while hoping to hear from Toby. While she was sorting laundry in the basement, Perry passed through the kitchen, quickly drank a cup of coffee, grabbed his lunch bag, and left the house without an umbrella. Later, E.J. and Obra-Jean came down for breakfast, ate some oatmeal and toast, and gathered their lunches and schoolbags. They put on their raincoats and boots and said goodbye to Leona as she passed through the kitchen from the basement. Almost as soon as they left, the phone rang. She answered "Hello."

Mother, it's me.

Toby? Where in hell are you? Where have you been and why didn't you come home last night? Why didn't you call? You've upset your father and me with your inconsiderate and immature behavior. What's the matter with you?

Nothing is the matter with me, Mother. I wanted to stay the night with a friend and I did.

Who did you stay with last night?

A girlfriend from school.

What girlfriend? Where?

At the apartment of a girl in my calculus class.

Where is that? What were you thinking?

I was thinking I'm an adult and I can stay with a friend without asking my parents' permission. My friend has an apartment near campus.

You call this acting like an adult?

Yes, I do.

Bullshit! You think you're old enough to take care of yourself? Up until now you've behaved more like a spoiled child than an adult. That's not how I raised you. I'm your mother and I'm concerned about your well-being.

Calm down, Mother. I'm fine. Nothing has happened. What are you so upset about?

Why am I upset? Are you kidding me?

Mother, I don't know why you're reacting like this?

Really, Toby? You think you're behaving like an adult? Listen, you're still living in your parents' home. We pay for your school. We buy your clothes and everything else you want or need. We take care of everything for you so that you can sleep all morning and—when you feel like it—go to school that we pay for. So, you don't need to have a job like me and your father. You can stay out till all hours of the night, doing whatever you do with god knows who, and not have to answer any of our questions about where you've been, who you were with, or what you were doing. You can take care of yourself? Well, why don't you start now? You're twenty. You can go to school and work to pay for it yourself. Then you can get up when you please, eat what you want when you want it, and do whatever without me asking you all of these questions or making demands on you. If you could do these things, then you would qualify as an adult.

Mother, you and Daddy decided to pay for my school. Any money you spend on me you decided on your own. I didn't ask you to do what you do.

I didn't hear you object either. Listen to me, Toby, if you want to keep on living in this house, you're going to have to answer to me and your father. Period. If you want to do whatever it is you want to do without our questions and rules, then start your own life now somewhere else.

Mother, why is it in order to live with you, I have to do everything the way you want? I'm not thinking about living on my own now but I could do it if I decided to.

Oh. You're not ready to live on your own. I see. But, you want to live in your parents' home but not respect our wishes.

I don't want to continue arguing about this over the phone. Can we talk when I get home? I've got to change and be back on campus in time for my one o'clock class.

Okay. I'll expect you here in the next hour and when your father comes home this evening, we'll all have a conversation together.

Fine, Mother. Goodbye.

Yes. Goodbye.

Leona realized that she had not been to the bathroom. She climbed the stairs, opened the bathroom door and again surveyed the disarray of towels and toiletries left by her family. She took off her bathrobe and nightgown and stood naked in front of the full-length mirror attached to the bathroom door. She looked at her still supple body. It was mahogany dark and smooth. Her breasts were still shapely despite having nursed three babies. After forty-one years and three pregnancies—four counting an abortion—she saw what men saw—a desirable, sexually experienced woman. She cupped her hands over her crotch and turned her head up towards the ceiling as tears rained down her cheeks. At eight o'clock, after having breakfast in the kitchen, she decided to call her boss at work.

Hello, Mister Becellus. Yes, this is Leona Moore. I'll have to take a personal day of leave. We're having a family issue here and I need to stay home until it's settled.

I'm sorry, Leona. Is it serious?

No, nothing serious has happened but our oldest daughter didn't come home last night and she just called. I need to talk with her when she comes home.

Okay. I've got a lot of work that needs typing. I'll get a girl from the office steno pool to do it.

Thank you. I'll let you know when I'll return to work as soon as I hear from her. And, I'll catch up on any work you have for me when I return.

That's okay. Good luck, Leona.

Yes. Goodbye Mister Becellus.

As she finished her phone call, Leona's mother entered the kitchen from her bedroom. After hanging up the phone, Leona seated herself at the kitchen table with a cup of coffee. Her mother took a cup from the cupboard and poured herself some coffee, adding milk and sugar from containers on the kitchen counter and seated herself at the table opposite Leona.

Good morning, Leona.

Good morning, Clemenza. How long have you been up?

Since about five. That was another terrible storm early this morning. It woke me up and it's still raining. This spring has been really wet.

Yeah, I know. Did you eat something?

I had coffee and toast before all of you got up.

Do you want me to fix you something eat?

I'm not hungry now. Maybe I'll have something later.

I won't have time to fix you anything later, Clemenza. So, if you're hungry, you'd better have something now.

I don't want anything now and I don't want to bother you.

I didn't say you were bothering me. Do you want to read the newspaper?

Maybe, later.

Later? Clemenza, why is everything always later?

I said I don't want to bother you.

And, I just told you you're not bothering me. I just want to know if you want something or not. Don't make a big goddam deal out of it.

I'm not making a big deal, Leona. You have so much on your mind, I don't want to add to your troubles. I really don't want anything. You don't have to let it upset you just because I don't want anything.

Fine. I'm just trying to be helpful.

How come you're home today? Is something wrong?

It's Toby. Your granddaughter stayed out all night and didn't let us know. She just called to tell me she's on her way home within the hour. I told my boss I would take a personal leave day to stay home. I need to have a serious talk with Toby.

Leona, she should have called you last night to let you know where she was.

Of course she should have called. Isn't that obvious? She really upset me. She's so inconsiderate.

Leona, she's still young. Don't get too upset with her. She's a good girl.

Clemenza, you know damn well how "good girls" can get into a lot of trouble. I'm her mother and it's my responsibility to see she doesn't make any foolish mistakes. I don't need you to tell me how to raise my daughter. You, of all people.

We all make foolish mistakes, Leona, even when our mothers try to warn us. I've made lots of mistakes.

Well, that's the truth.

I admit it and I wouldn't blame you or Toby for any mistakes.

Some mistakes are forever, Clemenza.

Yes, I know.

You should. Listen, I want you to clean the rooms upstairs today. There's a strange smell in E.J.'s room. The girl's room is a mess and so is the bathroom.

Okay, Leona. I'll start cleaning the upstairs. Do you still want me to fix dinner tonight?

No. I'll take care of it.

Clemenza got up from the table, took her coffee cup to the sink, washed it, and returned it to the cabinet. She retrieved a broom, mop, and bucket and headed upstairs. Leona also got up from the table and began cleaning up the rest of the breakfast dishes and replacing the breakfast food items in their proper places. Within the hour, Toby arrived home and found Leona sitting in the living room. Leona didn't look up when she heard

Toby enter the house. To Toby, she looked like a coiled rattler ready to strike.

Well, hello, Mother.

Skip the greeting, Patricia. I want to know where you were; who you were with; and why you decided to stay out all night and not tell me or your father.

Oh, it's Patricia now? Okay. Well, as you can see, "Patricia" is just fine. Nothing happened to "Patricia" so get that out of your head. I wasn't with a boy if that is what you're thinking; there were no boys around. My girlfriend at school . . .

Who is this girlfriend?

This girlfriend is Ronnie. Everyone calls her Ronnie but her real name is India Rhonda Sykes. Anyway, Ronnie is in my calculus class. We're the only Negro girls in the class. Actually, we're the only Negroes. She's really smart and a math major. She really understands calculus probably better than anyone else in the class. Sometimes, I thinks she understands it better than our teaching assistant.

Okay, how do we get to the fact of your staying out all night?

Well, Ronnie and I were talking after class about a particular calculus problem. I'm not sure I can even explain it to you and it's not that important anyway. In any case, we started talking about this problem and I suggested we get something to eat at the cafeteria. One thing led to another and she invited me to her apartment near campus to continue talking. We started talking about all kinds of things, things I haven't even talked about with some of my closer girlfriends. It was amazing. We talked about what's going on in Africa with these liberation movements and newly independent countries. We talked about Eisenhower and politics; about who might run for president in 1960. We talked about the Reverend King and the Civil Rights protests in the South. We talked about movies and television. And we talked about the fact that Ronnie has her own apartment.

How can a colored girl afford her own apartment?

Actually, her parents pay for it. They live in Chicago. They're both medical doctors and have a lot of money, I think. Her mother is Negro but her father is white. She came to school in Detroit because she wanted to be in a city with lots of Negroes. So, anyway, we talked and talked and then we realized how late it was. She suggested I stay the night in her apartment instead of heading home late on a bus.

You couldn't call to tell me this?

Mother, to tell the absolute truth, it was late. I was trying to be considerate. I thought you might be in bed and I didn't think it was such a big deal. Didn't you ever stay out late without telling your mother?

What I did or didn't do isn't important. You're my child and you didn't think I would be worried about you—our oldest child and elder daughter, who has never spent a night away from her family without us knowing where she was and who she was with—I wouldn't think it was a big deal?

Was it a big deal?

You're damn right it was.

Excuse me, Mother. I'm sorry. I'm really sorry but I'm old enough to take care of myself and I don't need to report everything I do to you.

Toby, we can't continue like this. You think you're all grown up and can do whatever you want. Your parents shouldn't be concerned. Well, clearly, you're not all grown up because your parents are concerned. So, we have to find a new solution.

I may not be your idea of an adult but, in my own mind, I am and I don't want to be treated anymore like a child, like Obra-Jean. I'm twenty years old and old enough to make my own decisions and lead my own life without having to consult with my parents.

But you're perfectly happy to have your parents pay for this life of yours.

You're correct, Mother, but I know that has to change and I can change it. I've decided to get a job on campus. I'll check job listings in the administrative offices tomorrow. I hope I can get an interview soon so that I can get a job this summer. In the meantime, Ronnie has already offered her apartment as a place where I can stay. She has her own bedroom and, in the living room, a couch that folds out as a bed. We can try being roommates for a while to see how that works. Otherwise, after I'm working, I could get my own place.

So, Patricia, you've already worked this out. I see. You would leave your own family for your precious independence.

You just said, as an adult, I should take care of myself; I think it's past time for me to do that.

Leona became silent. She had heard enough. She felt defeated in arguing with her daughter and didn't want to continue. She stood up, glanced at

Toby, and went into the kitchen. Toby, realizing that there would be no further conversation, went upstairs to change clothes and, when she was finished, left the house without saying goodbye to her mother. That evening, with all the family at home and dinner prepared—Toby had returned in time for the meal—Leona wanted everyone to sit at the table.

Obra-Jean, go call your brother and sister to come to the table for dinner.

Okay. What about Grandma?

Your grandmother is not eating with us tonight. She already ate in her room. Perry, put these dishes on the table for me. As soon as we're all at the table, I want to talk to Toby about her decision to move and leave her family to go live in some girl's apartment.

I thought you said it would be just the two of us talking with her after dinner? Why bring the kids into this?

Because Toby's decision affects our whole family.

Does it? Do her brother and sister really care?

I think they should care. If they don't, I'm going to make sure they do understand we're a family and we should stay together.

Leona, Toby's an adult. Maybe she's not the most considerate adult but she wants her own life, not our life. That's not unreasonable. Just because she wants her own life doesn't mean she's not part of this family.

You would think that, of course.

She's going to leave us at some point anyway, Leona. Why not now?

She should leave when she has definite plans and the ability to live on her own or get married. She doesn't have definite plans and she can't afford to live on her own yet and she doesn't have a husband.

But she wants to try. She'll have a job interview and a place to live temporarily with a friend who, I believe, welcomes her.

And what do we know about this friend? And what if she doesn't get a job? How is she going to pay for things?

Honey, we can ask to meet her friend. I wouldn't mind us giving her some money until she finds a job.

Perry, why do you always have this "things will work out" attitude?

Because, Leona, things always do work out, one way or another.

And, you would agree to let our elder daughter just leave this family for an uncertain life? Just like that?

Leona, here come the kids. Let's not talk about this in front of them. Please.

Kids, sit down and don't start eating until we've said the blessing. Did you wash your hands?

Yes, Ma'am.

Well, Patricia, thank you for joining your family for dinner for a change. It must be a special occasion that you've decided to grace us with your presence.

Gee, Mother, something smells good. What is it?

Spaghetti and meatballs. I helped Momma make the meatballs.

Yes, you did. Thank you, Obra-Jean.

I want us all to join hands and say, "Grace." God bless this food and this family and keep us all together. Amen.

Amen.

So, Obra-Jean, E.J., your sister has some news, don't you, Patricia?

Leona, can't this wait until after dinner?

No, Perry. Patricia, please tell us your news.

Yes, Mother. I told Momma and Daddy I'm going to move into an apartment near campus with a girlfriend. I'll try to get a job interview with the university administrative offices next week so I can make money to live on my own.

Can we come see you in your apartment?

Of course, Obra-Jean. My annoying little sister and my handsome baby brother can come visit anytime if you want.

I'm not annoying. Why are you always criticizing me, Toby?

Yes, Obra-Jean, you are not only annoying but also a devious, calculating liar.

That's enough, Patricia. This is not about Obra-Jean but about you.

Well, Obra-Jean, there isn't enough room in my friend's apartment. I'll be sleeping on a fold-out bed in my friend's living room temporarily. But you can come to visit if Momma and Daddy say it's all right.

I don't think it will be all right, Patricia. Your father and me don't know anything about this apartment or this girlfriend you'll be living with.

Mother, you can come see the apartment and meet Ronnie whenever you want.

I'm not interested in meeting anybody. Your brother and sister have their own home and beds here and that's where they'll stay. That apartment will be your world, your home. It's your choice. You're welcome to it. This family won't be a part of it. Isn't that right, Perry? Perry, isn't that right?

Leona, you can keep the kids from visiting their sister but you can't tell me what to do if I want to see my daughter or her new home and roommate.

Kids, as you can see, your father and me don't agree about this. Remember, I'm your mother. I'm the one who's going to see you're ready for the world out there. I've tried with your sister who has done nothing but ignore my suggestions and guidance all her life. Now, you see the result. She's leaving her family to sleep on a couch in a stranger's apartment. That's not the life I wanted for her and it's not the life I want for the two of you. And, it won't be your life. I'll see to that. I may have failed once with your sister but I won't fail with you two. Do you hear me?

Yes, Ma'am.

Obra-Jean, I want you and E.J. to clean up everything after you've finished eating and put the kitchen in order. Obra-Jean, you wash and dry the dishes and pans. I also want you to wash your hair tonight before going to bed and braid it into pigtails. Don't even think about talking back to me or giving me an argument. Just do it. You're looking like pickaninny. E.J., you put the food away, take out the garbage, and straighten up the kitchen. And both of you had better wear clean underwear and shirts tomorrow. Ask your grandmother to iron your uniforms. Perry, I'm taking the car and going to my sister's house. I'll be back when I get back.

— A Timely Visit —

Leona's sister lived in an apartment about a twenty minute drive from Leona's home. The apartment building, part of a new community near downtown Detroit, was built on land cleared of its buildings and residents through an urban renewal scheme. Blacks called it "Negro Removal." The new community called Lafayette Park consist of high-rise apartment buildings and low-rise, attached townhouses. Unlike the black neighborhood—called Black Bottom—that urban renewal destroyed, the new neighborhood was integrated with blacks and whites, mostly professionals. Leona's sister, Augusta Post, moved to Lafayette Park almost as soon as the first buildings could be occupied. The sisters occasionally spent evenings together at Augusta's one bedroom apartment because Leona needed to absent herself periodically from her own home and family. The sisters were friends—Leona's best friend—as well as siblings. Leona sat on the sofa while talking to Augusta who stood by the counter separating the galley kitchen from the living room.

Can I get you a drink, Sister?

A little bourbon and soda on ice would be nice.

So, Leona, why has my dear sister come to visit me without warning at this time of night? Trouble in Paradise?

I had to get out of that house. I didn't feel like driving all the way across town to my mother-in-law's place. I promise I won't stay long. I just needed to get away from Perry, the kids, and Clemenza for a while.

What's going on now?

It's Toby. She's decided to get a job on campus—if she gets and passes an interview—and move in with some girlfriend of hers from one of her classes.

Move in? My, my, that's a new and interesting development, isn't it?

I don't know how interesting it is. She'll be sleeping on a fold-out couch in the living room until she can get her own place, so she says.

Here's your drink, Sister. Move over so I can sit here too.

Okay. Thanks for the drink. Umm, it's good. I may need another after this one.

Don't forget you're driving home. So, who is this girlfriend?

Augusta, all I know is that her parents are wealthy and live in Chicago. They're both medical doctors. The father is white and the mother is colored. They pay for their daughter's apartment. Oh, and this girlfriend is a genius, I guess, at calculus. She's a math major. That's all I know.

And, why are you so upset about this? It sounds to me like a good move for my niece. She needs some independence. This is a good time for her to begin exploring the world without her parents watching her every move.

You sound like my stupid husband. Why am I upset? How could I not be upset? Shit. She's my daughter. She's twenty. She thinks she knows what this world is like but she doesn't know shit. She thinks she'll just breeze through everything because her father encourages her to do what she wants. Perry somehow thinks his daughter is on an equal footing in this world with his son. He thinks that a girl can make it just like a boy. And, worse, he thinks his daughter is on equal footing with white people. That, Augusta, is pure, dumb, stupid shit.

What's wrong with thinking like that, Leona?

What's wrong with that? Augusta, you know damn well what's wrong with that. You, better than most people, should know this world just doesn't work that way for women, especially colored women. Or, have you forgotten? Maybe, now that you have a good job teaching you've forgotten what you had to give up.

I haven't forgotten anything, Sister. I had to change my plans; that's all. Yes, some things didn't work out the way I wanted. But, I'm happy with what I'm doing now.

Are you? You may be happy but you're not doing what you said you always wanted to do.

Leona, you know as well as I do, when we grow up and get to know the world, we often have to adjust our plans. We realize some dreams just won't work for us. We have to find out for ourselves what does work, not necessarily what we dream will work.

Are you saying you aren't disappointed you couldn't follow your dream?

Of course, I'm disappointed but disappointment is a part of life. Not everything goes the way we want it to go. We learn from disappointments and make different and sometimes better choices.

Okay, yes, we all have disappointments but we don't all make good choices afterwards. I want my kids to always make better choices than me.

You can't be sure of anything like that, Leona. They have to live their lives and discover what works or won't work for them. That's life. Look, Sister, you've got your family, a home, a husband, a job, and a pretty good life. One child is in college and two others are in school. That seems like a pretty good deal to me. Where does all of this dissatisfaction and unhappiness come from? What's really wrong, Leona?

Perry said something.

Okay. Perry said something. Are you going to tell me what he said or is it a secret?

He said I'm insecure because of Clemenza.

That's not news, Sister. Isn't it true what he said? Haven't we been talking about this for years?

You know when Perry is guzzling his rum and coke, he starts saying all kinds of shit.

But isn't what he said true? Haven't we've agreed its true?

This is not about Clemenza. What's Clemenza got to do with this? I told him if I was insecure, if I had "fears and disappointments," I was using my experience to help guide my children. He thinks I'm hurting the girls by warning them about expecting too much in life.

Leona, maybe you're trying too hard. Kids learn somehow—from their parents, their relatives, other kids, their teachers. It's not your responsibility alone to help your kids understand what they might be up against in their lives. And, it's not your fault if they fail to learn some important lesson from you. You and they are only human like the rest of us.

You would say that.

Now, Sister, what does that mean?

Augusta, you know what I mean.

No. I don't think so. You should tell me, plain and simple.

If Clemenza had been a mother to me like she was to you, maybe my life would have been different and I might have made some better choices.

Why are you always blaming our mother? If Clemenza was as good a mother to me as you think she was, then why did I make some bad choices? I've told you many times, Leona, Clemenza was a mother, plain and simple—that's all. She was as good to both of us in her own way as she could have been.

That's easy for you to say. She was always a real mother to you but she wasn't a real mother to me. She wasn't a real, or a good, mother to me. How could she be? She left me when I was a child. I was raised by people I didn't even know, but she raised you as her own. She paid for your college. You lived with her until you went to New York. What did I get from her? Nothing.

How many times have we had this conversation, Leona? Really? A million times? Two million times? You're a broken record, Leona. Yes. Our mother paid for my college and we lived together but I still made some choices that didn't work out for me, and it had nothing directly to do with her.

Well, that was your fault. You were like Toby is now. You wouldn't listen to anyone even if they tried to warn you. So, you had a mother who loved you and kept you and you still went your own way and ignored her advice.

Leona, how could I have not gone my own way? We all go our own way. Right or wrong. Nobody's life turns out exactly the way they want it.

But you chose the wrong way even when you were warned.

And there was nobody to warn you?

Not my mother. A mother is the only one who counts to her daughter.

I don't believe that, Leona. What difference does it make if there is, or isn't, a mother? You were raised by people who took good care of you.

Who loved you. Our aunt was your mother. It's not her fault or our mother's fault if you made bad choices despite their advice.

It's not just the choices.

Then what the hell is it?

It's a feeling that your own mother wants you and cares about you and protects you.

You want to care and protect Toby. Does Toby feel you want and protect her?

She should. I've always been close and loving to her, her whole life. More than I can say for my mother.

But, does Toby feel your care and love or does she only hear commands and demands? Where's the love, Leona?

A mother who loves and cares has to be demanding. That's love, watching out for those you care about. That's what love is.

Well, I wonder how Toby feels about it.

Toby's headstrong like you and she's going to be disappointed like you.

And not like you? Toby is your daughter not mine. Toby is like you, Leona. You think our mother was not a good mother to you but you think she was a good mother to me. Well, she was a good mother to me and maybe she was not a good mother to you. But you and I are really very much alike, and Toby is like us. What I'm saying is each of us becomes who we are. A mother may make some differences but it's within each of us to figure out ourselves for ourselves. My mother didn't make me into who I am any more than she made you who you are.

But she loves you. She never loved me.

Leona, that's not true and you know it. She's always loved you, in her own way, true enough. She had to live her own life and she made a decision that affected your life, as well as mine. My god, the woman has lived in your house for four years now. You take care of her. She's always acknowledged you've provided her a home when she didn't have a home. What more do you want?

I guess I want what I can never have. I want a mother like you had, a mother who stayed with her child and loved her the best way she could by showing her love.

Dammit, Leona, our mother lives with you. Why doesn't that count? You want to remake the past? That ain't gonna happen, Girl, listen to yourself. You've got everything in your life, more than I have, frankly. Perry is right; you are insecure. Think about it. Just because you didn't have the mother you wanted, you think you can be the mother your daughters want. You may think you're a good mother, Leona, but your children may think otherwise. Maybe, Toby fights you because she feel she doesn't need you. Maybe, a good mother steps back and says to herself "I've done the best I can" and lets go of her daughter. I think that's what Perry meant by your insecurity. You want to be the mother you wanted not the mother your daughters want. Sister, take it easy. Take a break. You're doing a good job. Enjoy life. Let your family enjoy their lives.

Dammit, Augusta. This is hard. You don't understand the hurt in me. I can't make it go away. I try to be polite with Clemenza. I can thank her for taking care of the meals for us, for keeping the house clean. I can see that she tries to make up for what she did. What I can't do is forgive her and that is too fucking bad for me and for everyone else.

Sister, you need to have another drink.

I think I will. You know what?

Yes?

I'm gonna get another dog. I miss that mutt we had.

Cootie?

Yeah, good old Cootie. She ran away or somebody stole her. That dog wasn't good for anything. She was supposed to bark when someone came to the house but she would just sit there and watch.

I loved Cootie too. She was so sweet. What was she? Part cocker spaniel?

Yeah. But, she was too sweet. I want a big dog that barks and scares the shit out of people—maybe, a German Shepherd. That's what I want.

Leona, let me know when you get that dog because you won't see me around your house.

When am I gonna get my drink, Caesar?

In a moment, Sister.

Augusta, I had that dream again.

What dream is that?

The one where I'm at somebody's house party and this guy starts dancing with me and sticking his nasty tongue in my mouth. Then, he takes me outside—it raining some—and tries to rape me. Cootie is there but she doesn't bark.

Why do you have that dream? You always say that nothing like that ever happened to you. Tell me the truth; did someone try to rape you?

I guess that it was just a fear I had and still have. Maybe it's why I worry so much about Toby or maybe it's because I feel Clemenza didn't protect me. I don't know.

Here's your drink. Relax, Sister.

Leona and Augusta continued talking and drinking late into the night. However, both had early starts the next morning for their jobs and decided to end the evening at midnight. Augusta kissed her sister goodbye. Leona left the apartment and headed to the guest parking lot where she left her car. She thought about their conversation and felt her sister simply couldn't understand Leona's need, as a child, for her mother. Augusta, who always had her mother present in her life, well understood the irony that Leona now had responsibility for the woman whom she felt had abandoned her as a child. Leona continued mulling her thoughts until she finally went to bed. Perry awoke when she got under the covers.

How's Augusta?

Fine.

Did you have a good talk with her?

It was okay.

What did you two talk about?

What do you think we talked about, Perry? We talked about Toby, about you. I told her what Toby plans to do and how you support her as you always do and that I'm pissed about Toby. I'm pissed about you. And, I'm pissed that Clemenza was a terrible mother and that she's responsible for where we all are now.

How can you blame Clemenza for what our daughter decides to do? Or for how I feel about raising our children? Or for why you are always pissed about everything?

I'm not always pissed about everything, just about Clemenza, you, and Toby.

And what about you?

Well, I'm pissed that I might have been a different person with a different life if it hadn't been for my mother.

Really? Are you saying we wouldn't be married. That we wouldn't have these children and this life?

Maybe.

I don't know what to say, Honey. I've known all these years something made you unhappy. I thought if you had a husband who loved you and made a good life for you and gave you the children I thought you wanted, you could get over the fact you didn't have the mother you wanted.

Oh, I have the mother I've always wanted but she's your mother and my mother-in-law. She's my real mother, the woman who treats me like her own child. But she's not the mother who lives in my home and who I have to care for. That woman is my sister's mother; that's who she's been a real mother to—my sister not to me.

Clemenza loves you, Leona. Or, she tries to but you won't let her. You could be nicer to her.

Why?

Because she's your mother, for god's sake.

You can be nicer to her. The children can be nicer to her. I will never be nicer to her because she did something she can never undo. She left me. Left me—a child with strangers. She left and took the daughter she really loved. And the one she didn't love she left behind.

Leona, that's ancient history.

Yeah, sure, Perry. Goodnight.

The next morning—following her usual routine—Leona went to work. Her boss, Arthur Becellus, was happy to see her because he did not give his dictation to the temp who took Leona's place the preceding day. After getting him and herself cups of coffee, she sat in his office and took shorthand notes of the several letters she would type to companies that were under audit. In addition, he gave dictation for a report that needed to be sent to Washington. As Leona was reviewing her shorthand to make sure that she had everything noted correctly, Becellus inquired about her daughter, and Leona replied that she was unhappy with Toby's decision to move out of the house and live with a roommate in an apartment near the university campus. To Leona's surprise, Becellus confided to her that he was having similar issues with his son. Becellus seldom talked about his family or home life so Leona listened carefully, avoiding asking too many probing questions. Becellus's son had recently returned home from college in Ohio and announced he would not return to finish the last year of his degree. When Becellus demanded to know what he planned to do with his life, his son replied he had gotten a job at a food wholesaler in the Eastern Market district. He was thinking about eventually going into the restaurant business. Meanwhile, he found an apartment in Indian Village on the city's east-side, and was moving there immediately. Becellus was apoplectic but realized he was powerless to persuade, or force, his son to change his mind about school, taking this wholesaler job, or moving out of his parents' house. He confessed to Leona that something was afoot these days causing children to ignore and reject their parents' guidance. Leona had heard these kinds of laments from her friends and even some of her co-workers but she never expected to hear similar anguish from her white boss.

Throughout the rest of the workday, Leona tried to concentrate on Becellus's letters and report and to put Toby out of her mind. Usually her co-workers avoided Leona when she was busy typing but on this day another secretary, Mildred Carter, stopped by Leona's desk to ask why she missed work the day before. Leona, who did not like to discuss family or personal matters with colleagues, simply replied that there was a minor emergency at home, nothing serious, but it required her attention most of the day. Mildred, sensing Leona's reticence, decided it was unwise to continue an inquiry. Just as she was about to turn away and return to her own desk, Leona stopped her, noting that it was time for a coffee break, and asked her if she wanted to have coffee together. Delightfully surprised, the secretary agreed, and the two women walked together to the coffee urn, poured their coffee and walked through the office to the corridor where both stood smoking cigarettes, drinking their coffee, and talking. Leona did not offer any significant details about her "minor emergency" but she did listen to her co-worker who, given this rare opportunity to talk with another sister at the office, unburdened herself with a shopping list of complaints and grievances. Leona suppressed her amusement of this sudden confessional. Of all of the sisters in this office, she believed this woman to be the most serene and untroubled. Apparently, appearances weren't everything.

— A Breakfast Chat —

According to Moore family tradition, Sunday morning was a sit-down breakfast for the entire household. Everyone was expected to be present —bathed, groomed, and dressed appropriately. Pajamas or sloppy clothes were forbidden. Breakfast was served more or less promptly at ten. Everyone was to be seated at the dining room table (each family member had an assigned seat). This tradition began when Clemenza entered the household after the Moore family purchased their house four years previously. As a gesture of goodwill towards the family, but especially to Leona, Clemenza offered to prepare a special Sunday breakfast—as well as most weekday dinners—in appreciation for being given living space in her daughter's home. Instead of being rebuffed, as she expected, Leona was surprisingly amenable. In fact, after five weekdays of working at her job and herding a husband and three children, Leona was relieved to sit down and enjoy Sunday breakfast that Clemenza prepared. She complimented Clemenza's efforts and restrained herself from any criticism of her mother during the Sunday meal. Leona's restraint allowed the other family members to be more openly friendly to

Clemenza during this rare show of goodwill in the otherwise cool daughter/mother relations. Sunday breakfast was a treat for all.

The menu seldom varied although preparation of individual items changed from week to week. There was bacon, sausages or steak, eggs, grits or potatoes, and toast or biscuits. Sometimes, fried apples or grilled tomatoes provided a little variety to the menu. Coffee, tea, milk, and occasionally orange juice accompanied the meal. Everything was fresh and perfectly prepared since Clemenza had been a professional cook all of her adult life. When she had placed all of the serving dishes on the table, family members said a blessing and then served themselves in order of the youngest first so that Clemenza was always the last to plate her own food.

Leona insisted the children not talk during the meal. She relaxed this rule for Toby when she began college. Only after everyone had finished eating could the younger children join the conversation. Leona and Perry used the "adult" time to talk about their respective jobs especially the annoyances and gossip about fellow workers and bosses. Sometimes, they talked about politics—both were Democrats who detested Republicans and particularly the Eisenhower administration. More often, they talked about race and racism—white people were always difficult to understand and nearly impossible to like even the relatively good ones like Leona's boss, Mister Becellus. The younger children always listened intently to these discussions since both attended an all-white Catholic school in the neighborhood. Clemenza seldom joined these conversations because she was infrequently asked her opinion and she didn't want to risk upsetting Leona.

On the Sunday following Toby's decision to move out of her parent's home and take up temporary residence in an apartment of her friend,

Ronnie, the adults' conversation focused on Toby but, in actuality, it was a full-blown nuclear meltdown of Leona's mind.

I am not happy with this family. Patricia, I'm especially not happy with you, and because your father always seems to take your side in things, I'm not happy with him either. I'm not the bad guy here. So don't point any fingers at me. Besides, I don't want to hear what either of you have to say. I've heard it before, and you're gonna say the same things again. Well, this time listen to me and you, Obra-Jean and E.J., pay attention because if you don't get my message, I'm not gonna be happy with the two of you either. Obra-Jean, you're almost on my list anyway for not doing your homework assignment last week. Now, this is what I don't like: Patricia, you've had a good home and a mother and father who love you and have given you everything we could, maybe not everything you've wanted, but everything we could. I never had that from my own mother but you have. And, what do I get in return? Complaints, stubbornness, and rebellion. Do I get love back from you? No. You can't wait now to leave your home and family to sleep on a couch in some stranger's apartment. That's the home you want. Well, take it. See if I care. I'm done with you and I'm done with you too, Perry, for encouraging our daughter because you think she should do what she wants to do. I say no. She doesn't have a clue about how her whole life will be affected by what she wants. You two just think everything will work out fine. Well, more often than not it doesn't work out fine. There are plenty of women out there on the street who can tell you it didn't work out fine for them. I see them every day when I go to work. They're miserable, beaten down, and unhappy. They had big dreams. Oh, yeah. Big dreams. They were going to do this and they were going to do that. Well, you know what? They ain't doing shit. You, Miss Smartass, you quit Catholic school to go to Cass. Now, you're in college and you're gonna get a job and live in your own apartment and then what? You're gonna take some job from a white girl? Ain't gonna happen. Your fancy education ain't gonna protect you from white girls. They're gonna get the job you want, and you're gonna take what they don't want. That's how it works. I've failed to get this across to you but I'm setting my sites on Obra-Jean now. Obra-Jean, learn from your sister but don't be like your sister. Don't follow her path. Listen to your mother who loves you and follow my advice. I know what's best for you. You, too, E.J. If I had gotten just a little of the motherly love from my own mother like you kids have gotten from me, I wouldn't . . .

You wouldn't what, Leona?

Perry, I wouldn't be sitting in this damn dining room with all of you.

With that, Leona got up from the table, threw down her napkin, and went upstairs to her bedroom. Perry excused the kids to leave the table. He went to the living room and sat on the couch. Clemenza began removing the dishes from the table and returning them to the kitchen. That was the end of Sunday breakfast.

Leona spent the rest of the morning in her bedroom. At first, she tried to nap on the bed but her agitation was so intense she couldn't close her eyes or relax. She sat up, moved to a chair, and sat gazing out of the open window into her backyard. Through the trees she could see the rooftops of homes across the alley from her house. The foliage had grown so thick that she could not see any particular rooftop completely. Something about all of those other homes and all of those other families in those homes made her wonder if any of those other families were at all like her own. She thought about Toby. Why, she wondered, had her oldest daughter become so difficult and so ungrateful for the love, attention, affection, and care her mother lavished on her? How did that happen? Leona searched her memory for some event, some speech, some action that turned her daughter against her. She could not identify a single thing in their lives together that would have made her daughter behave as she did towards her mother. It was puzzling and distressing. Leona wanted to cry but Leona didn't cry. A breeze blew into the room. The fresh air smelled of flowers somewhere, but not from Leona's backyard because Leona was not a gardener. She never liked the idea of putting her hands in dirt and happening upon a worm. There had been enough of that when she was a child and when she and the neighbor kids played in the dirt surrounding their houses. It seemed, as she momentarily thought back to her childhood, that everything, then, was dirty—her clothes, her one pair of shoes, her hair, her body, her world. Coming back to the view out of the window, she reminded herself that her own house, her children, her person, her world would always be clean, neat, and orderly. She would not allow her children to wear any clothes that showed signs of dirt. She was adamant. They must stay clean, away from dirty things. One of the reasons she wanted her kids in Catholic school was because she thought that cleanliness would be stressed by the sisters. Everything in the school would be clean—Leona had noted that fact when she visited the school prior to enrolling her children. Her children would be clean when they attended school and they would stay clean in school. It was something of an obsession with Leona. It was a good thing, she thought. Something caught her attention. It was the horn of ship, probably one of the many ore carriers on the Detroit River carrying ore between cities as far away as Lake Superior and Lake Erie. Although the ship and the river were several miles from Leona's house, the sound carried effortlessly to her ear. She listened for the sound again. It was comforting. What would it be like to be on a ship sailing far away somewhere? Her reverie was interrupted by the smell of something burning, something like bread. Perhaps one of the kids was making toast. Whatever it was soon dissipated. There was always something to disturb her few moments of peace and quiet. When she re-focused on the view from the window, she wondered again about Toby. Leona sent Toby to ballet lessons when she was young. She had piano lessons. Leona enrolled her in special after-school classes at the YWCA. She took her to swim classes and art classes. Leona gave her everything a child could possibly want. What happened?

That afternoon, on her way downstairs to the kitchen, she noted that Perry was in the den watching TV with E.J. The girls were nowhere to be seen. Leona assumed they were in their room or had gone outside. Entering the kitchen, she saw Clemenza sitting at the table in the middle of the room. Clemenza looked up from a magazine she was reading, stared at Leona, smiled, and then looked away. Leona went to the refrigerator and retrieved a pitcher of ice water, poured herself a glass, and sat at the table opposite Clemenza. She glanced around the kitchen noting if everything was in its proper place. Seeing nothing amiss, she gazed at Clemenza. Her mother's short, graying hair was pressed into waves. Her face, although clearly showing her age, was smooth, the skin soft, and very dark. Leona never thought of her mother as any kind of beauty but here was this elderly woman who had a graceful, gentle countenance. She was small and compact, with thin arms and slender fingers. Her nails were unpolished but trimmed. She wore glasses without rims. She had always worn glasses as long as Leona could remember. Leona wore glasses too but only when she was reading or typing at work. Leona suddenly wondered what she herself would look like when she was Clemenza's age. Would she lose her shapely figure? Would her breasts sag or disappear like Clemenza's? Would she be like this old woman? Would she ever have the chance to sit at her daughter's breakfast table or live in her daughter's home when she was old and, perhaps, a widow or divorcé like her mother? Toby probably would never even have her own mother in her home. Leona felt a rush of anger but also dismay. She had invited Clemenza to stay in Leona's own home with her family. She gave Clemenza her own room. She asked nothing of Clemenza except to help with meals and housework. She provided her anything she needed—clothes, toiletries, spending money. She kept

Clemenza safe and secure. Why did she do those things for a woman whom she resented so thoroughly? Sometimes, she imagined taking something really heavy and smashing it against her head. She wanted to slap her. She wanted to yell at her. She wanted to call her a selfish, unfeeling, unlovable bitch. She wanted her to suffer, to hurt, to be shamed, to . . . Leona noticed that Clemenza had put down her magazine and looked at her as if she could hear Leona's thoughts. Had Leona somehow, inadvertently, said something out loud? Clemenza tried to smile again, to be friendly. Leona got up from the table and walked out of the kitchen. She met Toby who had come from her room upstairs and was heading to the den. They crossed paths in the dining room. Leona asked Toby if she would be home for dinner that evening. Toby replied that she planned to leave shortly for her friend's apartment and spend the night there. Leona turned away from Toby and walked towards the front door. As she looked around her living room, she saw, as if for the first time, their furniture. Everything seemed old-fashioned and worn. Perry purchased their furniture, without consulting her, from someone who got it from someone—probably some old white person who died and whose household belongings came into the possession of Perry's "dealer." Leona didn't know this as fact but she hated the mahogany furniture because of how it looked and because it belonged originally to someone else. Someday, she thought, as she headed out of the house to the front porch, she would buy all new furniture she liked. She would also buy rugs for the living room and dining room. She hated those bare wooden floors. On the porch, she leaned on the railing and looked up and down the street. There were a few neighbors out and about. One was cutting grass. Others were standing and talking. She noticed Obra-Jean across the street, sitting on the front steps of a house with a girl her age who lived in the house. Obra-Jean animatedly described something with her arms flailing and her hands pointing and making a kind of chopping motion. What could that conversation be about? Leona made a note to herself to ask her daughter what required such extravagant movements in order to make her point. At that moment, a neighbor woman walked by and greeted Leona. Leona returned the greeting and watched the woman as she continued down the street. Who were these people who lived on her block? She didn't know any of them personally except in this casual way. She had never been invited into their homes and she had never considered inviting them into her home. Why? It seemed to Leona that her whole world centered on her family and her work. Why did she not know another person in this neighborhood? Why was she not sitting on the front steps telling someone a story? There was a bigger world around her and it was completely unknown to her.

III

Obra-Jean Moore

— That School —
Spring 1957

It was a lie—a child's lie for sure but a lie nonetheless. On that rainy morning when Obra-Jean told her mother she didn't want to go to school, she had, in fact, completed her math homework and had studied for her exam the prior afternoon. She lied about it first to her brother knowing he would unwittingly repeat the lie to their mother, and then she lied directly to her mother as an excuse to stay home from school. Later that evening at dinner, she lied still again to her family about Sister Angelica because, in fact, she turned in her homework on time and aced her exam. It was not strange for her to lie since Obra-Jean learned to lie early during her fourteen years, and often because no one seemed to notice her lies except her sister. And this lie was complicated—the truth of which no one ever discovered. Obra-Jean lied because she had no prior experience with a situation that arose in Sister Angelica's class and she didn't know how to express or explain her feelings to herself or her family. The day before this particular set of lies several boys in her class teased Obra-Jean during recess about her skin color, her hair, her facial features, and her intelligence. As teenage white boys with virtually no contact with other black people, they picked up on the "jungle" trope popular in movies and TV. They called Obra-Jean a "monkey" who simply copied and repeated everything she heard and saw. "Monkey see, monkey do." This denigration of her appearance and intelligence stunned Obra-Jean. She thought to report the boys to Sister Angelica but while she was pondering this possibility, Sister Angelica announced to the class that she would create "teams" to solve difficult math problems for an in-class competition at the end of the spring semester. This was Sister Angelica's experiment to use her brightest students as mentors to increase math proficiency among her not-so-bright students. So, Obra-Jean was paired with Janette Fulgenzi—they were the two brightest students in the class. Janette was also considered one of the prettiest girls and certainly the most popular. To Obra-Jean she seemed perfect in every way. Although they never spoke to one another, both seemed to acknowledge that they were competitors at the top of the eighth grade. So, these two events—denigration by teenage white boys and pairing with the prettiest and most popular white girl in her grade—confounded Obra-Jean. Her explanation to her family at dinner of her dislike of kids at her Catholic school was, therefore, based in truth but clearly it wasn't the complete truth which she never revealed. These lies were the beginning of a way she found to manage life in her family and especially with her mother. As time passed, she became a very proficient liar.

On that same morning when her mother insisted Obra-Jean could not stay home, E.J.—according to his mother's instructions—accompanied Obra-Jean to and from school. They followed their customary route that took them past the public middle school where hoodlums—as Leona called them—were presumably inmates lying in wait for unsuspecting Catholic school victims. It was still raining and both children had the hoods of their raincoats raised over their heads. They avoided most of the puddles of water on the sidewalk but even when splashing though some of them, they remained dry because they wore their boots over their shoes as instructed by their mother. For most of the way, the siblings didn't talk. E.J. scanned the route constantly in case some kids from the public school were out and about. There were none, possibly because of the rain. However, as they neared their Catholic school, Obra-Jean broke the silence and asked her brother a question about the hoodlums their mother said beat up a kid from their school. E.J. shrugged and replied that he heard there was just some pushing and shoving. He thought that a white boy from their school had said something to a colored boy at the public school when everyone was heading home recently. In his opinion it was stupid kid stuff and no one actually got beat up. His explanation prompted Obra-Jean to make another inquiry. She wanted to know what he was supposed to do if someone did start trouble with them. E.J. assured her that no one would bother them. Their mother's apprehension was simply their mother being their mother. E.J. saw his role as protecting a dumb little girl to which Obra-Jean snapped that he was always saying stuff like that about her when she was not little, in fact as tall as E.J. and smarter than him. E.J. countered that his sister was dumb because she didn't know what was going on around her and next fall, when he began college at Wayne University, she would be walking to school on her own and this troubled their mother. Obra-Jean protested that she knew very well how to take care of herself. Besides, her brother was a skinny kid who didn't even know how to fight. She, on the other hand, knew very well how to take care of herself. She was in the eighth grade and a teenager and would start high school next fall. She reminded her brother that she told her parents that she didn't want to stay in Catholic school. She was the only colored kid in her class and she didn't like the other kids because she didn't feel she was included as a friend among her white classmates. Then, she repeated what she told him at breakfast: She wanted to go to Cass Tech High like her sister did. However, she knew their mother wouldn't approve because she had fought Toby when Toby refused to continue attending Catholic high school. Obra-Jean expected the same response from her mother. E.J. suggested she bypass their mother and go to their father who would back her up and agree to let her go to Cass. He added that she was his favorite child anyway and treated her like a princess. Obra-Jean pondered this thought as they approached their school compound, Saint Catherine, that sprawled over much of a city block. There was a large Romanesque-style church and rectory which contained living quarters for four priests. A separate building housed the sisters who taught grades one through twelve and held their bedrooms, kitchen, and dining room. Two separate large buildings contained the lower school and high school. E.J. headed to the upper school building and Obra-Jean entered the lower school building. He reminded her to wait for him after school at her entrance. Obra-Jean nodded and returned to her thoughts. Knowing her mother would object vehemently to her changing from Catholic school to public school, she wondered if going directly to her father would undercut her mother. If it had worked for Toby, why wouldn't it work for her? If, as E.J. said, she was her father's favorite, wouldn't he agree to let her change schools? Her father knew she was smart. As Obra-Jean had overheard in a conversation between her parents, he wanted his daughters to have the same opportunities as his son. And, he was willing to endure his wife's anger when things didn't go her way. This last point gave her hope. She could use her father as a weapon and shield against her mother.

Obra-Jean's classroom was on the second floor of the lower school. Long wardrobes lined each side of the central corridor. That's where Obra-Jean hung her raincoat and placed her boots. The eighth grade, like all of the other grades, had two classrooms and two teachers. Obra-Jean's homeroom teacher was Sister Mary Angelica who sat at her desk at the front of the room facing the rows of student desks. Across the hall, a lay teacher, Missus Celeste McManus, sat at her desk facing similar rows of desks. Obra-Jean entered her homeroom and took her seat at the front of a middle row and sat expectantly while Sister Angelica spoke.

Class, I'll collect your homework assignments now. Pass them up to the front of your row and those of you in the front row pass them over to Janette. Janette, when you've collected all of the papers, please arrange them alphabetically, as usual, and then put them on my desk. Right here. Thank you.

Class, are there any questions? Yes, Audrey?

Sister, I didn't finish my homework.

Why not, Audrey?

We had to visit my aunt who was sick. We didn't come home until late last night.

Well, that's an excuse but very poor planning on your part. See me after class, Audrey. Was there anyone else who didn't finish their homework? No? Okay. Now, today we are going to discuss ratios. Please open your textbook to page one seventy-three and start reading about ratios. After that, I want you to do the problems in your book and write your answers on a separate sheet of paper with your name and turn it in at the end of class. Yes, Obra-Jean?

Sister, I've already read this and the book doesn't explain ratios very well. When we have our class competition, I want to understand ratios better.

I don't understand what you are saying.

Sister, I have a book at home that gives a better explanation and there are more exercises.

Well, Obra-Jean, this is the book the school provides and it is the one all of your classmates are using so I think this is the one you will have to use for now. Don't you agree?

Oh, yes, of course, Sister. Yes, I do agree. Thank you.

Later during class recess, Obra-Jean stood in the hallway reading her math book. Most of the other kids used the recess to go outside or use the lavatory. Obra-Jean chose to stay near her homeroom in the hope that Sister Angelica would ask her a question or talk to her. Instead, Janette Fulgenzi approached.

Is that the math book you mentioned in class, Obra-Jean?

No. This one is mine. The other one belongs to my big sister.

Could you bring her book to school someday? I would love to look at it for our team competition.

She might not let me borrow it. She's in college and has a lot of math books because she's really good at it. She doesn't like for me to use her things.

Couldn't you persuade her? We don't have any books at my home and our school doesn't have a library.

What about the public library, Janette?

My parents won't let me go there.

Why not?

They say there are undesirable people in the library.

Undesirable people? What undesirable people?

I think that they mean people like you.

People like me? Like me, how?

You know, colored people.

Are you kidding me, Janette?

No, Obra-Jean. My parents don't like colored people.

And, they say that to you?

They don't say it to me, but they say it to each other when I'm around them.

Do they know I'm in your class?

I've never mentioned you to them.

Why not, Janette?

They would take me out of this school and send me somewhere else and I don't want to leave this school. I like it here.

So, you don't mind being in class with a colored girl?

I don't think like my parents. We're not taught in school to dislike people just because they're different from us. We're taught to love everyone unless they do some harm to us. I believe that's the right way.

Do you?

Yes, I do, Obra-Jean.

Janette, you've never been friendly to me. You've never talked to me before today.

You've never been friendly to me either, Obra-Jean.

I haven't?

You've never spoken to me.

You never spoke to me either, Janette.

I didn't think you wanted to talk to me. You've always avoided me.

I avoided you, Janette, because you never paid any attention to me.

I don't look at most of the kids in our class. I'm actually pretty shy. It took a lot of courage for me to come talk to you now. But, since we are going to be a team, I had a reason to talk to you. Maybe we could even be friends.

What about your parents?

We would have to be friends only at school, maybe eat our lunch together. I would really like to learn more math with you because I know you're really smart. We would win this competition.

So, Janette, we can only be friends at school? How would that work?

Isn't that better than not being friends at all?

Better, maybe, but not really good.

I know it's not the best solution but I would really like to be friends even if it's only at school.

Let me think about it. I'll let you know. I want to ask my sister about this and about her book.

You'll let me know tomorrow?

I'll let you know when I get an answer.

Okay.

All of the rest of the school day, Obra-Jean tried to suppress some of the excitement she felt in making friends with Janette Fulgenzi. The girl whom other students recognized as the smartest in their class wanted to be friends with her because she thought Obra-Jean was just as smart. After she and E.J. returned home, she was still thinking about Janette when E.J. reminded her to ask their father about high school at Cass Tech. Obra-Jean wanted to talk to her sister first but that was the night Toby didn't come home for dinner and didn't return until the next day. Therefore, Obra-Jean postponed talking to her father until she could speak with her sister first. The following night at dinner, when her mother berated Toby for deciding to move out of the house and stay in a friend's apartment, Obra-Jean realized her conversations would have to wait until some semblance of tranquillity returned to the Moore household. A few days later just before dinner, she went to the girls' bedroom where Toby was studying. Now that she needed information and advice from her sister, Obra-Jean adopted a more congenial tone to begin a conversation.

Toby, I think it's great you're moving into an apartment with your friend.

Why, because you'll have this bedroom all to yourself?

Yes, but no. It's because you're doing what you want to do not just what Momma wants. I want do something too that Momma won't like.

What bullshit scheme are you planning now, Lying Sister?

Could you not call me names? I really need your help. I'll tell you what I'm planning but can I ask you two small favors first?

Two small favors? Obra-Jean, you really are a wonder. Do I look like a fool to you? I know your tricks. I've seen you in action for fourteen years. Why has my snotty, scheming little sister become so sweet and polite? What does she want?

Am I snotty? Okay, sometimes I am, but I do need your help. First, I want to borrow that math book you have. Okay, I was looking at it when you weren't here. I confess, I was bothering your stuff but only because I wanted to learn more about a math problem.

I told you to stay out of my stuff.

I know, I'm sorry. I didn't take anything or mess-up anything.

Little Sister, I know you. You're not sorry but why do you want my math book?

There's this girl at school. She's a really good student and wants to learn more than what's in our school book. So, I want to take your book to school to show her because she and I are a team for a class competition.

Why can't she come here so the two of you can look at the book together and your smart big sister can give you two grade-schoolers some tips?

Her parents wouldn't let her come here.

Of course not. She's white, right? Her parents don't like colored people. Is that right? It's the same old story. I knew it would be like that if I went to Saint Catherine and that's one of the main reasons I wouldn't go there. Who needs that shit from white people?

I didn't know that was how you felt because I never heard you say anything.

You weren't part of the conversation, Little Sister. Our mother wants us to be "pretend" Catholics and all that bullshit. She didn't want to know how I felt about being the only Negro girl in my class. She only wanted what she wanted. Now, I don't know if I want to let you take my book to school for a white girl to use. For sure, she wouldn't do that for you.

If you feel that way, then I don't know if I should ask you a second favor.

Is it worse than the first?

Well, this girl doesn't think like her parents. She wants to be friends with me but, because of her parents, she can only be friends at school. I want you to tell me if you think I should agree to do that?

Obra-Jean, you've been in that school for what? Four years? For someone who watches everything and everybody, I can't believe that you are just now noticing what kind of school you're in? What's up? Why is all of this an issue now? Why do you want this girl to be your friend? Don't bullshit me.

Me and her are the smartest kids in our class.

Obra-Jean, don't talk like some ignoramus from the cotton fields. You know you can't say "me and her." That's low-life talk. I know you know better. It's "she and I" or "we're."

Toby, I know that. I was just talking between the two of us. I know the right thing to say, okay? So, we're the smartest kids in our class, okay?

Thank you. Now, do you want to be her friend only at school knowing you could never visit her home and she would never come here to visit you? Is that the kind of friendship you want?

That's why I'm asking you, Toby. If I knew the answer, I wouldn't have to ask you.

Okay, lose the attitude. I'll tell you, Obra-Jean. White people are funny—not ha-ha funny but strange and unpredictable and often very cruel. They may say they want to be friends but, sometimes, I don't think they know what it means to be a friend to a Negro. I've tried being friends with a couple of white kids at Cass but they always disappointed me because they couldn't really see me as one of them. I was always an outsider. That's how it seemed to me.

That's how I feel now at Saint Catherine. Is it the same at your college?

That's a different story, Little Sister. There are lots and lots of Negro kids at Wayne so I don't have to try being friends with white kids, and they certainly don't try to be friends with me.

Doesn't your new roommate have a white father? So, isn't she part white?

Yes, but Ronnie is a real Negro. She looks Negro. She talks Negro. She acts Negro. She's my soul-sister.

Gee, I wish I had a soul-sister.

Who would want to be a soul-sister to a snotty, self-centered, lying brat like you? You don't really think about anyone but yourself. But this girl at your school certainly won't be your soul-sister. On the other hand, you might learn something from her that could help you later on. Yeah. You might learn something. She could be useful. So, give the white girl a chance to disappoint you. And, yes, you can borrow my math book but don't mess it up. Now, what is it you want to do that Momma won't like?

I want to go to Cass in the fall for high school.

I knew that scheming mind of yours was working overtime. By the way, Momma definitely won't go for it. She's gonna go nuclear.

You did it. You went to Cass.

And, now, I'm moving out of the house because I can't live with Momma any longer. Do you want to see her really angry? Do you also want to leave this house because that's what it will come to.

No and no.

Well, if you tell her you want to go to Cass, that's what you'll have in your face—non-stop, fire-breathing, yelling-at-the-top-of-her-lungs anger.

Well, I want to go to Cass and I'm gonna ask Daddy to persuade Momma to let me go.

Even if somehow you could go, you would still have to live with her. You see how she and I get along. She will have you for breakfast and not with toast.

Then, maybe I won't live here.

How would that be possible? You don't have a job and couldn't find one to pay for an apartment. You're too young. And what Negro female high school student in this city has her own apartment?

I don't know but I have an idea how I could move out of here if I had to.

It had better be a fantastic idea because if it isn't, you can kiss your plans goodbye. Good luck, Little Sister. Now don't bother me anymore. I have to study.

Obra-Jean made her way downstairs with all that her sister said sloshing back and forth in her mind. When she reached the living room, she had made up her mind about two things: she would be friends with Janette and she decided it was time to talk with her father. After dinner when he settled into his armchair in the den by himself with his rum and coke, she moved a chair to sit beside him.

Daddy, can I talk to you about something?

Sure, Sweetheart. What's up?

Well, Daddy, you know I'm the only colored kid in my class at Saint Catherine but I also think Saint Catherine is not a very good school. For example, our math book isn't nearly as good as the one I got from Toby when she was at Cass Tech. She learned a lot more at Cass than she would have learned at Saint Catherine, and that's why I want to go to Cass next fall instead of staying at Saint Catherine.

I thought you didn't like math.

Well, I do like math but Sister Angelica isn't a very good teacher. There's a lot she doesn't know.

Okay, so I get that Cass is a better school but are you still bothered by those white kids at Saint Catherine?

No, I don't care about them. I think I would just learn more about a lot of things at Cass, like Toby did, than if I stayed at Saint Catherine.

Well, the reason we sent you Catholic school was because we wanted you to get a better education.

That's what I'm saying. I would get an even better education at Cass. Wouldn't I?

You're probably right. Did you talk to your mother about this?

Daddy, are you kidding?

Well, you're gonna have to convince her first.

Daddy, you know how she is. Everything I want to do she hates. She always finds reasons why I can't do something.

She does do that a lot lately, doesn't she? And my guess is she'll probably say no to Cass.

That's why I'm asking you. You can make her let me go.

Honey, I can't make your mother do anything she doesn't want to do.

But, Daddy, you did it for Toby. You convinced Momma. You have to try. I can't stay at Saint Catherine. I don't want to be the only colored kid in my class. Please, Daddy.

Obra-Jean, Honey, I didn't convince your mother about Toby. That's not how things work with your mother. She never agreed to let Toby go to Cass and she won't agree to let you go. You see, Baby, with your mother, I have to take the punches. Oh, she wouldn't hit me, not with her fists anyway. But, she will hit me and keep hitting me with her anger and I'll have live with that. I can take a lot but I can only take so much.

Daddy, this is important to me. I really can't stay at Saint Catherine. Yeah, I don't want to stay but I can't stay.

Why not?

There's a boy there who tried to force me to do things.

What things? Rape you? What happened? Did he hurt you? Who is he? Does anybody know about this? Does Sister know about this? Where did this happen?

He came up to me when I was alone in the cloakroom but he didn't hurt me because nothing happened. I kicked him in his balls and ran. I didn't tell anyone because this boy's father owns a big car business. I heard he gives a lot of money to the school. And, Daddy, if I tell you who he is, you'll only get into trouble if you mess with his son. I just want to leave Saint Catherine. That's what I want to do.

Dammit, Obra-Jean, You should have told me about this. I would have killed that kid. I'll still kill him. This can't happen to my daughter. Tell me who he is. I need to report him. He can't get away with this. I don't care who his father is. You're my daughter and this boy should be punished.

But, Daddy, he'll deny everything. Then what? How can I stay at that school if everybody knows what happened? All of those kids will call me names and it will be worse for me than it is now.

But, Honey, he tried to hurt you. He deserves to be punished.

Yeah, but I'm the one who'll be punished and, if you do something, you'll only get yourself and me into trouble.

Jesus. Let me think about this. My own daughter. This is horrible. Obra-Jean, I would give my own life for you. I can't let this be. I have to do something. Okay, maybe you're right. You can't stay at that school anymore. I'll talk to your mother but I won't tell her what happened.

She'll only make things worse, much worse, like you said. I'll say to her it's time for you to be with more colored kids and you'll get a better education at Cass. I won't mention Toby either because that will only piss her off even more. But, you know, your mother will still say no.

Why, Daddy?

Honey, your mother is not an easy person to understand. She wants to push you forward and hold you back at the same time. We've had a lot of arguments about this, and your mother is determined to see you raised her way.

But, why, if it's not what's best for me?

Obra-Jean, Honey, sometimes a mother can be right and wrong at the same time. I can't say if, this time, she is right or wrong. I promise you I will try my best to convince her. Okay?

Thanks, Daddy. I know you will convince her.

Honey, if I don't convince her, I'll have to tell your mother I've made a decision and it's final. I have to do it for you. I don't want anyone to hurt you, ever. You've gotta leave that school so that boy can't bother you again. I would kill him if I had a chance. Then, the police would kill me. What would happen then to you, your mother, and your sister and brother if I was dead? I don't know how all of you would manage. So, it's best for all of us if you go to Cass.

That night in bed, Perry waited until Leona settled beside him before he raised the subject of Obra-Jean attending Cass Tech. To his surprise, Leona didn't immediately object. She listened and remained silent. Perry asked if her silence meant she agreed Obra-Jean could change schools.

Leona replied without elaboration that Obra-Jean could do as she liked. She added, in a hostile tone, that everyone could do whatever the fuck they wanted. Then, she turned out her nightstand light, pulled the covers up to her chin, and fell asleep. Perry was dismayed and puzzled by this unexpected reaction. He instinctively felt the battle was not over. Nevertheless, he decided he could tell his daughter she could change schools. He left a note for her before going to work the next morning. Obra-Jean carried the note to school and, at the first recess, she walked over to Janette and held out Toby's math book.

Is that your sister's book? Oh, thanks, Obra-Jean, for bringing it.

Let's stay after school, Janette, so we can look at it together. I can tell my mother Sister Angelica wanted to talk to me about the math competition. Since I walk home with my brother, I can tell him the same story and ask him to wait a half-hour. Can you stay a little while too?

I don't know. I would have to tell my mom something. Oh, and I usually walk my little sister home from school. I'll have to tell her to walk home with her friends. But, okay, I will. Obra-Jean, I'll be lying to my parents.

It's not really a lie. We can talk about those things with Sister Angelica sometime and, then, we've sort of told the truth.

I like that. You know, you're smart and very pretty for a colored girl.

And you're very pretty for a white girl, Janette.

That's a funny thing to say.

Why is it funny?

I don't know. Why do you have to say: "For a white girl"? Why not "for a girl?"

I could ask you the same question. Think about it. Why am I pretty "for a colored girl?" Why not just "for a girl," like you said about yourself?

We can all see that colored girls are different from us.

"We" and "us" means white people? You're talking about how white people feel? All of you think colored people are really different? Different how? Why is that?

You look different. Your skin is darker. Your hair is very curly. Your face is different too.

Okay. There are differences. But, Janette, do you realize you look different to me? Your skin has no color. Your hair is so straight it would just hangs on the side and back of your head if you didn't use those barrettes to pin it up. Your nose is sharp, too, like a knife and you have no lips.

But I look like normal people.

Yeah, you look like normal white people. I look like normal colored people.

Obra-Jean, don't you think white people look nicer than colored?

Some do, some don't. White doesn't make them better looking.

Most colored I've seen are not as good-looking as white people.

In my family, nobody thinks white people are better looking than us just because they're white.

But my family does think they're better looking. They think colored people are ugly.

Janette, that's what you learned in your family. I learned something different in my family.

But, your family is wrong.

No, Janette. My family is right, and your family is wrong.

How can that be?

That's what we learn in my family. I believe what I've learned just as much as you believe what you've learned in your family.

You know I've never had a conversation like this.

Because you've never talked to anybody but white people. Right?

Yes, that's true. So this is how colored people think?

Not all of us. Some do think white people are better looking. Everything they see and hear tells them that. I think you're pretty not because you're white but because you're pretty even with your thin lips, sharp nose, and straight hair.

Maybe, that's how I feel about you too.

Well, it's a first step.

What do you mean?

Maybe, we can be friends after all.

I hope so. I really like you, Obra-Jean. What's your family like?

My family is like most families. I have a mother and father. My mother's name is Leona and my father's name is Perry. They are both old, about fifty, I think. We call my big sister "Toby" but her real name is Patricia. She's twenty and in college at Wayne. And I have a big brother who is eighteen. We call him "E.J." but his real name is Elgin James. He's a senior in high school here at Saint Catherine. Our grandmother also lives with us. Her name is Clemenza and she's my mother's mother. She's really old, about seventy. What about your family?

We have an ordinary family. I have a mother and father, too. My mother is about sixty. Her name is Alice. My father is even older than my mother. His name is Theodore. I have two sisters. Joyce, who is older than me, finished high school and got married. Judy is younger than me and is in the sixth grade here at Saint Catherine. She's the one I usually walk home. I also have two brothers. Joseph is the oldest of us all. He is married with three kids. Jerrold is next oldest. He's not married and still lives at home with me and my little sister.

Do you have a pet, Janette?

We have a cat. What about you?

We had a dog but it died. I have two goldfish but they're not much fun. I call them Lulu and Fred. What kind of house do you live in, Janette?

You know, it's like these houses around the school. It's brick and old and has two floors and a basement. We have a nice backyard where my mother grows roses. What's your house like, Obra-Jean?

It's not as big as the houses around Saint Catherine. It's all wood and has an upstairs, a downstairs, and a basement. Our backyard isn't very big either and there's just grass back there. No flowers or anything. Oh, there's a couple of big trees. I think they're maples. How long have you lived in this neighborhood?

Forever. It's the only house I've ever lived in. And, you?

I think we've lived in our house about four years. I was just ten when we moved here. Before that, we lived in an apartment building. Our apartment was really small and it only had one bedroom. My grandmother didn't live with us then. She came to live with us when we moved to this neighborhood. She lived with my Aunt Augusta before that.

Obra-Jean, you know more colored are moving into this neighborhood. My parents don't like it. They've been talking about moving somewhere else. I think they're planning to move soon to a suburb like Saint Clair Shores.

Isn't it all white?

I think so. That's why they want to move there.

What do you think?

Obra-Jean, I don't know.

Why don't you ask them?

I can't do that.

Why not?

I don't ask them anything about colored people. They would get mad at me.

But Janette, I thought you want to stay in this school.

I do because we're friends now. You're gonna stay in this school, right?

Well, actually, I don't think so. My father left me a note this morning. He says I can go to Cass Tech in the fall. That's where I want to study like my sister did.

Obra-Jean, you say you're leaving Saint Catherine? You won't even be here? We're just becoming friends and you're leaving?

I want to leave but you could come to Cass too if you still lived in Detroit. We could still be friends.

My parents would never let me go to public school. All of my sisters and brothers went to Catholic school. My family is Catholic. It's the only thing they believe in. Besides, I heard Cass has a lot of colored kids. My parents wouldn't like that at all.

My mother doesn't want me to go to public school either. But, my father thought it was a good idea. My parents aren't Catholic so my father thinks public school is okay.

This ruins everything if you go to Cass.

But, Janette, we can still be friends.

Oh, Obra-Jean, how?

If you want to, we can meet on weekends.

I'm really upset. I thought we would be together. Now you say we'll be apart at different schools. And, if my family moves, how will we get together?

Hey, if we're gonna be friends, we'll figure this out.

Obra-Jean and Janette developed a routine until the end of the spring semester of staying after school at least once a week so that they could study together. This was possible because Obra-Jean lied to Leona that Sister Angelica was tutoring her. E.J., as usual, was tasked to wait and accompany his sister home from school. Obra-Jean and Janette did not actually study. More often than not, they just talked about things on their mind like high school, black and white people, boys, and their changing bodies. Obra-Jean also told Janette about how excited she was because she found out that, as a high school graduation present for E.J., her parents had planned a summer vacation trip to New York City where she would see many famous sights. Janette wanted to be enthusiastic but she was disheartened that, having gained a new friend, she would be separated from her perhaps for a long time. She then decided to risk breaking their after-school routine and called Obra-Jean at home.

Hello, may I speak to Obra-Jean? I'm her friend, Janette, from school.

Just one moment, please. Obra-Jean, some girl from school wants to talk to you.

Thanks, Momma. Hello.

Hi, Obra-Jean. This is Janette. I was thinking . . . school is out in a couple of weeks and, after that, we might not see each other much during the summer especially when your family goes on vacation. What if we could take a bus downtown and walk around and window shop before then?

Oh, wow. That would be cool, Janette. I can go on Saturday.

You can? Great. Where should we meet?

How about in front of school? We can tell our parents we're going to an eight o'clock mass and staying afterwards for a catechism study class.

That's a great idea. We can meet in front of our school at eight. Let's talk at school tomorrow about Saturday.

On Saturday, the girls met as planned and took a bus downtown. They headed to department stores and looked in the street-level windows of Kern's, Crowley's, and Hudson's. They also visited some of the specialty clothing stores, like Winkelman's. Shoppers crowded the streets around the department stores. Automobile traffic was heavy. Buses bringing shoppers downtown lined up outside of the stores. Obra-Jean and Janette shuffled along with the crowd, stopping occasionally to look in the display windows. Janette stopped in front of a window with a display of summer dresses.

This is fun, Obra-Jean. Look at those dresses. I would love to have a dress like that one.

Really, Janette? Somehow I don't think it would look good on you.

Why not?

For one reason, Janette, a beige dress wouldn't look good with your dark hair and pale skin. It would look better on me because my skin in darker.

What about the dark blue one with the tiny pink flowers?

Yeah, I think that might be better you. It's too bad, though, you don't have any money. On our trip to New York this summer, I want to shop in the stores there. Maybe, my mother will buy me something nice for high school.

Obra-Jean, I wish I could go to New York. My family has never traveled anywhere with us. I guess there were too many of us kids and not enough money. You're lucky. It's just you and your brother going with your parents?

Yeah, my brother and my Grandma Post.

Your father is driving your car?

He'll probably do most of the driving. My father and mother might take turns. She can drive too. Do you want to hear how we're getting there?

Sure.

Okay, So, my father says he's driving down to Toledo. Then he heads east across Ohio to Albany in New York. Then he'll head south to New York City. It's a long drive. That's why my parents are taking turns. We're driving straight through and just stopping for gas and something eat along the way. My father is hoping some of the new highways under construction are finished so that the trip won't be too long. Anyway, we'll have to sleep in the car until we get to New York.

That is really exciting. I wish I could come too.

Me too. You would be more fun than my brother. He's so boring. All he talks about is his girlfriends.

Gee, Obra-Jean, you'll be gone for a couple of weeks in the summer and, then, you'll be in Cass Tech. We might not see each other for a long time. My parents told me yesterday they've decided to move to Saint Clair Shores this summer. They're sending me to a Catholic school there in the fall. My parents also want me to go to a Catholic college somewhere, eventually. They want a school far away from Detroit where, I think, there aren't any colored people. There's a small Catholic college in Indiana they're talking about.

Wow. They really don't like colored people, do they?

No, they don't. I wish I had parents like yours, Obra-Jean. They seem so nice, and they let you decide what you want to do.

Well, they don't always let me do what I want. But, yes, my father helps me a lot. If's funny, it's my mother who always has some kind of objection or warning about anything I want to do. She's that way with my sister too but not with my brother.

At least you can talk with your parents. My parents just tell me what to do and most things they don't even discuss with me.

Why don't you come live with us?

You're making a joke, of course, Obra-Jean. But, I think I would like living with you and your family. Thank you.

Hey, Janette, look at that streetcar. Let's take a ride on it uptown for a while before we go home. What do you think?

Gee, Obra-Jean, I've never been on a streetcar.

Come on, it will be fun. We'll ride up for a while and come back. We'll see stuff that might be interesting.

Somewhat reluctantly Janette followed Obra-Jean to the streetcar stop in the middle of Woodward Avenue and joined the cue waiting for the next streetcar. Within minutes one of the sleek new yellow streetcars glided to the stop. The girls boarded at the front and dropped their coins in the coin box and found a seat facing in the direction they were headed uptown. As the streetcar conductor clanged the bell to alert cars preparing to turn at intersections, the girls watched attentively as the streetscape passed by. Obra-Jean had taken this ride with her mother several times in the past and was familiar with the route. However, this time she began noting the different buildings. There were several theaters with marques advertising recent Hollywood movies. Large, ornate churches were interspersed with office buildings and shops. Further along the route was a factory that made and bottled Vernor's Ginger Ale. The glass front of the modern building allowed the girls to peer inside and see some of the bottling machinery. After fifteen minutes or so, they arrived at a park-like setting with huge, stately buildings. From her previous trips, Obra-Jean informed Janette that on one side of Woodward was the main Public Library and on the other side was the Detroit Institute of Arts—the art museum. Janette was impressed with the buildings and with Obra-Jean's knowledge. Obra-Jean suggested that they exit near the museum and library, take a little walk around the area and then board a streetcar to return downtown. As the girls walked along Woodward, something stirred an emotion in Obra-Jean that she couldn't identify. She was excited but by what? Was it being with Janette? Was it being on her own and exploring the city without her family? Could it be these grand, beautiful buildings in this park-like setting?

Just when Obra-Jean thought they might end their excursion and take a streetcar to return downtown, she noticed the Detroit Historical Museum. It was a much smaller building than the Public Library or the Detroit Institute of Arts and it was situated not in the park but on its edge on a side street. Obra-Jean remembered visiting the museum with her parents years ago and had never forgotten something inside. She wanted to show it to Janette who was hesitant and asked if they could enter without adult accompaniment. Obra-Jean assured her that kids were welcome and they entered the building. She headed to a stair that led to a lower level. She promised Janette that she would surprised and pleased by what was there. As they descended the stairs, they felt they were entering a different world. For, indeed, it was a world that no longer existed. Called the Streets of Old Detroit, the entire lower level was a re-creation of narrow cobble-stoned streets found in the pre-automobile city. The lighting was subdued. In fact, old street lamps and lanterns in shop windows provided the only illumination. Windows in storefronts provided views in to a variety of shops such as grocery, pharmacy, ice cream parlor, millinery, shoe repair, and hardware. There was a fire station, garage for automobile service, and police station. The girls wandered the streets and laughed at the sound of their shoes clicking against the cobblestones. They peered through the windows to see what the shops offered. They noted that there was nothing comparable to these shops in their own neighborhood. How different life must have been without huge department stores. Obra-Jean was also aware of something else that she admired but had trouble pinpointing. She liked the "feeling" of the streets. Was it the closeness of the buildings to the street? Was it the details of the storefronts? Was it the quiet of the place? Nothing in her world outside of this place was anything like this. She wished her world was like this. All the way home, she turned these thoughts over and over in her mind.

Upon returning home from her morning with Janette, Obra-Jean learned from her mother that Perry had decided to take E.J. on Monday to visit Perry's workplace at the DeSoto automobile factory. Therefore, Obra-Jean would be going to, and returning from, school by herself. This arrangement did not make Leona happy but she couldn't change Perry's mind. Since Obra-Jean would not have an escort, she was not to stop anywhere along her route to and from school and not to talk to anyone or get involved with kids from the public school. Leona was adamant. An unsupervised trip pleased Obra-Jean because she was certain she would enjoy the independence. However, she concealed her pleasure of her own good luck but expressed her annoyance at her brother's good fortune.

Momma, why doesn't Daddy ask me to go with him to visit his factory? Why is it just E.J.?

You're never going to work in a factory, Obra-Jean. Frankly, I hope E.J. won't work in a factory either. But, your father wants to show off his smart son—who's going to college—to his work friends and his boss.

I'm smart and I'm going to college too.

But, you're a girl, Obra-Jean. His buddies and boss won't be interested in a girl.

Why not?

Because, Obra-Jean that's how things are. You know girls are not treated the same as boys. I've told you this time and time again. Women are not treated the same as men. I've been trying forever to get you to understand this. You're always going to be considered less than a man. You may be smarter and more talented but you're never going to be treated like a man. Get used to it. Now, that's all I have to say about visiting your father's factory.

Monday morning, E.J. left with his father and Leona sent Obra-Jean on her way alone with a further warning about obeying her conditions not to talk or get involved with anyone along the way. Obra-Jean said goodbye and started on her usual route to school. Before she had traveled three blocks from her home of the nine blocks to school, she spotted a single car garage across the street she had longed to view up close but never dared to examine. The garage's overhead door was open, as usual in the morning, and there was a white man working inside. He was building some sort of large architectural model. She looked both ways for traffic and crossed the street in the middle of the block and stood in front of the open door. The man noticed her and asked her name. She told him then asked him what he was doing and why. He replied he was building a model of a section of downtown Detroit on Woodward Avenue, the city's main street, for a civic presentation. Obra-Jean recognized the location because she and Janette had recently been window shopping at department stores on that street. The model was someone's idea for changing that section of the street from a major traffic thoroughfare into a plaza for pedestrians. The auto traffic would be diverted to a tunnel to be excavated beneath the street. Obra-Jean was fascinated and began asking more questions which the man casually but thoughtfully answered. He was not accustomed to talking with young black girls or any girls who were interested in his model. Not even the neighborhood boys were interested in what he was doing. They thought he was some kind of crazy old man playing with model buildings in his garage. Obra-Jean had one more question before she had to hurry on and not be late for school. How did he learn to make models of buildings? He replied he worked for an architect and learned all about building plans. She wondered what an architect was and where they worked. She had never known about architects or what they did or where they did it. It was fascinating. She said goodbye and asked if she could visit again on her way home. He told her he only worked in the garage during the morning. He would be finished shortly for the day and would leave for his other work. She could stop by another morning when he was working. She thanked him and left.

Although she didn't realize it at the time, Obra-Jean was drawn to the man in the garage. It was what he did, not who he was that tugged at her. He could build things that looked like miniature versions of real buildings. Quite unconsciously, her thoughts returned again and again to his wonderful creations. There was so much mystery attached to his work. She couldn't begin to understand where to begin to understand what he was doing. Some process in her mind prompted her to ask her father where he had put her nearly forgotten dollhouse. It was a young girl's plaything her parents had given her when she was eight years old. For a few years, she played with it, arranging and re-arranging the furniture, pretending to imagine the people who lived in her dollhouse. Ultimately, she lost interest in it because it was such a self-contained and nearly immutable object. Perry told her the dollhouse was in a basement storeroom with all of the kids' old toys. Obra-Jean decided to retrieve it and have another look at the thing. As she was poking around in boxes full of old toys, she came across E.J.'s electric trains. She remembered how he played with his trains in the basement. He would never let her operate the controls. When he was not around, however, she did arrange and re-arrange the several miniature houses he had that formed a kind of town for his train set. She opened another box and discovered her dollhouse and a wrapped package with her name on it. In the package were drawings she had made when she was younger—drawings she had completely forgotten but which her parents had saved and stored. Most of the drawings were of houses—some from her imagination and others apparently from memory of houses she had seen. Seeing evidence of her earlier interest re-focused her attention on the dollhouse. It was as she remembered it—a large house unlike any real houses in her own neighborhood. The rooms on two floors were arranged side by side and the entire rear of the house was open as if the back wall had been sheared off to expose the interior. Obra-Jean had a strong desire to re-arrange, not the furniture, but the rooms themselves. She couldn't figure out how to do this. At that moment, her barely conscious feelings became concrete. She wanted to create out of her dollhouse a house of her own intentions —like some of her early drawings—and, she thought, the man in the garage could tell her how to do this.

One Saturday, Obra-Jean told Leona she wanted to go Pingree Park in their neighborhood. Some of the girls in the neighborhood were meeting there to talk about attending high school in the fall. This was another lie but Obra-Jean knew her mother would not impose her usual restrictions or demand detailed information because she approved of Obra-Jean socializing with other neighborhood black girls. Obra-Jean headed immediately for the garage in the hope the door would be open and the man would be working inside. It was her lucky day. Silvio Pugliese was, indeed, at work. When she stepped up to the door, he greeted her and asked her how she was doing. She told him she wanted to make a building—a small one like he created—but she didn't know how or where to start. To his credit, Silvio, an immigrant from Italy, felt this was an important inquiry despite coming from a young black girl. She was serious and so was he. He stopped assembling parts for a model building and invited her into the cramped garage leaving the overhead door open. He showed her blueprints on a table with diagrams of a building he was constructing. He explained the blueprints were based on photographs of actual buildings and then scaled to the size of the model he was constructing. All of this was, at first, a puzzle to Obra-Jean but, as he continued his explanation, the real and the conceptual easily interlocked in her mind. She understood the process. What she still did not understand was how he took the blueprints and made actual pieces of the model. He showed her his materials—wood, cardboard, putty, glue, and nails—and demonstrated, briefly, how he selected materials for a particular part of the model. As she watched, he constructed part of a model using a saw, scissors, and a knife. It didn't take long for Obra-Jean to completely synthesize the process from beginning to end. She thanked him, left the garage, and went to Pingree Park to think. When she returned home, she took another look at her dollhouse and considered what she would do with it. She made detailed drawings of the floor plan and of the exterior. She tried several different designs until one finally satisfied her.

She spent many days thereafter in the basement creating a design for her house. Instead of rooms side by side, she wanted a more complex arrangement on each floor with hallways and stairs connecting the rooms and floors as in her own home. She began dismantling the dollhouse using a small handsaw, cutting apart and reconfiguring the rooms until the dollhouse resembled the kind of house she knew in her own neighborhood. And, instead of being completely open on one side, the dollhouse was entirely enclosed with exterior walls that could be removed to reveal the interior. Obra-Jean was learning as she proceeded. She made many mistakes. Measurements were incorrect. Parts didn't fit together properly. But, instead of giving up, she used each failure to find a new solution. She learned quickly from her mistakes and in a very short time, mastered the construction sufficiently to reveal her intentions. The completed dollhouse was no longer, in fact, a dollhouse but a miniature building not unlike her own home or the houses in her neighborhood. Stepping back to admire her work, Obra-Jean grew dissatisfied. She had realized her intentions but something was lacking. She couldn't know it at the time but what she really wanted was an original design. So she put aside her project and began to explore and learn more about buildings. All during her work on the dollhouse her family noted her project but they seemed completely uninterested in what she was doing or why. Leona was simply happy her daughter was busy and, apparently, passing her time constructively.

— A Family Vacation —
Summer 1957

The Moore family, as Obra-Jean described them to Janette—her parents, Leona and Perry, the three children, Toby, E.J., and Obra-Jean, and Leona's mother, Clemenza—lived in a two story, four bedroom, wood-frame house built circa 1920s when their neighborhood rapidly transitioned from fallow farmland and lush woodland to urban settlement. However, Obra-Jean did not know anything of this history of her family home or its neighborhood nor would it have really interested her. There was a massive influx of European immigrants to Detroit at the turn of the twentieth century. The explosive development of the automobile industry spurred housing developers to build whole neighborhoods of single and two-family homes packed together on narrow lots for the rapidly growing factory worker population of Detroit. The Moore family's neighborhood on the city's east-side was typical. Families of European origin settled on land purchased or expropriated from indigenous people. Many of these settlers were actually second generation Americans but some were of recent passage across the ocean and not necessarily English-speaking. Germans and Italians especially flooded the neighborhood and established businesses and associations to create a coherent, if not necessarily cohesive, community. After the Second World War, blacks, who had migrated from the South during the first half of the twentieth century, were effectively confined to overcrowded, but thriving, ghettos near downtown. Black Bottom and Paradise Valley were the beating heart of Detroit's black community. As some blacks became more financially secure, they pushed out of these ghettoes into surrounding neighborhoods to create secure enclaves of working-class, home-owning families. As the black population grew, this process of expansion continued with blacks seeking housing in contiguous white neighborhoods further from the center. One by one, white families sold to blacks and then moved further towards the periphery of the city. As more and more blacks appeared in the neighborhood, more and more whites left it while often keeping their stores and enterprises in place.

When Leona and Perry decided to move from their one bedroom apartment in one of Detroit's black ghettos to their new neighborhood, there were already some black families in the mostly white district. Leona and Perry did not make friends with their new neighbors, black or white. They retained ties with long-time friends formed from their young adulthood in Detroit although many of these friends now lived at some distance from them. On the other hand, their children found many kids their age in the new neighborhood and immediately began to bond with their favorites. Toby the oldest sibling and elder daughter, found several girls her age with whom she became pals. These friends at first proved essential to her sense of black sorority because her parents planned to place her in an all-white neighborhood Catholic school—Saint Catherine. It was all-white because the white families in the neighborhood abandoned public schools, and the incoming blacks, who were seldom of the Catholic faith, sent their children to free public schools instead of paying tuition for Catholic school. The Moore family, although not Catholic, believed in good education for their children. They were willing to pay for it at some sacrifice to themselves. They saved for their children's education and sent them all to a black Catholic school in their old neighborhood. Now their intention was the same for their new one. In the year that the family moved—1953—they intended to enroll Toby in high school, and E.J. and Obra-Jean in grade school at Saint Catherine. However, against her mother's wishes but with the consent of her father, Toby decided not to attend Saint Catherine. Instead, she enrolled at Cass Technical High—a school that, unlike neighborhood public high schools, was open to enrollment by all of the city's youth who qualified. At Cass, Toby met kids from all over the city, black and white, from working-class and middle-class families. Eventually, the friends she made at Cass were more interesting than her neighborhood pals in whom she lost interest.

While E.J. made many friends with neighborhood boys and school pals, Obra-Jean was less social than her older siblings. She tended to stay close to home and found solitary activities to pass her time outside of school. When she and Janette Fulgenzi became friends at school, Obra-Jean grew more gregarious and interested in some of the neighborhood girls her age. Her friendship with Janette, however, was set in its own world, neither within Obra-Jean's or Janette's family or neighborhood. They were pals together with no other companions. While their time together outside of school was limited because of parental restrictions, when they could be together, they shared thoughts, hopes, and dreams. Both knew the summer of 1957 was a time of change because both were graduating from grade school to high school. Obra-Jean had persuaded her father to allow her to follow in her sister's footsteps to attend Cass Tech while Janette's parents were moving out of the city to the suburb of Saint Clair Shores. They would no longer see one another on a regular basis and the Moore family was traveling by car to New York City for a few weeks during the summer, limiting even what little time remained to be together before each teenager went her separate way to school.

Perry owned a 1956 four door DeSoto, a car built in the factory in which he worked. It was also the car he used for the trip to New York City. Spacious enough for three adults—Perry, Leona, and Clemenza—and two children—E.J. and Obra-Jean—the family car handled well on two- and four-lane roads between Detroit and New York. Sections of a new interstate highway system were under construction but few sections were ready for continuous travel across Ohio and New York State. Along the way, Perry insisted on a brief stop in Cleveland so that he could visit an old Army buddy. Leona was annoyed by what she considered both an unnecessary delay and the unusual warmth Perry showed for his friend. She finally insisted that Perry cut short his visit. The family then pushed on to Albany. There, they turned south and, before reaching New York City, they stopped in the town of Hyde Park. Since this was the first time after Cleveland that the family had stopped for something other than to buy gas, take a toilet break, grab a sandwich or snack, or simply stretch after hours of riding in the car, Obra-Jean was delighted to be standing on spacious grounds surrounding the impressive and imposing mansion that was the home of the late president, Franklin Delano Roosevelt, and his wife, Eleanor Roosevelt. Obra-Jean had often heard her parents and their friends talking long and lovingly about the Roosevelts, especially Eleanor. Obra-Jean understood, somehow, they had been good people and somehow black folks had benefitted from their being president and first lady. She didn't know exactly what they did but she was sure it was something good. There was a depression when FDR was president, and people were poor and, then, there was a war and Obra-Jean's father was in it although he, apparently, never shot at or killed anyone. She knew that Roosevelt died unexpectedly and another man, Harry Truman, became president and her parents liked him too. Roosevelt and Truman were both Democrats. That's something Obra-Jean heard over and over and that to be a Democrat was good because both of her parents and their friends and other members of her family were all Democrats. It was good to be a Democrat and bad to be a Republican. Eisenhower was a Republican. He was now president. No adult that Obra-Jean knew liked Eisenhower but they were very fond of Roosevelt and here she was standing in front of his home. It was huge and beautiful and beyond this home was the Hudson River. It was so wonderful that Obra-Jean thought that only good people lived well in big beautiful houses like this one. Maybe, someday, she would live in a house like this. For some reason, they could not go inside of the house and that disappointed Obra-Jean but they could walk around the beautifully landscaped grounds. After about an hour, Perry announced they would have to return to their car and proceed along the final stretch of highway to New York City.

Obra-Jean was lost in thought as they drove along the Hudson River through one little town after another. Just when she thought, as she had thought many times on this trip, that they would never reach their destination, Perry told them they were crossing a bridge into Manhattan. They were now in New York City. Obra-Jean stared uncomprehendingly at the size and number of buildings, and the crowds of people on the sidewalks, and the number of cars on the streets. The further they traveled the more dense and big everything became. The drive seemed endless with countless stops at traffic lights, sirens blaring from police cars, fire trucks, and ambulances. She never heard this kind of noise in Detroit nor had she ever seen anything to match this overwhelming complexity of buildings. Traffic slowed. It seemed to crawl forward. They were coming to a convergence of streets which were bounded by buildings aflame with electric lights and signs. Her father rejoiced that they were in Times Square. Obra-Jean could hardly take it all in at once. There were too many things to look at, too much that was unfamiliar, so much that was bewildering like the giant billboard of a man's face exhaling from his mouth an actual, enormous smoke ring as if he had just taken a puff from a cigarette. As their car passed out of Times Square, her father seemed suddenly confused and kept looking for something that would tell him where he was. He made a series of turns and then more turns until he stopped in front of a large building on a street with other large buildings. There was a neon sign on the front of the building that said: Hotel Le Marque. Perry said this was the hotel where they would stay for several days. Leona exited the car, then E.J. and Obra-Jean, and finally Clemenza who was sitting in the backseat with the children. Perry retrieved their bags from the trunk of the car. A bellhop came out of the hotel and put their bags on a cart and brought them inside. Leona led the family into the hotel while Perry got in the car and drove away to find a place to park it for their stay.

The hotel was a drab and depressing affair. Obra-Jean knew this was not her idea of a hotel as she had seen in magazines and on television. She also knew to stay quiet. The carpet was tattered and stained. The man at the front desk was not friendly. The family had reserved two rooms: one for Leona and Perry and one for Clemenza and the children. When Perry arrived after leaving the car in a parking garage, the bellboy escorted them up to their rooms which were on the same floor but not adjacent. The hallway was dingy, dimly lit and, again, the carpeting was old and worn. The rooms were small with a single dirt-stained window opening onto a narrow courtyard. The bathrooms were barely clean. Clemenza's and the children's room had two beds—a double and a single. E.J. would sleep on the single bed and grandmother and granddaughter would sleep together on the double bed. Obra-Jean could not understand why they had to stay in such an ugly, rundown hotel when, she was sure, there were nicer places in New York. But, here they were and this was it.

Over the next five days, the family walked, bussed, and subwayed around Manhattan. They also booked a tour. First stop was the Empire State Building. Traveling to the top, Obra-Jean gasped when she exited the elevator onto the observation deck, and the panorama of New York City spread before her like some enormous model of a city. She had seen some building models at the Detroit Historical Museum and in that garage in her neighborhood. She had asked detailed questions of the man building that model. It had impressed and inspired her and, now, looking down at New York City, she wanted to build something like this—not a model but a real city. She wanted to be an architect.

There were also trips to the Statue of Liberty, Rockefeller Center, the United Nations Building, Penn Station, and Grant's Tomb. As their tour bus drove along the docks of the Hudson River, Obra-Jean noticed several ocean liners. They were like huge buildings floating on the water. Their mass and distinctive shape with towering smokestacks left a strong impression on Obra-Jean. The endless residential streets of multi-story buildings side by side with no breaks between them made an even stronger impression. Unlike Detroit with its monotonous blocks of separate one- and two-story houses, New York had five, six story, and taller buildings that formed a solid mass for each block. There were no front lawns as in Detroit. There were trees but, instead of hiding the houses as in Detroit, they seemed small by comparison with the height of the buildings. She was fascinated by the stone stairs that led from the sidewalks to the second story of some buildings. She tried to figure out the intricate carvings and other designs on some of the fancier buildings but she had no way to describe or remember what she saw except that it was strange and wonderful.

When the family returned to their hotel, Obra-Jean sat on the bed and tried to picture what she had seen. She could only conjure fleeting impressions, fragments really. To her surprise, the one sight she had seen came back to her more completely than any other. It was the United Nations Building. This glass box, taller than most buildings in Detroit and completely unlike any of them, registered on her mind in a way she could not explain. At dinner in a restaurant in the hotel that evening, she asked her father if he could tell her something about the building. He could not. Gradually, she forgot about her fascination and started listening to her parents' conversation. They were going to see a musical after dinner, all five of them. It was a Broadway musical, Lerner and Lowe's *My Fair Lady*, her mother said very proudly. Everyone was talking about this musical and they were lucky to get five tickets although the seats were not together. All seats were in the balcony but the children would be seated together in one section and the parents would be seated together in another section. Grandmother Post had a seat by herself. They took a taxi to the theater, the first time Obra-Jean and E.J. had ever been in a taxi. Obra-Jean had to sit somewhat awkwardly on her grandmother's lap in the backseat with E.J. and their mother. Her father sat in front with the driver. After paying the driver, Perry herded the family to a line outside of the theater and shuffled along as the theater patrons slowly entered the front doors. Although Obra-Jean had been to fancy downtown theaters in Detroit, those theaters only showed movies. This was a theater for live performances, and Obra-Jean realized she didn't know what to expect. As the lights dimmed and the orchestra began playing the overture, Obra-Jean's excitement bewildered her. She hadn't realized there would be an actual orchestra which she could see from her seat in the balcony. When the curtain rose revealing the set—a street or square in London filled with people in different kinds of costumes made to look like they lived in some earlier time—Obra-Jean grabbed E.J.'s arm. When Eliza Doolittle began to sing *Wouldn't it be Loverly*, Obra-Jean started to cry to herself. At intermission, E.J. asked her what happened to make her cry. She couldn't explain herself because she didn't understand why she felt the way she did. In fact, she couldn't explain to herself what she was feeling except that it was as if the Streets of Old Detroit had come alive on the theater's stage.

Obra-Jean assumed the family would return to Detroit after their visit to New York City but that was not the case. Either she never paid attention to what her parents said about the trip or they never fully explained it to her because the trip was a present for E.J. Upon leaving New York, they headed south. Obra-Jean ceased being interested in their vacation because she didn't have a chance to shop in New York; she wanted to return to Detroit. Therefore, when her father announced their arrival in Atlantic City, Obra-Jean was annoyed. What was in Atlantic City? Her father parked the car and everyone got out and walked a few blocks past homes and stores until they reached the Boardwalk along the ocean front. This was the first time that either Obra-Jean or E.J. had seen an ocean. Detroit is on a river, actually a strait between Lake Saint Clair and Lake Erie. As impressive as those bodies of water were, they did not compare with the seemingly endless expanse of the Atlantic Ocean that filled their vision. A warm, moist breeze wafted across the Boardwalk. The sandy beach between the Boardwalk and the ocean was filled with white people in bathing suits, some sitting or lying on the sand, others running, playing, and entering or leaving the water. Obra-Jean wanted to walk along the Boardwalk and look at the shops and places to eat. She persuaded her grandmother to walk with her while her parents and E.J. stood gazing at the beach and ocean. Obra-Jean had never spent much time with her grandmother. She did not really know her very well. Prior to Clemenza coming to live with them in their new house, Obra-Jean had not seen very much of her grandmother who had lived with Obra-Jean's Aunt Augusta. She never knew why her grandmother came to live with them especially since it was clear to Obra-Jean that her own mother, Leona, didn't particularly like her mother. It was at that moment Obra-Jean realized Leona never called Clemenza "mother," only "Clemenza." If Obra-Jean had ever dared call her mother by her first name, Leona would, as she often said: "Knock you into next week." While Leona said such things with a somewhat joking tone, Obra-Jean knew there was something very, very serious about Leona and her mother, and about Leona and her daughters. Whatever it was she could not figure out.

The family did not stay overnight in Atlantic City. Instead, after a few hours on the Boardwalk, they returned to the car and Perry began driving west to Philadelphia. This was another destination that came as a surprise to Obra-Jean. She couldn't remember anyone ever mentioning Philadelphia and, frankly, she didn't want to go there, although she had no particular objection except she still wanted to return to Detroit. As Perry drove the car across the Delaware River into downtown Philadelphia, Obra-Jean had lost all interest in observing the surroundings. After much stop and go, left turns and right turns, Perry stopped the car in a residential neighborhood in front of a tall narrow house. When she asked where they were, he announced this was where his younger brother lived, and the family would be staying at his home for the next few nights.

Perry's brother moved from Detroit to Philadelphia nearly a decade earlier. Carson Moore owned an elegant Victorian house in front of which Perry had parked his car. Uncle Carson was a name Obra-Jean had heard many times but she had never met or knew him. It was already dark out and the house glowed with light from within. There were steep steps up to the front door like buildings in New York City. After her father rang the doorbell, the big wooden front door opened and a very slender man stood in the doorway smiling. Clearly expecting his guests, he welcomed inside his brother and, one by one, his brother's family. Obra-Jean was accustomed to being the last person introduced at any family gathering and she was not disappointed when, again, she was the last to be introduced. Everyone passed into the house with their bags. There was a central hallway with stairs on the right going up to the second floor. Left and right, there were rooms closed off, Obra-Jean noted, by doors that slid into the wall—something she had never before seen in a home. She later learned these were called "pocket doors." Carson immediately asked everyone to follow him upstairs where they would find their bedrooms. Leona and Perry had one bedroom, lucky E.J. had his own small bedroom, and Obra-Jean and Clemenza again had to share a bedroom. Once everyone got settled, they returned downstairs to the living room on the left of the entry hallway. It was well furnished and comfortable. Obra-Jean surveyed the room, taking in patterned rugs on the floor, paintings on the walls, lamps, vases, and covered bowls on tables, a chandelier hanging from the ceiling in the middle of the room, and a huge fireplace on the windowless long side wall. Tall, curtained windows at the front of the house screened the room from the street. Obra-Jean thought how uninteresting her own home was compared to this. Carson offered to get drinks for everyone and suggested that dinner was ready and for all to pass into the adjacent dining room and take a seat. He would sit at the head of the table nearest the kitchen and told his brother to sit opposite him with Leona to his left and Clemenza to his right. Obra-Jean and E.J. could sit left and right of Carson. Then something happened that Obra-Jean thought was strange. Another man who had not been previously present or introduced, entered the dining room with drinks and began serving them. He was much younger than Carson and—Obra-Jean thought—very handsome. He introduced himself as Philip Townsend, Carson's housemate.

Carson left for the kitchen and returned with a huge platter piled with fried chicken. Philip followed him, then, making multiple trips, brought on trays into the dining room several bowls and dishes containing mashed potatoes, corn on the cob, collard greens, lettuce and tomato salad, and cornbread. It was a feast spread across the large dining room table. After Carson was seated, he said a blessing and suggested that everyone help themselves by passing the serving dishes. Philip retreated to the kitchen. Obra-Jean listened closely to the adults' conversation. Everyone, including Clemenza, talked about Detroit and Philadelphia.

Perry wanted to know about his brother and his life. It was all new information to Obra-Jean but, eventually, she grew disinterested because no one asked anything about her. When the conversation began to wind down, Carson suggested it had probably been a long day for everyone and they all probably wanted to go to bed. However, he said he had a surprise and disappeared into the kitchen. When he returned, he carried a cake ablaze with thirty-seven candles. He began to sing "Happy Birthday" to Perry. Spontaneously, the family joined in. Carson placed the cake on the table and at the conclusion of the ditty blew out all of the candles. Obra-Jean was perplexed. Her father's birthday was still some days off. Why were they celebrating now? As if anticipating Obra-Jean's unspoken question, Carson explained that he knew he could not be with his brother on his actual birthday—by that time, the family would have returned to Detroit—so he wanted to celebrate the occasion while his brother was in Philadelphia. Philip then entered the dining room with plates and forks. Carson removed the candles, cut and plated the cake, then served Perry and the other family members. Carson went to the buffet, opened a drawer and produced a gift-wrapped package which he said was a present for Perry. Upon opening it, Perry withdrew a beautifully tailored burgundy cardigan sweater. Perry was delighted. Carson explained that he had knitted the sweater himself. This news astonished Obra-Jean. Later, when everyone had retired to their bedroom and she climbed into bed with Clemenza, she thought about Carson, her father, and Carson's friend, Philip. Something was going on here that she didn't understand but no one else seemed to take notice or spoke of it. Her last conscious thought before falling asleep was that her father was almost thirty-seven. That seemed very old to her.

Over the next few days, the Moore family visited several sights in Philadelphia especially the Liberty Bell and city hall with its massive statue of William Penn atop the building. During lunch on one of their excursions in the city, Obra-Jean was bored and daydreamed about home.

Philadelphia could not offer her anything of interest after New York City. She was certainly looking forward to being again in Detroit and, maybe, meeting Janette so that they could talk about school. Her attention suddenly shifted back to the adults. Something about her parents' conversation caught her attention and she focused on their remarks. Leona questioned Perry about Philip. Who was he? It was clear to her that, as Carson's housemate, he slept in Carson's house but where? Perry tried to change the subject by saying he didn't know about his brother's home life. Leona persisted. Perry suggested maybe Philip's bedroom was one of those in which they were sleeping. Unrelenting, Leona questioned where was he now sleeping. Perry tried to end the discussion by saying Philip probably slept in Carson's bedroom. Leona asked if that meant they slept in the same bed. Perry said yes and told Leona to drop the subject. How his brother lived was none of their business. Obra-Jean could not quite grasp the significance of this conversation but it stayed with her.

At the end of their visit when her father announced they should pack to return to Detroit, Obra-Jean became enthusiastic. Everyone thanked Carson for his hospitality and Perry invited his brother to visit him in Detroit. The return trip through the Allegheny Mountains of Pennsylvania intrigued Obra-Jean. It was unfamiliar landscape. She had seen mountains along the Hudson River when they traveled to New York City but they had not driven through them as they were doing now in Pennsylvania. There were long tunnels through the mountains and these were amazing to her. How did they make these tunnels, she wondered? Who made them and when? By the time the family reached Pittsburgh, however, Obra-Jean had become completely grumpy. Maybe, it was being cramped in the backseat with her brother and grandmother. Maybe, it was seeing so many unfamiliar things and meeting so many new people. Maybe, it was just fatigue. In any case, when they reached Toledo, she felt that her world was finally coming back into focus. A few more hours and they would be in Detroit, in their own home, and she would be in her own room.

After getting lost in Toledo because of confusing highway signs, and making several wrong turns, Perry finally found the so-called Dixie Highway to Detroit. Since he had driven most of the way from Philadelphia to Toledo, he asked Leona to take over until they reached the outskirts of Detroit. Dixie Highway was a four lane main road connecting Detroit to the southern states and was heavily trafficked with cars and trucks. Leona drove in the northbound curb lane to allow the faster traffic to pass her. She was an experienced but cautious driver. So, when a truck in the oncoming southbound traffic suddenly swerved into the northbound lanes in which she was driving, she instinctively, but unfortunately, turned the steering wheel to the left and slammed on the breaks. The rear-wheeled drive of the car caused it to fishtail so that the passenger side of the car faced the oncoming traffic. In the mayhem of the moment, their car slammed into the rear of a car in front of theirs crushing the front passenger side of their DeSoto. By the time the car, as well as all of the other traffic, came to a stop, the family in the DeSoto was shaken and confused. Leona looked around the car's interior. Her husband next to her was lifeless. He was bleeding from the head and chest. The odor of oil and gasoline mixed with that of blood. Obra-Jean was leaning into E.J. who, in turn, was leaning into Clemenza. All had their eyes open but they weren't speaking. Leona knew that Perry was dead. The rest of the family was alive but stunned.

Two sheriff patrol cars arrived to investigate the accident and to re-route traffic. Soon an ambulance also came and attendants placed Perry's body inside. Leona accompanied the body to a hospital in Toledo. A sheriff invited the rest of family—Clemenza, E.J., and Obra-Jean—into a patrol car and he drove them to the same hospital. When they arrived, Leona informed them that she had called her sister who, fortunately, was home and immediately agreed to drive to Toledo to pick up the family and bring them with their luggage back to Detroit. Meanwhile, Leona asked a member of the hospital staff to call the McFall Funeral Home in Detroit to transport Perry's body back home. By the time Augusta arrived, several hours had passed and Leona and family were beginning to recover from the shock of the accident. Leona was all business as she itemized all of the things that had to be done when they returned home. E.J. tried to assist his mother. Clemenza remained silent. Obra-Jean sat by herself and watched her family. She wondered if she should mention to someone that she was hungry.

The funeral service for Perry was, for the most part, a mix of emotions. Leona held herself together trying not to cry because she was still uncomprehending of Perry's death. Hers was an in-between place—knowing he was dead but magically believing he would re-appear alive and well. Toby followed her mother's example and showed no emotion but could barely tamp down her rage and grief. When she was in private, she cried uncontrollably. E.J. was the only family member who visibly cried at the funeral, and everyone avoided him as if embarrassed by his unchecked emotion. Obra-Jean did not cry. She was deeply sad about her father's death but worries of her own fate competed with her sadness. She felt her world had changed in ways she could not anticipate but only fear. Without her father, she imagined her mother being a complete and total bitch. Since Toby would be out of the house in her friend's apartment and E.J. would be in college, both of them would escape their mother's control. However, Obra-Jean would be constantly badgered by her mother, prevented from doing almost anything she wanted to do, and fearful her mother would revoke the decision that she could attend Cass.

Perry's other family—the Moore, the family of his birth—mourned his death uncontrollably. His brother, Carson, wept openly. His grief was surpassed in both intensity and volume by Perry's parents. His father,

Barry, nearly collapsed in his pew and had to be attended by Carson. Perry's mother, Estyllene—called Styll by most of her family and friends—couldn't console her husband because she was paralyzed with sorrow. She slumped next to him in their pew, her eyes tightly closed, tears streaming down her face. The women ushers in the church had to revive her with cold compresses. Perry's youngest brother, Mason, who sat next to Styll, displayed no emotion whatsoever and seemed disconnected from the sorrow around him. When it was time to leave the church, the women ushers helped Styll and Barry to their feet, escorted them out of the nave and down the front stairs to the sidewalk. Obra-Jean had never witnessed such a scene and, although she understood the emotion, she was put off by its open display. In her family, such carrying on was discouraged. It wasn't proper. That's what her mother told her all the time. "Mind yourself, young lady. Don't make a scene in public especially in front of white people." This unrestrained outburst of crying—losing control, making noise—was especially surprising coming from adults—old people particularly. When the extended family returned to the late Perry Moore's home, Styll and Barry had recovered their composure. Obra-Jean noted how quickly the mood changed among members of the family. Instead of grief, there was laughter and jokes. Styll seemed to become an entirely different person. She was the life of the party talking to everyone and telling stories about Perry and her other sons while eating from a plate of food prepared by Clemenza. Obra-Jean watched and wondered. Then, her mother said something to Styll that caused Obra-Jean to freeze. Leona called Styll "Mother." Obra-Jean had always noticed this title her mother gave Styll because she knew Styll wasn't Leona's mother; she was Leona's mother-in-law. Clemenza was her mother but, now, Obra-Jean was puzzled. Why, had Leona never called her own mother "Mother" only "Clemenza." Why?

— The New Reality —

The Moore household became exactly what Obra-Jean anticipated. Toby had already moved out of the house to an apartment with Ronnie and refused Leona's pleas to return home to comfort and help her. Following the funeral and facing a future without Perry, the full weight of being a widow nearly suffocated Leona. She cried as much for Perry's death as for her now uncertain future. Perry's life insurance policy would pay the expenses of the funeral but what about the house payment? Without Perry's income, how could she pay for the house and all of the other bills? She considered and quickly dismissed the idea of selling her diamond wedding ring. Her bank account had, maybe, a little over a thousand dollars that wouldn't last long if she used it for household expenses. After considering her income and expenses, Leona reached a decision about finances. She informed E.J. she could no longer afford to pay his tuition. He would have to get a job but that still wouldn't completely compensate for the loss of Perry's income. Her only idea was to ask Augusta and, maybe, her in-laws, for some money. As much as she hated relying on her family for help, she could see no other possibility.

E.J. for his part, got a job in order to stay in school. Following Toby's example, he eventually got an interview at the university administration and he was hired as a student clerk. Burying himself in his schoolwork and part-time job at college, E.J. spent very little time at home. Obra-Jean did begin classes at Cass Tech, as her father promised she could— Leona did not revoke the decision but she put Obra-Jean on a very tight budget. She was not allowed any extraneous expenses except those directly related to school. Obra-Jean took a bus to and from school. When she returned home after school, she was alone at home in the afternoon with her Grandmother Post. Although E.J. was occasionally home in the evening, he stayed in his room until dinner and then returned there or left the house for socializing elsewhere. Leona conceded responsibility for cleaning the house and preparing all meals to Clemenza because Leona simply didn't have the time, energy, or enthusiasm for housework, shopping, and cooking. She was moody and often crying to herself. Obra-Jean understood that her mother was upset. All of them were upset but they had their own lives to live. As a gesture of being helpful, she offered to assist her grandmother with meals and housework which Clemenza gratefully accepted. When Leona arrived home in the evening, she bored into Obra-Jean. She wanted to know daily what she did in school. She wanted to see her homework and tests. She wanted to know who she was with outside of school. She monitored all of Obra-Jean's life unrelentingly. There was nothing Obra-Jean could do that escaped Leona's notice. It was infuriating to Obra-Jean and she resolved that this surveillance could not continue. She would have a showdown with her mother but she needed an ally.

The phone rang at the Moore family home. Obra-Jean answered thinking her Grandmother Moore was returning her call. She was surprised by the voice at the other end. It certainly wasn't her grandmother but it was familiar. At first, she was confused then realized it was her grade school friend, Janette Fulgenzi.

Hi, Janette. It's a nice surprise to hear your voice. I didn't recognize it at first. How are you?

I'm fine. I started high school at Our Lady of Perpetual Sorrows here in Saint Clair Shores. It's so boring—the school, and not having my smartest friend to talk to. The kids here are dumb as dust. I really miss you and that's why I'm calling. Can we get together for a shopping trip downtown? I could meet you at Hudson's department store and we could spend some time window shopping.

That would be great. When do you want to go?

I was thinking of going two Saturdays from now. This coming Saturday I'm ushering at the Shubert theater downtown.

Ushering? How did that happen?

A friend of mine at school has been ushering there for Saturday matinees when the theater lets high school and college students usher for free admission. We get to see whatever play is on, and ushering is really nothing because often there are hardly any people in the theater. A lot of people have stopped going downtown now that there are shopping centers with movie theaters in the suburbs.

Ushering sounds like fun. I'd like to do that sometime.

Well, let's talk about it when we get together for our shopping day.

Okay. What time?

Ten? And, I tell you what, instead of Hudson's, let's meet under the big clock outside Kern's department store on Woodward Avenue.

Good. See you two Saturdays from now at ten.

Window shopping was an adventure for both girls. Dressed for the cool fall weather, each wore a heavy cardigan sweater over her blouse and skirt, attire that mimicked their Catholic school uniform. Together, they covered all of the downtown department stores and many of the women's specialty shops. They made mental lists of all of the things they would like to buy but couldn't. They even went into a few shops to examine the merchandise and prices. Neither had more than a few dollars saved from their weekly allowance and, therefore, a purchase was beyond their means. Interspersed with their discussion of clothes, shoes, and trinkets, each girl talked about her school and classes, the students, the teachers, and many other facets of high school life. Janette was particularly interested to hear that Cass Tech had kids from all over the city—different races, ethnic groups, and economic levels—while Our Lady of Perpetual Sorrows only had kids from the neighborhood, and exclusively from Catholic, middle class, and white families.

Obra-Jean, what's it like to be around so many different kinds of kids?

I like it. There are colored kids and white kids and a few kids from Asia. There are kids from pretty wealthy families, I think, because they dress really well not like the kids in my neighborhood. There are also kids who live in the projects. There are some really, really smart kids like you.

And you.

And me. There are kids into theater, into sports, into science, and into art. There's a girl who belongs to a singing group. She's from the projects. They sang at Cass and they're really good. She told me they might make some records at this new music company called Hitsville, or Motown, or something. Isn't that amazing? I like the theater group. I've been getting to know some of the kids in it and we sometimes stop at a place downtown for soda pop after school before taking a bus home. They know so much about so many things I've never heard about. You know, Janette, we were really isolated from everything at Saint Catherine. Cass Tech is a whole new world for me. And, there are parties after school at different places, and dances. I haven't been able to go yet because my mother won't let me but that might change.

You're lucky, Obra-Jean. I feel like I've gone backwards. My school is even less interesting than Saint Catherine. I don't know how I can last there for four years.

Oh, you will. You'll find something or someone interesting.

What kind of classes are you taking?

Janette, at Cass, you have to choose a curriculum. I'm in the science curriculum, like my sister was, so I'll study biology, chemistry, physics, math and, you know, the regular stuff like social studies, English, and Latin.

You're not taking all of those different classes at once, are you?

No, no. That's the curriculum. I'll take different combinations of classes during the next four years.

I wish my school had something like that. We just have the boring stuff and lots of religion and catechism.

I'm sorry about that. By the way, I can also take electives. I met this girl my age who's in the art curriculum. She's been telling me about her drawing class. Now that's something that really interests me.

Drawing?

Yes. I want to learn how to draw better. Can I tell you something, Janette?

Sure.

This science curriculum is to keep my mother off my back for the time being. It's not what I really want to do. Are you ready for this: I think, I want to study architecture in college and become an architect.

Architecture? An architect?

Yeah. You know, design buildings.

A girl who designs buildings? I've never heard of that. When did you decide this?

It's happening just now. I made up my mind when we went to New York City. I knew I was somehow interested in buildings but I didn't know anything about how buildings were made. I mean, it never even occurred to me that someone had to design each and every building there is. Our house was designed by somebody. My school was designed by somebody. I want to be that somebody who designs buildings. If I told my mother this, she would automatically say no way because she doesn't know anything about architects. She insists I study something she knows is practical so I can be, maybe, a school science teacher someday. And, right now, I can't go against her. That's why I'm studying science but I have a plan.

What is it?

I don't want to say right now but I'll tell you if it works out.

Great. Hey, do you want to get an ice cream or something at Hudson's cafe?

Sure but I've never been there. Have you? Where is it?

Oh, I've been there lots of times with my mother. It's on the mezzanine. It's not expensive. Let's go now while it's not crowded. We can take the escalator up.

Okay. This is fun. You were going to tell me about ushering. What's that like?

Wait a minute. We're almost at the cafe. Let's talk about that after we get a table and order. See, here it is. There's a table over there. Isn't this a nice place, Obra-Jean?

Yeah, and not too busy.

Excuse me, Miss, could you bring us menus and take our order?

I'm sorry but I'm busy.

Excuse me. Obra-Jean, she said she was busy. How could she be busy? There's hardly anyone here. Here comes another waitress. I'll ask her. Excuse me, Miss. Excuse me, Ma'am. Did you see that? She just ignored me. What's going on here?

Janette, let's go. I want to leave. I don't think they're going to serve us.

What do you mean? I get waited on all the time when I come here with my mother.

You're not with your mother. You're with a colored girl. They aren't waiting on us because they don't serve colored.

That's impossible, Obra-Jean.

It's not impossible. You'll see. Let's sit here a while longer, Janette.

Twenty minutes passed and none of the waitresses came to Obra-Jean and Janette's table to give them a menu or take their order despite Janette's repeated requests. Janette finally became convinced Obra-Jean was right and they gathered their things and left.

I can't believe what happened there.

Believe it. This is how they treat colored people.

But why?

They don't like us.

Why?

Because we're colored. Ask your family. They'll tell you. You don't have to have a reason.

I'm so sorry, Obra-Jean. I wouldn't have put you through this had I known. Listen, I'll tell you what. Let me make it up to you. There's a new play starting next week at the Shubert theater. Why don't you take my place and usher on Saturday? You'll love it and you'll see a play for free.

You don't have to do that, Janette. What happened was not your fault. That's the way some people are. My mother tells me that all the time. But, hey, I would love to go to the theater, especially for free. When we were in New York City, we saw *My Fair Lady* and it was wonderful.

Okay. All you have to do is arrive at the entrance a half hour before the theater opens its doors at one-thirty. Dress nicely. There will be other kids there. When the manager opens the door for ushers, tell him I couldn't come and you're taking my place. He'll tell you where you'll be stationed and what to do to seat the audience. It's simple and you'll have fun.

Wow. Thanks, Janette. I'll do that next Saturday. Hey, I miss you a lot. Let's get together again, soon, okay?

Obra-Jean arrived at one o'clock before the Shubert theater opened for the Saturday matinee. When leaving her house, her mother asked her where she was headed and she replied she needed some books to study that were only at the public library. This explanation seemed to satisfy Leona and Obra-Jean headed downtown instead. At the theater, she had to wait, as she expected, because all of the doors were locked. Several other young people gathered at the same entrance. Obra-Jean surmised they were also ushering. All of them were white. After a few minutes, one of the entry doors opened and a man motioned the young people inside. As Obra-Jean stepped forward, he looked at her quizzically, and she promptly stated that she was taking Janette Fulgenzi's place. At first, he seemed hesitant but then, glancing up and down the sidewalk, motioned her inside. He gave each of the young people an assignment in the theater and turned to Obra-Jean to tell her she would be in the upper balcony. She could take the stairs to the top of the theater. Programs would be at the rear of the center aisle for her to pass out to audience members. He handed her a card diagraming all of the seat numbers.

After climbing the stairs, Obra-Jean retrieved a stack of programs and awaited the arrival of the audience. By curtain time, no one had come to the balcony although there was a smattering of a crowd in the orchestra. Obra-Jean took a seat at the front of the balcony and watched a performance of *The Seagull*, a production of a Broadway touring company. Obra-Jean liked the play but it was somehow a hollow experience without a full audience and no one else in the balcony to appreciate it. She headed back to the lobby after the final curtain. There, the manager stopped her.

Thank you for ushering today. What's your name again?

Obra-Jean Moore.

Oh. Okay. Obra-Jean, thank you for ushering today. But, listen, I have to tell you if it were just up to me, I would let you usher again but I can't. I'm sorry to say but you can't come back to usher. My boss, Mister Nederlander, saw you in the balcony and he told me you couldn't come back.

Why is that? Because there was no audience?

No. Well, not exactly. Not directly. He doesn't want colored kids ushering in his theater because the audience wouldn't like it. I'm sorry. It's not my fault. It's the way things are. You understand, right? It's not you. Colored just don't belong here. Sorry.

Obra-Jean left the theater without saying another word. All the way home she thought about what had happened. She felt embarrassed. Actually, she was humiliated and couldn't put it out of her mind. This was the second time she was treated badly because she was black. Her mother had warned her this sort of thing would happen. So, she wouldn't ever mention this to anyone including Janette. However, Janette's mother upon close questioning of her daughter discovered, much to her dismay, that she was spending Saturdays with a black girl. This was simply intolerable to her and had to stop. The ensuing conversations within the family raised everyone's temperature to the boiling point. Janette was told never to associate with this "Obra-Jean person" again. It was for such reasons the family had left their old neighborhood for a safe white's-only precinct. To make sure future meetings would not take place, Janette's mother also made a decision—she would call this black girl's mother and tell her that under no circumstances would she allow her own daughter to socialize with a Negro. When Leona received this angry telephone call without any prior knowledge of her daughter having lied about her activities and was, in fact, socializing with a white girl, Leona gave a few choice pieces of her mind to Janette's mother before slamming down the phone. She didn't know who she was madder with—Obra-Jean or Janette's mother. She felt comfortable being furious with both and with everyone else in her family for good measure. However, she didn't confront Obra-Jean. She waited. She had no way to take revenge on Janette's mother but she could make Obra-Jean's life miserable. In myriad small ways she did to her daughter exactly what she did to Clemenza. All Obra-Jean knew was that Janette disappeared from her life. Janette stopped calling her and didn't answer Obra-Jean's calls. Obra-Jean never learned why. She did learn, however, that Leona's capricious ire could focus on her as well as on Toby and her Grandmother Post.

Obra-Jean tried her best to avoid irritating her mother. She followed her brother's advice and simply agreed with everything her mother said without any argument. The apparent loss of Janette as a friend was a hurt that would not leave Obra-Jean. To take her mind off both her mother and Janette, Obra-Jean began spending a lot of her free time in the local public library. There, she found a section with books on architecture. The selection was not extensive so Obra-Jean thought to visit the Main Library on Woodward and found an overwhelming variety of books many of which were non-circulating. As often as she could persuade her mother to let her visit the library, she sat in the Main Library reading room and looked through architecture books about Europe, America, and Asia. She was fascinated with the various types of buildings, the different styles of architecture, and the structural designs that made buildings tall or to cover enormous spaces. Everything about buildings and who created them fascinated her. She knew this is what she loved and would always love.

IV

Estyllene Baker Moore

— A Plan —
Fall 1957 to Fall 1958

Obra-Jean's first semester at Cass was liberating. It was a complete and welcome change from the rigid routine and monotony of her Catholic school. But life at home made her even more miserable because of the contrast between the constraints at home and the freedom of her new school not to mention her mother's barely suppressed anger with Obra-Jean for lying. She quickly reached a point where she needed to leave her mother's constant supervision, prohibitions, and antagonisms. During the semester, she pondered various alternatives. She considered staying with her sister but Toby had not gotten her own place and was still sleeping on the couch in Ronnie's apartment. Her Aunt Augusta lived in an apartment with only one bedroom and might feel imposed upon to share her home with her niece. She believed there was only one other possibility. She decided to ask her grandmother, Estyllene Baker Moore, about living in her spacious house. There were four bedrooms of which only three were occupied by her grandparents and her uncle. That left the guest room open for the perfect guest—Obra-Jean.

Hello? Grandma?

Hey, Baby. You'll have to forgive your old grandmama for not returning your call. I've been busier than a toothless dog with a bone. Your grandmama has been running all over town cleaning other folks' homes and doing errands for your poor old grandpapa. So, how are you doing, Sweetie?

I'm fine, Grandmama.

That's good. What has my smart and beautiful granddaughter been doing?

I'm studying for school right now. I've got all of these really good but hard classes—Algebra, Biology, Latin, Social Studies, and English.

Ooh, Baby, I don't even know what some of those things are you've mentioned. You'll have to explain them to me sometime when we can sit down and have a nice chat over tea and some of your grandmama's lemon bunt cake.

I'd love that Grandmama and I hope we can do that soon because I can't think straight around my mother. She's constantly complaining I'm not doing this or that right, and she makes it hard for me to concentrate on my work. Grandmama, the next semester starts in a month. You know my Momma is having a hard time taking care of things. She's been crying and angry and upset with me and Grandma Post.

Honey, I've been angry and upset too. Your father's death was like part of me died. Your mother is having a hard time right now. She's lost her husband. And, she's lost his salary. She's got two kids to take care of and she's got her mother to look after too. It's tough on her, Sweetie. She's got a lot on her mind and she's just got to think about a lot of things just to keep her family together. Isn't E.J. helping her?

No, not really. E.J. is always away from home most of the time—at college or at his job, I think. He's gone all day but doesn't forget to show up for dinner. Then, he's in his room or away somewhere maybe with his friends. Momma doesn't ask him for his help.

I don't understand why he's not helping her. I'll have to have a talk with that boy and tell him, as the man in the house, he has to step up to some new responsibilities. Both of you kids will have to be very considerate of your mother. This is not an easy time for her or for you and your brother. You'll have to be more considerate and understanding too.

She treats poor Grandma Post like she was a maid or something. Do this, do that. Poor grandma just does what Momma asks and doesn't complain. I try to help grandma but Momma seems angry about that. It's like she doesn't want me to be friendly to her. I'll tell you, Grandmama, I just don't want to be around my mother. Momma is always picking fights with me. She criticizes me all the time. She doesn't like anything I do. She says I can't do anything right. I know she's sad and unhappy but I don't want to be around her like this. I would do much better in school if, maybe, I could stay with you and Grandpapa for a while.

Oh, Obra-Jean, your mother would have a stroke and, after she recovered, she would make chitlins' out of me. No, no, no. She wouldn't like you staying here with me and your grandfather at all. Your mother likes to keep a close watch on her children, especially her girls. You know that. She's always been that way starting with your sister. Toby was like you. She wanted to stay with me all the time too so she could be away from your mother. But, your mother wouldn't stand for it and I know she wouldn't agree now with your staying here.

Grandmama, I know Momma wouldn't be happy about me staying with you but you could persuade her, you and Grandpapa. She listens to you. I don't know but she seems to like you more than anybody else in our family. She always says good things about you and Grandpapa.

You give me too much credit, Obra-Jean. Your mother is not someone who is easily persuaded. Your poor dead father didn't have good luck with your mother either.

But, Grandmama, please, I know you can convince her especially if you tell her that her life would be easier if she didn't have me around the house. She's always complaining about money. I just seem to be an extra expense and I get in her way. She finds fault in everything I try to do for her. Besides, she's got E.J., and he can do more for her than I can. She never complains about him. I think she likes him better than me.

Oh, Honey, don't say that about your poor mother. She would never love one of her children more than another. She just loves each of you differently just like she loves her mother and me differently but she loves us all. We're the only family she's got. But, I'll tell you, Obra-Jean, if she feels I'm taking her child away from her, she would have my scalp. She would put me in the doghouse and feed me scraps. Don't put your poor old Grandmama Moore on the wrong side of your mother. She's a pistol. I love her like she's my own daughter but I don't push her. I don't contradict her. I don't go against her wishes. If I ask her this for you, she's going to be really, really mad at me. She knows her own mind and doesn't like other people telling her what to do.

Grandmama, you're the only person who can really talk to her. She listens to you. She won't fight with you.

Oh yes she will, Obra-Jean. I don't want to tangle with your mother because it would be an unfair fight. I'm too old to outrun her. She would grab me like a chicken and snap my neck. I would be running around in circles with blood spurting everywhere. You don't want that for your poor old grandma.

Grandmama, if you talk to her in that calm and loving way you have, she'll listen. You'll make her realize that, with me out of the house, she can relax more. She'll know I'm with you, and you'll keep me in line. She trusts you. She's always trusted you. If Daddy got her to agree to let me go to Cass—and you know she didn't want me to go there—she'll certainly listen to you because she doesn't want you to stop loving her like your own daughter.

You've got a point there, Baby, but mothers and daughters are tricky business. There can be love but also the absence of love. It's not hate, exactly, just unloving indifference. And do you know why? Mothers know what daughters don't know but daughters think they know everything. I haven't had a lot of luck all these years in giving your mother advice. She certainly listens to me more than she listened to her own mother but she doesn't take advice easily. She's got a strong will. That's what your sister is like too. Strong-willed like her mother and, I think, maybe you're like your mother too. I think, though, that maybe right now she might be better off if she could rely on E.J. and not have to worry herself about you. You know everything your mother does, she does for her children. She loves you all equally. She may seem to treat you differently but she has her reasons. So far, you children have all turned out pretty good. Honey, never think your mother loves your brother more than you. She just knows a girl is going to have a very different life from a boy simply because she's a girl. So, she has your best interests at heart even if it seems to you she is tougher on you than on E.J. You'll see what a good mother she is when you become more grown and have a daughter of your own. But in the meantime, maybe right now the two of you need a little break from each other. Your mother could focus on a new life for herself, and you can concentrate on your schoolwork. Okay, I made up my mind or I've lost my mind. I don't know which it is. I'm gonna wrestle with the devil. Now, don't get me wrong; your mother is not a devil but you know what I mean. I'll talk to her. Maybe, I can convince her to let you stay with me and your grandfather. Maybe.

I know she will.

She may listen to me but it doesn't mean she'll follow my suggestion. We'll see, Baby. Say a prayer for your poor old grandmama. She's gonna "wrassel" with Goliath. Bye, bye, Honey.

Styll thought about the best way to approach Leona. A direct approach would be best but how to arrange that? When Perry was alive, he and his family came to his parents' home for Sunday dinner once a month. Styll was an excellent cook as were many older black women who had to create interesting and nutritious meals for their families without exotic ingredients or expensive goods. Traditional dishes created in the South during times of extreme hardship and deprivation also established a familiar repertoire of meals, the kind of meals Clemenza prepared for Leona and the kids. However, a day at the home of her in-laws meant not only a change in her weekly routine but also a day without Clemenza. Over the years of her marriage to Perry, Leona had developed a warm relationship with Styll because she welcomed Leona into the Moore family. More importantly, Styll was sympathetic to Leona, knowing her personal and family history and accepting her role as a mother to Leona

—a role Leona rejected for her own mother. It had been months since Leona had visited Styll, so Styll called Leona and set a Sunday date for dinner. She expected the children would attend as well but Leona pointed out she could not assure Styll that Toby would be present. Toby was living her own life now completely independent of her family. Leona would inform Toby of the dinner date but not insist she attend. An argument, at this time, was not what Leona wanted or needed.

The second Sunday of December was cold and windy. A light snow covered the ground. Leona arrived at her in-laws' house in a rental car because her insurance company had not yet replaced the family car that was severely damaged in the accident. Obra-Jean and E.J. accompanied her. Although Leona had been looking forward to the dinner, she wasn't sure how she would feel to be with her in-laws without her husband. There was hardly an occasion in their married life when both of them were not together while in the company of his parents. Perry was the magic ingredient that made socializing easy. Without him, she wasn't sure her in-laws would be completely comfortable with her. She rang the doorbell and Barry opened the door welcoming them inside. He hugged Leona and Obra-Jean but shook hands with E.J. The children left their coats in the entry closet and walked to the kitchen; Leona lingered, hung up her coat, and sat to talk with her father-in-law.

Styll was in a frenzy in the kitchen. She was stirring, sniffing, and tasting food in several pots and pans on the stove and in the oven. She offered her cheek for a kiss to the children then shooed them out of the kitchen because she needed to concentrate on her final preparations. Obra-Jean and E.J. rejoined their mother in the living room and sat quietly while the adults talked. Barry wanted to know how Leona was managing without Perry. She explained the hardest part was his absence from every aspect of her life. She was alone at night in bed. She didn't have him to discuss all the things couples discuss between themselves. There were chores she couldn't do and, although E.J. could do some of the things his father formerly did, he could not do them all nor was he reliable. She would have to find someone to help her. Having sole responsibility, now, to raise her children was overwhelming. She had all but given up on her older daughter, who seemed determined to live her own life apart from her family. Leona hoped E.J. would not follow his sister's path and she hoped she could guide Obra-Jean in a different direction from that of her sister. She informed Barry that her boss at the IRS was being very considerate of her new situation and promised her his cooperation in helping her adjust to her increased responsibilities. Barry turned his attention to Obra-Jean and E.J. and firmly advised them to help their mother and not create any new problems for her. They nodded agreement. Barry then changed the subject to talk about himself and his recent health issues, including kidney and urinary problems. His leg, which had been damaged in a horse-riding accident as a teenager, limited his mobility. Because he couldn't drive, he took a bus downtown to work, and Styll drove him to his medical appointments as well as taking care of all the household chores. He was so grateful to her for being with him and taking care of him all of these fifty years of their marriage.

Barry recounted for the children that Leona and Perry had been married for twenty years. They met when Perry was in his last year of high school. Leona, who was four years older than Perry, had already graduated high school in Hot Springs, Arkansas. She had married a man whom she persuaded to bring her to Detroit. Then, she abandoned him after a few months and got a lawyer who quickly obtained a divorce decree on the basis of incompatibility. Meanwhile, she saw Perry at a house party given by a mutual friend and they quickly got together. Having impregnated Leona, Perry quit high school during his last school year to work in an automobile factory. He and Leona also moved into Barry and Styll's home. Perry and Leona eventually married when Perry turned eighteen. This was after they already had their first child, Toby.

Barry then turned from the children to Leona to remind her that Styll had opposed her eldest son quitting school and marrying a divorced woman. Leona replied that she was well aware Styll was suspicious of her reasons for marrying a second time and so quickly. Leona decided to do everything to win Styll's trust and approval. She began by calling her "Mother" not "Styll" and she made herself indispensable to Styll who never gave live birth to a daughter of her own. Obra-Jean listened carefully to this conversation. Although she had heard some of these things before, they didn't mean anything to her previously. They weren't important then but now, she realized, they were very important and she wanted to know more.

In the presence of her father-in-law, Leona began to relax. She understood, even without Perry, she and Barry could get along with ease. She became more talkative telling Barry stories about her life with his son. She emphasized how much she loved him and what a good husband and father he had been. She praised Barry and Styll for raising such a loving, responsible, and kind man. She regretted her own children could no longer benefit from his guidance and example. E.J., she felt, had some of his father's qualities and probably would do well in his life. Obra-Jean was still very young and, without her father's presence, she might falter. In Leona's experience, daughters depended on their mothers but they needed their fathers too. A father was more lenient than a mother. That was how Leona viewed Perry in relation to their daughters. While she was talking, Leona noticed that Barry had begun to cry. When she asked him what was wrong, he replied that he missed his son who had been not only a good husband and father but also a good son. Styll came into the living room to announce dinner was ready. When she noticed Barry was crying, she told him that crying would not bring back Perry so stop it. Leona inquired about Mason, the Moore's youngest son who lived with them. Styll looked at the ceiling indicating Mason was upstairs in his room. She shook her head. Nothing more was said of him. He never joined them for dinner.

The dining room table had already been set. Styll now wanted Leona and the children to come into the kitchen and help her carry the serving dishes to the dining room table. Once everything was in place, they all sat down, said a blessing, and began passing the serving dishes. Styll had created a feast: Roast beef, mashed potatoes, fried corn off the cob, green string beans, stewed okra with tomatoes, baked sweet potatoes, cornbread, biscuits, a peach pie, and homemade lemonade. She had been cooking all morning having done preparation work the night before. There was mainly small-talk during the meal as everyone sampled the dishes. When the meal was completed and the table cleared, Leona joined Styll in the kitchen to help her clean up and put away the leftovers. Barry and the children went into the family room to watch television.

Mother, that was a delicious meal. Thank you so much for treating us with your fine cooking. I have to confess, I haven't had any enthusiasm for cooking since . . .

Baby, I know how all of this has come crashing down on you. It's terrible to lose a husband, especially one so young and when you still have youngsters to raise all by yourself.

It's hard but it would be easier if Toby wasn't so damned selfish and stubborn. I asked her if she could reconsider her plans to continue living with that friend of hers and move back home to help me with her sister and brother. Of course, she said no. Sometimes, I don't know. I can't figure out how things went so wrong with her. I thought I was being a good mother to her, helping her find her way, pointing out the things she needed to know, warning her of the dangers in life, and helping her in every way I knew. I didn't get any of that from my mother. I wanted to be sure my daughters did get what I missed. What was wrong with that?

Nothing was wrong, Baby. You did what any good mother would do.

Then why didn't it work with Toby?

Why do you say it didn't work?

Look how inconsiderate and hard-headed she is and the fact she only seems to think about herself, not about me or her siblings.

Now, Leona, don't get me wrong. I'm not taking Toby's side. Toby should be more considerate but she's a young woman going out on her own, finding her own way. You went out on your own.

Because I had to. Nobody, especially my mother, offered me a choice.

Well, yes, you had to be on your own. Toby is really only doing the same thing. The big difference is you didn't have a choice but Toby does. So, to you, finding her own way makes her inconsiderate and selfish but, to herself, she's just doing what we all have to do—find our own way. Now, if you'll let me offer you a little advice, I'll tell you to let Toby do what she has to do and don't show your disapproval. After all, what will you accomplish by always letting her know how much you dislike what she's doing? You can't make her do what you want so why go that route? Go easy with her. Accept that she has her own way of doing things even if you don't like what she's doing. The fact is she's an adult and can ignore you but I don't think she wants you out of her life. She just wants to have her own life as she wants it.

Mother, you really remind me of Perry. I see where he got his ideas. But, I don't know. If I had a mother like I'm trying to be with Toby, I would be so grateful.

Leona, Baby, you don't know what kind of person you would be if you had any mother other than the one you have. Now I know you don't agree and I can understand that but think about it. If you had your perfect mother, would you be the woman you are today—a woman who has lost her husband and has a young daughter to raise by herself and two grown children in college? Baby, you've got more strength and toughness and smarts to push on than a dozen women. You'll keep going and make your children go out in the world and take care of themselves. What you don't see in Toby is her independence. That's also how you are. And, I think also E.J. Now, Obra-Jean—that child is gonna need some special help and I want you to think about this. With all you have to take care of, with all of the problems you have to deal with on your own, maybe I could help you out by letting Obra-Jean live with me and Barry for a while? You need some financial help without Perry's income. We're too poor to give you money but we could ease your finances by having Obra-Jean live with us. That would mean you, E.J., and Clemenza could take care of your house without all of the additional worries about Obra-Jean. And, Barry and me would have some real company and help around this house. You know, your father-in-law is practically a cripple and he can't do much besides his job. Mason, well, that poor child just lives in his own world. I can hardly trust him to walk to the corner grocery store to buy a loaf of bread. Now, if Obra-Jean was staying with us, my life would be a lot easier. I would have someone who could really help me around the house. You wouldn't have to worry about Obra-Jean because I know she would mind me. She doesn't talk back to her Grandmama. What I say is law.

You would want Obra-Jean here? Why would you want that responsibility?

Leona, Obra-Jean is no baby. I can see she's growing up and becoming a serious person. She would be nothing but a godsend.

But, Mother, it's my job to raise her.

Leona, you've done your job and you'll continue to do your job because Obra-Jean will always need her own mother. But, right now, her mother has too many other things on her mind now. Maybe, you're not in the best frame of mind to love and care for a teenage girl. Barry and me have a lot of time on our hands. We've got a room for her. She wouldn't be any trouble to us. We can see she gets to her new school. And, you can come to visit her. She can come to visit you. I think this arrangement would be good for all of us. As I said, Barry and me could use some company because Mason spends most of his time in his room. It would be nice for us to have a young person around here. She could bring her friends here. We could have a good time.

Mother, she's my only daughter at home. What would the house be for me without her?

Look, Leona, let's just try it for a while. Let's try it, say, for the rest of this year of her high school while you're still getting your life re-organized. If you want her to come back to your home, we can decide to do that. It will be a trial period, a little breathing space for you. Look at it this way, you will have one less thing to worry about for a while. Then, when you've got things straightened out, if you want her to come home at the end of the school year, we can tell her that's what we all want her to do.

What if she doesn't want to come back home?

Baby, that's the question. Why wouldn't she want to come back to you?

Well, I am her mother and she should want to come back to be with me.

I'm sure she would come back. But, if we give her some time, we'll find out. Let's give it a chance, Leona. It would be temporary and it might be better for both of you.

But why do you think she'd want to stay with you?

It's just a hunch I have.

What about Mason? How would he feel about Obra-Jean living here?

Honey, Mason doesn't pay attention to anyone or anything. He wouldn't even know or care if Obra-Jean was here.

Styll's reasoning tempted Leona but she was not yet willing to let her younger daughter leave her home under any circumstances. Obra-Jean was now her responsibility alone and she was unwilling to share it even with her mother-in-law. While she was ruminating over her feelings, Obra-Jean came into the kitchen for a glass of water for Barry. Leona watched her daughter and noticed not the child she thought she knew but the daughter who was before her very eyes. Leona thought, maybe for the first time: Obra-Jean is no longer, in fact, a child. She's still young but there is a quality about her that Leona never acknowledged. Obra-Jean was aware and calculating. She also told lies. How had Leona missed this about her daughter? It was Obra-Jean's idea, not Styll's, for her daughter to leave home to stay with her grandparents. She somehow planned this. Leona made a sudden analogy to Toby's decision to leave home. Her daughters did not want to live with their mother. Why? What was Leona doing wrong? In that moment of contemplation and uncertainty, Leona conceded Obra-Jean was not her possession. Her daughter had a life of her own. She had a family that included more people than her mother. Styll was also a mother and she might help Obra-Jean to learn things Leona had been unable to teach her. She could try sharing her daughter for a while and it would please Styll. Leona needed Styll's love. If she relented on this matter, she would please her, and Styll would love Leona more. In that moment of insight and need, Leona decided to allow her daughter to stay temporarily with her grandparents. Leona conceded that this arrangement would also give Leona some much needed breathing space and ease her finances.

Obra-Jean moved to her grandparents' home after the New Year and before the start of her second semester at high school. She settled into her room on the second floor. She brought her clothes and most of her personal things except her goldfish—Lulu and Fred—which she flushed down the toilet. Her stuff filled Leona's rental car. Styll helped Obra-Jean and Leona to move Obra-Jean's things into the house and her bedroom on the second floor. The house was older than her own family home but very similar in layout. Since Obra-Jean had stayed overnight many times with her grandparents as a young child, she was accustomed to the house and the neighborhood. Styll made sure Obra-Jean was comfortable and had everything she needed like towels and face cloths. She would have to provide her own personal products for which her mother had given her a weekly allowance. The allowance would also give her a small amount of spending money for school. Styll didn't anticipate having any problems with Obra-Jean since she already knew Obra-Jean wanted to stay with her and her grandfather. She wouldn't risk being returned to her own home with her mother. Styll also was less concerned than Leona with Obra-Jean's private life. She knew her granddaughter was intelligent and not given to foolishness. Although any young person could make a serious misstep and find herself in a difficult or threatening situation, Styll expected, with a few gentle reminders, Obra-Jean would exercise due caution. This, in fact, Styll believed had been Leona's gospel to her children, especially the girls, from day one. However, Leona's preaching of caution in all matters is what drove Toby to rebellion. But, Styll mused, rebellion was Toby's nature not Obra-Jean's. Obra-Jean was, if anything, too conforming, or so Styll thought.

Obra-Jean rode two buses to reach Cass Tech as she had when traveling from her parent's home. It was a longer ride than from her home but she had allowed enough time to arrive in time to register for her spring classes with the head of her study hall, Mister Nathan Green. Imperious and unfriendly, Mister Green announced to the hundred or so students sitting and standing in the huge study hall that, when he called a student's name, the student should come forward and receive his class schedule, all of which were carefully typed by Mister Green's secretary. Obra-Jean was seated near the rear of the study hall and had some difficulty hearing the names being called but thought, finally, she heard her own and walked quickly to the front of the room. Upon retrieving her schedule, she noted her classes—second semester algebra, social studies, English, Latin, and biology. It was a typical array of courses for a second semester science student. Her schedule also included two periods for study hall and a half hour lunch break. Her first class was at eight in the morning and her last class ended at four. It would be a long day but only an hour longer than her classes at Saint Catherine. It was now eight in the morning and time for her first class.

At the end of her school day, she returned to her grandparents' home via the same bus routes. Styll welcomed her home and told her to get ready for dinner at six. Styll, Barry, and Obra-Jean sat at the kitchen table to a much simpler meal than Sunday's dinner. Styll had made a pot of beef stew.

How do you like school, Baby? Tell Grandmama what it's like. I want to hear everything.

Grandmama, the school is big. I think there are eight floors. The cafeteria is on the top floor. There are elevators. We can take elevators up to the cafeteria. There are so many kids—all kinds of kids from all over the city. You know there wasn't another colored girl besides me at Saint Catherine. At Cass there are lots of colored girls and boys. The head of my study hall is a colored man. He's kind of scary because he's so serious and doesn't stand for any fooling around. He told one kid who wouldn't stop talking to get his things and leave the building. I mean the sisters at Saint Catherine were strict but they weren't scary like Mister Green. When he gave me my schedule, he warned me that I wouldn't remain at Cass if I didn't continue to follow the rules, do my work, and behave like a lady, and he meant it.

That's a good thing, Obra-Jean. Young people need to know there are rules and proper behavior. That's what your parents have been teaching you all of these years.

Yeah, I know but somehow this was different. This was like the real world. Do you know what I mean?

Honey, everything is the real world.

I guess so but this was a more grown up real world.

I get what you're saying.

Obra-Jean, what are your classes?

Oh, Grandpapa, I have second semester Latin and English, algebra, biology, and social studies.

That's a lot of different classes.

Yes, it is. The teachers seem to be nice. They're also very serious and have lots of rules about attendance, class behavior, and doing our assignments. We also have to be prepared to recite in class.

How is that different from your Catholic school?

I guess it's not really different but I like the way things seem to work at Cass. It's like it's up to us kids to do what's right. Not because of some punishment but because it's our responsibility.

You've already learned that?

Yes, Grandmama.

Well, I think you made a good choice to go to Cass.

I think I did too. I've already got homework for tomorrow so before I start, is there anything that you want me to do?

No, Honey, I'll take care of the dishes and the kitchen. You go on and do your homework. Your grandfather will probably sit in his chair and read. I may watch a little television later and you can join me if you want.

Okay. I'll go upstairs and see you later.

Barry watched his granddaughter leave the kitchen. Styll got up from the table and began clearing the dishes. She hummed some tune while working. Barry stood, steadying himself by holding on to his chair. His bad leg threw him off-balance and he always had to be careful before taking a step lest he fall. If he broke his hip or leg, he could end up in a hospital and never recover. Before leaving the kitchen, he turned to his wife and spoke.

Styll, that child is going to do well.

I know, Barry. She's been under Leona's thumb her whole life. Now, don't get me wrong, Leona is a really good person. But, she's been holding Obra-Jean back just like she tried to do with Toby.

But Styll, if Obfra-Jean's out from under Leona, she just might go too far if you're too easy on her.

I'll keep an eye on her. Don't worry. If I see she's going too far, I'll let her know.

I hope when you do, it's not too late. Leona would never forgive you if something happens to her daughter. You've never raised a daughter. You were too easy with our son and look at him now.

What's wrong with Carson?

You know damn well what's wrong with him. He's not a real man.

What do you mean by "not a real man?"

You know what I mean.

Well, I don't like what you're saying. Besides, is it my fault he likes men instead of women?

Yes. You were too soft with him. Now he's a grown up into a sissy living with another man.

Philip is his housekeeper.

Don't bullshit me, Styll. He may keep his house but he also keeps his bed.

What do you know about it?

Do you think I'm a fool? I know what I know.

How do you know? You've never been to Carson's home.

I asked Carson and he told me.

Then he was being honest with you.

Honest and a sissy.

What does that have to do with Obra-Jean?

I'll tell you. Leona may have the right idea about her children. She's tough with them. You may mess things up by being too easy.

Like I messed things up with Carson? You didn't have anything to do with it?

I saw he wasn't like Perry. He was a mama's boy. You wouldn't let me be tough with him.

Tough? You wanted him to be like Perry. He wasn't like Perry. Never.

He could have been if we had both been tough with him.

No, Barry, No. Carson was always different even as a child. You can't make people into who they aren't.

We've had this talk too many times, Styll. Do what you want with Obra-Jean. If things go bad, it'll be your fault and your fault alone. I won't have Leona blaming me for anything.

Styll, who, during this conversation, seemed to be concentrating on the dishes, was, in fact, keeping an eye on her husband, ready to steady him if he faltered. She and Barry had argued about Carson for years and she had heard all of his complaints before. It didn't bother her. She was more concerned that her husband was becoming more unsteady. Barry really needed a cane or walking stick as he hobbled out of the kitchen towards the living room. Styll relaxed, stopped humming, and focused on the dishes.

— A Clean House —

In addition to being a housewife, caretaker to her husband, and a mother to her son, Mason, and granddaughter, Obra-Jean, Estyllene Baker Moore was a domestic who worked in the homes of several different white families and individuals. She was dedicated and efficient. Once a month she made the rounds of her clients' homes. They lived in houses and apartments within the city of Detroit. One of her favorite clients was a Jewish family that had a large comfortable home in an all-white neighborhood not too distant from Styll's. Styll drove to her clients' homes in an older model Chevrolet. The Bergenstein were married with adult children who lived in their own homes. Howard Bergenstein was an accountant with an office downtown. Harriet Bergenstein was a dance teacher in a private Detroit school. Both worked on the day Styll came to clean their place. Styll had keys to their house which she safeguarded in her own home. Although their house was generally tidy, Styll could spot dirt, dust, and debris everywhere that no one else would ever notice. She moved through the upstairs rooms quickly since the Bergenstein only used their bedroom and the bathroom. She chuckled to herself that Howard frequently missed the toilet bowl and peed on the ceramic tile floor. Then she turned her attention to the main floor—living room, dining room, study, kitchen, and washroom. She liked to listen to soap operas on the radio while she worked and would often slow down working to catch a particularly choice conversation between main characters. Fortunately, the Bergenstein had radios on both floors so she never missed a line of dialog. After vacuuming and dusting, she honed in on the kitchen. The sink, counters, and floor were filthy according to Styll's standards and she scrubbed, wiped, and polished all of their surfaces until they sparkled. Once these rooms were pristine, she took all of the dirty clothes and soiled linens—mainly sheets and towels—from the bathroom hamper to the basement laundry. She had noticed some stains on one of the sheets and used bleach to help remove the spots. Once they were washed and dried, she ironed the clothes and sheets, folded them and returned the clean clothes to the bedroom and the linens to the upstairs linen closet. Then, she sat down in the kitchen after she made herself a sandwich with some of Harriet's chicken salad, and garnished her plate with a whole dill pickle and some potato chips. She finished off her lunch with a cola from the refrigerator and some cookies from a package in a cabinet. Her work finished, she locked the front door and left to return to her own home which always looked as if Styll needed a full-time cleaning lady for herself.

Another of her favorite clients was a single, middle-aged man. He owned an apartment in a building on the Detroit River. For one person, his apartment was large with two bedrooms, living room, kitchen and bath. Richard Storer designed the displays for windows in Hudson's downtown department store. He was very good at this and applied his flair for display to his apartment which was filled with exotic objects, art, and brilliant textiles. Cleaning his apartment was a challenge for Styll because she was always afraid of breaking some precious object or spoiling the effect of an arrangement Richard expended so much effort to achieve. Richard told her repeatedly in his soft Southern drawl not to worry. He would rather have a clean apartment than concern himself with something that could always be redone or replaced. Nevertheless, Styll was extremely careful in his apartment and never broke or damaged anything. When cleaning his bedroom, she noticed a stack of magazines that were out of place. As she flipped through them, she found one that was unlike the usual *Life*, *Newsweek*, and *Better Homes and Gardens*. It had a young man on the cover in a very revealing bikini bathing suit. She turned the pages and there was photo after photo of naked or nearly naked young men. Styll looked at the photographs more closely. Something struck her: These men were like pin-ups of women in magazines meant to titillate men. But why, she thought, would a man want such a magazine with pin-ups of men? Styll was no innocent but she had never really thought about her bachelor client except that he was a bachelor. Well, she decided, he liked men. Then, something Barry said to her when she first went to work for Richard came back to her: He called Richard "light in his loafers." The phrase hadn't meant anything to her and she had ignored it but now she smiled to herself. Her husband had been right. Richard was "light in his loafers." Her own son, Carson, she knew, was like Richard—only her own son had the courage to live with another man and accept the disapproval of his father. As she was putting the magazine back in its place in the stack, a new thought came to her, about Toby. Was Toby, who was now living with another young woman, a woman who liked other women? Was her conflict with Leona for most of her life not about Toby's stubbornness or inconsiderateness but about Leona's instinct that her daughter was headed for a completely unconventional life, a life with another woman and not a man? How had Leona divined this? What were the clues? Styll would have to find out because, for the first time, she had a real concern about Obra-Jean.

— Styll, Emy & Evy —
Spring to Summer,1969

Styll had two sisters. The three of them were the Baker girls. One sister was married with no children of her own. The other sister, in Styll's opinion, was definitely not marriage material. This was her younger sister, Emyllene Baker. Among other things, Emyllene was a drunk, a drug addict, and a whore. In other words, she was an embarrassment to her family. From an early age, Emyllene proved herself uneducable and averse to any sort of parenting or help. Not only her parents but also her sisters had tried unsuccessfully to right a course Emyllene had chosen. She was as determined to be a blight on the Baker family name as she was certain to be an agent of her own destruction. Emyllene liked men, or she liked what men could do to, and for, her. She was an unashamed slut whose only work experience and job was prostituting herself for a little spending money or a bed to sleep in. She had boyfriends who were as marginally situated in conventional social life as she was. They kept her out of the rain and snow most times but soon lost interest in whatever part of her body she could offer for their pleasure, perversion or disease. Emyllene, for reasons that Styll could never understand, would come to visit her home, not for a meal or a place to sleep or company or even money or a favor. She just came and stayed less than half an hour and wouldn't be heard from again for months, sometimes for years. Styll never invited her sister to sit down and never offered her food or drink as she customarily did with any other visitor to her home. Emyllene would simply come into the living room and stand or wander restlessly from one part of the room to another until, without any visual or aural signal, terminate the visit and walk out of the front door with barely a goodbye.

As Styll was listening to her favorite soap opera on the radio and cleaning up her kitchen from breakfast—Barry had earlier left for work and Obra-Jean for school—the doorbell rang. Styll came out of the kitchen and walked to the front bay window in the living room to see who was at the front door. It was Emyllene. Styll might have pretended not to be home but, she thought—her sister was her sister. She wouldn't stay long, a half hour or so would pass quickly enough, and Styll could resume her household work. She opened the front door, and Emyllene strolled in as if she were visiting royalty taking time out from her busy day to share her gracious presence with the peasants.

Well, good morning, Sister. What brings you here so early in the day?

I was in the neighborhood and thought I would see my favorite sister.

You were in the neighborhood? This is the only neighborhood you know.

Oh, Sister, that's not true. I get around this city. My mens take me all over Detroit to really fine neighborhoods, much finer than this one. We visit beautiful homes and dine in the finest restaurants. I know more of this city than this neighborhood. I know more than you think I know.

I see. I stand corrected. Have you visited your less favorite sister as well?

Evyllene doesn't seem to appreciate my company. She told me not to come back to her house ever again. But I don't need her because you've always been my favorite sister anyway, the only sister who understands me and has been nice to me. You welcome me into your home.

Then, why don't you have a seat, Emy. Can I get you some coffee and a biscuit?

Sister, that would be lovely. May I sit here in this chair?

Go right ahead. I'll be just a moment. Cream and sugar for your coffee?

That would be very nice.

Where's your boyfriend?

Which one?

Uh, I think you called him Slash.

Oh, him. Well, Mister Slash has disappeared. I've got me a new man—Thomas. He treats me nice. I'm staying in his room now. It's in a house just a few blocks away.

Styll rolled her eyes but tried to keep a pleasant smile on her face. She indicated to her sister that she needed to go into the kitchen to retrieve the coffee and biscuit. She put a little butter and honey on the dish with the biscuit, poured the coffee, added cream and sugar, and put the dishes on a tray before returning to the living room.

Okay, here you are. I'll leave this tray on the coffee table. So, Emy, tell me about this Thomas person.

He's a little younger than me.

Emy, please explain something to me. You are, what, fifty? How much younger is Thomas? Is he still in high school?

You're such a kidder, Sister. I don't like them that young.

Slash was, what? Twenty?

Twenty-five and a high school graduate, mind you.

Oh, practically an old man. Why are you running around with these boys?

Honey, young boys like what I've got.

And, what exactly have you got except a couple of holes like every other woman?

I know how to use them, and boys like what they can do with them.

Including Thomas?

Right.

So how old is he?

He's thirty-two.

Oh, my gosh, he's practically a senior citizen.

That's why you're my favorite sister. You can always make me laugh. Now, let's talk about something else.

Like what, Emy?

I've been thinking about something, Sister.

Yeah? Thinking, huh? Thinking about something? About what exactly?

I've been thinking about our mother.

Our mother? Which mother are you talking about? You and me didn't have the same mother.

Yes, but we were raised by the same mother—Corrine, Daddy's second wife.

They weren't married, Emy. They just lived together but they didn't marry.

Did I know that?

I thought you did.

Maybe I forgot. Corrine. She was my mother, right?

Yes, I'm afraid she was.

But she was not your mother or Evyllene's mother.

That's right, Emy. She was your mother, not mine. And, she was the mother of all of those other kids she had before she met our father.

What was she like? I don't remember her too well.

She was a lot like you, to tell the truth. She wouldn't listen to anybody. She was sleeping with other men while she was with our father. She didn't really know how to raise us and, frankly, didn't care. Evyllene and me tried our best to raise you after she left our father. But you ignored us and did things your own way.

Well, I like my mens and I like to have a good time. I never wanted all of this home and family stuff you have here although you have a beautiful home and a lovely family. I'm free and can go my own way. If my mother was like me, then good for her.

Okay. So, Emy, why are you here today?

You're not really telling me anything about my mother. Did she love me?

How would I know? I don't know what was in her head.

How did she treat me?

Like she treated the rest of us, Emy.

Sister, did your mother love you?

I think so.

How do you know?

I felt it even when she was upset with me about something. It was the same with our father. I felt his love. Didn't you?

I didn't feel that anybody loved me. Not Daddy, Momma, or you, or Evyllene.

But me and Evyllene loved you or tried to.

I never felt it.

I'm sorry, Emy. I'm really sorry. We really tried.

The conversation paused. Emyllene ate her biscuit and sipped her coffee. Styll turned away from her and stared out the front window. She was upset by her sister's claim that no one in the family loved her. In truth, Styll thought, Emyllene was unlovable. Could she, Styll, have been more loving? Styll returned her gaze to her sister and looked long and closely at her. Here was a sad soul, someone who claimed to be having a good time doing exactly what she wanted but who really wanted something she felt she never got. Emyllene, having finished her biscuit and coffee, looked up from her dish and stared at Styll.

I'm sorry too, Sister, but that's the past. I have my mens. Well, this has been fun. This is the first time I've ever had coffee and a biscuit at my sister's house. What happened? Why now? Are you feeling sorry for me?

Emy, you are my sister. I want to love you.

But, I'm not a sister you love. Right?

I do care about you but I will say honestly I don't know that I love you. I do care about you and wish you took better care of yourself and let your sisters help you.

Well, I can take care of me. My mens can take care of me. I don't need you or Evy. Thank you, Sister, for the coffee and biscuit. Till next time. Goodbye.

And, Emyllene left the house with the same air of departing royalty waving to her subjects. Styll was puzzled. What had come over her sister to visit now and to ask if her mother loved her? This was an episode from one of her soap operas only no one died from a brain tumor. Styll returned the tray with the coffee cup and dish that had held the biscuit to the kitchen and resumed the task of straightening up the room while making plans for dinner. Barry loved her fried chicken. She thought that would be an easy choice to make since she already had everything she needed. She thought Obra-Jean would like chicken as well. Since she had several hours before she needed to start preparation, she decided to call her other sister, Evyllene, to find out if she was home. In fact, she was and invited Styll to come by for a brief visit. The sisters' homes were back to back to one another but each faced a different street and were separated at their backyards by an alley. Styll only needed to walk out of her house through her own backyard, cross an alley, and enter the backyard of her sister's house. It was something she seldom did so it was with a sense of adventure she went into her sister's house.

Her sister, Evy, met Rufus Jackson, the man she married, in Georgia. He was a free-lance mason who worked by himself, for himself, and made a substantial fortune as a laborer and contractor. After he and Evy settled in Detroit, he bought the vacant lot behind Styll's house and built a solid brick house for his wife. They never had children. Styll always admired her sister's house because it was much more substantial than her own home but felt sorry that there were no children to enjoy it. As was her habit, Styll knocked on the side door of the house instead of ringing the doorbell at the front door. Evyllene invited her inside and they went up a short flight of stairs to the kitchen and sat at a table in a little dining area within the kitchen. Evyllene put fresh squares of gingerbread on a plate and placed it in the center of the table. She poured cups of coffee for both of them.

What's with Emy coming to your house? What garbage pail is she living in now?

Evy, she says she's staying nearby with her new boyfriend.

That whore. Styll, why do you even let her into your house? She's probably diseased and filthy. You didn't let her sit down, did you? She might have fleas or something.

Yes, I did let her sit down. I suddenly felt very sorry for her and something else. I felt, maybe, I could help her. She's our sister after all.

Styll, we tried and tried to help her. She never wanted our help, For all I know, she still doesn't.

Evy, I'm not sure. She asked about her mother.

Another whore. I still can't believe our father had anything to do with that trashy woman.

Daddy wasn't a saint, Evy. He liked women just like Emy likes men. If she was a whore like her mother, what was our father who lived with a whore? What was he?

Yeah, but Daddy kept a home and a job and he tried to raise us proper. Ever since we were young, we worked cleaning houses to make money. Emy's job was making money with her body. You met Barry, got married, and left Georgia for Detroit. I got married and followed you.

Then, Emy followed us. She never could get a man to marry her so she became a whore.

We're judging her, Evy. Emy's just trying to make it in this world like everybody else. Now, Daddy did want us to be proper ladies. But our mother was the one who really raised us before she died. She put us on the right path. Emy's mother wasn't like that so Emy missed out.

How did she miss out?

She asked me if her mother loved her?

She asked you that? What the hell did you say?

Evy, I told her the truth. I didn't know.

That's not the truth. Styll, you know that's not the truth.

But I didn't know if her mother loved her. She really didn't seem able to love anybody.

Yes, you did know. You were there when Daddy and Corinne got into it one night. He beat the shit out of her in front of us because she said she never wanted to have his baby. She couldn't stand Emy and she couldn't stand him. You were there, Styll. She left him right after that. Oh, wait a minute. You weren't there. Now I remember. I told you what happened later.

You know, I forgot that. I guess I wanted to forget it.

Well, that's the truth, Styll. Emy's mother didn't want her. She never loved her or our father. She didn't love us. But, we didn't care because we hated her.

Oh, Evy. Our family was a mess. How did we survive? No wonder poor Emy is the way she is.

Poor Emy, my ass. She's just like her mother.

No. She's not really like he mother. She wants love but she's getting it from the wrong people. What is so sad, Evy, is she never had a chance to learn about love from a mother like Corinne.

She had a chance with us but she didn't take it.

That's not fair, Evy. If Corinne had been our mother, we might be just like Emy.

No, Styll. We tried to love Emy. We tried to help her grow up but she wouldn't listen to us.

But we were only her sisters not her mother. That's a big difference. No one can replace a mother.

No. No. No. That's not it. Styll, a mother or a father isn't the only person who makes a child the way she is. It takes aunts and uncles, grandparents, teachers and friends—you name it. All kinds of people—inside and outside of a family—help a child become a good person. Think about it. You've brought your granddaughter into your home. Why? Because you want her to find out who she is. She can't do that with her own mother. Styll, I'm telling you because I believe it. People can change no matter what kind of parents they've had or even if they had no parents at all. We are in charge of ourselves.

Well, listen to you, Evy. When did you become the wise sister?

Styll, I've always been the wise sister. You've just never listened to me. Now, tell me, how are you doing?

Do you mean how I'm doing about Perry's death?

Yes.

Evy, Perry was my pride and joy. He was a beautiful baby and a beautiful man. He gave me a daughter-in-law I love, and three wonderful grandchildren who are going places. When he died, I swear, something in me died with him. But, you know, Evy, life goes on. I said goodbye to Perry at the funeral and now I'm moving on. I've got a crippled husband to take of and a son who is a sad critter, bless his heart. Mason is a grown man in body and a child in his head. All I can do for him is love him. He'll never leave my house till I die. This, Sister, is what life is about. This is the life I have. I'm doing my best to be a good Christian wife, mother, grandmother, and sister. I don't know any other way. My beautiful Perry is gone. I have to focus on the ones who are still alive.

Bless you, Styll. You know I'm here to help in any way. But, now, I've got to get ready to go shopping so, Big Sister, you go home.

I'm on my way, Little Sister. You don't have to tell this sister twice to go home. Thank you for the ginger bread. And, maybe, I'll take a couple of more pieces with me for later because they're so good.

Honey, take the whole plate. I certainly don't need to be eating them. See you later.

Styll grabbed the plate of gingerbread squares, said goodbye to her sister, and started to return home through her sister's backyard. She paused in the alley before opening the gate to her own backyard. Looking up and down the alley, she thought about all of the years she and Barry had lived in this neighborhood. They knew almost every family on their block. Some were just nodding acquaintances but others were friends with children who had grown up with her children, attended the neighborhood schools with them, and visited at one another's homes. Now, most of those kids had moved away to other neighborhoods or even to other cities. She seldom saw any of them when they returned to their parents' homes for brief visits. As she thought about it, she seldom saw any of her neighbors except for the few who attended her church across the street and at the corner of her block. She looked at the backyard of her neighbor's house on the left of her own house. She remembered a time when the family in that house raised chickens in the backyard coop with a rooster that would crow in the morning. A rooster was better than a clock she thought. A vivid thought came to her mind of her neighbor swinging a chicken in the air by its head in order to break its neck and kill it. The way the bird fluttered and screeched came back to her as did the blood that flowed from the knife cut to the neck administered to drain the carcass. Styll had certainly de-feathered and cleaned a fair number of chickens in her own day and knew, intimately, the smell of blood and guts and the sheer violence administered to the bird to render it as tasty, aromatic fried chicken. Now, she bought packages of cleaned and dismembered chicken parts at her local grocery store. She looked at the house to the right of her house and thought about the time the wife ran from the house in the backyard stark naked screaming for her life as her husband followed wielding a butcher knife. Fortunately, another slaughter did not occur because neighbors intervened and saved the woman. No one called the police and, somehow, the couple reconciled. She looked further down the alley and saw the flames and smoke billowing from a neighbor's house. That was a memory from years ago. The house was nearly destroyed. Two children died in an upstairs bedroom. The remaining family moved and a young couple purchased the wreck and rebuilt the house. Styll never became friends with them simply because neither she nor they made an effort. The thought quickly passed her mind. She opened the gate to her backyard, walked to the side door, and entered her own home.

After doing laundry, paying bills, placing a bet with a numbers runner who stealthily came to her side door everyday, she sat and took a little rest before starting dinner. When Obra-Jean returned from school and then Barry from work, she announced they would sit down to dinner at six-thirty. She called Mason to come downstairs and join the family at the table. After dinner and after the kitchen was put into order, Styll sat down with Obra-Jean to inquire about her school.

How are your classes, Baby?

I really like my teachers, especially my Latin teacher, Missus Tatkin. I didn't think I would like Latin but she makes it easy to understand. She's a little strange. She says something is wrong with her tear ducts. She won't let anyone come near her because she's afraid of some kind of infection that would affect her tear ducts. It's kind of funny but, otherwise, she is really good. She's strict like the sisters at my Catholic school but a lot less scary. She smiles and really appreciates when a student says things correctly. She's complimented me a couple of times for knowing the nouns and verbs and knowing how to use them. She also gives me lots of "A's" for my homework. I'm doing really well.

How about your other classes?

I'm learning a lot and getting good grades on all my assignments. Really, the teachers treat me well. All of them are white, you know. I think it was a good idea to go to Cass. I really like it. The kids are so different from Catholic school. They seem to know so much about so many different things. It's fun. I like it. I want to take an art class in the next school year. It's not in our curriculum but I can take it as an elective.

Obra-Jean you're taking on a lot of extra school work but I guess you can handle it. Have you talked to your Aunt Augusta about taking art? You know she was once an artist.

I knew that, Grandmama. I really should talk to her. That's a very good idea.

Have you made any new high school friends?

There's one girl. Kyra Smith. She's in the art curriculum and she's the one who got me thinking about an art class. She's really a good artist and she wants to be an art teacher.

Do you still want to be a science teacher?

I don't know. I don't think so. I never wanted to be a teacher. That was my mother's idea.

Well, Baby, you don't have to decide now. Try out different things until you find the thing that you really like. By the way, do you want to invite Kyra over for dinner sometime?

I don't know. We'll see.

Obra-Jean was ambivalent about Kyra who had become her best friend at school when they took the same English class. Like many students at Cass, Kyra came from a working-class family. She had two older siblings —a brother and sister—and two younger siblings—also a brother and sister. As the middle child, she possessed an easygoing affability that attracted and promoted friendships with other students. Obra-Jean intrigued her because of her obvious intelligence. But, her self-assured aloofness kept Kyra at a distance. However, when Kyra was having trouble with an English lesson, she decided to ask Obra-Jean for help and was encouraged when Obra-Jean quickly and thoughtfully responded. Obra-Jean was not much interested in making friends at school. However, Kyra's request for assistance broke through Obra-Jean's self-imposed isolation and fostered development of a somewhat tentative friendship. The two classmates began to find opportunities to meet in school outside of their English class as Obra-Jean began to press Kyra for information about her art courses. Unlike Obra-Jean who had no social life outside of school, Kyra engaged a wide social network of friends who partook of activities and events of interest to high school students, such as movies, roller skating, music clubs, and house parties. Kyra tried unsuccessfully to persuade Obra-Jean to accompany her to a whites-only roller-skating hall that set aside one Saturday afternoon a month for blacks to attend. Kyra explained that a lot of high schoolers roller skated to R & B music. It was great fun and a chance to be with some really exciting black kids. Obra-Jean had never roller skated in her life and had no interest in starting to learn or to be with exciting kids, black or white. There were over a thousand kids at Cass and none of them had particularly interested her. Kyra almost gave up trying to entice Obra-Jean into some kind of after-school activity when off-handedly she mentioned that there would be a house party given by a fellow art student the next Saturday evening. It would be a chance to listen to music and have fun. The student and his family lived in an Indian Village mansion which, Kyra noted, might be Obra-Jean's one-shot chance to see the inside of one of these opulent homes. Intrigued, Obra-Jean agreed to attend. Kyra explained that she had a white friend, another art student, who had access to his parents' car. The friend would drive them and a couple of other students to the party.

Parties, such as this one, were usually arranged when the party-giver knew that the parents would be absent from the home on the night of the party. Attendees brought their own drinks and refreshments and settled into whatever rooms in the house were available to them. Rock and roll music played on the record player quite loudly while clusters of partygoers talked, drank, and smoked. Obra-Jean and Kyra were the only black teens at a party of some fifty young people. Kyra recognized many fellow art students from Cass and introduced Obra-Jean to them. To her surprise, Kyra saw that Obra-Jean socialized quite easily. She was a master of small talk as well as skilled in handling more serious discussions of current events and popular music. Kyra was delighted and felt something more. As the evening wore on and both she and Obra-Jean had a few cups of the cheap wine they brought with them, Kyra nudged Obra-Jean into a dimly lit library where there were couples making out. Kyra put her arm around Obra-Jean and feeling no resistance, kissed her on the mouth. Obra-Jean responded by returning the kiss but then suggested that they rejoin the main party. There were more parties after that one that they attended together. To Kyra's dismay, Obra-Jean began withdrawing from socializing with her and eventually declined all further invitations. In the words of her grandmother, Estyllene, Obra-Jean did try different things until she found the thing she really liked. Kyra wasn't that thing.

— A Farewell —

Styll received a telephone call from Receiving Hospital, the city's public hospital. She had been designated as next of kin by a patient, Emyllene Margaret Baker, and the hospital was now calling to notify her that her sister was in a serious, possibly terminal, condition. When Styll hung up the phone, her thoughts began to crowd in upon one another. What had happened to her sister? How could her condition be fatal? Who did she need to contact? Should she go to the hospital immediately? Impulsively, she called her sister, Evyllene, who, when she heard what had happened to their sister, quickly suggested that Styll should come to Evyllene's house as quickly as possible and she would drive them both to the hospital. Styll told Barry about her sister and suggested that, given his condition, he stay home with Mason. She would ask Obra-Jean who was in her room if she could accompany her to the hospital. Both women hurried to Evy's house. The drive to the hospital was nerve-wracking because they were traveling in rush-hour traffic. Then, when they arrived, they couldn't immediately find a place to park the car. When they finally reached the front desk for patient information, Styll was crying and both Evy and Obra-Jean were trying, unsuccessfully, to calm her. They reached the emergency center where they were told they would find their sister. When they entered her cubicle, Styll's legs gave way and she collapsed. Obra-Jean and Evy managed to lift Styll into a chair.

Emyllene lay in a hospital bed attached to intravenous tubes and a heart monitor. Her face was bandaged. She was unconscious. A nurse entered and Evy besieged her with questions. The nurse told her that Emyllene had been beaten and stabbed multiple times. She had lost a lot of blood. Her wounds were extensive and deep and she had internal injuries. Also, the assailant had slashed her vagina and rectum. The hospital had done all that could be done. It was unlikely she could survive so much physical damage. Evy began to cry. Obra-Jean roused Styll with a drink of water and explained to her what the nurse had just reported. Styll struggled out of the chair and wobbled over to her sister's bed. She took her hand and called to her. One of Emyllene's eyes was battered shut but she managed to open the other and focused on her sister's face.

We're here, Baby Sister. It's me, Styll, and here's Evy and my granddaughter, Obra-Jean. We're here and we're gonna stay here with you. Who did this to you?

Emyllene nodded her head slightly and seemingly attempted to speak but there was no sound. Styll leaned in close to her sister's face and repeated: "Who did this to you." Emyllene tried to mouth a word. Styll asked her if she could speak a little louder. With great effort and barely audibly, Emyllene said: "Slash."

Obra-Jean found two chairs to place to either side of the bed and Styll and Evy sat down. Each held a hand of their sister and cried. They didn't move for an hour. When the nurse returned, she checked the heart monitor. It had flatlined. She felt for a pulse and held her hand close to Emyllene mouth to see if she were breathing. Assured that the patient was dead, she told the women that they should say their farewell, leave the cubicle, and make arrangements for the body.

Styll never determined if Slash had killed her sister because Slash was found dead, bludgeoned almost beyond recognition. There was no grave for Emyllene's body and no funeral. Styll had her sister cremated and her ashes remained in an urn that she placed in a closet. After a short period of grieving, Styll returned to her regular routine. Something, however, was nagging her and she decided to have a talk with Obra-Jean.

Baby, let me get to the point. My sister didn't deserve to die as she did. However, she chose a life that put her in danger and, despite everything anyone said or did to warn her, she went her own way. Now, I know you are not like my sister. You're smart. You have a plan for your life. You were raised by people who really love you. My sister had none of that. But, you do and so I'm saying to you don't ever let yourself be tempted to do anything that will bring you harm. Your body is sacred, so protect it. Your mind is your gift, so protect it. Your life is yours alone to safeguard. Don't give it to someone else. Do you hear what I'm saying, Obra-Jean?

Yes, Grandmama, I understand.

I know you understand but are you really listening? Your mother has entrusted me with her most precious gift—her daughter—and I don't want to betray your mother's trust. So, Obra-Jean, it's up to you to listen to your grandmother and to your mother and do what's right for you. Always. You'll help your old grandmother to sleep well at night if I know I can trust you.

You can trust me, Grandmama.

Lord, Child, I hope so. I surely hope so. You don't want to send your Grandmother to an early grave because it anything happens to you, that's where your mother will see that I'm headed. And you better believe it.

V

Patricia Tobias Moore

— Toby Makes Her Move —
Summer to Fall 1957

Her father's death reaffirmed and justified for Toby her decision to move out of her family home. She could never be her own person as long as she lived with her mother. And as much as she truly loved Leona, she couldn't continue what seemed to her to be pointless fighting over Toby's life choices. But Toby's long-standing difficulties with her mother were not, she finally admitted to herself, the primary reason she decided to move. It was her infatuation with India Rhonda Sykes that tugged Toby from her family's home into Ronnie's apartment. Toby told herself she liked Ronnie's intelligence and air of sophistication. Ronnie was also biracial and stunningly sensual—qualities Toby at first dismissed as being irrelevant to her attraction but which she later realized were essential to her infatuation. In contrast to Toby who was a full-bodied, dark-skinned, young woman, Ronnie was slender like a fashion model and very pale. Like many black women, Toby straightened and curled her hair but kept it short, close to the contours of her head. Ronnie's hair was naturally curly and hung in waves to her shoulders. However, she usually pinned it so that her hair was swept up and back exposing her long neck. Both women loved to joke perhaps as relief from their intense seriousness about their studies and their evolving social and political beliefs. They both loved their conversations and debated differing points of view. When Ronnie offered Toby a temporary place to stay in her apartment near campus, Toby recognized this as a providential gift allowing her to leave home immediately and start an independent life as a student and worker bee. She settled, she thought temporarily, into Ronnie's apartment before Perry died and used this as an excuse for not returning home to help her mother with the house and her siblings. Toby and Ronnie became roommates. Their first days together were a period of learning the basics of each other's lives.

I thought your name was Toby.

That's what I'm called, Ronnie, but "Toby" is just a nickname. My middle name is Tobias which is kind of weird. It was the name of my great-grandfather on my father's side. When I was a kid, I asked my parents why I was called "Toby." My father told me he gave me the name "Tobias" and "Toby" for a nickname. He never explained why he would give his daughter his great-grandfather's name. I mean, why didn't he name my brother "Tobias?" It was my mother who named me Patricia. I never liked being called "Patricia," "Pat," or the absolutely hideous "Patty." It's just not me. I mean do I look like a "Patty?" I've always felt that way about my first name as long as I can remember. I don't know why she named me Patricia. There is no Patricia in my mother's or father's family but weird names or weird choices for names are part of my family's history. You know about my little sister, Obra-Jean. I mean what kind of name is that? It's so countryfied. So down home.

Toby, "Obra-Jean" sounds like a French word to me when you say it real quick. It sounds like *aubergine*.

And what is *aubergine*?

It's French for "eggplant."

You're kidding. My sister was named for an eggplant?

It could be, Toby. Why not?

I don't think my parents even knew any French. How could they have chosen a French word and why?

Maybe, they heard it and liked it but changed it to a sound that was more familiar, and the spelling followed from their pronunciation.

That's really a funny idea. My sister is an eggplant.

Is she dark-skinned like you, Toby?

Oh, definitely. All of the women in our family are dark-skinned except my Aunt Augusta. Obra-Jean is the darkest. The men—my brother and grandfather—for some reason, are all light-skinned but not as "ofay" as you. My father was light-skinned too.

So, maybe that's the answer. Someone who knew the French word thought your sister reminded them of an eggplant in color.

She's not that dark, Ronnie.

Hey, it's just an idea.

You seem to know a lot of things, don't you?

It comes directly from my parents. When your mother and father are both medical doctors, you get to know a lot about a lot of things. You see, my mom grew up in Atlanta and went to school at Meharry Medical College in Nashville. My dad was born and raised in Chicago and studied medicine at Northwestern University. They met at Northwestern Hospital where they both interned. Somehow they fell in love and got married. My father's family disowned him. They didn't want any "jigaboos" in their oh-so-white family. I'm their third child. Like you, I have a sister and a brother. My brother is a lawyer in Chicago and my sister is a housewife with two children also in Chicago. Our parents took us to theaters. We spent a lot of time in libraries and museums. We traveled across the United States, Canada, and Mexico and we went overseas to Europe and North Africa. Both of my parents speak some French and a little Spanish. They are actually both quite amazing. They supported my decision to come to school in Detroit.

I don't know anyone like you, Ronnie. You're not the typical Negro girl. I think you're very classy and easy on the eye.

Listen, Toby, I know my life is different from that of most Negro girls in this country. I've had a lot of privileges. My parents always made us kids aware we've had advantages. They said we should use them to help lift up lower class Negroes. As doctors, my parents have tried to improve the lives of poor Negroes. They want me and my siblings to do the same. We're members of the so-called "Talented Tenth."

Talented Tenth?

That's what W.E.B. DuBois called the Negro elite that is supposed to uplift our race.

I guess you read that somewhere, huh?

Of course but I also heard it from my parents. Over and over and over. It's my mother's mantra.

Did they name you "India" because of their travels?

That's funny. I never thought about it but guess what? My sister's name is "Ethiopia" and my brother's name is "Holland."

Wow. That's cool. So, why do you call yourself "Ronnie" instead of "India?"

Because I like the sound of it. It sounds like a man's name.

A man's name? You don't think of yourself as a man, do you? You sure don't look like a man. In fact, you are one of the sexiest-looking women I've ever met.

Sexiest? Hardly. Anyway, it's nice to know you find me attractive. I think you're quite attractive yourself. Anyway, I like "Ronnie" because I think it's ironic that this bourgeois, Negro sister is living the good life. I study what I want. I'm free to be with anyone I like. And I'm completely independent like a man. This sister has power.

Independent? Don't your parents pay for your school and apartment?

Yes, they do but not directly. I have a trust fund I use to pay for everything myself.

A trust fund? You're a rich bitch?

I'm richer than most Negroes I know but I'm not really rich. I'm just financially secure and definitely a bitch.

Holy shit.

Ironic, yes? I guess you could call me "I," for "India," "Ronnie." Get it? "I-Ronnie." Now, what about you, Toby?

Let's see. My family is strictly working-class. My dad worked at DeSoto. He was killed in a stupid car accident when my parents were returning from a trip to New York City. He died just before his birthday. I was crushed. I cried for days. He was so good to me.

I'm sorry.

Yeah. Well, my mom is, shall we say, a "tough cookie." She's a secretary at the IRS. We have butted heads since I was little. But, she means well and she's been a really good mother. The problem is she couldn't let me be who and what I wanted to be because she was afraid of something. She always said she just wanted me to understand what my future would be like. But, something else was going on with her. She's doing the same thing to my little sister. It's strange.

Mothers and daughters.

Right on. Anyway, she made me take ballet lessons. I mean can you see me as a ballerina? Come on. I looked like a ox lumbering around the dance floor. No illusions here.

You're probably being a bit hard on yourself. I think you're quite graceful.

Oh, thank you. I'm a graceful ox. She also made me take piano lessons.

So, did my mother. And, tennis lessons and . . . are you ready for this? Ballet lessons.

180

Well, at least you look like you could have been a ballerina.

If you think you were an ox, I was a water buffalo. I may look like a ballerina but I dance like an elephant. Wait. An elephant is actually more graceful. If a cow could dance, that would be me.

Both women had a good laugh. The easy self-deprecating humor brought them closer together. They sat in the living room of Ronnie's apartment near the campus of the university. Toby's stay was intended to be temporary until the university's administrative department hired her, and she could afford to pay for a place of her own. Toby, in fact, hoped she could get settled in something near the campus fairly soon, in a matter of weeks at the most. There were lots of inexpensive apartments in the neighborhood because the district was working-class with an older stock of buildings not in the best of repair or upkeep. In other words, they were perfect for low-budget college students. Wayne University was a commuter school of mostly locals with relatively few students seeking housing on or near the campus. Toby imagined the lack of competition for a place would allow her a quick and inexpensive find. However, her plans didn't proceed as expected. She was unable to get an interview for an administrative office position until the fall semester. Meanwhile, Ronnie seemed content to extend Toby's stay indefinitely at no cost to Toby. Now that Leona was head of the household, Toby felt that moving home would change nothing between mother and daughter. They would simply resume fighting over everything Toby wanted to do. In truth, Toby wanted to be with Ronnie.

When classes resumed in the fall, the administrative office finally scheduled Toby's interview. She was confident she would be a good candidate because she could type. Her mother, a secretary, had insisted that Toby—and E.J.—learn to type while in high school by taking a summer course. Toby also imagined such tasks as filing she could learn quickly on the job. She knew other students who had such low-level jobs in campus offices and, in fact, the university liked to hire students for part-time work because of their education, communication skills, and social manners. They were also cheap labor since they could also be paid less than full-time staff. From having done some investigation, she knew the probable fifty dollar monthly rent she would pay for a room could be covered by her salary with a little left over for food and utilities. She could live modestly.

Toby and Ronnie drank white wine, something that was new to Toby because her parents didn't drink wine and never kept it in their home because it was associated with "winos" and "riff-raff" as Leona called anyone she felt below her class. As presented by Ronnie, wine seemed sophisticated to Toby. And Ronnie impressed Toby as such an elegant as well as beautiful young woman because she was so comfortable and knowledgable about things like wine. Ronnie could talk about all kinds of subjects seemingly in depth. She had first impressed Toby with her understanding of calculus. She had also impressed her teacher with her understanding. She was an outstanding student. She also knew history and geography and sciences and food and Broadway shows and classical music and philosophy and, well, her knowledge went on and on. In addition, she was very analytical, could tell a good story, and was persuasive in her arguments. To Toby, she seemed perfect.

I know you said your parents encouraged you to come to Detroit for college, but why did you come to school here instead of going to Harvard or someplace like that? You just don't seem like any of the other students at our school. I really feel working-class compared to you.

Toby, you're charming and smart and beautiful. Yes, your family background is working-class but you're a classy girl. You've boosted yourself into the striving middle class and intelligentsia. I'm sure you're aiming next for the aristocracy.

I mean, really, can you imagine me as an aristocrat? Well, I would like to be presented to the Court of Saint James. But, really, I do want to be classier. Classy like you would be good enough for me.

Oh, come on, you're classy enough already. Believe me. So, about my parents. They wanted to me to apply to Harvard and Yale or the University of Chicago. I didn't want to be with a lot of white kids in a completely white environment. I thought about Howard in D. C. In fact, that was my first choice. But, you know, I wasn't interested in Washington, Boston, or Chicago. I certainly wasn't interested in New Haven. I thought it would be an interesting experience to live in Detroit. This is the biggest and baddest industrial city in the country. It has a huge Negro population of working-class people. Although my parents agreed with my decision, they also wanted me to think about studying in Africa eventually. You know the independence movement is gaining momentum in parts of Africa and it would be an exciting time to be there to witness it all. But, for now, Wayne is a good school especially for what I want.

That's math, isn't it?

Oh, no. I like math but art and art history are what I really like.

Ronnie, you like art and art history? What could you do with art or art history after you graduate?

What do you mean what could I do, Toby?

Wouldn't you have to get a job or make a living as an artist or something? What Negro women have worked as artists? I've never heard of any. My Aunt Augusta tried it and gave it up.

I'm sorry your aunt didn't make it. Maybe she just didn't have what it takes. True, there haven't been many Negro women artists for sure. A few did succeed like Edmonia Lewis in the nineteenth century. In this century, Augusta Savage, Lois Mailou Jones, and Elizabeth Catlett have made reputations for themselves. Toby, this is a new era. Negroes are going to do a lot more things than they've ever done before. There are more opportunities. However, I not particularly interested in being an artist. I just want the knowledge and the skills.

God, if I told my mother I was going to study art, she would have a stroke. She has hammered me, my sister, and my brother that we have to be practical, always practical. We have to prepare ourselves for work we're sure we can get so we can support ourselves and our families.

See, that's a working-class mentality.

Okay, my father worked in a factory but he had a different attitude. He encouraged me to do what I wanted. He was the one who let me quit Catholic school and attend Cass Tech. I think he understood that I was not going to be a copy of my mother. He didn't know what I would be. Hell, I didn't know what I wanted to be. But he wasn't afraid for me. It's funny, you don't really appreciate someone until they're no longer around. I loved my father but I don't think I really showed him how much I loved him. It's only now that he's gone that I wish I could tell him how I feel. He was special.

I'm really sorry about your dad. He must have been a real counterweight to your mom. It's funny but I actually understand her point of view, Toby, although I don't agree with her. You come from a typical working-class family in Detroit, right? Your mother is a secretary and your father worked in an automobile factory. You have their perspective on life and opportunities for Negroes. My parents have a very different perspective.

Probably, their class, as professionals, has given them exceptional opportunities and experiences. And, of course, my father is white. He's used his race to protect and support us. My parents have encouraged their children to consider all possibilities and to go for it. If we fail, we won't have failed because we limited ourselves for trying. I've thought of doing different things. Maybe I'll be a lawyer like my brother.

See, Ronnie, you can think like that. I can see that attitude might work for you and your family because you've had advantages my family never had. But I can't afford to think like you because I don't have a trust fund like you do. I have to make it on my own and make sure I can survive. My family has given me a little help in the past. They sent all of us kids to Catholic school but I can't expect much help from my mother now. I wouldn't ask her anyway. Even if she could help, my mom wouldn't help me. If I told her I was going to do something that wouldn't be a ticket to support myself and a family, she would gut me like a chicken.

But, Toby, why shouldn't you take chances? We're talking about your life. Our world is changing. We won't allow ourselves to live under the restrictions and discriminations that our Negro parents, grandparents, and their parents suffered. We're a new generation. We have all kinds of opportunities if we go for them. You're living in your mother's world of fears and limitations.

How do you ignore what our parents teach us?

You don't ignore it. You evaluate it and develop your own viewpoint. That's what you're already doing when you moved out of your parents' home. Just take that further. Imagine what you really want in your life, and do it.

But, see, you have that kind of confidence because your parents allowed you to have it. I don't have that kind of confidence.

I think you do but you have to take risks. You won't have the confidence if you aren't willing to try and even fail. You've got to try.

Maybe.

Toby sat in the outer office of the personnel department head for university clerical employment. Several other students were in the same room awaiting their turn to be called in for their interview. When she heard her name, Toby rose, shook hands with a middle-aged white man who invited her into his office. He introduced himself as Mister Harry Ostrowski, administrative assistant to the department head, and invited Toby to have a seat in front of his desk. He smiled, sat in his desk chair and opened a file on his desk. He confirmed that he was speaking with Miss Patricia T. Moore. Toby mentioned that she preferred to be called Toby. He smiled again and continued to call her Miss Moore. He wanted to know her previous experience and she explained she never had a job because she had been in school most of her life and her parents had supported her until now. She added that her father had recently died in a car accident and her mother was now supporting herself and two other children—one in high school and the other also at Wayne. Ostrowski then wanted to know about Toby's major, and Toby replied she hadn't yet decided but had done very well in math in high school and in her college calculus classes. She had thought about possibly teaching math as a public school teacher upon graduation. She was now taking an advanced calculus course. Ostrowski seemed surprised by this information and asked if she had taken any accounting or statistics classes because the university could use staff with good math and accounting skills. She had not taken accounting or statistics but offered that she could if that would help her employment possibilities. Ostrowski nodded as if agreeing. He then made some notations in her file and said she would hear from his office by the following week. He then rose, shook her hand, and said goodbye pointing to his office door.

Toby was pleased and surprised by the interview. There was so much that wasn't said or asked but it seemed to her that Mister Ostrowski might have been impressed with her. She knew she looked good in her best dark blue dress with a silver necklace. She was well groomed with a little make-up, mostly lipstick. Her mother—she smiled to herself—had provided her a good-grooming role model although Toby normally resisted wearing any kind of makeup or jewelry. She thought about accounting and statistics courses mentioned by Mister Ostrowski. It was something she never had considered because she didn't know the first thing about accounting. No one in her family had ever mentioned accounting as something someone could do, The fact that Mister Ostrowski suggested this to her implied, at least, he thought this was more than a possibility for her. If she got the job, she would look into it. Frankly, it appealed to her more than teaching math to a bunch of snotty-nosed kids like her little sister.

As Mister Ostrowski promised, she got a letter signed by him offering her an entry-level position as student clerk trainee beginning immediately. She could work twenty hours a week during business hours and could arrange her coursework so she would have five blocks of four-hour work periods. Given her present course schedule, Toby thought that she could manage the work conditions, meet her current courses, and still have plenty of study time. She would be very busy but she would be making enough money to cover rent for a room. Now, she needed to look for a place to live.

I was thinking, Toby, there's a two bedroom place one floor up that's really nice. I had a look at it yesterday and it's in pretty good shape. A new coat of paint maybe and some other work and it would be move-in ready immediately. I could move there and we could share the apartment.

But, Ronnie, how much is it?

It's two-hundred and fifty a month.

Are you kidding me? That's way out of my league. I couldn't afford anything like that. Have you forgotten that I'm the poor college student. I couldn't split that kind of rent with you.

I know you couldn't split the rent but how about this? I rent the apartment and you could pay for a bedroom in it for what you would pay someplace else.

I can only afford about fifty bucks a month. That wouldn't be fair to you.

Oh yes, it would be. See, I would like a bigger place anyway and having you as a permanent roommate would be fun. You know, someone to help out with the place and share meals. We could each have our own lives but we would be good company for each other. We have a lot to talk about. Don't you think?

Ronnie, you would do that?

Of course, because it makes a lot of sense. We make a good team. We're pals. We like a lot of the same things. We're both getting ourselves ready for the world out there. We're both smart, beautiful, and cultured. Oh, yes, you are beautiful and cultured, my dear. We can go to the art museum together. We can go to the theater. We can do all kinds of things. Wouldn't it be great?

Whoa. Let's slow this down. Where is this coming from, Ronnie? Are you really sure about this? I mean, I would love sharing an apartment with you. I would especially love sharing one that was nicer than anything I could afford on my own. But, we haven't known each other for very long. It sounds like we would be more than just roommates. Are we ready for that? Besides, I won't have the kind of money for theater and all that. I'm practically Skid Row.

Oh, I see. You're right of course. Maybe it's too soon. Maybe you've got other plans. I'm sorry I was rushing things because I was really excited about this apartment.

Well, it's not that I have other plans. We just don't know each other that well. We would both be giving up some of our independence.

What about this then? Let's try it for a little while since I want to get the apartment anyway. If it doesn't work out for both of us, we can both go your separate ways.

That seems more sensible. Oh, my god, I'm beginning to sound like my mother. Forget I said that. I like your plan. We're both on the same page.

Great, Toby. I'll check with the landlord and see if we can move in. Let's have a glass of wine and drink to our new home.

Toby informed her mother of her plans and, immediately, got the reaction she expected. Leona was not pleased. Why, she wondered, would this roommate of hers want to share an apartment the roommate was mostly paying for? What's in it for her, she demanded? Toby repeated the reasons Ronnie gave but Leona was not satisfied. Something just wasn't right about this. Leona raised objection after objection to the point Toby began to feel, perhaps, her mother was right. However, instead of agreeing with her mother, she became more emboldened and told her mother she had decided to enter the deal with Ronnie and that was that. As soon as she spoke, her boldness faltered and she began to wonder if Ronnie was to be trusted. Sure, Ronnie was enthusiastic about their sharing an apartment but how long would her enthusiasm last? They were only recent friends, after all. Maybe, Ronnie would get bored with her and ask her to leave. Then what? Well, she could still find her own room. It wouldn't be as nice as living in a big two-bedroom apartment in one of the best buildings in the university district but it would be okay. The more she thought about her mother's objections the more she regained her confidence in her own decision and in Ronnie's genuine friendship. Ronnie had no reason to be deceptive as far as Toby could see. She also had never shown any sign of being capricious. If anything, she deliberated every move carefully and made firm decisions. Toby decided Ronnie could and should be trusted.

Toby's desk in the administrative offices of the university was in an open work area of many such desks with many student clerks like herself. After a few days of employment, Toby realized the university used a lot of paper to keep track of tens of thousands of students and hundreds of faculty and staff. Everything was done by hand or with manual typewriters. She worked with a group of student clerks who processed course grades into transcripts for each of the university's students. It was tedious and repetitious work that had to be exacting. Clerks constantly double-checked the work of their colleagues to ensure that courses taken and grades were correctly posted in all details to the appropriate transcript. Although the work was not particularly interesting, Toby found her fellow workers to be very intriguing. The clerks, mostly young people like Toby but not all current students of the university, represented a cross-section of the city. There were whites and blacks—but more whites than blacks—men and women—but more women than men—a few Asians, and to her delight, a small cadre of black Africans. Since she had encountered whites at Catholic school and Cass Tech, whites were not the folks that attracted her attention. The black women and the Africans intrigued her the most. The black women were all types—every shade of color imaginable from dark black through deep brown, like herself, to mocha, tan, and high-yellow shades like Ronnie. In appearance, they ranged from extremely attractive and fashionably dressed to homely as sin and barely presentable. Many were friendly while others were shy or aloof. It was a wonderful collection of women. Surprisingly, to Toby, there were no black African women. Mostly, there were young black African men with full heads of very wooly hair carefully shaped and cleanly delineated around the face and neck. She was struck by their hair because men and boys of her world kept their hair very short, practically down to the scalp or heavily oiled or greased and pressed close to the skull by a stocking cap made from a woman's nylon stocking and worn at night, as her own father and brother had done for years. She wanted to meet some of the Africans but did not want to behave inappropriately. She didn't know how they would perceive a young woman as herself making an introduction. She thought she would watch and see how socializing at work functioned. Meanwhile, she chatted with friendly black females and made a few casual friends with whom she could catch a sandwich and a cup of coffee during their break.

Toby noticed one of her co-workers was often staring at her, not for long periods of time, but briefly and intently. Toby was puzzled. The woman was *aubergine*, that is, about as dark as any black person she had ever seen even among the Africans who were often very dark. At first, Toby thought it was something about the way she looked or behaved but the co-worker expressed no particular interest in, or emotion regarding, Toby. She would simply stare momentarily then look back at the papers on her desk. Toby decided to speak to the woman during a coffee break in the employee lounge.

Hi there.

Are you speaking to me?

Yes. Sure. I hope I'm not bothering you. I just wanted to say hello.

Hello. Can I help you? Did you want something?

No. Just hello and to introduce myself.

Really? Why?

I've seen you but we never had a chance to talk. I'm Toby Moore and I sit one row over from your desk.

I know where you sit but I didn't know your name.

As I said, I only wanted to say hello. I hope I'm not bothering you.

No, you're not bothering me. I'm Ondine Mahmoud.

Nice to meet you, Ondine. Are you a student at Wayne?

Yes, in education. I graduate this year. What about you?

Oh, I'm a math major and probably heading towards education too but, lately, I've had a different idea.

Yeah. What's that?

I was thinking about accounting but I haven't looked into it yet.

It could be interesting.

That's what I'm thinking. So, how long have you worked here?

A couple of years.

Do you like it?

The work's okay. The other women here aren't very friendly. None of them really speak to me. That's why I was surprised by you.

That's strange. They're friendly with me. I don't know why they wouldn't be friendly with you.

Well, I guess I'm not the type other colored women find easy to like.

Really? I don't know why. I certainly hope we'll have a chance to talk sometime but I've only got a minute right now before I head back to work. I really only wanted to say, "hello." By the way, Mahmoud is an interesting name.

I know. It's Egyptian. In school, kids always made fun of my name and they made fun of me. They called me "Mud." For a long time I hated that name but now I like it. You can call me "Mud" if you want to. I don't mind. I'm sorry you have to run.

Yeah. Well, I better get moving now. I've got a lot of work to finish today. Bye, Mud.

Goodbye, Toby.

Toby returned to her desk and resumed work. At the end of her shift, she headed for the exit and encountered one of the women with whom she had developed a more cordial relationship. They talked about their workday and the classes they now had to prepare for and attend. As they walked along sharing stories and bits of gossip, Toby thought to ask her colleague about Ondine. What did she know about the large and very dark woman who sat one row over from Toby's desk? Her companion thought for a moment and tried to put the description to a face but no one came to mind. Toby tried to be more specific but still got no identification from her colleague. It was strange because the woman was so distinctive. Toby and her colleague departed ways at the library and Toby continued on to her calculus class in State Hall.

When she returned to Ronnie's apartment later that afternoon, her roommate wasn't home. There was a note, however, from Ronnie reporting the landlord had agreed to lease the new apartment to her. They could move in as soon as possible and the remaining rent for the current apartment would be applied to the new apartment. Toby immediately thought of packing but decided to wait until she discussed plans with Ronnie. Right now she needed to study for her classes and get started on some papers that were due next week for her English Literature and Sociology courses.

Ronnie arrived home later than usual. She noted there was nothing cooking and asked Toby what they should do about dinner. Toby suggested they get some Chinese take-out. It would be ready quickly and cheap. Ronnie joked about what wine to serve with Chinese and got on the telephone to a nearby take-out place to make an order. She and Toby agreed a large order of shrimp fried rice would do for dinner. And two egg rolls. When the food arrived, they sat down at what served as their dinner table and quickly dispatched the meal. But before turning to their studies, Toby told Ronnie about her experience with the strange *aubergine* woman at work. Ronnie was amused. She asked Toby why she was attracted to the woman. Why was she important enough to Toby that Toby would be concerned about the woman? Toby replied she was intrigued by the woman's guarded friendliness in conversation because she had only stared at Toby without smiling while they were working at their desks. Ronnie shrugged off the matter and retreated to her room to study. Toby remained in the living room and tried to put the *"aubergine"* out of her mind by turning her attention to her own studies.

Toby aced all of her classes. She had that kind of intelligence. Although math was her greatest strength—something she could master with minimum effort—her vague thoughts of becoming a math teacher wobbled. After all, being a public school teacher was her mother's suggestion or, rather, her expectation of Toby. Her ever-practical mother had repeated her expectation so often that Toby had assimilated it without critical evaluation. However, her new job and the idea, first proposed by her interviewer, Mister Ostrowski, that Toby might consider accounting as a career smothered teaching math until, as a goal, it no longer breathed in Toby's head. Being quick to see new paths when prodded by both Ronnie and Ostrowski, Toby saw a dim light shining in the direction of business school. She wondered why she had never considered this possibility before. The answer was obvious. No one in her family or acquaintance was in business or had studied business practices. Not a single black person in her world had ever attended business school. There were teachers, lawyers, doctors, clerical and factory workers, but no one in business. Well, she thought, why not? Just because it had never before been a possibility, why couldn't she take a step in that direction? Her next step, then, was to consult the university catalog and investigate the course of study for a business degree. She also decided to discuss business school with Mister Ostrowski since he had opened this mental door for her. When she finally got an appointment with him, she was surprised he wasn't encouraging so she asked him directly why he was not supportive.

Miss Moore, I suggested accounting and statistics courses to you because I thought they would help you in your present clerical work, and position you for a possible future permanent employment here in university administration. The coursework would be consistent with your employment opportunities. Business school is another matter. Frankly, business is a male-dominated field, and I don't think a female would find the business environment encouraging to her development or success.

I hear what you're saying, Mister Ostrowski, but I'm willing to take the chance.

Maybe you are but I think you would find the experience very frustrating and unrewarding. Men, quite possibly, would not accept you as their peer. You might even find the business school environment hostile.

Does the university tolerate such conditions for its female students, Mister Ostrowski?

Miss Moore, the university has rules and standards but the university cannot monitor every individual's behavior. Business is a male environment both in the university and in our society. That is a fact.

But, these days, a lot of facts are changing. Whole countries are changing the facts of their existence and their future. It's also happening right here with us Negroes. We are changing the facts of segregation and discrimination.

Well, I'm glad you brought up the question of Negroes, Miss Moore. You are an attractive, neat, and intelligent young lady. You fit in here very well and all reports indicate you do your job excellently. But, if you will not be offended, I should point out to you that you are also a very dark-skinned Negro, and a woman, and neither of those facts will endear you to the white faculty and students of the business school. Here, in this office, we are inclusive. The business school is not. I can't change that. The dean of the college can't change that. The president of the university can't change that. The business world is not ready for women and, especially, dark-skinned Negro women. That's how our society is.

I see. So, if I were a white male, I could become part of the club.

I'm sorry that's the way it works but, as I've said before, you have a career here. We appreciate your work. Stay here and you will continue to do well.

Do you mean I might even have your job someday?

We don't currently employ women or Negroes in supervision.

Because they are not qualified? No, because they are women or Negroes. I see, only white men are qualified. Well, thank you for your time, Mister Ostrowski. By the way, that's a nice tie you're wearing. Did your wife buy it for you?

Why, yes, she did.

It's nice to see that women are good for something. Goodbye, Mister Ostrowski.

When Toby left Ostrowski's office, she headed towards the business school. The administrative offices where she worked were in a converted four story warehouse building at the north end of campus. To reach the business school offices which were located in an old mansion—a remnant of the former residential neighborhood that the university was rapidly transforming—Toby headed south traversing nearly the entire several blocks of the campus and passing new classroom buildings, old houses, and apartment buildings. One of the city's main north-south streets bisected the heart of the campus with endless automobile traffic. Toby crossed the street at an intersection with a green light. Many students were out and about, some coming and going from classes, others standing or sitting in the few open areas chatting with friends. She knew very few of her fellow students but she did spot a fellow from one of her classes and waved to him. He waved back.

Toby felt free on this campus. She felt part of a world far removed from her family home. This was independence. This was the life she wanted, not the constant supervision of her mother or the petty squabbles of her siblings. She had outgrown her family's neighborhood of working-class one- and two-story homes and her neighborhood pals when she decided to attend Cass. Cass provided the first steps to freedom. There were kids from all kinds of different backgrounds. The teachers were nothing like the sisters in Catholic school. They were real people not the servants of some bishop or pope in Rome. What Cass offered in liberation was magnified tenfold at the university. There was more diversity, more opportunity, more freedom. She felt open to it all. She was living now with another young woman who was sophisticated and knowledgable in ways Toby was only beginning to comprehend. Sure, Toby knew she was smart but she also knew she was inexperienced. She was beginning to realize how small was her world. There was so much she didn't know. She would learn a lot and quickly, she thought, from Ronnie. Her reverie as she walked the campus came to an abrupt end when she reached the mansion housing the business school offices. Toby walked up the steps, opened the door, stepped inside and found the main office where she obtained an application for the college, thanked the clerk, and headed to the library where she filled out the application. Later, she obtained the supporting documents and letters, then mailed the application and waited for a reply. She had already decided that, since she met all of the academic requirements for admission, if she wasn't accepted, she would file a formal complaint with the university. If that failed, she would investigate legal action although she didn't have the slightest idea who she could turn to for a lawyer. Fortunately, none of these measures were necessary. She was interviewed and told, in a much more discreet way, some of the things Ostrowski had said. A month later she received her acceptance letter to begin study during the next fall semester.

Leona was stunned. How did her daughter ever get such an idea? What in hell was she thinking? Negroes didn't do well in the business world. For one thing, Negroes often didn't support Negro businesses because, rightly or wrongly, they thought white businesses were better. Most black businesses that Leona knew were small and not very efficient or attractive. There were small take-out restaurants selling barbecue and fried shrimp; and small groceries that often had poor produce and unsanitary conditions; and there was the occasional shop with merchandise that appealed to a certain lower- and working-class aesthetic. The most successful businesses were barber shops, beauty parlors, and churches. Leona didn't think you needed to go to business school to operate a beauty parlor and certainly not for ministering a holy-roller church. Although she didn't know it, her feelings and attitude were perfectly in line with those of Mister Ostrowski. When Toby came by her mother's house for a Sunday visit, Leona was ready to pull the pin of her verbal grenade.

Toby, you know I want you to have a good life. You are intelligent and, I guess, you're doing well in school, as usual. I thought you would take your mother's advice and prepare yourself for the world we live in. But, no. You want to live in a world that doesn't exist for colored people. That's the reason I haven't agreed with many of your decisions. It's as if, as smart as you are, you can be as dumb as our old dog was when it comes to making decisions. Why your father encouraged you to be this way is a complete mystery to me.

Momma, Daddy knew me better than you do. He knew I would do what I thought I should do even if it didn't seem like the wisest thing to you. Business school is what I want and, I think, I will succeed. Of course, I can't predict the future but neither can you. That's why I want to take the chance. Okay, I could have done things your way and then what? I would be doing something I don't want and something that would never make me happy.

Do you think I'm happy being a secretary? And a widow? And raising three children by myself? I've done what I could in a way I thought would bring all of us some security. And also give me a little peace of mind.

Momma, I know you didn't have a lot of choices or opportunities in your life. And, yes, you did what you thought was possible. Well, I'm in the same situation. But the times they are changing. I have more choices and opportunities than you did. Just because I can't predict the future doesn't mean I should ignore possibilities and forget about being happy.

Toby, are you going to open a business? If so, what kind of business?

I don't know, Momma. Maybe, I'll be an executive in somebody else's business.

An executive? A female colored executive? Have you seriously lost your mind? What world are you living in? Certainly not this one.

I know there aren't many Negro women out there in business. Someday, there will be more and I could be one of them.

Toby, do you know your Aunt Augusta was like you? She had the same kind of dreams. Do you know where those dreams got her?

Yes. She's a school teacher.

That wasn't her dream. She wanted to be an artist but couldn't make it.

Momma, some dreams fail. So what? She's a teacher instead of an artist. She seems happy. She's not living on the streets.

You know, Toby, you go right ahead. Do what you want. I give up on you.

Momma, don't give up on me. You can encourage me. We can hope for the best and accept what comes. Anyway, I've decided about business school. I begin classes next fall. What follows, we'll just have to see.

Toby was agitated by her mother's opposition to business school but she was also determined to follow her instinct. She wanted to unload about her mother with Ronnie. First, however, they had to attend to their new apartment. After they moved, they both spent time trying to organize their things and assess their needs. Toby needed a bed. They both wanted some attractive and comfortable furniture for the living room and a real table for the dining room. They decided to explore second hand furniture stores where they found a number of things that were in good condition and responded to their decorating tastes. Once the apartment became more livable, they sat on their new old sofa with glasses of wine and unwound.

Ronnie, my mother is impossible. She's opposed to me going to business school. She really believes I'm making a mistake.

Then prove her wrong, Toby.

Nobody proves my mother wrong. She's always right. I'm guessing your mother isn't like that?

My mother is somewhat complicated. She went her own way and became a doctor. She married a white man. She understands her children and can be very supportive. However, she has certain limits.

I've never heard you mention your mother setting limits.

Doctor Sykes, as I like to call her, can bring down the hammer.

Ronnie, this is the first time I've heard you say anything like that about your mother.

That's because she seldom puts up any barriers.

You say, "seldom." Are you implying she put up one for you, Ronnie?

Toby, Dear, maybe this is the time to talk about some stuff now that we've become official roommates.

Like what stuff?

You know, Toby, I had a feeling from when I first met you that I could talk about certain things and you would understand. When you began mentioning the "*aubergine*," I thought, well, Toby has a pretty sophisticated view of people.

Where is this going, Ronnie?

Toby, I'm trusting in your sophistication, okay? So, in high school, Toby, I had a girlfriend.

We all have girlfriends.

Well, this was a real girlfriend. We had a very, very close relationship.

How close is "very, very close?"

Sort of like lovers.

Lovers? Oh. You mean it was more than holding hands or a friendly kiss on the cheek.

I mean it was a lot more, definitely more than holding hands or a friendly kiss on the cheek.

Well, are we talking about naked bodies and body parts that don't usually come into contact with one another, especially when it's someone else's body part that comes into contact with your own?

Okay. So, it wasn't exactly naked bodies, at first. Well, not completely. And different people's body parts did eventually come into contact.

So, it was sort of sex.

Maybe, more than sort of.

You "got it on."

Yeah. We "got it on."

Care to share any details? You've got my complete attention now.

There was this girl, Athena Poole. She and I were in this private girls' school together in Chicago. She was very sexy and very popular with other girls, not because they wanted to have sex with her but because she seemed a goddess. I mean she was gorgeous. Even the teachers were somewhat in awe of her.

And, so, did you worship this goddess?

We kind of gravitated to each other, me being Miss Smart, and she being Miss Gorgeous Goddess. I knew I was attracted to her but I didn't think it was anything more than what other girls felt. You know, infatuation. You understand that, right? Sure, you've got your *"aubergine."* Then, one evening the goddess and I took a walk on the school grounds. It was pretty dark but we were together and felt safe. We came to a grove of trees where we couldn't be seen by anyone and she kissed me on the mouth.

Yeah, and then the body parts started connecting?

Not at the beginning. It got a lot more involved and "getting it on" later in a dorm room.

Involved and body parts connecting?

I was in love with her.

Before or after the body parts connected?

After we tried a lot things with each other. It was great.

A lot of things? Am I being too, as they say, prurient? So, tell me what happened?

We had an intense sexual relationship. However, she was going to college at Howard. I wanted to go there too to be with her. Doctor Sykes found out about our relationship and said, "no." Then I came to Detroit.

So, your mother isn't so broad-minded, so to speak.

Actually, I would say she is broad-minded. In this case, however, she didn't like Miss Athena Poole and told me so.

She didn't like the gorgeous goddess? Why?

Turns out, Athena had a reputation I didn't know about. Doctor Sykes discovered this from some other parents. She wasn't exactly opposed to my loving another girl, just this girl. Apparently, Athena was not from what Doctor Sykes considered a good family. She called her a common slut with more emphasis on the "common" than on the "slut." And that was that. No daughter of hers was going to be in the company of a common slut.

I'm liking Doctor Sykes. I'd like to see her and my mother together. So, Athena was "then." What about "now?" Are you still interested in other girls? Does all of this here mean you are interested in me?

Toby, have you noticed that we are living together in this apartment?

Of course, I've noticed. But I never got any hint you might be interested in me other than as a friend and roommate.

And I thought the same about you. Toby, I really like you and certainly admire you.

And . . .

Well, how about you, Toby? Have you ever been interested in another girl? Are you interested in me?

You know, Ronnie, I guess I've thought about other girls but I've never had a sexual feeling for a woman or a man.

What about the "*aubergine*?" You seemed attracted to her.

It wasn't a sexual feeling.

How do you know? Maybe you don't know what a sexual feeling is.

Hey, maybe, I don't know. I've never experimented.

So, Toby, how would you know if your attraction involved the possibility of sex?

I guess I would have to try it and see what happens.

Now the seed has been planted. Shall we see what grows?

— Toby Makes Another Move —
Spring to Summer 1958

As summer vacation approached, there was no let up of administrative tasks. There was the wrap-up of paperwork from the spring semester just concluded and the preparatory paperwork for the next fall semester. Toby, like her co-workers, was a drone keeping the hive buzzing. In fact, she was busier because many student workers took off the summer for vacation and their workload fell on people like Toby. While Toby had focused intently on her work, she occasionally indulged in office gossip. Mostly, the conversations were amusing but not sustaining and her interest drifted off. That is until talk between two black female co-workers touched on one former employee.

Girl, what was with that black bitch?

She was just mean . . . and ugly.

Ugly as sin and big as an elephant and black as coal.

And those clothes. We know she lived across the tracks but did she have to look like a train ran over her?

And that hair. That bitch's head never saw a straightening comb. She just let it look like a pile of nappy wool. Why they ever hired her is beyond me.

She never talked to anyone but, then, who would want to talk to her? When she did speak, she was nasty and rude. Good riddance, I say. I hear she graduated so she won't be coming back here in the fall.

I'm curious, Brenda. Who are you talking about?

Hi, Toby. By the way, do you know Joyce?

No but I've seen you around. Nice to meet you, Joyce. Anyway, who were you discussing?

You've seen that big, black, ugly girl named Ondine. She sat one row over from you. She stared at people all the time for no reason.

Sure. I know who you mean. Yes, Ondine. Ondine Mahmoud. I spoke to her a couple of times. She seemed friendly to me.

Not to me. That bitch was always mean. Right, Joyce?

She was mean to me too.

What do you know about her, Toby?

What do I know? Not much, really, Brenda. She was in education and I think she graduated. Joyce, how about you? Do you know anything?

I know she studied biology. I think she lives on the east-side. That's about it.

Why do you ask about her, Toby?

I was just curious, Brenda. I liked her. She was fascinating. I would have liked to know her better.

Oh. Pardon me, Toby. Well, I'm glad she won't be coming back to work here. She brought the whole place down with her ugliness and attitude.

Well, if everyone talked about her like you do, Brenda, no wonder she seemed mean.

Toby, she was mean and ugly when she first walked through the door.

That's right, Brenda. I was here her first day and she practically told all of us to get out of her face.

Why would she do that, Joyce, unless you and Brenda treated her like you talk about her?

Really, Toby, she didn't belong here. You can't be nice to a person like that. Ugly is as ugly does. A bitch is a bitch.

As they say, Ladies, it takes one to know one. Well, I've got some work to finish before I leave. See y'all later.

Did she just insult us, Brenda? Why is she standing up for that woman?

Beats me, Joyce.

Ronnie was Toby's perfect audience. She listened intently, remembered details, and encouraged Toby to explore her feelings. One early evening after dinner, they sat together on the sofa in the living room with glasses of white wine and tried to unwind from their busy day. Toby wanted to discuss her conversation with Brenda and Joyce.

Do you remember, there was this woman at work who was kinda fascinating? Her name is Ondine Mahmoud.

The "*aubergine*." What about her?

Well, she was a big girl.

Meaning what?

She was tall and a plus size and she was very dark, darker than me and not conventionally attractive.

Okay, Toby. You're describing a beast.

See, Ronnie, that's how some of the other gals in the office felt about her.

But you didn't?

No. She was fascinating, as I said.

Okay, so she was big, black, and unconventionally attractive. Toby, I know the type but what made her fascinating?

I told you, I often saw her staring at me. Apparently, she stared at some of the other girls.

Staring how? I stare at people. You probably stare at people. What's strange about staring?

I don't know. It was the intensity but also the disinterest. She would stare as if she was trying to figure out something.

About you?

That's what I don't understand, Ronnie. I finally spoke to her one day and she was reserved but friendly.

Is that odd?

Not really. Here's the thing. The other girls must have treated her badly. She probably thought I was like them. But, when I spoke to her, she was polite.

Did you like her?

Ronnie, I didn't even know her. I just was curious about her staring and thought I would start a conversation to know her a little bit.

So, Toby, what's this all about?

That's what I'm trying to figure out. You're very light-skinned. Also pretty and smart and wealthy. As a Negro, you probably never encountered the kind of abuse she may have experienced.

You're right. I don't know firsthand but I've certainly heard stories from friends and family.

Yes, but knowing is not the same as experiencing.

I agree, Toby. Tell me this, though. Why does this particular girl, whom you've spoken to maybe a few times and really don't know, concern you so much? You said she no longer works in your office.

You know what? Even though none of the other girls liked her, I wanted to know her. Something about her was intriguing as if she had stories to tell that I wanted to hear.

You're fascinated with the downtrodden, the outcasts, the misfits. Is that it?

I'm fascinated with you Miss India Rhonda Sykes and you don't fit any of those categories.

Maybe, I do, Toby.

How so?

I knew many girls like me at my private school. Their families had money and a good life. Yes, they were mostly light-skinned like me. We high-yellows have unearned advantages over our darker sisters simply because our female Negro ancestors were raped by white men. And, our families may have taken advantage of their skin color and appearance to get some of our society's rewards. But that doesn't automatically make us the most successful of insiders.

It doesn't hurt either.

Okay, Toby, you're right. I get your point but understand my position too. This girl is fascinating to you because she was an outcast among your colleagues for all the reasons you've mentioned. I'm simply asking you why you're so focused on her. I've heard you mention her more than you've ever spoken about your father, for example. You never talk about him. Why not?

My father was a good man. He took care of his family. He had a good job and he worked hard. He was always encouraging me and my siblings. I loved him. I cried for days when he died. What more is there to say? I miss him. I wish he hadn't died in a stupid car accident.

Think about it, Toby. Here's your father, a man who means so much to you and your life and you can sum him up in a couple of sentences. And, then there's this *"aubergine."* It seems you can't stop thinking about her. What's up with that?

Ronnie, my father is dead. He's not coming back. Talking about him won't bring him back. It only makes me angry that he died so young and for no reason.

Talking about the *"aubergine"* won't bring her back either.

Okay, you want the truth? I think I was attracted to her.

Really? Sexually?

I think so. Yes, definitely.

That's your type?

Ronnie, I didn't even know I had a type. I've never thought about it. I always liked smart girls like you. You're one of the smartest I've ever met. I don't know if Ondine is smart but she seems very intelligent. And something else. That's what I can't figure out. That something else.

That's what attracts you, the something else?

Maybe, it's her strange personality and looks. She totally lacks the kind of look most women want. She's outside of our ideas of an attractive woman.

She's a primitive?

Ronnie, that's kinda derogatory. But, she is primal. She's unadorned. She's elemental.

Toby, are you saying that's what turns you on about her? Would you like her to be your girlfriend?

You know I've never had the kind of girlfriend you're suggesting.

A boyfriend?

Are you asking me if I'm a virgin?

Yes.

I told you the truth when I said I never had a sexual attraction to a woman or a man. And, I've never had sex with anyone, Ronnie.

How about with yourself?

If you want to know, Ronnie, yes I have.

It's good to know. Welcome to the club, Toby.

You've already had sex with a girl.

Several, in fact.

With a boy?

Never. Not at all interested. You're living with a practicing lesbian.

Well, I guess I have a lot to learn about you and from you.

Does that mean that you want some lessons, Toby?

I'm not there yet.

Well, if you get the urge, I ready, willing, and able.

Ronnie leaned over to Toby and kissed her on the cheek. Toby turned and kissed Ronnie directly on her mouth. They embraced, stood, and walked hand in hand to Ronnie's bedroom. From that moment, Toby became a gradual sexual partner to Ronnie. It didn't happen all at once in a explosion of passion but in a slow, teasing kind of seduction. Toby was, as she acknowledged, a novice to sex. It turned out, as she admitted, that sex with a woman or a man was not something in which she had devoted much interest. She didn't recognize herself as a particularly sexual creature having always preferred the margins to her schoolmates' adolescent discussions of sex. When asked about her seeming indifference, Toby deferred, deflected, and dismissed all talk of sex as not worth her time. Even her mother's talk to her at the onset of her menstruation consisted mainly of how to avoid getting pregnant. Most of Toby's friends thought of her as asexual, a unicorn. Her intelligence and intellectuality gave her a free pass on teenage obsession with sex. Now in college and living with another young woman, she was learning she didn't know she had an interest or enthusiasm for an exciting and scary invasion of her body by another person, and for reciprocation. Life became, suddenly, more complex and thrilling and more wonderfully satisfying.

— An Unexpected Proposal —
Fall 1958

Leona invited Toby to Sunday dinner as a gesture of reconciliation. When Toby asked if she could bring Ronnie, Leona guessed that, to see her daughter, she would also have to see her daughter's roommate. Leona knew she had lost the battle to direct Toby's life. For the first time as a mother, she pivoted, almost gracefully, with an outpouring of motherly love that persuaded her daughter to visit. Once she got Toby's consent, she also asked Obra-Jean to be with the family. Obra-Jean was excited to come because she hadn't seen her sister or brother in a few months and was particularly eager to tell Toby about her life in high school and living with her grandparents.

Sunday arrived, Clemenza prepared a feast—baked pork chops, candied sweet potatoes, green bean casserole, apple pie, and sponge cake. The entire Moore family sat down to dinner with their guest, Ronnie. Leona was in a rare mood; she was happy to have all of her children together. Each one had stories to tell about their school, what they were learning, and what they were thinking about their futures. Toby described her excitement about having begun business school and some of the possibilities for future employment after graduation. E.J. was taking advanced math courses and planned to enter the education college so that he could become a high school math teacher. He was also dating a fellow student, Vergie Thomason, whom he would like to invite to a Sunday dinner soon. Obra-Jean effused about her high school. She was so happy to be among other black students and away from Catholic school. She loved her classes and off-handedly mentioned that she was taking an elective art class. Leona's goodwill instantly imploded. She could see no value in taking art. It was not something that would benefit Obra-Jean. It was not practical. It was a waste of time. No, she forbade Obra-Jean from taking more of these superfluous classes. That was her final decision. Ronnie, who had remained mostly quiet during the meal decided to risk Leona's wrath. She told Leona about her own decision to take art and art history courses because she thought learning about different things actually opened a person's mind to new possibilities.

Ronnie, how would that benefit a young colored girl who already doesn't have a lot possibilities in life?

Missus Moore, all of us may not have a lot of possibilities in life. But we can always expand our minds as we learn more about the world. Who we are inside of us is as important, if not more important, than who we are to the rest of the world.

Excuse me, Ronnie, but your parents are rich doctors, right?

Not rich but well off.

And, your father is white. True?

Yes, Ma'am. Very white.

So, Ronnie, you're not really like the rest of us ordinary working-class colored people, wouldn't you say?

I've had certain advantages, Missus Moore. But any of us can and should improve ourselves even if it is only for ourselves. You've encouraged your children to get a good education. Why shouldn't they open their minds and develop their talents as much as they can? Why should Negroes remain uninformed, untrained, and underdeveloped simply because we might not have the opportunities to use all of our gifts? The fact that we have gifts might come in handy someday. An unexpected opportunity might come our way. We might make an opportunity because we have the necessary skills. I should tell you, Missus Moore, I'm not taking art and art history classes because I want to be an artist. I've decided I want to be a lawyer. Art and art history help me to learn and memorize facts. I have to use my research skills. There's a lot of organizing of ideas and reasoning through partial or conflicting information that would make me a better lawyer. I also want to be a lawyer who knows about art, history, and everything else that interests me.

Well, you can afford it, Ronnie. My daughter needs to finish her education and find a job. Girls from my kind of family can't be all of the things you can be.

I get it, Missus Moore, and that's where we can help one another. This is my proposal. If Obra-Jean wants to take another art class, I'll pay any expenses. I'll also pay any expenses for the one she's presently taking.

Leona, not to mention the rest of the family, was stunned into silence. Leona knew she would sound ridiculous if she objected to Ronnie's offer. She felt she had been outmaneuvered and, wisely, replied that, if Ronnie wanted to waste her money, it was not Leona's place to tell her otherwise. But she couldn't help issuing another warning to Obra-Jean to be sensible and realistic about her future. The dinner conversation drifted off into inconsequentialities until everyone got up from the table. Leona and Clemenza cleared the dishes. E.J., Vergie, and Ronnie struck up a conversation while Obra-Jean asked Toby to come with her to their former bedroom upstairs where she closed the door.

Toby, I want to tell you something. I want your advice but only if you don't laugh at me and make me feel bad like you always do.

Oh, Little Sister. My scheming, conniving, lying little sister. Here we go again. What's your scheme this time?

You know you don't always have to be nasty to me. You think I've been a brat in the past. Maybe I was. My life is different now. So try to be nice to me. What I want to ask you about is this. I want to be an architect.

Oh, shit.

Come on. What do you think?

I think you've flipped your wig. A female architect and a Negro? Why not president of the United States?

You're in business school. I'm not laughing at you, Toby.

That's because you don't have a sense of humor or a sense of irony. I'm making fun of you not because being an architect is ridiculous. But because you really think you can become an architect. I know I can become an accountant because that's what I'm studying in school. Maybe I won't be successful but I will be an accountant. How can you become an architect? Just because you want to be one?

I know I have to get into architecture school and graduate. Then I have to get a job as an architect and then design buildings.

You make it sound so simple or simple-minded. Little Sister, what you're talking about is like saying you want to go to the moon. How would that be possible?

I know it would be hard but not impossible.

You would have a hard time, Obra-Jean, even if you got into and through architecture school.

You're in college. I mean, you've started business school and that wasn't easy. Why would it be so much harder for me?

Well, it was easy for me to get in to business school, maybe easier than architecture school. I'm guessing I'll graduate and I'm guessing I'll get a job. I'm taking a big chance. You would be taking a bigger chance.

But do you think I can do it?

This is what I think, my bratty, snotty Little Sister. I think you're too smart and too clever for your own good. Therefore, you're going to do whatever you decide to do. You've already quit Catholic school for public school. You managed to move out of Momma's house into our grandparents' house. That is amazing. You may be the real deal because you are a lying, scheming, conniving, double-dealing, smart-ass little sister.

Gee, Toby, thanks for being such an understanding big sister. I can always count on you to give me shit and then try to wipe it off. So, here's my plan. I finish high school in science, to please Momma, while taking drawing classes. I go to Wayne for a year and take some of my required college courses. Meanwhile, I'll apply to architecture school at the University of Michigan and the University of Detroit.

You've got it all figured out just as I suspected.

You think so?

Yes, and listen, if Ronnie can help you with classes, I can help too with a little money. Just ask and I'm there for you.

Thanks, Big Sister. I hope you mean what you say because there is a favor I want to ask.

How did I not see that coming? Just shoot me in my fat, stupid head.

I want to take drafting courses in addition to the art classes. I want to know how to make good architectural plans.

Of course you do. I see my little sister is already covering all of her bases. As I said, you're the real deal. You had all of this worked out, didn't you?

Gotta stay on top of these things, Big Sister.

After dinner, Toby offered to help Clemenza in the kitchen while the rest of the family and India had moved to the living room to continue their conversations. When she was a little younger, Toby was very close to her grandmother—a relationship, she gleefully sensed, that irritated her mother. Of the three siblings, Toby was the least inclined to accommodate her mother's moods and fearlessly defied her demands. In fact, she particularly enjoyed annoying her mother by being especially friendly with Clemenza. Toby genuinely loved her grandmother and tried as best she could to show her affection and to help her whenever possible around the house. In Leona's presence, Clemenza never expressed her own loving feelings towards Toby but in private—mostly in her room—she and Toby spent many hours talking about Toby's dreams and plans. Clemenza even shared some stories of her life as a way to explain why Leona treated her as she did. She asked Toby to keep their discussions to herself lest they come to Leona's attention. When Toby moved from her parents' home, her contact with Clemenza was limited mostly to occasional telephone calls. So, the Sunday dinner was a rare occasion for the two women to be together if only briefly. While cleaning the kitchen, Clemenza wanted to hear more from Toby about her school and classes as well as her future plans. Clemenza also probed discreetly and delicately into Toby's relationship with Ronnie which Toby honestly disclosed. Although Clemenza was not surprised to learn that the roommates were also lovers, she was concerned if such a relationship might affect Toby's life and career. Toby was unconcerned about the future. She was going to live the life she wanted and face whatever problems as they arose. Clemenza marveled at the assurance of her granddaughter and wondered if living with a fairly wealthy young woman had not given Toby a false sense of security. Toby laughed. She explained to Clemenza that her sense of security came, not from a wealthy partner, but from her own willingness to risk venturing out into the world free from her mother's fears.

Before returning to the rest of the family, Toby thought to inquire about her grandmother's health, well aware, as she was, that Clemenza had several long-standing medical issues. Clemenza acknowledged that, as she grew older, she felt increasingly worn-down by her ailments but she somehow kept going. Toby asked when she had last seen a doctor and was startled to learn that her grandmother had never had a physical exam in her life. She had always relied on drugstore over-the-counter remedies. Toby offered to accompany Clemenza to see a doctor. She would ask Ronnie to borrow her car and drive her grandmother to an appointment. Clemenza thanked Toby and promised her that, if she felt really bad and the drugstore medicine didn't help, she would accept her granddaughter's offer. Toby embraced Clemenza, hugging her tight. Tears rolled down Toby's cheeks.

— In-Laws —

Ronnie received a letter from her parents. Although they communicated infrequently, she didn't expect a letter to portend anything out of the ordinary and, therefore, didn't open it immediately. It was only after dinner the same evening when she and Toby were talking about a movie they might want to see that Ronnie remembered the letter, opened it, and read it out loud to Toby. It was brief and to the point. Her parents were inviting her to come to Chicago for their thirtieth wedding anniversary. There would be a long weekend of dinners and parties with the extended family and friends. Her mother added a postscript noting that Ronnie's parents would pay all expenses for her trip. The parents planned the anniversary weekend for the first week of November. Toby was pleased by the invitation and urged Ronnie to attend. Ronnie felt conflicted. Although she would like to celebrate her parents' anniversary, she wanted Toby to accompany her but the invitation did not provide for a guest. Ronnie knew that, even if she could bring Toby, Toby couldn't afford the trip on her own and wouldn't allow Ronnie to pay her expenses. Besides, where would Toby stay in Chicago? Ronnie had not disclosed to her parents the nature of her relationship with Toby and was not prepared to reveal it now. Why would she want to bring a roommate to Chicago for her parents' anniversary celebration? Toby was sympathetic since she had not disclosed the nature of their relationship to her own family but she also had an idea. What if they both went to Chicago—Toby would pay her own way because she had saved a little money—but Toby would stay in a hotel and they could avoid the problem of explaining Toby to Ronnie's parents? She and Ronnie could be together during the weekend when Ronnie was not required to be with her family. Ronnie thought this was a good idea but, now, it didn't seem quite right to her to keep secret from her parents both Toby's presence in Chicago and their relationship. Maybe it was time to say what was what. Toby began to understand and appreciate Ronnie's forthright way of operating in the world but this still amazed her. Would she really disclose to her parents that she was living in a lesbian relationship? What would they say and do? Would Ronnie want to find out?

Doctor Belinda Carter-Reese Sykes and Doctor Alvin Joseph Sykes were neither upset nor pleased by their daughter's announcement that she and her girlfriend were coming to Chicago for their anniversary celebration. They had the choice of including Toby in their plans or not. Opting for graciousness over protocol, they informed Ronnie that she not only could, but also should, bring her girlfriend to all of the festivities. Although Ronnie was mildly surprised by her parents' response, Toby was not. She felt that her deceased father might also have been as gracious. Maybe, even her very-much-alive mother might be accepting since she seemed to be letting go of some of her controlling instincts and animosity. Ronnie decided to drive to Chicago to save Toby from paying airfare and she booked a hotel room in the Loop to further reduce Toby's expenses. On Saturday afternoon, when Toby and Ronnie arrived at the home of the Doctors Sykes on Chicago's South Side, they were both warmly welcomed. Everything was as Toby expected. Their home, a two-story brick structure, was substantial, beautifully appointed with Swedish Modern furnishings and decorated with Dutch landscape paintings, framed historical prints of African tribal royalty, and Chinese ceramics. Toby also was not surprised by the very formal greeting both parents gave to their daughter—a tentative embrace and a light kiss on the cheek. Toby shook hands and, then, she and Ronnie were invited to take seats in the living room.

The opening conversation at first put Toby at ease. Belinda inquired about Toby's studies. When she was satisfied that she had heard enough, she turned to Ronnie and repeated the same inquiry. Toby began to feel uneasy. This was not really a conversation but the opening salvo into what could become an inquisition. Something about the brusqueness of Belinda reminded her of no other than her own mother. Belinda was really a coiled snake awaiting an opportunity to strike, but at who? Was she about to rip into her daughter or her daughter's girlfriend, or both? Alvin intervened and suggested that they move to the dining room where the table had been set for a light lunch. Toby and Ronnie were seated opposite one another while the Doctors sat at each end of the table. Lunch was a consommé, green salad with pear slices, and grilled salmon. As the conversation continued, Belinda wanted to know about her daughter's apartment. Ronnie explained that the two-bedroom apartment was in an older four-story building a few blocks from the Wayne campus. There were many apartment buildings in the area, mostly occupied by university faculty and students, and it was very safe. Belinda wondered if Ronnie and Toby shared a bedroom. Ronnie replied that they each had a bedroom. What then, was the nature of their relationship, Belinda pursued? Ronnie looked directly at her mother, then glanced at her father, and returned to face her mother. She replied that Toby was her girlfriend. They had a romantic relationship. Toby thought she would choke on her salmon. Belinda turned to Alvin and said something about regretting having sent their daughter to a private girls' school. Perhaps if she had not been immersed in a single-sex culture, she would have taken to bonding with men instead of women. Then, she turned to Toby and asked what her family thought about their relationship. Toby looked at Ronnie and, then, at Belinda and said that her mother had invited them to a family dinner. Although she had not explicitly told her family about the intimacy of her relationship with Ronnie, she and Ronnie were both warmly welcomed by them. Belinda placed her napkin on the table next to her plate with its uneaten salmon. With her hands folded on her lap, she looked at Toby and asked her to talk about her family. Who were they? What was their background? What did they do? Toby first mentioned her dead father, then identified her mother, brother, sister, aunt, and grandparents and filled in what she knew of their background and current occupations. In the case of her brother and sister, she mentioned their future plans.

That's an interesting family you have. Well, Detroit is the motor capital of the world, I suppose, and my understanding is that there isn't very much culture there. So, what do your people do to enrich their lives?

I guess they watch a lot of television, go to movies, and visit with family and friends.

Oh. Do they attend concerts or museums or theater?

Not really but my aunt is the culture-lover. She's traveled a lot and lived in New York City. She was an artist but now, as I said, she is an elementary school teacher.

School teacher. I see. That's honorable. India, Dear, I'm puzzled. What exactly do you have in common with these people?

Mother, that's a mean question and I'm surprised that you would play the class card. The people in Toby's family are lovely, intelligent, and very hard-working. They may not have had the advantages you and Father enjoyed and that you provided for me. But they are good and loving people. I enjoy their concern and support for one another. I love being with them and with Toby.

Well, that's discouraging. Apparently, all of our money was wasted on your upbringing and education. We had aspirations for you to take a profession, marry in your class or better, and raise children who could aspire to even higher levels of achievement. It's called, Dear, "improving the race" and, although your father is white, he understands that we Negroes must constantly rise up, generation after generation, so that we can equal or surpass whites. I'm afraid you are spoiling our dream with your working-class girlfriend. Just as you almost spoiled things with that disreputable girl at your school.

Mother, thank you for being completely honest with me but I disagree with you. Toby's family is "raising up the race" by working hard and being responsible citizens and a loving family. They are no different from you and Dad except you have more money and think that, somehow, money makes you a better class of people. Your questions are rude. Your attitude is elitist. Apparently, after my upbringing and all of the resources you've lavished on me, I've learned a different set of values. I'm with Toby and I think Toby and I will leave now. I don't plan to return for the anniversary events. We'll find other things to enjoy during our stay in Chicago. Thank you for the delicious lunch and goodbye.

Ronnie and Toby stood up from the table, left the dining room, and exited the doctors' house. They headed back to the Loop, walked around, talked about the visit, and decided to catch an early movie. After the movie, Toby noticed a bookshop. In the window was a book on Chicago architecture and it occurred to her to take a closer look at it inside the store. The book had color photos and text describing historic and modern buildings in Chicago. Thinking of Obra-Jean's improbable dream of becoming an architect, she impulsively bought the book as a gift for her sister. Before heading back to their hotel, Toby and Ronnie stopped at a small Italian restaurant for dinner. During their meal, Ronnie proposed that, for the remainder of the weekend, they should visit Grant Park, the Art Institute of Chicago, and attend a concert at the Auditorium Building. Toby listened uneasily. Something didn't feel right to her. She didn't like walking out on Ronnie's parents and their celebratory weekend. Yes, Ronnie's mother was rude and denigrating to Toby but so what? Toby knew she came from a working-class background—she wasn't ashamed of the fact—and she had not had the experiences or advantages of Ronnie—something she had already admitted to Ronnie. She admired—maybe adored—Ronnie and was grateful to have found such a generous, attractive, intelligent, and loving partner. Ronnie seemed quite at ease with Toby's family. In fact, she seemed more comfortable in the company of the Moore family than with the Sykes. But, and this was the issue that was troubling Toby, Ronnie's family was her blood family and they were about to celebrate their thirtieth wedding anniversary. All of Ronnie's family would be present and, Toby reasoned, so should Ronnie, with or without Toby.

When they finished their meal and headed back to the hotel, Toby ventured to express her concerns to Ronnie. Ronnie listened politely without interrupting but she clearly was not receptive to what Toby was proposing. Toby persisted, emphasizing that Toby was not at all upset by Belinda's attitudes and opinions. Perhaps having fought with her own mother for many years over differences of opinion gave Toby some insight that mothers and daughters might agree to disagree and still maintain their unique relationship. As Toby expressed these thoughts to Ronnie, she had to simultaneously check the reality of her own relationship to Leona. Was she as accepting of Leona as she was encouraging Ronnie to be with Belinda? Toby's self-examination produced a big, painful "No" and at that moment, Toby admitted to Ronnie her own failings in understanding and accepting Leona and conceded that Ronnie's dilemma was no different from her own. Toby's admission touched something in Ronnie that caused her to pause in her anger toward her mother. In that pause, she saw her mother from a different perspective. Her mother was a product of a particular striving black culture that, apparently, advanced and encouraged the ideas she expressed. That her mother accepted these ideas and expressed them in such an insensitive way might be a flaw in her character but it was only a flaw. Belinda had always been a good mother who thought only of the best for her daughter. Because of her upbringing and experiences, Ronnie had developed different ideas for herself than those espoused by her mother, and she lived her life accordingly. It might be possible that mother and daughter could coexist with their differences. They would disagree; they would argue; they would fight but they would be true to their own selves as mother and daughter.

When they reached their hotel and returned to their room, Ronnie thought to place a telephone call to her parents' home. She hesitated. Toby asked her what was happening and Ronnie replied that she couldn't call her mother and give in to her mother's class prejudices regardless of family ties. Her mother was wrong and also insensitive. Although attending the anniversary events during the weekend was important as would be the presence of the entire family, Ronnie felt she had to make a choice. The woman and family she loved meant more to her than her family of origin. Maybe someday she and her parents might find common ground but today—during this visit—was not that time. Ronnie and Toby spent the remainder of the weekend enjoying Chicago then headed back to Detroit. Although she didn't discuss the matter further, Toby was distressed but, for her own well-being, she resolved to heal the rift in her own relationship with her mother instead of harassing Ronnie about her parents. At the next occasion of seeing Obra-Jean, Toby surprised her sister with the book of Chicago architecture. Obra-Jean was delighted and thanked Toby repeatedly. The book was a kind of affirmation for Obra-Jean—she understood it as a blessing from her sister and approval of her dream.

VI

Augusta Post

— A Night at the Opera —
Summer 1958

Ever since Perry's death during the summer of 1957, Augusta wanted to do something special for her sister, her young niece, and her mother. Having listened to Leona's constant complaints about finances, and about being a widow with three children who were making her life miserable and being a daughter of a mother who didn't love her but who was now in her care, Augusta wanted to release some of the pressure she felt was building up in the Moore household. The New York Metropolitan Opera was coming to town during the summer of 1958 for its annual visit to the Masonic Temple. Although not an opera fan, Augusta reasoned that a night out at the opera might be an experience her relatives would enjoy and put them in a better frame of mind. Friends had told her that even for opera novices, the Metropolitan's productions were unrivaled by any other theater in Detroit. Augusta explained her plan to Leona and asked if she would like to attend as Augusta's treat. At first, Leona expressed disinterest—she didn't know anything about opera; she was too distracted by all of the things on her mind; and she was tired and depressed. She couldn't imagine spending a long evening out with Clemenza and Obra-Jean. Augusta persisted by explaining that was precisely the reason she invited her. But Leona hardened her stance—she wouldn't enjoy herself. Then she suggested asking Obra-Jean and Clemenza to go without her. Augusta tried one more time to convince Leona but, being rebuffed, took her suggestion and asked her mother and niece. Clemenza voiced some of the same objections as Leona. She appreciated being asked but she would not enjoy herself. She countered that she would love to see Augusta sometime. Maybe Augusta could pick her up in her car and they could spend an afternoon or evening together. Augusta promised to do that soon. Obra-Jean, on the other hand, was overjoyed at the invitation and told her aunt that she would certainly like to see an opera for the first time. With that settled, Augusta ordered tickets for a Friday night performance.

When summer of 1958 came—the summer after Obra-Jean's first year at Cass and after she had moved to her grandparents' home, she grew anxious about the impending performance. She told her aunt she didn't have anything nice enough to wear to the opera. Augusta suggested they go shopping downtown and buy a new dress for Obra-Jean who knew exactly what she wanted. She remembered from her trip to New York City that the most attractive women at the theater she attended wore simple black cocktail dresses. That was what Obra-Jean wanted. She and Augusta visited every department store and several women's fashion shops until they found a dress that matched Obra-Jean's vision and Augusta's pocketbook. When she tried it on and looked at herself in the mirror of the fitting room, she saw herself as a young woman and no longer a child. Augusta suggested they buy a fake pearl necklace for the dress and a pair of black high heel pumps. Then the fashion statement would almost be complete. Obra-Jean would have to wear makeup—a little lipstick and some facial powder. Her aunt would take her to the beauty parlor for a real hair styling.

The night of the opera was warm and humid. As a crowd of mostly white people ascended the steps to the Masonic Temple, Obra-Jean felt self-assured. Her aunt also opted to wear a black evening dress and the two of them made an elegant pair. Obra-Jean was now as tall as her aunt and, although her figure was not yet fully developed, she possessed a kind of slim gamin quality associated with Audrey Hepburn, one of Obra-Jean's favorite actors. No one could have told Obra-Jean she didn't belong in this crowd. She knew she looked good and she knew she was good— smart, beautiful, confident, and having some knowledge of the real world.

The opera was *Tosca*. Obra-Jean and Augusta read the program notes presenting a synopsis of the story and describing the kind of music Giacomo Puccini created for the principal characters. After the house lights dimmed, the opening ominous chords caught Obra-Jean unaware. Then the bright lilting melody that followed pulled her into a story of love, honor, and death. Although she could only guess at what the Italian lyrics meant, the music seemed to capture the mood and feelings of the characters. At the first intermission, in the foyer, Obra-Jean and Augusta were both excited by the production. Even if they could not fully grasp all they witnessed, they knew it was powerful theater and unlike anything else they had ever seen. In the final act, after a firing squad executed Tosca's lover, Cavaradossi, and Tosca leapt to her death from atop Castel Sant'Angelo in Rome, Obra-Jean burst into tears. She was saddened by the unexpected ending but she was also thrilled by the experience of the theater. She thanked her aunt for making the evening possible and promised her she would never forget this kindness shown her.

— About That Plan —
Fall 1958

Leona had asked Obra-Jean to spend a Sunday at home with her brother instead of at her Grandmother Moore's house. During her visit and out of a sense of politeness toward an adult, Obra-Jean mentioned to her mother she wanted to say hello to her Grandmother Post who sequestered herself in her room after dinner. She knocked on her grandmother's door, was invited in, and sat in a chair to chat with her. Clemenza, seated on her bed, asked Obra-Jean about school and inquired if she liked living with her Grandmother Moore. Obra-Jean replied she loved being with her grandparents and that Grandmother Moore was kinder to her than her own mother. They could talk about a lot of things she could never discuss with Leona. Clemenza felt this was an opportunity to say some things to her granddaughter for the first time. She liked Obra-Jean. In fact of all of her daughter's children, she admired her the most for her intelligence and determination. Now was a chance to let her granddaughter know something about herself. This was the beginning of a story Clemenza told her granddaughter, Obra-Jean:

Your mother, Leona, was my first child. She never knew her own father. He was not the father of her sister or her brothers. Now, you've never met the brothers because they were born and live in Hot Springs. That's in Arkansas. Leona's father was a slick young man named Duke. He talked me into having sex with him after he gave me some liquor. I was young, only sixteen at the time. I hadn't tasted alcohol before and didn't realize it would remove most of my inhibitions—that is, if I had any, which I didn't. I was surprised when I became pregnant. By that time, Mister Duke was gone, and I didn't know where. Then I had your mother. I guess I made some mistakes because I didn't know better.

Clemenza told a long tale. She revealed details of her life and shared thoughts about feelings that she had long withheld from her own daughters. She told these things to Obra-Jean because she felt her granddaughter would not only understand but would benefit from the information. After their conversation, Obra-Jean said goodbye to Clemenza and returned to the living room to be with her mother about whom she now knew a great deal. She could see her mother differently.

Your grandmother doesn't want to come out of her room, Obra-Jean?

I guess not, Momma.

What did she say to you?

She asked me about school.

Is that all?

She wanted to know how I liked living with Grandmama and Grandpapa Moore.

So, what did you say?

I said that I liked being with them.

Is that all?

Yeah. That's all.

You don't seem to have much to say to me.

What should I say, Momma?

233

Don't you miss me and your brother?

Yes, of course I do.

Well, how would anybody know? You're so silent with me. You must have had a lot to say to your grandmother. You were in her room a long time.

It didn't seem like a long time. We just sat. She talked mostly. That's all.

I really think it's time for you to come back here to live in your own home, Obra-Jean.

But Grandmama Moore wants me to stay with her. She says I keep her company.

What about me? I need some company too.

You've got E.J. and Grandmama Post. So, why do you need me here? You only complain about everything I do.

I want you here, Obra-Jean, because you're my daughter.

You don't complain about E.J. because you like him.

Of course I like him. I love you both. Do you really think I don't like you? Do you think that's why, as you say, I only complain about everything you do?

Yes, I do.

Listen, Obra-Jean, what I don't like is the fact that you don't pay attention to what I tell you. Your brother does. It's that simple.

So, why should I come back here?

Because this is your home. Your grandparents' house is not your home.

Grandmama and grandpapa need me there. I help them a lot around the house.

I can see you don't really care about me. You're not concerned if I need help. You and Toby are just alike. I show you nothing but love and you just run away. Okay, so if you are happy at your grandparents' home, stay there. I can get along without you. I don't need you here but just remember this conversation when you want something from me.

You're not being fair, Momma. You said I could stay with grandmama and grandpapa.

I only agreed to let you stay there a short while. I didn't intend it to be permanent.

Momma, I need to stay at least until the end of the semester then, maybe, I could come back.

And, then, you will argue that you need to stay just a little longer until the end of the school year and then on and on. You are determined to have things your way. Okay, Obra-Jean, I don't want to fight with you. You're as hardheaded as your sister and I guess you've stopped listening to me, your own mother, just like your sister did. I've tried to help you girls understand life and not make mistakes like I made. You're just wearing me down and I don't have the energy anymore to try to show you the right way. Listen, do what you want to do. I don't care and I won't talk about it anymore. Just don't come to me when things don't work out the way you want. I've done my job as your mother. You're on your own now. Maybe your Grandmother Moore will have better luck with you.

Momma, I'm doing really well in school and so is Toby. What are we doing wrong?

You're not looking ahead. That's what's wrong.

Momma, I'm sorry I'm not doing what you think I should do but I'll be okay. You'll see.

Oh, yes. I'll see. Please, I'm done. Finished. We don't need to talk about this anymore. Oh, by the way, I was talking to your Aunt Augusta. She wants to talk to you.

Do you know why?

It's something about a trip she's planning.

Where to?

Europe, I think. I'll find out more in a week when I go to see her. She's invited me to dinner for next Sunday.

Is E.J. going too?

He says he has other plans with his girlfriend. I'll spend the day with my sister since, obviously, none of my own children want to be with me.

A week later, Leona groomed and dressed herself in a dark blue skirt suit as if she were heading to her office for work but, in fact, she was preparing for her Sunday visit with her sister, Augusta, who lived in fashionable Lafayette Park—a new neighborhood created by urban renewal near downtown. The drive—in a new model Plymouth that replaced the car totaled in the accident that killed Leona's husband, Perry—was relatively quick because the distance between her and her sister's home was only a few miles. She took a familiar route, first, through the neighborhood called Indian Village. This neighborhood of luxurious old mansions for Detroit's elite was named for its residential streets, Seminole and Iroquois, not directly for the indigenous people who lived in the area before the arrival of European settlers. Passing quickly through this enclave, she then headed past undistinguished blocks of one- and two-story homes packed together in monotonous districts for Detroit's industrial workers. After the expansive green park-like setting of Elmwood Cemetery, these neighborhoods suddenly gave way to glass and steel towers of Lafayette Park. Leona steered her car into the driveway and parking lot for guests near the crisp, machined elegance of her sister's apartment building, a residence that looked like a giant metal and glass cereal box.

It was early afternoon and Leona expected to spend most of the rest of the day with her sister, returning home only after dinner, drinks, and lots of Augusta's favorite recorded music. Augusta buzzed her into the building and Leona took an elevator to the sixteenth floor. The building was silent. Exiting the elevator, Leona turned right in the carpeted hallway that stretched from one end to the other end of the building. Before she reached Augusta's apartment, her sister opened her door, stepped into the hallway, greeted Leona enthusiastically, and waved her inside. Augusta was dressed more casually than Leona. She wore beige linen slacks and a purple silk blouse. Leona noticed Augusta was wearing the matched set of silver earrings, necklace, and bracelets that Leona gave her sister as a birthday present earlier in the year. Leona put her purse on a small table near the door and walked into the spacious living room with a wall of floor to ceiling windows that provided a view of downtown Detroit. Augusta liked modern furniture that highlighted the rigid geometry of the apartment building. Several framed contemporary prints on the walls and a couple of brilliantly colored textiles draped over the sofa provided some color in the otherwise monochrome decor. The plush white carpeting absorbed nearly all sounds. Leona settled on the light gray sofa while Augusta retrieved drinks and snacks from the open galley kitchen. Augusta knew her sister only drank bourbon with a little soda so she brought out an ample supply of both with a bucket of ice on a tray she placed on the glass-top coffee table in front of the sofa. Augusta preferred white wine and, therefore, brought out a glass for herself with an open bottle of wine chilled in a bucket. After pouring herself a drink, she offered a toast to her sister.

Here's to my favorite sister.

I'm your only sister, Augusta.

But, Leona, you're still my favorite.

I see you gave me the good bourbon this time.

I always give you the good bourbon—only the best for my favorite sister.

Augusta, this favorite sister stuff is a little tired. You know if I wasn't your sister, you wouldn't give me the time of day.

Why do you say that? It's certainly not true. You are my only sister and I love you.

Augusta, my dead husband would be the only person who would believe that.

What's with you today? You're crankier than usual.

What's with me? My husband's dead. Toby has moved out of the house and is living with that woman near the university. She hardly has any time for me. She doesn't call me. We don't talk unless I call her and when I do, she doesn't have much to say. It's some of the same with Obra-Jean who's living with her grandparents. She doesn't seem to need me anymore either. We hardly ever talk unless I call her. I think they both blame me for everything including killing their father. I can hardly sleep worrying about them and about how I'm gonna pay all of my bills without Perry's paycheck.

First of all, Leona, Perry's death was an accident.

Of course it was. I just can't get over Perry dying like that. I blame myself even though I know it wasn't my fault. That truck was coming at us, cars were going every which way. I know I panicked and just tried to get out of the way of the cars in front of me. Now Perry is dead.

Leona, listen, nobody blames you. An accident is an accident. It was bad luck. Thank god, nobody else in your car was injured or killed. Perry is dead. You won't forget that but try to focus on the good times you two had together. What about that trip to New York? You said you loved it.

Yeah, I did love it.

So, why not remember other good stuff?

I've tried but I just wish Perry hadn't died. We'd been married twenty years. That's a long time to be with someone. I miss him. My daughters aren't making my life any easier, especially Toby. I lost my husband and now I feel like I've lost my daughter. I swear, I don't know what it is she thinks I did to her to make her so angry with me. I tried my best to steer her in the right direction. I tried to make her aware of what she would face in the world. I tried to prepare her for whatever life she might want for herself. I tried to do what our mother never did for me. I wanted Toby to have a good sense of herself and of the world she would be living in. I even had her and her roommate to dinner. What am I doing wrong?

Leona, I've heard your complaints about Toby ever since she decided to leave Catholic school. And I always say you did your best. Toby is a good person. She's making choices maybe you wouldn't choose for her. But she's doing what she feels is best for herself. I don't ever hear you say these kinds of things about Elgin James.

E.J.? E.J. has always been very steady. He's been obedient to his parents. He always did well in school. He listened to me and never caused me or Perry any trouble. He's a good kid. I expect he'll finish school, get a job, get married and raise a nice family of grandchildren for his mother. He never fought me like Toby did. And, then, there's Obra-Jean who somehow persuaded her grandparents to let her live with them.

You let her do it, Leona.

I know I let her do it. Mother Moore pleaded with me to let Obra-Jean stay with her while I sorted things out at home after Perry's death. I did feel overwhelmed having two kids at home. My job, a house, and our mother who, well, that's another subject. All of it was too much. I was thinking that, well, for the time being, if Obra-Jean wasn't constantly under foot giving me trouble and doing things in an ass-backwards way, I could pull my life together. Then, she could return home and I would be in a better frame of mind to deal with her.

So, what was wrong with that plan?

Obra-Jean just doesn't want to be with me. My own child doesn't want to be with her mother. She's like her sister. What the hell is wrong with them?

Leona, how about I refresh your drink? Did you try the shrimp? And those cheese puffs are delicious. Come on, Sister, eat and drink and put your children out of your mind. You're here to relax today. I made us dinner for later. You'll love it. It's your favorite—baked chicken and rice. What would like to hear on the record player? A little Sarah Vaughn, or Dinah Washington, or Johnny Mathis?

Give me Dinah and you can play Johnny too since I know he's your favorite. Augusta, while you're up, could you get me a glass? I want to try this white wine.

Wine? Really, Leona? You don't usually drink wine.

I know. I always thought wine was for white people and winos.

Well, I'm not white or a wino.

Yes, but you've spent a lot of your life with white people and you've let them contaminate you. Sometimes, I wonder if you're still colored.

I'm as much a Negro as you are.

You're a lot lighter than I am.

Honey, we had different fathers, that's all. I guess your father was darker than mine. I look more like my father and you look more like our mother.

Oh, lucky me.

Come on, Leona, you are the beautiful daughter and always have been. Even after three children, you still have a good figure. You've got beautiful hair like an Indian princess. The boys were always after you. I should have been as lucky as you.

You're attractive too—slim, light complexion, nice figure. What have you got to complain about?

Attractive, maybe, but not beautiful. Almost any woman can make herself attractive. But beautiful? I don't think so. Either you are beautiful or you're not.

Men find you attractive, Augusta. The problem is you don't have any interest in men.

I've never found the right man. The men I like don't seem to like me.

Maybe, you're looking at the wrong men.

Who are the right men, Sister?

The men who do like you.

How can I be interested in someone I don't find interesting?

It's easy, Sister. You just do it.

Easy for you to say. You found the perfect man you liked.

Did I?

Leona, Perry was a perfect husband. He was very handsome with that café au lait complexion and wavy black hair. He had a good body too and a flat belly. You could tell the man had muscles when he was in a T-shirt. He worked hard, made a good life for you, and he loved his children. He even agreed to let our mother live with you. He was a good father and a faithful husband. If I had a man like that, I would have married him too.

That shows how much you know, Caesar Augusta. Guess what? A lot of women were attracted to him. He was gorgeous and could be very sweet and seductive. Yes, he could charm his way into a lady's heart when he wanted to. Hell, he even charmed the nuns at the kids' school. Perry would lay on the charm and they would just giggle and say, "Oh, Mister Moore." And, he was fun too. We had some good times together. We went to different clubs but we really liked to go to the Flame Show Bar. They had all of the great entertainers—Billy Eckstine, Sarah Vaughn, Lionel Hampton, Count Basie. Everybody who was anybody performed at the Flame and we were there. Some of our friends would go with us and we would have a party. We were still young and ready for action. You know, we would dance and drink all night long. Everybody was arguing with everybody else and laughing at jokes. Sometimes, it seemed that the women knew more dirty jokes than the men. Perry really knew how to party. He was the life of the party. He could talk about anything. I don't know where he got all of his information but he had a lot of opinions about everything, especially politics. He hated Republicans and loved his Democrats. He even said if any of his kids became a Republican, he would disown them. He was kidding because that man loved his children more than anything. He was a good father more than he was a good husband. As I said, he knew how to have a good time that is until he drank too much. Then he was somebody else.

I know he could get a little high but it sounds like you're implying something else.

Let's just say that Perry could be a very different person when he had too much to drink.

How so, Leona?

He wasn't always the kind of person everyone thought he was. Meanwhile, you say he was faithful. Perry was a lot of things but faithful wasn't one of them. You just don't know.

Perry wasn't faithful to you? You never told me that before.

I don't tell you everything. But, he's dead now. So, you need to know he couldn't keep his dick in his pants.

Leona, really? How do you know?

Perry found a lot of women to satisfy him besides me, his wife.

I know you're serious but, since we talk all the time, I can't believe you'v never mentioned this before.

I did mention it but you thought I was only kidding. You were convinced Perry was a prince who could do no wrong. That's what everyone thought especially his mother.

244

Yes, I heard you kid him about other women but you always sounded like you were making a joke. He never seemed to be bothered by your kidding him. In fact, he used to smile when you joked about other women.

Yeah, he smiled that smile. But why would I joke? I was serious.

But you made it sound funny like a joke not like you actually meant it.

I made it sound funny because I wanted to kill him. If I didn't make it sound funny, I would have killed him.

Leona, do you hear what you're saying?

Of course, I do. Why do you think I've been blaming myself for his death? I feel guilty not for the accident but because in my heart I thought he deserved to die for cheating on me.

Leona, don't do this to yourself. Wanting to punish him doesn't mean you deliberately killed him. Oh, my poor sister. How do you know he cheated? How long was thing going on with other women?

I suspected something as long as we were married. But, I only caught him after Obra-Jean was born.

So, why did you stay with him if he was cheating on you?

I loved him and I hated him. It's all the same. I just couldn't be indifferent to him. I found out about a woman he was screwing. You know, Perry would, from time to time, say he was going to have a drink at a bar with Henry, his buddy from work. Or, he claimed he would go by Henry's apartment for a few drinks. Well, he may have had a few drinks with Henry as a cover story but he was headed to see one of his bitches. I found all of this out later on. Anyway, one day, a bitch called our house asking for Perry and let slip something about Perry she couldn't or shouldn't have known.

What was that?

She asked for him by his middle name.

I didn't know Perry had a middle name.

He never used it so it's something she shouldn't have known. Apparently he told it to her because he didn't want her to know his first name. She asked for Alexander.

That was his middle name?

Yep. I asked him about this woman. He made up some kind of shit lie that she was a waitress at a bar where he and Henry went for beers. She said he had left his cap there. She said Henry gave her his number and she was calling to tell him she put his cap in a safe place for him to pick up. I cussed her out and hung up the phone. When he came home, I came right out and told him I knew everything including who this woman was. I said he could choose between us but he couldn't have us both. One or the other, I said. He smiled that smile and said he would never choose any woman but me.

Smiled? This is amazing, Leona. But I wonder. What if Perry really was, in fact, spending his time with Henry at a bar or at his apartment?

Why would he spend so much time with Henry?

Because they were good friends?

They may have been good friends but Perry was using Henry as his cover to see his women. He didn't deny there were other women.

You haven't said that he admitted it either. Leona, were there other women after the woman who called?

He let things cool off for a while. He thought he was real slick, and I was some kind of dumb bitch who couldn't put two and two together. I found out about another of his women who he had been seeing before the one I caught. A friend of mine saw them together in a liquor store and happened to mention what she saw to me. After I confronted Perry, I told him he could keep his women but not to put his filthy hands on me again. I was closed for business.

No, Leona, you didn't.

I did. No more dipping into the honey pot for him.

Leona, no. What did you expect he was doing if he was not having sex with his wife?

He was probably doing what he always did. There are plenty of women who were happy to satisfy him.

And, what about you?

Frankly, I didn't miss it. I can take care of myself.

Are you hinting at what I think you're hinting?

A woman's little helper.

It just goes to show that what looks like a perfect marriage is anything but perfect.

There's no perfect man or marriage, Augusta.

I can't help asking this question. After what you've said, why do you still think I need a man?

I don't think you need one. You just might find out that one is handy. Speaking of which, you haven't mentioned dating a man in years. What's up with that?

I told you I haven't found the right man.

Or any man. Are you even interested in men?

Why would you ask that, Leona?

Maybe men aren't your thing.

What would my thing be?

I don't know. You tell me.

Leona, let's just say if the right man came along, I would certainly take an interest. Let me pour you some more wine. Now, we haven't talked about your finances. Money must be a little tight for you living on one income. Correct? I suppose our mother contributes something from her savings.

Yes, money is tight but Clemenza isn't any help. She doesn't have much money herself. I pay for nearly everything she needs.

Well, I can help you out there, Sister. How about if I pay for all of mother's expenses and a little extra for you? That way, with Toby working and living on her own, and E.J. working and making some money for his schooling, and Obra-Jean living with her grandparents, you'll have, what, only the expenses for the house, a car, household, and yourself? Right? Do you think you could manage then?

It would be tight but I could get by. I think Perry also had some kind of death benefit from his job that will put a little more money in the bank.

Then everything is cool? Am I correct?

We'll see, Augusta.

As the afternoon faded into evening, and as the sisters talked about everything and anything, Augusta excused herself momentarily to warm up the chicken and rice casserole she prepared for dinner. Augusta was not much of a cook but she did have a few dishes she did well. She also set the dining room table and when the casserole was warmed, she and Leona sat down to eat. Augusta waited expectantly for her sister's reaction to the meal. Leona knew that her sister was not a great cook but she did enjoy the casserole. She had two helpings. After dinner, and after the table was cleared, the sisters returned to the living room sofa for more drinks. Leona requested another bourbon and soda since she could not develop a taste for white wine.

Dinner was delicious, Augusta. Now, tell me about this trip that you're planning.

Okay. It's a three-week trip. Next summer, I fly to New York and catch a flight to Paris where I'll spend four days. Then I fly to London for three days. After that, I fly to Vienna for two days. I take a train from Vienna to Italy to stay for a week. First I'll visit Venice, then Florence, and finally Rome—all by train. Then, I fly from Rome to Spain and stay in Barcelona for two days, and take a train to Madrid for two days before returning home. It's a package tour for about thirty people. I think it would be fun. It will be a first for me and I want to take Obra-Jean along so we can have our first overseas experience together. I'll pay for everything. It will be my gift to my niece. What do you think?

You want to take a teenager on a trip to Europe for three weeks? Obra-Jean will make you crazy if you aren't already crazy.

We'll have fun, and I'm not her mother.

You'll find out what it means to be a mother.

Oh, Leona, she'll love it, and I will love it too. Think of the stories she'll have for you and her friends. This is a great opportunity for her and, maybe, when she comes back after all that time with her aunt, she'll appreciate her mother more.

Pour me another drink, please.

Okay. But what do you say?

It's fine with me. Maybe she'll get some good sense from her aunt because she sure hasn't gotten any from me.

You underestimate her and yourself. I think you've been a good mother to all of your children. Obra-Jean is very smart like her siblings but she's young and inexperienced. She's grown out of that childhood phase. I see it all the time with my students. Most of them grow out of it and are fine. That's what I think will happen with Obra-Jean and this trip will help her by opening her up to a bigger, more interesting world. You won't recognize her when she returns.

I hope not.

— And More Plans —

Augusta lived some distance from the elementary school where she taught seventh grade. The school served a neighborhood that had a mixture of white and black families with blacks in the minority. It was what was called a "changing" neighborhood meaning whites were moving out as more blacks moved in. The homes were mostly single family, two-story brick structures in a variety of faux-European historic styles. The homes were substantial, centered on large plots of land and set well back from tree-lined streets. As blacks moved in, their goals seemed to rival those of their white neighbors in upkeep of their homes, land, and possessions. New greenery was planted in front and behind the houses. Wood trim on the houses was freshly painted. Nearly every backyard of black-owned houses was adorned with lounge chairs, picnic tables, and barbecue grills. The smell of grilled and roasted meat wafted through the neighborhood. This was a middle class district for black professionals such as teachers and lawyers. The whites were mostly well-paid factory workers and some professionals. The class and racial differences created two communities within the neighborhood and isolated one from the other—cordial in casual meetings but distanced socially and culturally. These distinctions carried over into the school where Augusta taught.

Her seventh grade English classes were large but the young students were mostly attentive, bright, and orderly. There was always an occasional unruly student who needed to be sent to the principal's office or even suspended from classes, and there were minor clashes between groups of black and white kids. Nothing really disturbed the serenity of the school. However, each semester, there were fewer and fewer white students and, as the black school population increased, a different mood settled over the school. It was more animated and vibrant. Black and white teachers noticed the difference and white teachers were undecided if this mood portended a positive change or the beginning of a decline in school discipline and order. An uneasiness permeated the staff as a perception of their differing perspectives came into focus. The divide was not strictly along racial lines. Some black staff were not pleased with the shift and agreed with the white staff who felt the same. This was the opening of a rift among blacks and whites as well as between blacks and whites. Augusta favored the changes; she wanted a school more focused on black children and their community but found herself on the outs with some of her black and white colleagues.

Augusta was a reasonable person not given to conflict or to being disagreeable. She preferred to discuss issues and to find common ground. However, as the racial changes progressed, she found her position rebuffed by those who disagreed. Some colleagues stopped speaking to her. She felt increasingly unhappy in her school and in her work. The pleasure of teaching which she had always enjoyed began to sour and she pondered her alternatives. Although the Detroit public school system had many black teachers, a few principals, and some administrators—public school employment had long been one of the few professional options open to blacks—there were limited promotions because of racial discrimination to the vast central administration of the system. Aware of these restrictions, Augusta nevertheless inquired about a promotion. She was told that such a promotion was impossible without a graduate degree which she did not have. This was a big, but not insurmountable, obstacle. Augusta decided to take a leave from teaching at the end of the school year and enroll in a master's degree program in education administration at the University of Michigan. She applied, was accepted, and started classes during the summer of 1955 commuting to and from Detroit to Ann Arbor. In just over two years after intensive coursework, she completed her degree and applied for an administrative position and promotion within the Detroit public schools. As a single woman with both experience in the classroom and an advanced degree, she was an excellent candidate. The fact that she was also light-skinned, attractive, and well-groomed with a professional affect, favored her promotion and assignment to a district office where she would assist in overseeing the operation of schools in one area of the city comprising several mostly black neighborhoods. Augusta realized quickly enough that her assigned district was treated quite differently from some of the other districts that were predominantly or exclusively white. Many of the indicators of success in a school district such as graduation rates, college applications, and academic achievement were below those of predominantly, and all-white, districts. Instead of the central administration providing more qualified teachers, more counselors, more financial resources, more after-school options for sports, the arts, and college preparation, the central administration provided less of everything. She knew this was blatantly unfair to the students, teachers, and parents who paid their taxes like everyone else, and to the community which, she felt, was diminished and penalized for nothing more than being predominantly black and working-class. What could she do? After giving the matter a lot of thought and discussing it with her friends, she decided to return to a teaching position at her elementary school. But, before returning, she also decided to take a long vacation to Europe. She thought this would be a great opportunity to bring her young niece along so they could both explore the wonders of the Old World. It might have seemed an odd choice of travel for Augusta because, since living in New York City, she had become much more interested in African history and culture as well as the achievements of black women. She had considered a trip to Africa, instead of Europe, but decided to wait and see what African countries were like after the wave of independence movements across the continent had run their course. For the present, Europe was her cultural destination.

Augusta arranged a meeting with Obra-Jean by inviting her to lunch downtown on a Saturday. She picked up her niece in her car and they rode together. Augusta decided to park her car in one of the many parking garages instead of one of the surface parking lots. For some reason she thought a garage would provide greater protection from theft or vandalism. After parking and exiting the garage, they walked to a restaurant near Harmonie Park, were seated, and ordered soup and sandwiches.

How's my niece today?

I'm good, Auntie.

And how's school?

I love Cass Tech. It's so different from Catholic school and the building is huge. I have to run from class to class so that I'm not late. At my Catholic school I just walked across the hall from one classroom to another. That was it.

Well, I'm pleased you like it. Cass is the best public school in the city. It's the best school, period. You couldn't get a better education in a private school. Keep up your grades, as I know you will, so you can get into whatever college you want. I know it's a little early for you to be thinking about college since you've only been in high school a year or so but what are you thinking about now?

You know my mother wants me to study something practical so I can get a teaching job when I graduate.

To put it mildly, Leona is a very practical person.

Well, I've been taking the science curriculum so I could, maybe, be a math teacher someday.

But that isn't what you really want to do. Am I right?

Yeah. I don't want to teach math or anything else. I want to be an architect.

That's a surprise. Wow. Tell me about that.

I've been interested in buildings ever since I was little. Remember, I wanted a dollhouse for Christmas one year. Not because I wanted to play with dolls but because I wanted make a house but I didn't know how. A dollhouse was the only thing I knew.

It's funny you say that because I never saw you playing with your dollhouse. Your mother was annoyed she bought it for you. You ignored it.

I wanted to change it but I didn't know how to do that. I didn't know how to ask anybody to help me. It wasn't until I saw this old white man in our neighborhood who was working in his garage. It opened onto the street where E.J. and I walked to school. I could look inside when I passed by it on my way to school. He was working on this big model of downtown Detroit buildings. You could see the streets and the buildings like Hudson's department store. I watched him build it. I even asked him questions. I wanted to do something like that. I tried to figure out how I could build models. I asked this man to help me and he showed me what to do. I rebuilt my dollhouse in our basement. My daddy helped me with the tools but I rebuilt it all by myself. My mother said I was too old to be playing with a dollhouse but she left me alone.

Wait a minute. You were in a garage with an old white man? Were you all by yourself?

Yeah, but I made sure he left the garage door open so I could get out of there in a hurry.

Oh, my niece. And your mother worries about you. You're not quite as innocent as she thinks you are. I guess I have a lot to learn about you. But, listen, Obra-Jean, I know you and your mother don't agree on a lot of things, but she isn't always as unreasonable as you think.

To me she is unreasonable. Always.

Well, I'm glad you did what you wanted to do.

Yeah. So, when we went to New York City, what interested me the most were the buildings. They were so big. There were so many of them. They didn't look anything like buildings in Detroit. I really liked them and I wanted to make my own buildings. That's when I got the idea of being an architect.

I see. That's really wonderful but you know there haven't been many women architects, and even fewer Negro women architects. But there were a few. Let's see. I remember that Helen Eugenia Parker worked here in Detroit on Trinity Hospital. It was the first hospital in the city for Negroes. Elizabeth Carter Brooks worked in Washington, D.C. Beverly

Loraine Greene was the first licensed architect in this country. So, you won't be the first in Detroit or in this country but there sure haven't been many Negro women in architecture.

Gee, how do you know all of this?

Obra-Jean, I did a lot of research and reading about us Negroes, especially Negro women. We need to know about our own people.

Well, I'm glad I won't be the first Negro woman architect but I hope, at least, that I will be one of them.

I hope so too. Even so, you will have to climb over some very big hurdles—and I'm not saying you shouldn't try or that you won't succeed —but you need to understand what you want won't be easy to get.

I'm willing to work hard. That's not a problem for me. I know this is what I want.

Your mother is not going to be supportive. As I said, she's very practical and what you want to do is not what she considers practical. You won't ever convince her and that's only going to be your first obstacle. The next is getting into an architecture program at a university. That might not be a big hurdle because of your excellent grades. But being a young black woman may prevent you from being accepted. However, let's say you get into a good school. Then, you'll be working in an all-male environment and probably an all-white male environment. That's going to be a killer. A black woman facing nothing but white men? Take it from me, you have little chance of winning. But, let's say, again, you finish your degree and then look for a job in architecture. Your choices will be all-white, all-male architecture companies and offices. Who would take a chance on a Negro woman? That's a hurdle even I can't imagine you going over. But, let's say you find an office that hires you. What are they going to let you do? Design a building? It's hardly ever happened. Beverly Loraine Greene may be the only Negro woman who worked for a large architectural company. She worked on projects for Edward Durell Stone and Marcel Breuer.

I'm amazed you know all of this.

Obra-Jean, I had know for myself what Negro women have accomplished. My sorority sisters are a wealth of information. I need this kind of knowledge to inspire my students.

So, I could be one of the few Negro women architects. Right?

A big "maybe."

I think one day it could happen to me.

You could be right. It could happen as unlikely as it seems. It could happen. That's why you should follow your dream. Do it or you will always wonder why you didn't try. As you say, someday you might succeed.

If other Negro women could do it, I could do it too.

I'll help you in any way I can. I hope you know that. One of us is going to make her dream become real. Mine didn't. Now, let's talk about a trip. Your mother told you I'm planning a trip to Europe, and I want you to come with me.

I would love that, Auntie.

Okay. It's a three-week trip this coming summer. We'll travel with a group of about thirty people. We'll have guides so we won't have to guess at what we're seeing and we'll have someone to answer our questions. We start in Paris and finish in Madrid. In between, we'll see major cities in England, Austria, and Italy. Isn't that exciting?

Oh, yes. We'll stay in hotels?

Of course. You and I can share a room if that's okay with you. Sharing will actually save us money.

Good.

And, mostly, we fly from country to country. However, we'll also take trains in Austria, Italy, and Spain.

Wow.

There will be lots of buildings for you to see and museums and so many different kinds of sights.

Auntie, what about the food?

We'll eat what they eat in each country.

Won't there be a lot of strange stuff to eat?

Strange, maybe, but it's a good thing to try food you've never tasted.

Are you sure about that?

Come on, Obra-Jean. This will be an adventure and that means taking chances with the unfamiliar. If you think you can become an architect, you better start with facing a lot you don't know or understand. But, don't worry. I'll bet when you see new things to eat, you'll want to try everything.

Auntie Augusta, why are doing this for me?

That's a good question. It's because, Obra-Jean, I don't have any children of my own and I never will. I think you and your siblings are all smart and finding your own ways in this world. But, you are my special niece because you figured out you needed to get away from your mother. Don't get me wrong. I love my sister. She's a good person and a loving mother but she isn't ready yet to deal with the world you'll be living in. She doesn't understand that our world is changing slowly around us. I think more changes are coming, maybe big changes. You'll be able to take advantage of those changes if you are prepared. That's what I believe.

Momma doesn't see things the way you do.

I know that. She and I have talked about it. She's going to fight you not because she doesn't want what's best for you but because you represent another fight she hasn't been able to fight.

Do you mean with Grandmama Post?

I don't want to say too much but, yes.

She doesn't like Grandmama.

Yes and no. It's complicated. She loves her mother, maybe too much. But Leona has unshakeable resentments because she thinks our mother hurt

260

her. She hasn't been able to forgive her. You should ask your grandmother someday about that. I don't want to try and explain it.

Grandmama Post already told me everything.

She did? Good for her. I didn't want to say anything because some things should be told by the people involved not by people, like me, on the sidelines. As I was saying, your mother is fighting a battle and you're caught in the middle. Just stick with your plans like your sister did. You'll be all right and I'll be standing by you.

Leona was surprised to receive a telephone call from her sister inviting her to meet at a restaurant in Greektown for dinner. Leona was not accustomed to eating in restaurants in the city. Detroit restaurants had a long, unfortunate history of either excluding blacks or deliberately providing poor service as a snub and a warning not to return. Most blacks simply ate at home or at the homes of family or friends. Or, when dining out, they patronized black-owned restaurants instead of facing the humiliation of being turned away or feeling they had wasted their time and money for an unsatisfactory dining experience at white establishments. Leona had, therefore, never been to Greektown, a block-long restaurant district on the eastern edge of downtown and a short walk from Lafayette Park where Augusta lived. While Greektown restaurants mainly had white clientele, most were not overtly discriminatory against blacks. Augusta and her friends and colleagues from work occasionally dined in a particular restaurant because it was cozy, friendly, and inexpensive. It also had a liquor license and the food was abundant and delicious. Augusta had visited the restaurant often enough so that waiters recognized her and seated her at a table midway between the front door and the entrance to the kitchen at the rear. Other white restaurants used these undesirable locations, especially near the kitchen, for their rare black customers as if to show their disdain. Augusta knew the menu and had several favorite dishes. She thought her sister would enjoy both the restaurant and the food. When she arrived and mentioned her reservation for dinner, she was seated at one of the more desirable tables after which she ordered a glass of Greek wine and awaited the arrival of her sister. While waiting, she glanced towards the front of the restaurant and through the windows saw her sister standing outside peering in. She waved and Leona opened the door and entered. The maitre d' asked if she was with Miss Post and, getting an affirmative, escorted Leona to Augusta's table.

Leona, how do you like this place? Isn't it nice and aren't the waiters friendly?

I never expected anything like this. This place is a lot smaller than I thought it would be.

Well, yes, there are, what, about sixteen tables?

It seems so.

And wait until you taste the food.

Am I going to like it? I've never had Greek food before.

Oh, it's mostly things you already know. There are lamb, beef, and chicken dishes and fish too.

I'll stick with chicken.

So, look at the menu section with chicken. The menu tells you how it's prepared and what comes with it. Do you want some wine or a drink?

What are you drinking?

Greek wine. It's called retsina.

Okay, I'll try that.

Waiter, excuse me. Could you bring me another glass of retsina and my sister will have one too?

Yes, Madam.

Yes, Madam? Augusta, did I hear him right?

I told you they were very friendly and polite here.

What are you having for dinner?

I'm ordering grilled fish and an octopus appetizer.

Octopus. Oh my god. Really, Augusta? I don't even want to see it when it comes to the table. Is the fish fresh? I wouldn't want to eat anybody's old fish.

Oh, it's fresh and it comes whole with the head.

Whole with the head? I don't think I'm gonna like this place. Who eats fish with its head on?

It's good that way. You'll see. So, how is my favorite sister?

I wish you would stop saying that because it sounds so phony.

Leona, maybe it sounds phony to you because you have never believed I really love you.

Sure you love me. Here's the waiter.

Ladies, here are your glasses of wine. Are the ladies ready to order dinner?

Yes, I'll have the whole grilled fish and my sister will have roasted chicken with rice.

Ma'am, the fish comes with rice and salad. Would you like anything else? We have a delicious lentil soup.

I would like the octopus appetizer but no soup for either of us.

That's one octopus appetizer, one grilled fish, and one roasted chicken with rice. Would the ladies like a complimentary hummus with pita bread?

Yes. I would and I think my sister will try it as well.

Right away, Ma'am. Your meals should be out shortly.

What do you think? Isn't this nice? I love this place.

I don't see any other colored people here.

Oh, Leona, you know our folks don't like restaurants. They've had too many bad experiences but, I think, when Negroes learn they are treated well here, they'll come.

And when they come, the white folks will run away.

No they won't, Leona.

Yes, they will. They always do. You'll see. Just wait. After all, I'm your "favorite" sister. Why now?

Well, for one thing, before Perry died you were so involved with him and your family you never had time for the two of us to get together like this.

And you, Sister, were also always too busy with your work, school, and your bridge club.

Speaking of which, Leona, I was invited to substitute at another bridge club that my sorority sister, Betty, belongs to. It has a whole bunch of woman I don't know too well. A couple of them are school teachers, like Betty, but this one woman who works in the post office is a pistol. She's got to be one of the meanest, nastiest woman around. She's got a mouth like common streetwalker and an attitude that would scare a rattlesnake.

Sounds like a real bitch. What's her name?

That's funny. It's a kind of weird name—Habboey. Habboey Gant.

What kind of name is that?

Beats me but she's married and plays pretty good bridge if you can just tune out her nastiness.

Is that what you say about me?

Come on, Leona. You're not that bad.

Really. Ask my family. They think I'm a witch . . . and a bitch.

They love you, Leona. Listen, I work with kids and they can be difficult. You're a mother. You're bound to have conflicts with growing and grown children. Wait till they have their own families. They'll come around.

I'll be dead by then or abandoned in the old folks home.

Oh, Leona, no you won't. Your children will always take care of you. By the way, how is everything at home?

It's pretty much the same. Clemenza takes care of the house and all of the meals. E.J. is, well, doing whatever he does. He has a steady girlfriend, you know. I hardly see or hear from Obra-Jean. The house needs some work. It's beginning to look like something in Dogpatch and so is the neighborhood.

You could move to Lafayette Park near me.

And what about Clemenza?

Oh, I see your point. I guess there's nothing you can do for now.

Especially since you won't let Clemenza live with you.

Okay, you got me there. I'm selfish. I wanted my own space for myself when I moved back here from New York. Unlike you, I don't want to live with and take care of my mother. We didn't get along because she never supported my being an artist. Honestly, Leona, she's a lot like you. You are the good daughter, not me. You put up with her. I can't. That's it. Now, listen. The other thing I wanted to tell you is about my trip to

Europe with Obra-Jean. She's very excited about it, and I want to tell you what we're going to do.

Augusta reviewed the itinerary of the trip in detail and highlighted some of the sights they would see. She talked about the hotels, the flight to and from Europe and the plane and train travel within Europe. She explained they would be in a group with a guide and that she and Obra-Jean would see and learn a lot of new things. She thought this would be a special opportunity for her niece and the two of them would become great friends. In the middle of Augusta's discussion of the trip, the octopus appetizer and hummus with pita bread arrived then their main courses. Leona ate silently. Augusta didn't notice, at first, that her sister was not showing any enthusiasm or interest. When Augusta did notice, she began to limit the things she wanted to say. Finally, she stopped talking. When Augusta looked up from her meal, she saw that Leona was glaring at her.

Well, Augusta, that's all very nice for the two of you.

What the hell is the matter now, Leona? You sound peeved.

Me, peeved? Why should I be peeved?

I don't know. I thought you agreed to let your daughter take this trip. But now you're behaving as if something's wrong.

Wrong? Nothing's wrong. It's just that you're taking my daughter to Europe for three weeks. Just the two of you . . .

There'll be . . .

I didn't finish, Sister. Just the two of you for three weeks so you two can become great friends.

Yes, what's wrong with that? You knew I wanted to be closer to my niece.

Why don't you take your own daughter?

Leona, don't be ridiculous. You know I don't have a daughter.

Oh, yes, that's right. I have two daughters. One of them has left me. The other wants to leave me. You, conveniently, want to help her by being her best friend.

I'm not trying to take Obra-Jean from you. We're going on a trip together so she can expand her knowledge of the world.

And so the two of you can become great friends.

Friends, yes. Why do you keep stressing that? You seem to be suggesting I want her to become my daughter. I had no such idea.

Oh, really? You've always given her special presents, taken her to concerts and plays, even the opera—things you never did for E.J. or Toby. How do you explain that?

Leona, I never guessed you were upset because I showed Obra-Jean special attention. Both of your older children got so much attention from you and Perry. Obra-Jean seemed to get a lot less attention from you because you were so pre-occupied especially after Mother came to live with you.

Mother. So, that's it. I got Clemenza and you get Obra-Jean.

Leona, you're talking like a crazy person. You're not making any sense.

Oh, no? I got stuck with Clemenza because you moved to New York and when you moved back here, you didn't have room for her. As for our brothers, well, they weren't about to take her in with their families.

Okay, Mother came to live with you after I left for New York. She couldn't afford to stay in our old apartment alone. When I returned, my new apartment didn't have room for her. I didn't want to make room for her. I admit that. Now, I have to correct you. Our brothers would have taken her but she didn't want to live in Hot Springs. So, now, suddenly, I'm taking Obra-Jean from you? She's not living with me. She's at your mother-in-law's house, not my apartment. You let her stay there. I don't understand what you're saying. You're making me out to be some kind of villain here. I'm only trying to be kind to my niece.

Obra-Jean at my in-laws? That's temporary. Meanwhile, you swoop in and want to carry her off to Europe where you can become great friends. To me that means you want her to depend on you and not on me. Didn't you tell her you would help her anyway you can? And, to become an architect? Of all the stupid-assed things I've heard from my daughter, that is the most stupid-assed.

Leona, is that what's bothering you? Listen, your daughter is smart, talented, and she has ambition. Maybe too much ambition but why should you or anyone else try now to make her believe she can't become who or what she wants to become?

You know the answers, and I don't need to tell you.

Yes, I know her dreams might be a little unrealistic but why shouldn't she try? She seems to understand the barriers and, yet, she believes she can succeed. I say let her try. If she fails, she fails. I failed and had to take another path. She might have to do the same. That's life, Leona.

And that would be a wasted life. A mother's job is to steer her children in the right direction. She explains the world to her children and makes sure they really understand. She keeps them from making terrible mistakes. She takes responsibility for teaching them. And, she lives with the consequences.

Fine. That's what a mother does. I only want to be her aunt and friend. I don't want to be, nor can I be, her mother. Obra-Jean won't confuse who's who in her life. You, Leona, are her mother. I'm her aunt. I wish you could get over whatever it is that makes you talk so crazy sometimes. It's really tiring, Leona, to constantly have these arguments with you. You're unhappy about our mother. You're unhappy about your daughters. You're unhappy with your life. Deal with it and stop putting your anger on everyone else. I'm your sister. I've told you again and again, I love you and I love your family. I only want to do something for my niece to make her life better. It's something you can't do for her. But, you're her mother so do the things only a mother can do. If you want to be a good mother, love your child and love not just who she is but also who she wants to be.

I do what I do because I love my daughter. Why didn't my mother love me?

Leona, really? Clemenza loves you . . . in her own way for sure, but it's love. She's always loved you. But, Clemenza is not and cannot be the mother you somehow want her to be. She's not the mother I wanted her to be. This is the other side of the coin, Leona. You have to love your mother for who she is just as you have to love your daughter for who she is. And, dammit, Leona, how about you love yourself for who you are?

Clemenza didn't abandon you, Augusta, like she abandoned me.

Listen, if I've told you once, I've told you a thousand times, she didn't abandon you. You were not abandoned. Do you think she left you because she didn't love you? She left you in Hot Springs with her sister. Our Aunt Iris didn't have any children of her own. So, she adopted you and our brothers. She was a real mother to you and to them. She loved you and raised you until you were old enough to go out on your own. And, yes, our mother left you behind but not because she didn't love you. She thought you would be better off with her sister.

Why didn't she leave you too?

Leona, she brought me with her to Detroit because I was only a baby. But, you know what, Leona, it occurs to me right now that you're as angry with me as much as you're angry with Clemenza. You're jealous of me and for what? Do you think I got her love but you didn't?

Yes, I do.

Well, you're wrong, Sister, dear. Clemenza was loving to me as long as I did things the way she wanted. She's just like you. No difference. Look at it this way, Leona. Who is the woman living with you today? Do you feel her love?

She cooks and cleans the house, if that's love.

Is that love or is she just your servant?

I don't know the answer.

Well, how about this? Do you love her? Apparently, not, since you act like you can't stand the sight of her. So, what's your complaint?

Okay, do you want to know my complaint? Clemenza was a whore.

Leona, lower your voice. These people in the restaurant will hear you.

Do I give a damn? I don't care what these people think? Listen, our mother was a whore. In Hot Springs all she did was screw one man after another.

Leona, please don't act the fool in this restaurant. Sister, lower your voice. I would like to return here someday. Understood? Jesus, Leona, first it's "my mother abandoned me," "my mother didn't love me," now it "my mother was a whore." What's with you? If Mother was a whore, as you say, I was too young to know it. If she did sleep with a lot of men, what choice did she have? How could she keep herself and her children fed and housed without men taking care of her? And, what difference does it make now what she was?

I saw her with lots of men. I saw what they did for her. That's what she taught me.

Are you saying you became a whore too?

What did I know? I did what my mother did until I found that fool, Farrell Broadstreet. I got him to bring me to Detroit. Then, I dumped his sorry ass for Perry. That got me three kids and a husband who screwed everything with one or two legs.

Leona, let me get this straight. You're saying Mother was a whore who set a poor example for you. Then she abandoned you because she didn't love you. Now, it seems to me that leaving you behind with Aunt Iris was a blessing for you. You were living with a woman who showed that she loved and cared for you. Consider yourself lucky. Aunt Iris, not Clemenza, was the mother you needed. In any case, Sister, that's the past. Stop blaming yourself. Stop blaming your mother. Stop blaming Perry. Stop blaming me. Stop blaming everyone. It's not going to do you any good. If you did what you felt you had to do, it got you here. You've got a good life. The rest is all past. That's it.

No it's not, Augusta. I live with everything that's happened to me. Daily. Constantly.

For god's sake, Leona, we all have history but we have to make peace with it. Give it a try for a change. You're not who you once were. And, you're not your mother. You are the woman who is seated opposite me at this table in this restaurant right now. That's it. That's who you are.

I hear you, Augusta. Lower your voice. These people will hear you.

Sister, you are really special. You need another drink. I need another drink. I need two drinks. By the way, why are women called whores. But the men who have sex with them are just horny? Why is it that what a woman does with her body to earn money for a family is a disgrace? But, what men are doing is just satisfying their needs?

Because we're women not men.

Well, you're right but thank god we're women.

Why is that?

Because we know how to do something men don't know.

And what's that?

We can bring life into this world. Men can't grow a child in their bodies.

Spoken like a woman who never had a child. Excuse me for getting a little loud. You see, this in one of the reasons white folks don't like colored people around them. We're loud and talk nasty. Are they looking at us?

Oh, Leona, nobody here is paying any attention to you or me. They have their own problems. I'm glad you can unload.

Thank you, Sister. We haven't solved anything for me but I feel a lot better. I'm lucky I have you as my sister. By the way, that wine tastes like cow piss.

When was the last time you had a glass of cow piss? Never mind, Sister. I'll finish your wine and order you a different drink. Let's eat. Our food is getting cold. Waiter.

— Vacation in Europe —
Late Summer 1959

Augusta and Obra-Jean took a Boeing 707 jet flight to Europe. They were the only black people on the plane. The flight attendants were courteous and seemingly treated them no differently than any of the other passengers. Neither Augusta nor Obra-Jean seemed concerned about their treatment because they were both a little anxious about the newness of the experience and potential danger of flying so fast and so far from one continent to another over a very large ocean that was very far below them. When the dinner meal was served, they weren't sure they could eat or hold down their food in fairly jittery stomachs. Nevertheless, they ate, and heartily, and had no further digestive problems. Sleeping was more of an issue and both squirmed restlessly in their seats, sitting upright and unable to stretch their legs. To pass the time, Augusta decided to teach Obra-Jean some simple phrases like "good day" and "thanks" in the languages of the countries they would be visiting. They practiced *bonjour* and *merci* for France, *guten tag* and *danke* for Austria, *buon giorno* and *grazie* for Italy, and *buenos dias* and *gracias* for Spain. A quick study, Obra-Jean mastered the phrases immediately and wanted to learn more words. Augusta thought it better to tackle more words as the occasion arose during the trip. By the time their plane landed outside of Paris at Orly, they were groggy and unsettled due to lack of sleep. Immigration, retrieving their one suitcase each, and customs were disorienting enough but then they re-joined their group in the arrival hall and began to relax as the tour leader took charge and explained the transfer by bus from the airport to their hotel in the city.

They arrived in Paris in the early morning and the city was alive with traffic and pedestrians. Their bus slowly wandered through Parisian streets until the tour guide announced they had arrived at their hotel in the city center on the Left Bank. It was not what Obra-Jean was expecting for a hotel. In fact, from what she had so far seen, Paris was not anything like she expected. Her most vivid images of cities, other than Detroit, were New York and Philadelphia. She was completely unprepared for how different a city in Europe would look compared to one in the United States. The streets were narrow. The buildings seemed to come almost to the curb and they were continuous without gaps between buildings. And they were several stories high and mostly made of stone and decorated with ornate projections and even human figures. Shop signs and advertising were in French as were street signs—

something she considered odd until she realized it was her lack of awareness that was odd. The automobiles looked different. The pedestrians dressed differently. People sat at tables on the sidewalks, eating and drinking. It was a lot to take in all at once and Obra-Jean, after the jet flight and very little sleep, was overwhelmed. She wondered if this was all a mistake. Maybe, everything she thought about her future was a mistake. Maybe, her mother was right. Stick with what's known; follow a well-defined path. She was afraid to reveal her thoughts to her aunt and possibly risk spoiling the trip so she sat quietly and apprehensively.

The tour group, which was white except for Augusta and Obra-Jean, disembarked from their bus and proceeded into the hotel. The lobby was not on the first floor, as even Augusta expected but, instead, up a flight of stairs. There, on the second floor which was called the first floor (she later learned the entrance floor was called the ground floor), was the reception desk behind which were three young men dressed in dark business suits with white shirts and dark ties. They collected passports, discussed room assignments with the tour guide who distributed copies of the hotel registration form, and finally handed out keys to the bellhops who accompanied their assigned guests to their rooms on various floors of the hotel. An open cage elevator that rose within the iron stairwell carried small groups up to their appropriate floor. Augusta and Obra-Jean were escorted with their suitcases to the hotel's third floor. When they entered the narrow room, they saw a large bed and to either side small tables. A door within the room opened onto the bath where crammed inside was a sink, small bathtub, toilet, and another fixture that looked sort-of like a toilet. They later found out this sort-of toilet was a bidet and was used to wash one's private parts. Augusta and Obra-Jean laughed about this after the bellhop left their room. The one window in the room offered light but no view except of adjacent buildings. A ceiling fixture provided the only artificial illumination. This was to be their retreat for the next few days.

Their tour of Paris took them to many favorite tourists sights—Notre Dame Cathedral, the Eiffel Tower, the Champs-Élysées, the Triumphal Arch, and the Louvre Museum. Obra-Jean was most excited by the architectural monuments because of their grand scale and rich decoration. Augusta appreciated her niece's enthusiasm and hoped her witnessing firsthand these impressive structures would help develop her own sense of architectural design. However, for Augusta the real treasure of Paris was the Louvre. As they walked the seemingly endless corridors crammed with paintings, she felt something she had long suppressed. Each time she came upon a work she recognized, she felt an impulse to know the secrets of its power. Was it the subject or the composition of a painting, or the beautiful human figures, or the way a three-dimensional reality was fixed on a flat two-dimensional surface that made a picture powerful? How was this magic achieved? She stood before Peter Paul Reubens' series of massive paintings of *The Life of Marie de'Medici*. How in hell did one man conceive and create all of these paintings, she wondered? There was so much to explore and so many rooms to visit that Augusta suggested to Obra-Jean they call it a day, leave their tour group, and find a nice cafe in the neighborhood on the Left Bank where they could sit, have something to eat, and watch life in the Paris streets before returning on their own to their hotel.

Aunt Augusta, the menu is all in French. I don't know what anything is. How can I choose?

Of course, the menu is in French. We're in France, my dear, but don't let that worry you. I've learned enough French in high school to figure out the menu. I often used French in my early days when I thought I was hot stuff. I also know a little something about French cooking so let me suggest that we both get one of Paris' famous sandwiches—a *Croque Monsieur*.

What's that?

Basically, it's a heated ham and cheese sandwich with a white sauce.

That sounds good. Why is called *Croque Monsieur*?

I think *croque* means crunchy and *monsieur* means mister. It's a crunchy ham and cheese sandwich for a man but us ladies can eat it too. By the way, speaking of French, you should consider learning more languages while you're in high school. Languages are easier to learn when you're young and they'll stay with you longer. They might also be very useful to you later in life.

What languages should I take?

I recommend French, of course, and maybe Spanish. German could also be useful.

That's a lot of languages.

Better to learn them now than later. Shall I order us two *Croque Monsieur* and what would you like to drink?

Coca Cola?

Honey, we're in Paris. You can have bottled water or a glass of wine. That's what I'm ordering for myself.

Okay. I've never had wine. Wow. This is fun.

Garçon, deux Croque Monsieur et deux vin blanc, s'il vous plait.

Oui, Madame.

What did you say to the waiter?

Two *Croque Monsieur* and two white wine, please.

Wow, I hope I can do that someday, Aunt Augusta. By the way, I know we're taking pictures of everything but I think I would like to make some drawings too.

Really? What would you like to draw?

The buildings. I know we'll have photographs when the film is developed but I want to make drawings because they'll help me to look at the buildings more closely, and I'll learn to see them better.

That's really interesting, Obra-Jean. I used to sketch for my paintings. I drew people, objects, views of the city. So I know what you're saying. Sketching is a way of looking and learning. Of course. Did you bring a sketchbook?

I didn't think of it. I should have but it didn't occur to me to do that until now.

Okay, then, we have to find a shop that sells paper goods.

There really are shops like that?

Oh, yes, my Dear, they're called *papeterie*.

We'll look for one after lunch. Here are our sandwiches now.

During their lunch which Obra-Jean was surprised she enjoyed, Augusta wanted to know more about her niece's studies at Cass. Obra-Jean explained that the drawing classes helped her to understand different drawing materials and how they could be used on various papers. More importantly, her instructors taught her to look closely and analytically at things in the world around her and to devise methods of making different kinds of lines and marks on paper to suggest the shapes, shadings, and textures of things she observed. Drawing was a presentation of observations on a piece of paper. It seems so simple in concept but it is very difficult to produce. She struggled, perhaps for the first time in her young life, to acquire the skill. Her teachers reminded her that continuous practice was the only way she would succeed. Augusta understood this perfectly since she had learned the same processes in her studies to become an artist. Her admiration for her niece only increased as she realized how much alike they were. She felt a sudden sadness as she contemplated her niece giving up at some point on her dream because the path forward was too difficult even for someone as gifted, intelligent, and determined as Obra-Jean.

Almost as if Obra-Jean could read her mind, she shared a new project with her aunt. Obra-Jean had begun taking mechanical drawing classes at Cass. It was highly unusual for girls to enroll in mechanical drawing and her counselor, Mister Green, was reluctant to allow her in the class. Obra-Jean explained her reasoning that, to become an architect she needed to know how to make architectural drawings as well as sketches. Mister Green was not persuaded that she could even become an architect to which Obra-Jean countered with all of the arguments she had rehearsed with her family. Green was not a man to be contradicted by a student, especially a black female student, and he told her she could not enroll in a drafting class. She left Green's office and practically ran to the mechanical drawing instructor's classroom. It was a break between classes. She introduced herself to Avery Harrison, explained what she wanted to do and why, and requested his permission to enroll in his class. He was a little startled by this black girl's request. He had never had any girls in his class and could never have conceived that a young black girl would want to learn mechanical drafting. But, right before him was this determined teenager who seemed far more committed to her quest than most of his students—all young and mostly white males. It was a quandary because he could not override Mister Green's objections. So, he struck a bargain with Obra-Jean: she could learn mechanical drawing with him after her classes. He would tutor her in the basics and she could practice on her own. For Obra-Jean this was a perfect solution. She would stay after classes two days a week with her tutor and practice drafting at home. Later, she learned she would need a drafting table, some drafting equipment, drafting pencils, and, of course, drafting paper. She asked Toby and Ronnie to honor their pledge to help her with school, purchased everything she needed, and set up her table in her bedroom. She quickly learned the basics from her tutor and, for the first time, understood how a three-dimensional building was transformed into two-dimensional drawings—floor plans detail the footprint and layout of the building; elevations show the facades; and sections, cut through the building, reveal the inner relationships of spaces to the structure. To say that Obra-Jean felt empowered by this knowledge is not to say much. She felt she knew the secrets of creating buildings. Everything about a building could be shown in precise, measured drawings.

Upon hearing all of this, Augusta sat back in her chair, inhaled her cigarette, and looked intently at her niece. She smiled and congratulated Obra-Jean for her steely focus. She would probably not only succeed as an architect but also become a very good one. Their lunch concluded, Augusta paid the bill, stood and took a look around the street, and noticed a *papeterie*.

Oh, look, Obra-Jean. My goodness, there's a *papeterie* right across the street. See that store with the red sign over the door. That's what we're looking for. Let's see what they've got. Careful of this traffic crossing the street. Watch out. We made it. Oh, Obra-Jean, look in the window at the beautiful papers and books of paper.

Auntie, let's go inside. I think I see what I want. Oh, Auntie, look at these books. Look at the paper. It's perfect for sketching. It's so beautiful.

Why don't you get a couple of them so you'll always have one handy? It's my treat.

Thank you. I guess I need some pens or pencils or something to draw with.

Maybe, this will work. It's a pen with an ink supply built in, and you can change the ink container when the one you're using is empty. Make sure you get several refills. Is there anything else you want to buy?

That's it for now, I think, unless you can suggest something else.

Not really. Well, if you need something else, there are these kind of stores all over Europe. So, don't worry about running out of paper or ink or if you want some different drawing materials. You might decide to use another type of sketchbook and something other than ink.

Thanks, Auntie. You sure aren't like my mother. She would have called all of this "nonsense."

As I said, my sister is very practical, but not a bad person. Now, let's pay the bill and see more of this fabulous city.

In fact, their visit to Paris ended much too soon for them before their group flew to London. All of Obra-Jean's doubts and misgivings upon arrival in Europe evaporated. After Paris, London was less exciting to her. Although the streets and buildings didn't seem as lovely as those in Paris, they did now seem familiar. This recognition suggested to Obra-Jean that she was already becoming accustomed to European cities. However, she began to look at differences she noticed between Paris and London. Saint Paul's Cathedral didn't have the mysterious otherworldliness of Notre Dame either outside or inside. Buckingham Palace was huge and impressive but not as grand as the Louvre which, she had learned, was originally also a palace. Augusta, again, was less interested in London's architectural monuments than its museums. The National Gallery had so many famous paintings that Augusta could hardly believe what she was seeing. Right before her eyes was Leonardo da Vinci's *Holy Family*. While she was glad to see Leonardo's *Mona Lisa* in Paris, it was, in fact, less impressive than this larger, more ethereal and mysterious painting. She stared at it long after her group had moved on to another room. At the British Museum, Augusta spent almost the entire visit looking at the so-called Elgin Marbles, figure sculptures that the British Lord Elgin had removed—the Greeks say stolen—from the Parthenon in Athens and brought to London. Their muscular forms and expressive gestures reminded her of sculptures by Michelangelo in the Louvre. She could not bear to part from this group of sculptures when she was told the group was leaving the building.

Already a kind of weariness was settling over Augusta and Obra-Jean. While they were thrilled to see all that they were seeing, the constant movement from place to place was tiring, and they were beginning to forget what they saw where. Arriving in Vienna, they admired the relative smallness of the city compared to Paris and London, and they thought the grand palaces were, indeed, grand but somehow a lot of things were beginning to look like a lot of other things. Obra-Jean did note that most of the big, important buildings in each of the cities visited so far all had very similar architectural features and she wondered about this. She remembered she had seen similar looking buildings in New York, Philadelphia, and even Detroit. Why was this? What did it mean? As her enthusiasm began to wane, she asked her aunt if she could skip the visit to the museum that day and stay in their hotel. Augusta understood her niece's growing saturation with Europe's wonders because she felt it herself. And, although she agreed to her niece's request, Augusta knew she herself could not miss a visit to the Kunsthistorisches Museum. There, she stood stunned in the presence of a room full of paintings by Pieter Brueghel the Elder. The exquisite detail of the natural world and the deft depictions of Flemish peasantry in ordinary activities made her cry. She tried to describe the paintings to her niece and explain her reaction over dinner at a restaurant in the city center. They each ordered the famous Vienna schnitzel and devoured it.

Just as they thought that they were growing tired of touring, they arrived in Italy after an overnight train ride from Vienna to Venice. Although they knew generally what to expect of Venice, they were, nevertheless, astonished by the sight of a city literally seeming to float on a body of water. The novelty of canals instead of streets of car traffic amused them. Saint Mark's Square transfixed Obra-Jean with its broad plaza surrounded on three sides by the measured uniformity of buildings and the wildly exotic Saint Mark's Cathedral as the focal point at one narrow end of the plaza. As she gazed at the church's front, she couldn't help but notice the four bronze horses atop it. These huge metal sculptures were such an odd crown to a church that she smiled and remembered other buildings that she had seen that similarly struck her as unusual. There was a tall building—the Chrysler Building—in New York City that had metal sculptures way up high, and that building's pointed peak reminded her of the towers of Saint Stephen's Cathedral in Vienna near the hotel where they stayed. All of these relationships made Obra-Jean ponder:

What connected something in one place to another something someplace else? As she stood facing Saint Mark's Cathedral, she turned to her right and, through a small plaza and beyond a wide canal, she noticed a church that seemed to float on the water. San Giorgio Maggiore (Saint George Major) seemed familiar and completely novel. What was it, she wondered? It had a high peak like a house but with pillars in front. She had seen this kind of arrangement again and again even in the United States. Why? It would not be until the end of the trip before she received an answer to her question.

Their stay in Venice was brief, and quickly they were on a train to Florence. This was Obra-Jean's first daylight train ride, an unanticipated adventure of speeding through the Italian landscape. After crossing the Apennine Mountains into Florence, Augusta and Obra-Jean were convinced this was their most favorite city thus far. They loved the narrow streets, tightly grouped buildings of stone, and the sudden, unexpected openings upon plazas filled with crowds of tourists. There was so much to see, so many palaces, churches, and a bridge with little buildings on it that arched across the Arno River. Obra-Jean wanted to wander but she had to remain with their tour group. On the day they were to visit the Uffizi Gallery, she asked her aunt if could she skip the museum and just walk around on her own and sketch. She promised that, after an hour or so, she would wait for her aunt in the big square near the entrance to the Uffizi Gallery. Augusta considered that her niece was becoming a seasoned traveler and being on her own posed no danger provided she remained alert and could find her way back to the Piazza della Signoria adjacent to the Uffizi. Obra-Jean left to explore. Augusta, who had long anticipated entering the Uffizi, felt a rising excitement. There were paintings she felt compelled to see firsthand as if being in their presence would be a life-changing experience. Since she had already undergone such an experience in Paris, London, and Vienna, she couldn't imagine being overwhelmed again. Then she entered the room with Alessandro Botticelli's *Birth of Venus*. Gazing long and inquisitively at this large painting, Augusta became lost in it. The alabaster nude figure of Venus, gliding on the sea while standing in an enormous shell, was both real and unreal. Human figures drifting in the air and a woman approaching the naked Venus to enshroud her with a cloak were beautiful beyond words. Although Augusta looked at as many paintings as she could bear, nothing moved her as much as Botticelli's painting. When she finally returned to the Piazza della Signoria, Obra-Jean was waiting for her. They discussed what Obra-Jean had seen. She confessed that she was less interested in particular buildings than in how the use of stone created uniformity among buildings. She was surprised that some buildings, like the Duomo and Baptistery, used pink, white, and green stone for decoration. These effects with building materials were unlike anything she had noted in other European cities.

Rome was the tour's last stop before Spain and, again, Augusta and Obra-Jean were feeling overloaded with so much more to see and understand. Nevertheless, both were awe-struck by Saint Peter's Square, the Basilica of Saint Peter, and the Vatican Palace. With all that she had already seen, the interior of Saint Peter's Basilica left Obra-Jean stunned and intimidated. She couldn't comprehend how such a vast, ornamented interior could be enclosed in massive stones yet bathed in the most subtle and calming light. She thought it should be like a enormous cave and, instead, it was like, well, nothing she had ever experienced except, perhaps Pennsylvania Station in New York or the Michigan Central Depot in Detroit. While Augusta was also impressed with Saint Peter's Basilica, the Vatican museum dismayed her because of the crowds and the sheer immensity of the place with room after room filled with things one couldn't possibly take proper time to inspect or appreciate. However, when she arrived at the papal apartment decorated by Raphael, she found a way to plant herself in front of a wall fresco called *The Mass at Bolsena*. It was not the whole painting that intrigued her but the vivid portraits of Swiss soldiers in the lower righthand corner. Their velvety garb with flowing, multi-colored skirts seemed so at odds with their intense focus on the main scene of Pope Julius II witnessing a miracle at a mass. Augusta was still lost in thought about this painting when she and her niece later entered the Sistine Chapel. Both of them gasped at the profusion of paintings on the ceiling and walls. How did one man create such a huge painting on a ceiling high above the floor? Even with their guide's explanation, they were still disbelieving of what appeared before their eyes. The entire room was incomprehensible even after hearing their guide's explanation. After visiting still more tourists sites—the Roman Forum, the Colosseum, and the Pantheon—Augusta and Obra-Jean conceded that Rome had, in many ways, topped all of the other European cities by the quantity and majesty of its architecture and paintings. They both also learned that Rome was the source of inspiration for much of the art and architecture they had seen elsewhere. Rome was mother to her European and American children and her children's art and architecture were sisters to one another.

The day before they were to leave Rome, Obra-Jean suddenly had an idea. She remembered the night, a year ago, when she and her aunt went to the Metropolitan Opera that was visiting Detroit and saw Giacomo Puccini's *Tosca*. There were three buildings that served as settings for the story—the church of Sant'Andrea della Valle, the Palazzo Farnese, and Castel Sant'Angelo. She wanted to see these places, if they really existed. To her delight, they did exist and seeing the interior of Sant'Andrea brought back the memory of the first act with Tosca, Caravadossi, and Baron Scarpia in this very church. The Palazzo Farnese astonished her as a work of architecture. She could hardly believe that this massive building had been a palace for a cardinal of the Catholic church. Disappointed that it was not possible to visit the interior because the building now housed the French embassy, she nevertheless sketched the grand facade to remind herself of the variety of architectural features and yet the disciplined order imposed upon the whole structure. The last setting of the opera, Castel Sant'Angelo, was a complete surprise to Obra-Jean. She didn't realize how large it would be nor that it was round like a huge stone drum. The enormous sculpted angel hovering high above the topmost story was a dramatic contrast to the monumental solidity of the building. Her guidebook explained the odd design—Castel Sant'Angelo was originally the tomb of the Roman Emperor Hadrian that, in a later age, was converted into a defensive bastion, and that was the reason for its shape, size, and fortress-like appearance. Making a connection between these actual buildings and their use as settings for an opera triggered something in Obra-Jean. It would be years in the future before this insight could be put to use by her.

During their walks through the streets of Rome, Obra-Jean noticed shops with the sign *"Liberia"* and she wondered what that meant. Since she was taking Latin at Cass, she hypothesized that the word might derive from the Latin word *"liber"* for "book" and *"liberia"* might be a bookstore. Augusta suggested they go inside one such shop and see for themselves. Upon entering the first shop they saw, Obra-Jean was astonished by the quantity of books that filled the floor to ceiling shelves and stood in piles on tables and even on the floor. The shop was a virtual warehouse of books. On one table, a book lying face up caught her attention. On the cover was a picture of Castel Sant'Angelo. She picked it up, browsed the book, and found that, although the text was in Italian, there were black and white pictures of many of the buildings she and her aunt had seen in Rome. She decided she wanted the book and, using some of the Italian she had practiced during their visit, said, *"Quanto?.* The elderly man behind the counter, who looked up from reading his newspaper, replied to her: "Five dollars, please, *Signorina*." Obra-Jean smiled and bought the book, replying to the clerk *"Grazia, Signore."* At that moment, Obra-Jean embarked on a life-long habit of collecting books on architecture. Now she had a book on Roman architecture in addition to the book—a gift of her sister—on Chicago architecture.

Spain was far more relaxing than the previous countries because Augusta and Obra-Jean opted out of much of the touring, except for Barcelona. Obra-Jean had not expected much after all that she had already seen but she joined the tour of Barcelona and when they stopped at Antonio Gaudí's unfinished church of the Sagrada Familia, she was amazed. She knew that the completed part was made of stone but the stone had become sculpture and the sculpted towers were unlike anything she had seen or dreamed possible. Even after all of the wonders she had explored, she found this fragment of a building somehow more moving and deeply memorable than everything previously viewed. In Madrid, at the last minute, Augusta decided to join the tour to the Prado Museum in the hope that she would see something that would revive her flagging interest in touring. Diego Velásquez's *Las Meninas* did that. This large, formal portrait of members of the royal family was such an odd presentation compared to many other royal portraits. It seemed more like a behind-the-scenes photograph than a record of stiff, unfeeling royalty. Even after all that she had seen in the previous weeks, this painting revived her enthusiasm and re-awakened some impulse to create again.

Before leaving Europe the next morning, Augusta and Obra-Jean joined the tour group for a final dinner at a restaurant near their hotel in the city center. Many folks in the group had become friendly with them over the course of the tour. There were people mainly from New York, Illinois, and California but also a few from Virginia, Georgia, and Texas. The restaurant had arranged a single long table for the group. Augusta and Obra-Jean found themselves seated between Southerners and across from Californians. They had spoken previously with most of these folks during the course of the tour and everyone seemed relaxed and full of stories that they wanted to tell. There was a lot of list-making—sorting out the truly memorable experiences from the more commonplace. While the adults treated Obra-Jean as a young person whose opinions were not of particular interest to them, they were fascinated with Augusta's observations. It was not lost on Augusta that her white audience expected she was speaking to them for herself and for all black people. She was careful in her remarks.

I decided to take this tour because, like you, I wanted to know more about the sources that were a foundation for our own culture in the United States. After all, the earliest immigrants to our country came from Europe and much that has been created in our country owes its origins to Europe's creativity and genius. I have to say that being in Europe, I now understand better than I could ever appreciate before that Europe itself owes much of its culture to Italy. The art, architecture and much else in France, England, Austria, and Spain originated in Italy from ancient times almost up to the present. That is why, for me, the most impressive things I've seen on the entire trip were in Italy, especially in Florence and Rome. For me, nothing that I've seen in all of the countries that we visited quite compares with the magnificence, beauty, and grandeur of Saint Peter's Basilica and the Vatican. The amount of talent, thought, and money that went into their creation are a high point of European civilization. I will never forget what I've experienced. I have to add, however, for an American of the Negro race, Italy and Europe are not the only cultures that have created greatness. My people were not immigrants to America; we were enslaved in Africa and brought to America in bondage to build a new country with our uncompensated labor. We created great palaces, tombs, and mosques in Africa and we made wonderful cultures as well. However, unlike Europeans, we were not allowed to use our heritage in building America and so much of what my ancestors created in Africa is not known today or, sometimes, not even acknowledged. But, in Africa, there were great civilizations long before Europe became Europe. There was Egypt and Songhay, Ashanti, and Dahomey. The first European explorers who traveled to Africa returned home with stories of the wonders of the continent. So much of that is now forgotten today but it happened. I tell you this so you'll understand that, as great as Europe is, it is but one civilization among many that flourished all over this planet and, although Europe is inspiring, Africa is the continent I look to for my cultural, artistic, and spiritual nourishment.

When Augusta had finished, much argument ensued among her fellow travelers just as she anticipated. But, she was content to have made her point, not to have changed anyone's mind about their belief in the priority and superiority of European culture, but to claim a place for African civilizations. Obra-Jean was startled and deeply impressed by her aunt and squeezed her hand under the table to let her know how much she loved her knowledge and boldness. In addition to being authoritative with all of these white people, her aunt helped Obra-Jean understand that art comes from art. Someone somewhere creates something and someone somewhere else is inspired by it. Americans knew about Europe and copied what they saw there. Americans did not know about Africa and that caught Obra-Jean's imagination. While she knew a little about Egypt, she had never heard of the other African civilizations and wanted to know more. Augusta explained that Songhay, Ashanti, and Dahomey designed and created wonderful buildings some of which still survive. If Obra-Jean wanted to know more, she should go to the main library and look for books about Africa. There she could see for herself what Africans created—in addition to the pyramids of Egypt, there are the great mosques of Songhay and the royal palaces of Dahomey.

As the group was leaving the restaurant heading back to their hotel nearby, one woman stopped Augusta and Obra-Jean to introduced herself as Neallie Boyd. She was from Lubbock, Texas and was impressed with

Augusta's views on art. She, too, was a teacher and an artist and wondered if Augusta would join her for a drink at a bar. Augusta explained that she felt responsible to accompany her niece back to the hotel but Obra-Jean interjected that she would go with some of the other members of the group. Assured that her niece would be in good care, she joined the Texas woman and they walked to the nearest bar and sat at a table outside and ordered drinks.

Miss Post, I'm so delighted you agreed to have a drink with me on our last night in Madrid. I'm sorry I haven't introduced myself earlier but I saw how much you were devoted to your niece and I didn't want to take any time away from your visit with her. But, I have to tell you how fascinated I was with your lesson in cultures and I want you to know how much I agree with you.

Thank you. Please call me Augusta.

And, call me Neallie.

Sure, Neallie. Was there anything in particular I said that caught your attention?

Yes, When you said, "Italy and Europe are not the only cultures that have created greatness," that really stuck in my mind. I'm afraid like so many people like me . . .

You mean white people?

Well, yes, so many white people are taught that Africa is just an uncivilized continent and its people are savages.

And that's why we were brought to this continent by the millions in slavery so that we could be civilized?

Yes, that's more or less what we learned.

And, now, you could believe something else?

I realize I'm ignorant because I never questioned what I learned. When I see a beautiful woman like you and a lovely young girl like your niece, I know it wasn't the culture of this country alone that made you who you are. You and your ancestors, going all the way back to Africa, have your own history and cultures. Slavery may have interrupted those connections but there is something deep within you that still links you with Africa and its greatness, at least that's what I understood from your comments. That is what impressed me when you spoke at dinner.

Thank you, Neallie. To tell the truth, I've had to learn about Africa on my own. It wasn't part of my upbringing or formal education. In fact, many Negroes I know are often ashamed of Africa but that is because they believe the negative and distorted views that pervade our culture.

If you think it's bad among Negroes, you must know how horrible it is among white people.

I know only too well.

So, here we are in this beautiful city. I think Madrid makes me think beautiful thoughts.

How so?

Here, I feel free of Texas and all of the chest-thumping about how great America this and America that are. My goodness, our country is barely two hundred years old. What can a country accomplish in two hundred years?

A lot if you use enslaved labor but you mean things like automobiles and television.

Well, yes, Augusta, you're right again. Where would this country be without the free labor and creativity of Negroes? Automobiles and television are great inventions but what has American culture created that might really be lasting? We still don't encourage and nurture the talents of all of our people. And, yes, I'm thinking of you in particular. How many women must there be like you who aren't given opportunities and support? For that matter, how many women are there like me who don't get opportunities and support? Really, Augusta, we're in the same boat.

But, I think, you have a few more oars in the water than I do.

Well, maybe, one day all of us women will have as many oars as men.

You're right about that, Sister.

Their conversation continued much later than either of them expected. Finally, conceding that it was very late and they had an early start in the morning, they finished their drinks, paid their bill, and headed back to their hotel. In the lobby where they realized they were parting for different floors, Neallie leaned over to Augusta and kissed her on the cheek. Augusta returned the gesture with a kiss on Neallie's cheek. A brief but intense embrace followed.

The next morning when Obra-Jean awoke, she was surprised that her aunt was not in bed nor did she seem to be anywhere in their room. Obra-Jean surmised that her aunt, in fact, had not returned since the previous night. At first, she felt a bit alarmed but just as she was planning to call the front desk to make an inquiry, a key turned in the room door and her aunt entered.

Good morning, Auntie.

Hi, Baby, were you wondering where I was?

I was about to call the front desk and ask if they knew anything.

Well, you know I started talking with that woman from Texas and we went for a drink. Afterwards, we came back to the hotel and we both wanted to continue the conversation even though it was getting very late. Nevertheless, we went to her room and talked all night long until now when I came back to you just in time for us to get ready for a quick breakfast, pack, and leave for the airport.

You talked all night?

Yes, oh, Obra-Jean, we have so much in common, and Neallie is really a fascinating woman.

Neallie? Fascinating? Auntie, I may be only sixteen years old but, already, I'm a accomplished liar. And, as a liar, I can detect someone else's lie a mile off. You talked all night? I don't think so.

Hah. Well, you embarrass me. I'm glad to learn that, in addition all of your other fine qualities, my niece is nobody's fool. Excuse me, Honey, for assuming you're innocent or naive. Obviously, you're not. That was a clumsy lie on my part because the truth has to remain between the two of us. Okay? So, what really happened was last night I was with a delightful woman, and we enjoyed each other in ways I haven't experienced in a long time. Your Aunt Augusta allowed herself to be pleasured by another woman. I'm not ashamed. This is who I am. Does that upset you?

Auntie, it's not a big deal. I understand you had a fling. I've kissed a girl. We held hands. We might have tried something more but we didn't. So, I get it. If you want to talk more about what happened, we can talk on the plane but, now, let's get ready for breakfast. By the way, I love you, Aunt Augusta. You are more important to me now than ever before. Thank you for trusting me and being honest and I won't ever say anything about your adventure.

Augusta and Obra-Jean's return flight home was uneventful. They spoke a bit more about Augusta and Neallie's night together but, because they chatted so much during the tour, both felt completely talked-out by the time they reached Detroit. Leona met them at the airport and drove Augusta to her apartment and then drove Obra-Jean Leona's home, not to her grandparents' house. Obra-Jean told her mother she was tired and wasn't ready to tell her all about the trip. She hoped she could wait until the next day to recount to her mother everything she had seen and experienced. While Leona understood her daughter was tired, she was miffed she wasn't given even a brief report just to show how much her mother mattered to her. The next morning, however, Obra-Jean joined her mother and brother for breakfast and gave an enthusiastic telling of all of the things that had impressed her, including her Aunt Augusta's farewell speech.

Momma, it was so much fun and I learned so much. Aunt Augusta was so nice to me. I didn't feel like a kid with an adult. I felt we were more like sisters, more like me and Toby but Toby still treats me like a baby sister.

You're still very young, Obra-Jean.

I didn't feel young with Aunt Augusta and nobody in Europe treated me as if I was a youngster. They treated me like an adult.

You're my child. E.J. is my child. Toby is my child. You're my children and will always be my children. When you are grown up and have your own children, you will still be my child.

I hope when I grow up and have my own children you won't still treat me as if I was a child.

If you still act like one, I will.

You don't treat E.J. like a child.

Hey, don't get me into this. I didn't say anything.

Obra-Jean, you know I'm not talking about E.J. He doesn't act childish. He's very adult. He respects his mother. He listens to me and makes good decisions, not like Toby or you.

Are you still your mother's child?

Do you mean Clemenza?

She's your mother, isn't she?

She gave birth to me. That's all. Your Grandmother Moore is more a mother to me than Clemenza.

But Grandmama Post is your real mother and you are her child.

Clemenza will never ever be a real mother to me and I don't want to talk about her anymore.

When can you take me back to Grandmama Moore's house?

You can go today if you don't want to be with your mother and brother. Pack your things. The sooner you are out of here the better.

Augusta invited herself to visit her sister on the Saturday following her return from Europe. She wanted to give her own assessment of the trip's effect on herself and on her niece. Leona suggested they sit in the living room while Clemenza was in the kitchen preparing dinner.

Obra-Jean said she enjoyed the trip to Europe.

And I enjoyed traveling with her. Leona, she was a very good travel companion—no problem at all—and she seemed so interested in everything.

Yes. That's great.

Leona, what the hell? You don't sound pleased. Now what is it?

I'm pissed. Just as I thought, she seems to like being with you more than she likes being with her own mother. She would rather live with Styll than with me.

Leona, Honey, how many times do we have to go over this? You're her mother. She's growing up and moving away from you because she's becoming her own person. She'll come back to you when she needs a mother. Right now, she needs people who can help her sort out who she is. A mother gives direction. The rest of us help her see the possibilities of that direction.

That should be a mother's job too.

Well, okay, but your daughter doesn't want your help right now.

And you and Styll are making sure she won't come to her mother.

Your daughter is making her own decisions, Leona.

And you think those are good decisions?

They're not bad decisions.

In my opinion they are.

Then, that's between you and your daughter. If you want me to stay out of her life, I will but I don't think that is in your daughter's best interest. She's had a wonderful experience in Europe, perhaps something that will change her life. If you don't want me to do the things I can do to help her become who she wants to be, then, okay, I'm out of it. She's your daughter. You always know what is best for her.

Augusta, my daughter is all that I have. Toby has left me. E.J. will leave me. What will I have?

You have a sister and a mother and your husband's family.

So, I should let go of my daughter?

Not let go. Just give her room to grow even if growing means being with other people and making decisions you wouldn't make for her.

I wish you had a daughter to understand how hard it is to hear what you're saying.

Well, that chance has passed me by. But, I will always be your sister, your only sister and, I'll say it again, you're my favorite sister.

Thank you, Sister.

VII

Clemenza Bevin Post

— So That is the Story —
Fall 1958

During Obra-Jean's Sunday visit with her mother—after she had moved to her grandparents' house and long before she made the trip to Europe with her Aunt Augusta—she intentionally made a sketchy and incomplete report to Leona about her conversation with her Grandmother Post. Although it was not an outright lie, it was a deliberately redacted response to conceal things she learned about her mother that she didn't want her mother to know she knew. In fact, Clemenza used the occasion to confess many things she had withheld far too long from her own daughters. Knowing Obra-Jean's sensitivity to the conflict between Leona and Clemenza, and Leona's treatment of Clemenza, she sensed her granddaughter might be a perceptive but discreet listener, as Toby had been a few years earlier. She asked Obra-Jean to have a seat in her armchair beside the bed where she sat and, after a few questions about school, she opened her heart and soul to her granddaughter. As she spoke, she seemed to slip into a kind of trance.

Your mother, Leona, was my first child. She never knew her own father. He was not the father of her sister or her brothers. Now, you've never met the brothers because they were born and live in Hot Springs. That's in Arkansas. Leona's father was a slick young man named Duke. He talked me into having sex with him after he gave me some liquor. I was young, only sixteen at the time. I hadn't tasted alcohol before and didn't realize it would remove most of my inhibitions—that is, if I had any, which I didn't. I was surprised when I became pregnant. By that time, Mister Duke was gone, and I didn't know where. Then I had your mother. I guess I made some mistakes because I didn't know better.

You see . . . in my day, children weren't precious or anything like that. Parents didn't fuss over them. They didn't make them feel like they were something special. They were just children, like kittens or puppies. Yeah, like puppies. They were cute, sometimes frisky. Some were really smart and made the others look kind of dull, like part of a litter. The ones that stood out got more attention. I won't say, they got more love, because all of the children, or most, at least, were loved, but not like now. They were loved because they were alive and might have a life. A lot of them didn't have much of a chance at life. They might have been born sickly or feeble-minded. Some died in accidents. They were burned or broken or poisoned. There were so many ways that children could die and did die. We mourned every death but life didn't stand still. The living went on living. There were always more children, sometimes too many. They ran away. They got lost. They disappeared. Mostly, they grew up and found their place in the family. They did what they were told. They made their own plans like school or work or family. The smart ones—the ones that were really clever or had talent—they stood out. Yes, indeed. They went their own way. They figured out what they wanted and found what they needed to become what they dreamed. Sometimes, they kept their dreams to themselves. Maybe because to tell someone what they wanted might spoil their plans. Telling somebody might make their plans seem stupid or crazy. Other folks might see something wrong with their dream. They might discourage or make fun of them. Sometimes, the dreamers had their own doubts. Their dreams were delicate things, very difficult to hold on to. It was better to be quiet and just act when the time seemed right. Of course, you know, not all dreams come true. Maybe most fail or turn out not to be what was expected. Expectations are dangerous dreams. They can crush your ambition. They can destroy your hope. They can ruin your life. That's why some parents stifle dreams. They warn their children not to aim too high, even if they have talent. You have to be born into a pretty special family with money and education to aim high. A poor parent—a single mother, like me—couldn't encourage my children to aim high. I struggled because I was poor. I didn't want my children to struggle like I did. But, I couldn't let them aim for something that was too high for them. I wanted them to know their place in life and have sensible expectations. I said, don't aim too high but try to do better than I did. Go for a little something more but not too much more. The really bright ones, I knew, wouldn't listen. They would go off chasing their dream, expecting who-knows-what, and be crushed. The ones with less talent made something simple of their lives. It wasn't a lot or anything spectacular. They were settled and secure and got on with life.

Your mother listened to me. Your aunt didn't. Your mother had a husband who made good money. She has her own home, and family, and job. I think she's happy or she could be happy if she'd let herself be so. She raised you like I raised her. She likes what she has and she wants that for you. Do you like what you have? See . . . That's what we have to ask ourselves. Do we like what we have? But there are some bigger questions. What do we want that we don't have? Can we expect to get it? See, I didn't want much. Just a home. Some money. Peace and quiet. I didn't want a husband. I didn't want children. I got both but not because I wanted them. My husband, well, he was a good man. He wanted children and a home and a wife who would take care of all of that. So, I got some of what I wanted but I got even more of what I didn't want. I left my husband. I left my children except for your Aunt Augusta who was a baby. The other children grew up and went their own way. As I said, I loved my children but they weren't what I wanted in my life. I gave them what I could. I gave them what I thought they should have that I could give them. Whatever else they wanted, they had to find on their own. I didn't pretend. I didn't lie. I didn't intend to be mean or cruel to them. In my own mind, I don't think I was. I just wanted them to know what I could give them and what I couldn't or wouldn't. See, that's the difference today. Parents want to give everything to their children. They want to give love that they may not feel. They want to give things they can't afford. They want to give knowledge they can't provide. I've seen parents today who think they can and should do everything for their children. That, to me, isn't good for children or parents. Children begin to believe they can have whatever they want. Their parents treat them as if they deserve what they want. See, I don't think the parent should do that. In my day, "No" was the first lesson of life. "No" sounds hard but it's an important word. "No" means that's the end of the conversation. There is nothing after "No." The child that learns the meaning of "No" is ready for this world. Understanding "No" keeps you in your place whatever that is. "No" reminds you of limits. It reminds you of barriers. It reminds you to be cautious. Be cautious of people, and places, and things because you have no control over them. That's all of the instruction you need to be a part of this world. "No" makes the walls of your life. You live inside the walls of "No."

I was no great beauty. Nobody had to tell me that although some folks did. I learned it for myself when I was told "No," that boy won't like you. "No," that dress is too pretty for you. It would look better on your sister because you're too dark for it. "No," we don't want you at our party. "No," I like your sister better. You see . . . "No" helped me to know how to understand my world. Then, one day I heard "Yes." It was a man who wanted me. He looked pretty good to me. I was young. Sixteen. He was, maybe, twenty or more. His hair was slicked back with lots of grease. He had big white teeth and a little, thin mustache. He wore an old suit, maybe handed down to him by an older man in his family. Maybe he got it when his father died. His white shirt was too big for him. So the collar, which was fastened, was loose around his neck. His shoes were old. They were worn and not polished. Maybe, he too lived in a world of "No." But he smiled at me. We were at a house party in our neighborhood. I went with my sisters. They were pretty and had nice dresses, not new, but clean and nice. One of my sisters gave me her old purple dress with white polka dots all over. It was sewn up to hide the rips and patches. It was clean, though. I washed and ironed it myself. It just hung on me because I didn't have much in the chest or behind. I looked more boyish than girlish and my hair was short, almost too short to straighten with a hot comb. I didn't have stockings, just socks. Black socks and flat shoes They were my only good pair and also black. I did have a little red bow in my hair. I knew I didn't look good but I didn't care.

At the party, I stayed near Iris, my oldest sister. She had been dancing with other girls. Girls did that when they didn't want men putting their hands all over them and rubbing their crotches into the girls' privates. I was watching all of this when this guy was suddenly standing next to me. He smiled with his big white teeth and said, "Hello." He introduced himself as Duke. I already knew that wasn't his name because I had seen him before. Girls in my neighborhood made jokes about Duke who thought he was hot stuff. In their minds, he was just another poor, do-nothing colored boy. He had a job, of sorts. He worked at a gas station and cleaned the work areas and the toilets and, sometimes, helped with car repairs. You could see the grime under his fingernails. But he was nice. Polite. He asked me if I wanted a drink. He had brought a pint of whiskey to the party and pulled it from his suit jacket pocket. I had never drunk whiskey before or any kind of alcohol. We didn't keep it in our house. Liquor was too expensive. I didn't give a second thought to taking a drink that was offered me. I said yes I would like a drink and put the bottle to my mouth. It smelled strong and the neck of the bottle also smelled of Duke's bad breath. I swallowed a mouthful and coughed. There was a burning sensation inside me and I noticed I was breathing heavily trying to catch my breath. I tried to smile at Duke. He took a swig from the bottle and then offered me another drink. I took a smaller swallow without coughing afterwards and I felt even warmer and happier. I looked at Duke and he was grinning. I felt his hand behind me. He was squeezing my butt. His hand pressed between my butt cheeks and then he patted me on my back. He suggested that we go outside—it was dark—and get some fresh air. He took my arm and guided me out the front door around to the side of the house. I was beginning to feel lightheaded. He reached under my dress and pulled down my panties. He stuck his thing inside of me. I was surprised but not afraid. He was rocking back and forth. In and out. It began to feel good. I felt real good. So this is what all the girls were always talking about. Well, I liked it. I really liked it and I liked Duke, even with his bad breath and dirty fingernails. I let him kiss me while he was rocking and rolling. Suddenly, he shook and squealed. Nobody told me this is what happens to a man when he comes. I was kind of frightened because I thought he hurt himself but then he relaxed and thanked me. I guessed he liked what happened. I liked what happened. He pulled out of me. I pulled up my panties and smoothed my dress. He asked me if I wanted to go back to the party and I said yes.

Duke disappeared after that night. I guess he did me because he knew he was leaving town. I later figured out that I was pregnant. Duke was the first man I was with but there were more after that. Many more. And after I had my first baby—that was your mother—there were another four. Only three survived . . . your aunt and your two uncles. One of the men I was with became my husband, for a while at least. I left him and most of my kids. They were not what I wanted. I wanted a home and peace and quiet. The world said, "No."

My family lived in Arkansas. That's where I was born. I was the third child of seven. My father was dead by the time I was born. My mother lived with another man who gave her more babies after me. Actually, there was more than one man. My mother wasn't sure which one was the father of any of them. We older girls knew what men wanted. We weren't afraid to get pregnant because we knew children meant more help around the house. It might also mean a little extra money when the children got bigger. They could get some work to do like cleaning white folks' houses or whoring. We weren't ashamed to be whores because we didn't need anybody's approval. We weren't church-going people and we didn't believe all of that "Thou shall not" stuff. We were as poor as could be but we got on.

Hot Springs is where we lived in Arkansas. It was a popular town because of the hot springs where white people bathed to cure their ailments. That's what they thought. There were big fancy hotels for tourists who came from all over to bathe in the springs. There was money too. A colored girl, who was smart and could make herself attractive, could service white men who were looking for a good time. You may not believe this but sometimes white women were looking for a good time with colored girls, and white men were looking for colored boys. The girls could service colored men too. But the colored didn't have much money. Anyway, I found some decent colored men who gave me a little money and kept me and my kids in our house and food on our table. My kids didn't go hungry. I couldn't give them much more than food and old, worn, hand-me-down clothes. I felt bad that they looked like poor kids but they were poor kids. They had no toys or books or anything like that. They had to play outside of our house. It was nothing more than a falling-down wooden shack with a tin roof. There were no flowers or grass outside of our house, just dirt. That's where they played—near the house in the dirt. We didn't have a bathtub or running water. We just had an old tin tub for bathing and a pump near the house for water. There was an outhouse—you may not even know what that is. It's a small shack with a bench inside with a hole in it. And when you have to relieve your bowel or bladder, you sat on that hole. The place always stank but that was how it was back in those days. I had a stove. We used wood in it to make a fire. Actually, it was good for cooking but a little smoky sometimes. Believe me, I felt lucky I even had what little I had.

That was my life until I decided it wasn't for me. I saved a little money and left Hot Springs. I went to Detroit because I heard there were good jobs. I could cook. I did it for my family and I thought I could be a cook in Detroit. I left your mother and my boys in Hot Springs with my sister, Iris, and took your aunt with me to Detroit. Your aunt was the youngest —she was my baby—but the smartest of the bunch. I thought I could give her a chance in Detroit she wouldn't have in Hot Springs. My other children were old enough to take care of themselves. They were safe with Iris. I didn't worry about them.

I got lucky when I came to Detroit. I found a job cooking for a white family. A colored woman I met in Detroit cleaned that family's house. She was no cook so she suggested me to them and they hired me. I made more money than I ever had whoring in Hot Springs. Back in those days, almost all colored folks in Detroit lived in one section of town called Black Bottom and Paradise Valley. It was a crowded neighborhood with ramshackle buildings. People were crammed together in small rooms. At first, I found a room with a couple of other woman. Then I got a single room for me and Augusta. After I made more money, I got a little apartment. I sent Augusta to a Catholic school. It was the best school in the neighborhood. Maybe, that was a mistake because she began to get big dreams for her life. I warned her not to aim too high. Colored girls can't dream too many dreams. She didn't listen. Anyway, your mother wrote me and said she and her brothers wanted to come to Detroit. Like I said, I had a little money but a small apartment. I couldn't take in three more children. So, I told her, "No." Don't come to Detroit. Well, she married some stupid boy. She persuaded him to move her to Detroit. Her brothers stayed in Hot Springs where they still live. Your mother and her husband arrived and got a room in a house. Now, your mother graduated high school in Hot Springs. She learned to type and found some kind of job typing in Detroit. When she made a little bit of money, she ditched her husband and got a divorce. Later, she met your father, Perry. They got married and had your sister, your brother, and you.

Now, I know you've noticed that Leona never calls me "Mother." It's always "Clemenza." She calls your Grandmother Moore "Mother." It bothers me but I understand Leona. She feels I abandoned her. In a way, I did. But I left her with people who could take better care of her than I could. I had done all of the mothering to her I could. There was nothing more for me to do. She could figure out how to take care of herself. That is what she did and still does. What I did or didn't do for her, though, bothers me now. She thinks I didn't love her. I did and still do even though you know how she treats me after all of these years. I've tried to explain to her and I've tried to show her how much I love her but nothing changes her mind. That's your mother. She's just like that. Well, maybe I made her like that by leaving her behind. I don't know. We can't undo what we've done. We can't be who we aren't. I'm not the best mother. Maybe I'm not even a good mother. I couldn't have been any different and I couldn't have done things any other way. It was all I knew and I did what I did. So, now, I live in payback and I'll die in payback.

I want you to know all of this, Obra-Jean, because your mother is trying her best to be a good mother to you. She worries about you and your sister and brother. She wants you to get what you need and have a good life. She's not thinking about what you want. She doesn't understand that her children want something different from what she wants. She thinks she's protecting you, not hurting you. She thinks she knows what's in store for you in your life. She doesn't want you to make the mistakes that she made. Honey, she can't help being who she is. Don't forget that she loves you and will always love you.

Now, I want you to do me a favor. I want you to try real hard to understand your mother. Listen to her. Don't fight her. Don't misunderstand me. I'm not saying you should do only what she wants. No. You have to do what you want. Just don't fight her about it. I think the way to do that is to listen to her. Don't get upset. Tell her you love her and respect her. You know she has your interest at heart. Tell her you have to live your own life just like she's done. You might make mistakes. She can say she warned you. But, you can learn from your mistakes. You'll ask her for advice even if you've made up your own mind. You know she's your mother but you won't always have her to help you make your own decisions. You have to learn how to do that by yourself when she's gone. Let me give you a big kiss and a hug. Now, go back to your mother.

Clemenza moved from her bed to her armchair after her granddaughter left her room. She glanced around her small room at the back of her daughter's house. There was one window that faced the rear yard. The window was open; a screen prevented insects from flying into her room. Puffs of air made the curtains flutter momentarily. There was a single narrow bed. Beside it was an overstuffed armchair and a small wooden table with old *Ebony* and *Jet* magazines. She had read every article in both publications but, from time to time, she liked to look at pictures of black people. Some were of happy occasions; others were of tragic events. They all reminded her of the situations in the life she had lived and of people she knew. She smiled to herself then felt a tear slide down her cheek. What if she knew back then what she knows now? Why did she tell her granddaughter all of those things about herself? Why did she tell her to love her mother? Did her own daughter love her? Is that why Leona was so angry with her own mother all of these many years because of love? Or, did Leona really hate her? Was it love and hate? Leona acted like she hated her but maybe she behaved like that because she loved her. Clemenza looked around the room again. This was a prison. This was her prison cell. She was being punished. Was she being punished because she was a bad person, a bad mother? Why was Leona still so angry? Yes, Clemenza had left Leona in Hot Springs with relatives but they took good care of her; they didn't abuse her. In fact, Leona liked Clemenza's sister, Iris, who had agreed to keep Leona and her brothers. Her sister was married but had no children of her own. She was happy to have Clemenza's children to look after and raise. Clemenza wrote letters to Leona telling her about her new life in Detroit, how she found work and was making money. She told Leona to be a good girl and behave. What she didn't say was why she left Leona behind in Hot Springs or why she took Augusta with her but not Leona and the boys. She didn't say: I miss you. I love you. I'll bring you to Detroit if I can. She didn't think it was important to say these things at that time. Nobody had ever said things like that to her. How could she have known those words were important to Leona and would be throughout her entire life? Now, she was Leona's prisoner, and Leona's ill-will was her punishment for not knowing what to say so long ago.

Clemenza Bevin was impregnated by a man named Duke—the only name she knew for him. When she gave birth, Clemenza called her child Leona Bevin. Clemenza later married Calvin Post who was a handyman in Hot Springs. He worked hard and made a little money. He met Clemenza when she was a good-time girl in one of the joints black men —married and single—frequented after long days of work. He knew

Clemenza sometimes had sex with several of these men and one night he asked her if she would have sex with him. He would pay. She accepted. After that, he wanted her more frequently and Clemenza, not being a fool to men's needs, suggested she would live with him and take care of his home which was a rented shack with an outhouse in the black section of town. Calvin thought it was a good deal even if it required that he also let Clemenza bring her young daughter along to live with them. This arrangement seemed to work for Clemenza—she had a man of her own and a place to live. Clemenza and Calvin agreed to get married and that was the beginning of the end. Calvin's attention turned to Leona who was still a child. Clemenza, again, not being a fool to men's needs, left Calvin, got a divorce but kept his family name, and moved in with her married, but childless sister, Iris. She resumed hanging out in joints and finding more men to sleep with and pay her for it. The result was three more living children—twin boys, named Leander and Titus, and a girl named Augusta to whom Clemenza gave her married name—Post. Sleeping with several men wasn't providing enough money to keep her growing family. Clemenza decided she would have to do what other women, and men, were doing and that was to head to a northern city where there were good-paying jobs for black people. She packed one old suitcase and, with Augusta, left for Detroit leaving Leona and the twin boys in Hot Springs with her married sister.

Clemenza loved her life in Detroit. She had a little apartment where she and Augusta could share a bed. Augusta went to school, a good Catholic school. She was smart and clever. Clemenza could see she was making plans, big plans. She wanted to go to college after high school. She wanted to become a famous artist. She had talent. Her teachers told her so. She wanted to study art and she knew she would be great someday. Clemenza thought these were childish dreams that Augusta would abandon as she grew older but they weren't abandoned and, in fact, became more central to Augusta's life. She talked about art. She went to the art museum. She went to the library to look at books about art. Art was her obsession. Clemenza fought her insistently but, ultimately, Augusta ignored her mother.

Clemenza learned from her sister in Hot Springs that Leona had married and decided to follow Clemenza to Detroit; Clemenza's sons wanted to stay in Hot Springs and did so because Iris really seemed like a mother to them. Clemenza wanted Leona to know that she could not provide a place to live for her and her daughter's husband. If they came to Detroit, they would have to find their own place. She could help them find a room but that was all. When Leona arrived in Detroit, she told her mother not to concern herself with the daughter she had once left behind. Leona could take care of herself. Clemenza was relieved but, then, she felt Leona's animosity. What had happened? They were together again. Why was Leona angry? Clemenza decided not to fret about her elder daughter. She was married. She could raise her own family now. Everyone would be fine. Detroit was a good place for Clemenza and her daughters.

After she settled in Detroit, Leona left and divorced the man whom, in fact, she hated because she met a new man whom she really loved and wanted to marry. Perry Moore was handsome, light-skinned with straight wavy hair, employed, and still a teenager. He had a job on an automobile assembly line, a job he started without finishing high school. For a black man, he made good money and he was wise enough to save most of it while living at home with his parents and brothers. When he met Leona at a friend's house-party, he courted, dated, and impregnated her. They lived in his parents' house and married before the birth of their child. Their daughter, Patricia, was born in 1937. Perry nicknamed her Toby in memory of his great-grandfather, Tobias. The nickname stuck as did a nickname for their second child, Elgin James, who was born in 1939. Perry, and then everyone else, starting calling him E.J. With two children, they needed more room and moved from his parent's house to a squalid one bedroom apartment with a Murphy bed in the dining room. Their apartment building was typical of housing for blacks in Detroit. Its absentee landlord gained substantial rent for substandard vermin-infested housing. If rats and roaches paid rent, the benefit to the landlord would have been extremely profitable. When their third child, Obra-Jean, was born in 1943, the family's sleeping arrangements were compromised and underscored the inadequacy of their apartment. Leona and Perry occupied the bedroom; Toby and Obra-Jean slept on the Murphy bed in the dining room, and E.J. commandeered the couch in the living room. Two adults and three children in such a cramped, fetid space pushed Leona toward wanting a house with a bedroom for everyone. Perry didn't think they had enough money saved to make a downpayment on a house they could afford and he didn't think any of the neighborhoods in which most blacks lived were desirable. Leona persisted; Perry relented and started looking into white neighborhoods to which blacks were moving.

A combination of unforeseen circumstances forced the issue of a house for the family, fortunately, at a time when they had barely managed to save enough cash for a modest downpayment. Augusta had left Detroit for New York leaving her mother alone in their shared apartment. By 1953, Clemenza could no longer afford the rent on her own. Much to her surprise, Leona suggested Clemenza live with her family. She explained they wanted to buy a house and there could be a room for Clemenza. Not having any other options or stable finances, Clemenza agreed to move in with her daughter's family after they arranged to finance their purchase by a land contract with the house's white owner. Clemenza was hopeful this arrangement would allow a new relationship with her daughter. At first, after everyone settled into the new house with three upstairs bedrooms and, on the main floor, a separate bedroom off the kitchen for Clemenza, she believed her daughter had overcome her animosity. However, Clemenza quickly realized no such reconciliation would ever take place. Leona could barely conceal her contempt for her mother and enjoyed being cool and dismissive of her. No one would speak up to Leona because the mere mention of her behavior unleashed a stinging rebuke. No one wanted to join in Clemenza's misery by creating an alliance with her against Leona. Leona roared and everyone, even Perry, sought refuge. Clemenza sheltered in her prison room. She looked out the window and then at the table with the magazines. The room was quiet, still, and lonely.

— A Summer Outing —
Early Summer 1959

There was a crowd of several hundred people waiting at the dock on the Detroit River. The morning sun was still low in the sky and a breeze coming from the direction of the river cooled the crowd waiting patiently for the loading ramp to be lowered from the Sainte Claire, one of the two Bob Lo boats. Folks were dressed casually for the heat and for the excursion downriver to Bob Lo Island just north of the mouth of Lake Erie. The crowd was mostly white but a number of blacks clustered in groups within the still, expectant crowd. In one such cluster was Clemenza who had been invited by Estyllene to accompany her, Barry, Mason, and Obra-Jean on a daylong visit to Bob Lo where they would picnic and enjoy the amusement park rides. Styll had included Clemenza in the outing so that she would have a companion for conversation during the excursion because neither Barry nor Mason had much to say about anything and Obra-Jean had agreed to join the trip only if she could bring some books to read for her impending trip to Europe with her aunt. The women all wore sun hats. Barry had a straw hat. Mason was bare-headed.

Both the Sainte Claire and her sister ship, the Columbia, were tied up at the dock. When one ship reached Bob Lo and then began the return trip to downtown Detroit, the other ship began chugging down the river to Bob Lo. The Sainte Clair would make the first morning voyage. Both ships had three decks and were propeller-driven. They bobbed in the wake of waves from passing ore carriers that ceaselessly plowed the river and Great Lakes between the ore mines in northern Minnesota and the industrial factories in cities along the waterways like Detroit, Toledo, and Cleveland. The Sainte Claire was the more distinctive of the two ships because of its flying bridge fanning out from the wheelhouse rising above the top deck.

As the hour approached for departure, the crowd became more animated. Everyone awaited the signal of the lowering of the gangway in order to rush on board and claim a coveted spot on an upper deck with a view of the Detroit side of the river. Since the boats docked facing upriver, the Detroit side view would be on opposite side of the ship until, upon leaving the dock, the ship made a wide U-turn heading downriver. Because none of the adults in their group would be able to move quickly enough to claim a Detroit view when the gangway was lowered, Obra-Jean and Mason were tasked to race onto the ship and rush up the stairs to the top deck. Obra-Jean knew she could sprint through the crowd up to the deck; she wasn't sure if Mason could keep up with her. When the moment came to board and the crowd surged ahead, Obra-Jean grabbed Mason's hand and pushed ahead. Clemenza and Styll were surprised at the speed with which Obra-Jean and Mason moved and disappeared into the crowd. They, and Barry, who was slowed by his damaged leg, lagged behind confident that they would eventually find Obra-Jean and Mason in a prime spot on the upper deck. The women each carried a picnic basket for the group's lunch on Bob Lo. Clemenza made fried chicken, deviled eggs, and a peach pie. Styll prepared ham and cheese sandwiches—Barry's favorite—potato salad, and a pound cake. They would purchase beverages at Bob Lo.

When the captain sounded the whistle indicating that the ship was preparing to depart, Clemenza, Styll, and Barry had finally reached the upper deck, located Obra-Jean and Mason who had commandeered deck chairs for them all, and arranged themselves along the perimeter of the walkway that formed a continuous path around the entire ship. As the Sainte Claire pulled away from the dock and started forward, it began a slow U-turn in the river to head towards Bob Lo Island. When the ship swung around for its downriver voyage, the Moore family watched the skyline of Detroit come into view. Within minutes the ship passed under the Ambassador Bridge linking Detroit and the USA to the city of Windsor in Canada. Detroit's industry hugged the shoreline as the ship passed beyond the bridge. Soon the smokestacks, factories, and mountains of industrial raw materials and industrial waste came into view. This sprawling, smoking, stinking industrial community was the real reason for the existence of Detroit. At the heart of this city within the city was the Ford Motor Company River Rouge Complex—an industrial city within an industrial city within an industrial city. The acrid fumes and dense smoke wafted over the river and saturated the ship as it passed the Rouge River—the open sewer of this industry—which carried the visible toxic effluent of manufacturing into the Detroit River and on to Lake Erie. Once past the Rouge complex, the landscape became green, the air seemed fresh, and the river ahead promised entry to the bucolic setting of Bob Lo.

The boat ride was well under the two hour mark when the captain's whistle signaled arrival at the Bob Lo Island dock. Bob Lo was the familiar name for Bois Blanc Island. Opposite the town of Amherstburg, Ontario, Bob Lo was on the Canadian side of an imaginary line in the Detroit River dividing the United States from Canada. Again, the ship made a tight U-turn in the channel between the island and the Canadian shore to dock facing upriver in preparation for the return trip to Detroit. Even before the captain's whistle, many of the excursionists had already begun making their way from the upper decks to the gangway. Styll, Clemenza, and Barry wanted to wait a bit so as not to get caught up in the crowd but, again, they sent Obra-Jean and Mason ahead to find a table in the picnic area for their lunch. The crowd quickly disembarked clearing the way for the elders to slowly make their way off the ship, down the gangway, and back on solid ground. They easily located Obra-Jean and Mason since the picnic area was only a short distance from the dock. When they reached the picnic spot and began arranging the park's table for lunch, Obra-Jean announced that she wanted to take Mason to the amusement park located a further distance from dock. They would have lunch after they returned from taking some of the rides, particularly the roller coaster and dodge-em cars. With that announcement, they left.

Styll and Clemenza settled down to chat while Barry spread a blanket on the ground, lay down, and took a nap. The two women had never been close friends but they were cordial to one another over the years their children—Perry and Leona—had been married. Both realized the awkwardness of their relationship since Leona always was more loving and responsive to Styll than she was to Clemenza. Early on, Clemenza explained to Styll that she was not jealous. She accepted her daughter's scorn as punishment for what Leona perceived as her abandonment by her mother. Styll, not having a daughter of her own, felt guilty about displacing Clemenza as Leona's "mother" but she relished the attention and devotion. Both women accommodated themselves to Leona and both were able to understand their own place and to sympathize with the other's place in Leona's life. Both watched with dismay as Leona, in an effort to prove she was a good mother, unwittingly pushed her own daughters away from her. Clemenza thanked Styll for taking Obra-Jean into her home. Obra-Jean seemed happy. She was completely involved in school and, as far as anyone could see, she was developing into a mature and confident young lady. One of the things that seemed odd about her was the fact she was not dating boys. She expressed no interest in boys.

In fact, Obra-Jean didn't seem to have any friends, either boys or girls, according to Styll, except for one schoolmate named Kyra Smith whom Styll successfully persuaded Obra-Jean to invite one time for a Saturday lunch. Obra-Jean never again invited Kyra or any friends to Styll's home and she never seemed to spend time with friends outside of school. Styll confided to Clemenza that, at one point, she wondered if Obra-Jean would follow Toby's path and live with another woman. Clemenza felt certain that Obra-Jean would not be a second Toby although she couldn't explain why. Styll wondered aloud about Obra-Jean's commitment to school. It was the only thing that seemed to interest her, the only thing she discussed. She had always been a good student so it wasn't unusual that she continued to be at the top of her class. But, Styll noted, there was something about Obra-Jean's involvement with school that was difficult to comprehend. Obviously, Obra-Jean wanted to learn things but she seemed to have some ultimate goal that Styll could never draw out of her. In her own way, Obra-Jean was as opaque as Mason. Maybe that was why uncle and niece got along so well. Styll looked in the direction of the amusement park rides as some inchoate thought passed through her mind.

Clemenza, our granddaughter could do great things someday. She's determined to be an architect. She's studying like crazy to learn how to make blueprints. I never even thought of such a thing but she spends hours after she returns from school working at that drafting board in her room. She's set up a table in the corner of her room with the drafting board on top. She's got some kind of lamp that she moves and swivels over the table so she's got a lot of good light. I've looked at some of her drawings when I've cleaned her room and they look just like blueprints. I don't know where she gets all of the information she uses to make these drawings but they look like the real thing to me. But what do I know?

Styll, that child has always been smart . . . I think, too smart sometimes. She's a lot smarter than the rest of us because she always seems to get what she wants. She sure knows what she wants. She doesn't let much get in her way. You know she tore apart that beautiful dollhouse her parents gave her for her birthday when she was a child. I thought she was destroying it but, it turns out, she was rebuilding it the way she wanted it to look. When she was finished, she showed it to me. I thought it looked like something someone made who did that sort of thing for a living. It was beautiful, more beautiful than the dollhouse. And, it was clever too. She made it so she could remove the outside walls and the roof and you could look inside. I asked her how she knew how to do this and do you know what she said?

No, what?

She said she just figured it out. Now, I don't think that a child as young as she was then could just figure things out like that. Someone must have taught her how to do that. But she insisted it was all her own idea. Isn't that something?

You know, Clemenza, I think Obra-Jean has a life that she's keeping secret from us. There's something about her that just doesn't add up. But she is a good child. She's respectful and very helpful around the house. She's made friends with Mason and nobody has been able to do that, not even Barry and me. She's as much of a mystery as he is.

Do you think it was a good thing she got out from under Leona?

That's hard to know. Obra-Jean loves her freedom. Lord knows Barry and me don't try to run her life for her like her mother would if she was living at home. But Leona has a keen eye. She would figure out something was up if Obra-Jean was living at home.

So, maybe it's a good thing she's living with you, Styll. Obra-Jean will become who and what she wants to be. None of us, especially her mother, will interfere with that.

Time will tell, won't it?

When Obra-Jean and Mason returned to the picnic area, the grandmothers had set out the luncheon and had already begun to eat. Obra-Jean and Mason joined them. Styll called to Barry who roused himself from his nap and came to the table. During lunch, Obra-Jean described the excitement of the roller coaster and dodge-em car rides. She joked that Mason had refused to join her and, instead, stood watching and waiting until she had finished each ride. Following the meal, Obra-Jean excused herself to read her books for the trip to Europe. Clemenza and Styll packed up the remains of lunch and decided to take a walk in the wooded area of Bob Lo park. The day together and the lunch had lessened a lot of the formality that had long existed between the two women. They began to share stories about themselves and their lives. Styll, sensitive to Clemenza's complete lack of a sense of humor, decided to coax her into laughing. She started by telling silly jokes that left Clemenza baffled and unresponsive. She then decided to risk an off-color joke to see if a little sexual humor would bring a smile. It worked and Styll realized that she now had a tool to make Clemenza laugh. Styll started talking about her dead sister, Emyllene, and gradually worked up to a description of her sister's whoring which she bragged took place with many mostly younger men. Clemenza listened attentively. Styll continued. She described her sister's hospitalization and death. Clemenza was completely taken in by the tale. The women stopped in their tracks as Styll continued with the story. She said that she arranged for the funeral home undertaker to come to the hospital and retrieve her sister's body to prepare for embalming and burial. When the body was ready for viewing at the funeral home, Styll went with Barry, Mason, and her sister, Evyllene. An undertaker escorted them to a basement room where the embalmed body was kept in its casket before being moved to a formal viewing room on the main floor. Styll said that she started crying as soon as she entered the room and saw the casket on the opposite side some distance away from her. She hesitated to approach it.

I had my handkerchief up against my face and I was crying like a baby and making all kinds of noise and acting the fool. Evyllene was holding my arm and pulling me forward. I kept pulling back but she was determined that we would look into that casket. We were about ten feet from it when I looked up and saw the face and started crying even more. I tried to wipe away the tears so I could see clearly and finally, I got a good look. I stopped and squinted. I jerked back. I leaned forward. I turned my head this way and that way so I could get a good look in the dim light. Something looked funny. I tiptoed towards the casket, looking and squinting. I raised up and bent down, leaning this way and that way, all the while tiptoeing forward. Then, I stopped just in front of the casket and got a good look at the face. I said to myself "Is this Emy? This sure don't look like Emy. Who the hell is this?" I called Evy who was a couple steps behind me and told her to bring her butt up to the casket and take a good look. I said "Evy, this ain't Emy. This ain't our sister. Who in hell is this?" She looked and said: "Well, it sure ain't Emy whoever it is." I turned to the undertaker and said: "What the hell did you do with our sister, Emyllene Baker? Where is she? This isn't her." He looked at me and then he looked in the casket and excused himself and went into another room. He came back in a few minutes and said that there had been some kind of mistake. If this body wasn't our sister's body, they must have brought the wrong body from the hospital. I got right up in his face and said: "You find my damn sister or else you'll be in one of these caskets." He left the room again and came back with a big smile on his face. "Missus Moore, my apologies. Your sister's body is here.

Somehow, the identification tags just got mixed up. We're sorry. Your sister is right here and ready to be viewed. We'll give you a special casket for free and give you a discount on the funeral costs and even provide some flowers. Please just don't make a fuss about this little mixup. We're very, very sorry and we want you to be happy with our service." So, I said to him: "If you want me to be happy and keep my big fat mouth shut about what you Negroes messed up here, you won't charge me for anything and you'll give my sister a 'Cadillac' casket and the best funeral possible with flowers and everything." He stood still for a moment. I could see he was making all of these calculations. Then he took both of my hands and said "We would be happy to send off your sister with no financial obligation at all to your family. You folks deserve the best we have to offer." He then motioned for us to follow him into the next room where Emy's body was with a lot of other bodies. She looked like she was sleeping. Me and Evyllene started to cry like Niagara Falls and left the room. When we got outside of the funeral home, we busted out laughing until our sides hurt.

Styll made Clemenza laugh. Clemenza kissed her on the cheek and thanked her. She grabbed Styll's arm and they continued walking through the park until they returned to their picnic area. The sun was already past its apogee. The heat of the summer day was becoming oppressive. The group gathered their things and proceeded back to the dock to join the queue for the next boat back to the city. The sister ship, the Columbia, was waiting. A smaller crowd boarded so there was no need to scramble for a good spot on an upper deck. In fact, the older members of the group didn't want to climb any stairs and they remained seated on the city-side of the lower deck. By the time they reached the downtown dock, the sun was again lower in the sky which blazed with color. Making their way to the Moore's car, they boarded and headed first to Clemenza's home. When they arrived at her house, Clemenza, before exiting the car, thanked Styll and Barry for including her on their outing and bringing a little joy and companionship to her life. She then turned to Obra-Jean, who sat beside her on the back seat, and told her that she loved her. She was proud of her and she wanted nothing more than that her granddaughter succeed at whatever she wanted. Clemenza hugged Obra-Jean, said goodbye to all, and headed to the front door of the house. When Clemenza was safely inside and waved from the front door, Styll drove off and headed back to the Moore residence. After they settled into the house, Styll asked Obra-Jean if she had enjoyed herself. She replied that it was one of the best days of her life. She was so happy to be with people she loved.

VIII

Brothers

— Perry —

Perry Moore and his brothers—Carson and Mason—were born within six years of each other to Estyllene Baker Moore and Barry Moore. As the eldest son, Perry assumed responsibility of protecting and educating his younger brothers. They were closer to one another than with other boys in their neighborhood. For reasons his parents never understood, Perry seemed to hover over Carson—from the time he was about twelve years old—and acted more like a parent than a brother. He created a kind of cocoon around Carson that no one outside of the family was allowed to penetrate. Their parents did not question this new dynamic because Carson didn't seem to mind Perry's guardianship. Carson, in turn, assumed the role of mentor to his younger brother, Mason. Thus, the three brothers bonded together. Carson and Mason remained close to each other especially after Perry met Leona, married her, and they began their own family. As the first son, Perry was his father's favorite. Barry wanted to name him after himself but Styll objected, and the couple settled on Perry instead of Barry Junior. Carson, who was named for Styll's deceased brother, was his mother's favorite. A bond between mother and son was so obvious to all that Carson was almost inevitably called a "Momma's boy." Instead of dodging this appellation, Carson relished it and stayed close to his mother until, as a young adult, he abruptly moved away from his parents' home in Detroit to live in Philadelphia. With both Carson and Perry gone, Mason became the lost child. Named by his mother after her maternal grandfather, Mason who was born with a aversion to human contact, had a severe learning impairment that became apparent only after he reached school age. He learned slowly, if at all, and, aside from the attention Carson and Perry showed him, he seldom registered in the minds of his parents although he lived most of his life sequestered within the confines of their home.

Perry attended public schools as did his brothers although Mason was quickly shunted into a special school for children with learning disabilities. Although Perry didn't finish high school because he started work on an automobile assembly line, Carson did graduate. Perry was drafted into the Army during the Second World War but never left the States. Carson was also drafted but was ultimately rejected from service for reasons he never explained or that anyone ever questioned. He then began college during the war and finished after the war ended. Mason was not developmentally qualified for the draft and dropped out of his special school after he turned sixteen. As the three brothers, by design or chance, went their separate ways, they remained brothers essentially by a link to their mother, Estyllene Baker Moore. Ever gregarious and fond of her sons, Styll tried to bring her boys together for family occasions. Carson eventually opted out, and Mason never really could opt in. That left Perry, with a wife and three children of his own, to fulfill Styll's desire for an extended family. She longed for a daughter but the one she did have died at birth.

In everyone's opinion—that is, family and friends—Perry was a loving husband and father, and a dutiful son. He was never particularly close to his own father, Barry—despite being his father's favorite—but he maintained a cordial, matter-of-fact relationship with him that felt sufficient to both men. With his mother, Perry was more relaxed and personal. He was swift to fulfill her requests and prompt to assist in her needs. He accompanied her for medical visits. He went shopping with her when she made rare, large, household purchases. Often, Perry's wife, Leona, went along because she enjoyed Styll's company and wanted to maintain more of a daughter—than daughter-in-law—relationship with her. Styll grew fond of Leona not only because she liked her but also because she became the daughter Styll desired but never had.

As much as Perry loved his own daughters, he felt closest to his son, E.J. Elgin James—named for his paternal grandfather, Elgin Joseph Moore—was smart, handsome like his father, and devoted to him. Father and son were a little male colony within a female province. Although E.J. was never much interested in sports, he humored his father by playing catch with baseballs and footballs. Perry worked a standard daytime shift at the DeSoto automotive plant. He started work in early morning and generally returned home early afternoon, that is, if he didn't stop for beers with his co-worker and friend, Henry Hatcher. When he first began work at the factory, he, like most other men, spent his shift on the assembly line doing repetitive tasks that involved installing and securing various components, inside and out, to the automobile body. Over many years of such work before and after his service in the Army, he impressed his supervisors with his suggestions and diligence. Since he had been promoted to the rank of sergeant in the Army with some authority to command other men, his supervisors decided to make him a foreman in charge of a small section of the assembly line. This was a rare opportunity for a black man at the time, and Perry stepped into the role with firmness and assurance. He quickly gained the respect of his fellow workers—black and white—because of his intelligence, competence, and fairness, and he treated his job as a precious gift not to be spoiled by hubris. He became an ideal boss.

In 1957, the year of the automobile accident in which Perry died, he had wanted his son to see him at work and to learn how his father collaborated with other men to make an automotive assembly line a smooth pairing of human labor with powerful machinery. He asked E.J. to request permission from his teacher, Sister Mary Concordia, to skip his classes one day towards the end of the semester so that he could accompany his father to the auto plant. The nun was reluctant to agree because E.J. was one of her best students and a day of lessons lost was difficult to make up at the end of the semester. However, E.J. turned on his charm—something he had learned from his father—and promised Sister Concordia he would make up any lessons after school. Sister was still reluctant. E.J. then had his father call her. Their conversation was cordial. Perry emphasized that this visit was part of what Perry considered his son's education, in fact, something he could not get in a classroom. It was important for a young man like E.J. to see how men worked together and how his father contributed to that cooperation. Perry was so reasonable with Sister and so complimentary of her instruction for his son that Sister finally relented only with a reassurance that any lost work would be made up. Perry assured Sister this would be the case because he would see that his son kept his promise.

The day of their late spring visit, E.J. rode with his father in the family car to the DeSoto plant on the city's far west side, on the border in fact between Detroit and the suburb of Dearborn. Perry parked his car in the employee parking lot and with his son walked into the employee entrance of the assembly line building. Perry greeted his fellow workers and proceeded to the office of his white supervisor. He knocked on the door and upon being bidden to enter, introduced his son to Thomas Knox who stood momentarily, shook hands with E.J., and sat down in his chair without suggesting that Perry and E.J. also take a seat. Knox asked E.J. about his school and nodded in agreement that Catholic schools were the best in the city. He then asked E.J. what he planned to do when he graduated, maybe work with his dad in the factory? He suppressed his surprise when E.J. said he was going to college to study advanced mathematics and become a teacher like his aunt. Knox congratulated him on his ambition and excused himself, indicating to Perry that he and E.J. should now leave his office. After father and son were a safe distance from Knox's office, E.J. questioned his father.

Dad, was Mister Knox a little upset about something?

E.J., take a lesson from what you've just experienced. Mister Knox was friendly up to the point that he realized you were not just another factory Negro. When you told him you were going to college, he understood you were already thinking outside of the limits that white folks, like Mister Knox, set for us Negroes. You see, his own sons work in this factory and he probably resents that you might rise above them. I don't want you to work in a factory. You'll be a professional not a factory worker. Your children might be aristocrats. Our family is gonna keep rising up in this world and not be held down by anyone who tells us to stay in our place. That's why I wanted you to meet him and for him to meet you.

Does Mister Knox think you're just another factory Negro?

Yes. He and his bosses know I have some smarts and they've given me a chance to use them but within limits. I've gone as far as a Negro can go in this factory. In their minds, a factory is the only place good enough for me and you. Remember that what other people think about you is not what you have to think about yourself. You set your own goals and go for it. If you don't make it or other people won't let you make it, at least you tried. Always try. Got that?

Yeah. Wow, this is better than school.

But school is what will keep you out of here. Your dad didn't have the opportunities you have so this is my life, and I love it. But, I don't want it for you and I don't think you want it for yourself. You want to be a math teacher after college, right?

Right. I'm sticking with math and teaching high school.

My smart son. You make me proud, E.J. Now, come on, I want you to see the assembly line and meet some of the guys.

Perry and E.J. walked down the section of the assembly line for which Perry was foreman. Perry called out the names of several different men and pointed to E.J. and announced this was his son. All of the men had heard talk about E.J. and how smart he was and that he was going to college after high school. They smiled and waved. Some quickly shook his hand. After Perry had explained his section of the assembly line, he actually had to return to supervising and he left E.J. in a little cubicle that served as Perry's office. After a lunch break, Perry had arranged for his friend, Henry Hatcher, who was also a foreman, to take E.J. on a tour through the rest of the factory while Perry returned to work. E.J. rejoined his father just as Perry's shift was coming to an end. Perry asked E.J. to step inside his office while he had a brief chat with Henry. Perry inquired of the factory tour. Henry told him everything went well. E.J. was curious about everything and seemed to understand the complexity of the factory assembly line. Perry thanked Henry for taking time to be with his son. Then, in a lower voice and leaning in close to Henry, he asked him when they might get together for a few beers. Henry smiled and promised Perry he could come visit Henry's apartment sometime soon. The men shook hands warmly, said goodbye, and Perry joined E.J. in his office. Together they exited the factory to the parking lot, entered their car, and drove onto the street that would take them home.

E.J. told his mother and sisters about his visit. He tried to describe all that he saw and all of the people he met. Since neither his mother nor his sisters had ever seen the factory where Perry worked and, although Perry talked about his co-workers—he never really talked about his work—they asked lots of questions about everything E.J. told them. Although E.J. was fascinated by the factory's organization and complexity, he couldn't imagine himself working there like his father. He knew his father liked his job and that he was good at it but E.J. was sorry this was the life his father had lived and would continue to live. For his own life, E.J. told himself he would never follow his father's path. He would, instead, create a very different life for himself and his future family. He would become a teacher like his Aunt Augusta.

— Carson —

While Perry's brother, Carson, was still in high school, he got a job as a delivery boy for a grocery store in his neighborhood where many older adults were too infirm to do their own shopping. In his round of deliveries after school, he came to know many families in the neighborhood. One was an elderly single man, Horace McGrew, who often tipped Carson quite generously for his delivery service. Carson would often take a few extra minutes to chat with the man and, sometimes, even sit and talk for a while when invited into the man's house. The man was unlike other men his age in that he wore expensive tailored clothes, had a very refined manner of speech, and looked intently and—Carson thought—seductively at the youngster. Carson found himself daydreaming about being seduced by the man and wondering what that would be like. He hoped someday he would find out. However, it was another male teenager who seduced Carson, and he then realized he was heading in a direction that was both unexpected and fraught with danger. From stories he heard from other kids in the neighborhood and at school, he knew his evolving interests and actions would have to be secret. However, he felt he could confide in his brother, Perry, who to his surprise only cautioned him to be careful. Perry told him what men did sexually with other men—Carson never inquired how his brother knew these things—and he assured Carson he could trust Perry to discuss anything he wanted to know. Following Perry's advice, Carson decided to conceal those parts of himself that might inform others of his secret desires. Sadly, one result was his distancing himself from his family and most of his friends. However, when he was drafted, he disclosed his secret life to the military and was immediately classified 4F—unfit for the Army. He thought this was his good luck.

Without fear of entering the Army and the war, Carson applied to and enrolled at Wayne University (not yet then a State school) and majored in education. His studies took many years because he could only attend school part-time due to his work schedule as a janitor in a downtown department store. When he graduated, he learned that the Philadelphia public schools were hiring teachers. He applied, was hired, and moved to the city of Brotherly Love where he found a brother, Philip Townsend, who became his live-in lover.

— Barry & Mason —

Barry, father of Perry, Carson, and Mason, was a charming man to everyone except his sons. Even for Perry, clearly his father's favorite, Barry was remote, gruff, and moody—often after having a few too many beers. He frightened his sons because an aura of threat radiated from him like a stove gives off heat. He was never violent but as the tone of his voice shifted from neutral to muffled, the boys stayed clear of him. Styll found this amusing because she knew her husband posed no physical threat to her sons; she would not have tolerated that and she explicitly told Barry so, repeatedly. Instead, she appreciated that her husband's manner was far more effective than her scolding and lecturing in forming the boys' behavior. As a result, her sons were well mannered, polite, and deferential to adults and this, she thought, was a necessity for three black boys to learn in order to survive in a world outside of the security of their home.

In 1919, Barry migrated to Detroit from south Georgia where he had met Estyllene Baker when both were teenagers. They married and decided to move north because of the prospect of work and the hope they wouldn't be treated as abusively as they had experienced in the South. Detroit in the 1920s was a boomtown because of the automobile and associated industries. Blacks found jobs and made more money than was ever possible in the South and this was the case for Barry and Styll. As lucky as they were in finding work that paid well, locating housing was much more difficult because blacks were limited to a few tightly circumscribed areas of the city. One such area was a neighborhood on the city's westside transversed by Warren Avenue, a major east-west crosstown artery. The neighborhood consisted of single and double family houses. These were substantial structures on narrow lots owned or rented by more prosperous blacks. However, as more blacks migrated to Detroit and sought housing in better black neighborhoods, they rented rooms in homes of settled families and these houses became overcrowded. Although the swelling population created problems of privacy, communicable diseases, and social tensions, it made a very vibrant, diverse, and creative community. Blacks created small businesses like grocery stores, hair salons, barber shops, and cleaners. Musical talent, nurtured in church choirs, also came from these neighborhoods. Mostly, however, blacks worked in the city's many automobile factories such as Packard Automobiles where Barry found work. Styll, who was raising her boys, began working during the day as a cleaning woman in the homes of whites to bring in extra income. The couple saved enough money to move from a room in someone else's house to a home of their own which they rented and eventually purchased in their westside neighborhood. The house was old and needed many repairs and improvements but it was their house and they made it more to their liking over many decades of investment and hard work. They added on a bedroom and sitting room at the rear of the house, and remodeled the kitchen and upstairs bathroom. The children all went to neighborhood elementary, secondary, and high schools. They made their own friends with children of similar backgrounds and circumstances but only Perry associated with a few of the neighborhood boys. He also became the only son who dated girls and he was a favorite with the prettiest girls in their neighborhood.

Barry never talked to his son about having sex with girls. Styll, who felt such a conversation was her husband's job, also said nothing to Perry. She worried, however, that her son would make some girl pregnant and not take responsibility for the consequences. Therefore, when her son brought a girl to their home for a visit, Styll would discreetly ask the girl if she were being careful. Often embarrassed and frequently uninformed about sex, girls would shy away from Styll's inquiries with denials of culpability on their part or on Perry's. Then came Leona. Perry announced he had a new girlfriend he had met at a party. She was a little older than he was, beautiful and smart, and had a job typing in an office downtown. She had been married and divorced and she was in love with Perry. Barry was amused. Styll was unhappy. A divorced woman was not what she wanted for her eldest son. It was already clear to her that her second son, Carson, was not interested in girls, and the youngest son, Mason, did not attract girls even though he expressed a sad, bewildered, but unfulfilled, interest in them. All of her hopes for the future of their family rested with Perry and she wanted him to finish high school and choose a wife carefully. Perry, however, knew he wanted Leona, and

Leona wanted him, so the deal was done. Besides, she was pregnant with Toby. He couldn't marry Leona until he turned eighteen so Leona moved into the house of her future in-laws. She quickly ingratiated herself to Styll by helping her with household tasks and showing her genuine affection by calling her "Mother." Styll succumbed to Leona's charms. She acquired a daughter she had always desired. When he turned eighteen, Perry, already a father, married Leona in a civil ceremony with only two witnesses present—a neighborhood friend of Perry, Preston Kabule, and an office mate of Leona, Lois Bayliss.

Barry was injured in a work accident that broke his left femur. He received inadequate care at the emergency room of the city's public hospital, and the leg never properly healed. From then on, he walked with a limp and had great difficulty climbing stairs. To accommodate his infirmity, the Moore family built the addition onto the rear of the house with a bedroom for Barry and a sitting room for the family. Barry still had to climb stairs to use the only bathroom in the house but he could manage that with difficulty.

Perry and Leona lived in one of three upstairs bedrooms. Of the other bedrooms, one became Styll's private quarters after she stopped sleeping with her husband, and the other was shared by Carson and Mason. This arrangement worked reasonably well until Leona became pregnant with E.J. Perry then had to move his family to an apartment, leaving Barry, Styll, Carson, and Mason in their house. However, Carson moved to Philadelphia after he completed his college degree. Mason was left without a friend or companion in the house except his parents. He was always a solitary child and now a solitary adult. He seemed to have no interests other than playing with an electric train he received when he was twelve. When weather permitted, he sat in the backyard and he took on simple tasks assigned to him by his mother like walking to the corner store for a loaf of bread. His father seldom spoke to him. Mason pretended to listen to the radio while his mother's soap operas were broadcasting but he never really understood what was going on or much cared. Something in him kept his mind engaged but no one could discern what that was because he never expressed a longing, desire, or need. He was completely self-contained and relied on his family only for meals but accepted whatever else they provided. When Obra-Jean came to live in the elder Moore's residence, Mason seldom spoke to her or even appeared to notice her presence. She tried to talk with him but his responses were nearly mono-syllabic and disengaged. It was a complete surprise to her when, one evening while she was studying in her bedroom —the bedroom that formerly belonged to Perry and Leona—Mason stood at her door watching her. When she noticed him, she asked if he wanted to come in and sit down. Silently, he entered the room and sat in a chair next to her bed where she reclined. For the first time, she really noticed Mason. He was handsome like a younger version of her father. In fact, he also looked a lot like her father. Obra-Jean realized she was attracted to him.

Hi, Mason. Nice to see you. Did you want to talk about something?

No.

Okay. You can just sit in that chair if you want. I'm doing my art project. Did you take art in school?

No.

What was your favorite class in school?

What?

Didn't you study something in school? What did you like?

Nothing.

Nothing at all?

No.

I'll bet that you learned something. How about, let's see, spelling? Can you spell "dog."

"D," "O,"...

"G." See, you did learn something. Now, "dog" in Latin—that's another language that I'm studying in high school. Dog in Lain is "*cane*." Say, "kah-nay."

"Kah-nay?"

Yes, "dog" is English—that's our language. In Latin, it's "cane" . That's "C," "A," "N," "E."

"*Cane.*"

That's good. Do you want to learn some other Latin words to spell?

No.

Do you know how to draw?

Yes.

337

Do you want to draw with me? I have paper and pencils. We can draw together sometime. Would you like that?

Yes.

Mason abruptly got up and left the room leaving Obra-Jean puzzled. However, he returned on successive nights and they began making drawings together. Soon, Mason began to speak in short sentences and ask Obra-Jean questions but at a certain point, he would suddenly leave her room. Styll, who noticed these occasional visits on her way to and from her own bedroom and thought them harmless, never spoke to Obra-Jean, Mason or her husband about them. Mason's periodic conversations with Obra-Jean continued after she graduated high school and began college. After she finished college and moved to her own apartment, Mason reverted to his solitary life and his mysterious inner world. When he died the year after his mother passed away in 1990, that left only Carson, the last of the three Moore brothers, alive.

IX

Ondine Dash-Mahmoud

— Welcome to the Family —
Fall 1959 to Fall 1961

When Augusta returned with Obra-Jean from their trip to Europe in the summer of 1959, she planned to leave her job at the central administration and return to the Charles Shellington Elementary School where she previously taught. Reinforcement for this decision came from her niece, Obra-Jean, who responded so enthusiastically to the travel experience that, now, Augusta wanted to help directly transform the lives of more of the city's black students. She learned that the position of principal was open at her old elementary school so she applied and was immediately assigned there before the new school year started. Since the last term, there had been a major turnover in the school's administration and faculty. Several of the white teachers, as well as the principal, left at the end of previous school year to work in suburban districts and in parochial schools. With many openings to fill, the public school's district administration hired new teachers and assigned some of these replacements to Augusta's school. The new teachers were mostly recent university graduates with little or no teaching experience. All were black and female. Augusta saw this change as potential for a shake-up in how things worked within the school. Perhaps, with this new cadre of black women, the educational experience for the children could become more attuned to black sensibilities and black culture. It was her hope. She wanted to meet the new faculty and assess their outlook, preparation, and intelligence. As she worked through the group of her new colleagues, one by one, she was not inspired. These were certainly qualified women but without a mission or zeal. They had a job and would persist as long as they could or needed to until they got married or found a better placement at a more prestigious or better endowed school. One woman, however, stood out from the pack. She was large—both tall and broad— and she was very dark-skinned with short, closely cropped hair. She looked formidable with a "Don't fuck with me" attitude. Her students were terrified of her and, consequently, hers were the best behaved classes in the school. She also seemed to be a good teacher with a very professional command of the lessons, an ability to hold her students' attention which was always lagging, and superior workplace habits. She would be an outstanding teacher, and Augusta wanted to get to know her. In the otherwise empty faculty lounge, Augusta found the woman sitting alone during a break between classes.

Hi, there. May I join you? Would you like a coffee or something?

Of course you may join me, Principal Post, and, yes, I would like a coffee. Black, like me, please.

I like that. I'm hearing excellent things about you and your classes. I'm very impressed. You're probably one of the best new teachers in this school or any school. Your students are learning much more and are much better prepared than kids in any of the other classes. Everyone has noticed.

Thank you, Principal Post. I had hoped that you would notice. Let's pray that my students continue to learn and grow.

How you do it? How have you managed this progress in such a short period of time? Who taught you?

Actually, I was here before you came. I've been teaching here since last year after I graduated from Wayne. This is my second year at Shellington. But, to answer your question, my mother taught me.

Your mother was a teacher?

No, not really. I mean she taught me but she wasn't a professional teacher. She was a wise woman who had to raise six children by herself after our father died. She taught me to believe in myself. To stay focused. To work hard at everything. And, not to let people tear me down. You know there are people who think they are so much better than everyone else. Some of them work here. Some of them are the other teachers.

Has someone said or done something to you?

Most of my life I've heard people call me a big, black, fat woman who is also ugly as sin.

Someone here has said that to you?

I haven't heard it here yet but I see it in how they look at me and how they behave towards me.

Yes, you are a big woman and dark-skinned. But ugly? I don't think so. I think you're grand, quite striking, in fact. You have a powerful presence. To my eye, you are lovely and, yes, beautiful but maybe not in a conventional or stereotypical way. Hasn't anyone ever told you how beautiful you are?

My mother did and my family.

Well, she, and they, got it right. I agree with them but let me add that I'm not here to judge your appearance. I hope you won't judge me by my appearance until, at least, you get to know me. What I do want to know is how you operate in your classroom to get such good results from your students.

That's what you want to know?

Yes, of course, that's what I want to know. It's my job to know how to make this a better school and to get better results from our students.

You want to know how a woman like me can be one of the best teachers in the school? It's as if you believe someone else, who isn't me, could do what I do without being me. Principal Post, I do what I do well because I know who and what I am and how that affects other people. It's not just about teaching. It's about being. I am being me, completely me. Do other teachers want to be me and look like me?

It would be dishonest for me, of course, to say, yes, they want to look like you.

But I bet you could imagine them wanting to look like someone who was as pretty as you.

You flatter me. By the way, I've never thought that I was pretty but it would be dishonest for me to say a woman might prefer to look like you than me. It's our culture that sees beauty only a particular way.

So, understand, Principal Post, it's about how I look. That is my not-so-secret advantage in the classroom. I get my students' attention and hold it because they are mesmerized by this big, black, fat woman.

Allow me to correct you. Big, black, large, and beautiful woman. I hope you see I'm mesmerized too. Listen, we both work here and I hope we can be friends as well as colleagues.

You, the principal, want to be my friend?

Yes. Why not? I hope you don't think that just because I'm a principal I'm not also a human being like everyone else.

Okay, but why do you want to be a friend to me?

As I said, I think you're grand and gifted, and you are confident in who you are. You're a treasure to this school. I'm completely fascinated to know you and I want you to know me.

You want to know me for me?

Yes, I do, of course.

Okay, let's start. I'm Miss Ondine Mahmoud, commonly known by some folks as Mud.

Mud?

Yeah. Black as mud.

I can't call you that.

Yes, you can. I like that name because nobody else has it.

Are you serious, Miss Mahmoud?

Very much so, Principal Post.

Okay. Then, it's Miss Mud. I'm Miss Augusta Post but please call me Augusta. I welcome you to the Charles Shellington Elementary School.

Augusta, just call me Mud.

Both woman had a laugh and, Ondine—realizing the time—excused herself to leave and teach her next class. During the remainder of the school year and over the next years, Augusta and Ondine continued to chat about Ondine's effectiveness as a teacher as well as other school matters. Their conversations, always in the faculty lounge, became more informal. Ondine seemed to relax as she determined that Augusta showed sincere interest in her as a person. She finally decided to take a chance with Augusta and invite her for dinner to her apartment in the Palmer Park neighborhood. There, they both could relax over drinks and enjoy a good meal together. They might even become more than friendly colleagues at their school.

Palmer Park is an older fashionable neighborhood at the northern end of Detroit. It shares a name with a large public park fronting on Woodward Avenue. At the southern end of the park is a dense cluster of low-rise apartment buildings, some constructed before the Great Depression and others after the Second World War. Unlike the rigid grid of streets that define most of Detroit, Palmer Park's tree-lined streets curve and offer surprising vistas of handsome Art Deco and modernist residences. Ondine's building was one such Art Deco gem. When the warm fall evening for the meal arrived, Augusta found a parking spot a block away from Ondine's apartment building. The leaves were already beginning to turn colors and drop to the ground. Although the evening was warm, Augusta draped her beige cashmere sweater over her shoulders. She walked a block to Ondine's building, buzzed Ondine's apartment, and entered the building taking the elevator to the fourth floor. When the elevator doors opened and Augusta peered in both directions to decide which way to walk in the hallway, she heard Ondine call to her and turned left reaching the door in which stood her host and colleague.

Welcome, Augusta. Come on in.

Delighted, Mud. Thank you for inviting me. This is a beautiful building, and the neighborhood is so quiet.

Do you want to give me your sweater, Augusta? I'll hang it here in the closet. You can leave your purse on the table there if you want.

Thanks, Mud. Umm. Something smells so good.

We'll see how good it is. It's a Middle Eastern dish we're having that I learned in my family. I hope you'll like it.

Well, I love trying new dishes.

Come on into the living room and have a seat. I've put out appetizers— an assortment of olives, three different cheeses, cucumber slices, and hummus.

Hummus? I love hummus.

How do you know about hummus?

I order it sometimes at my favorite Greek restaurant. It's ground chickpeas, olive oil, and spices. It's a Middle Eastern favorite served with pita flat bread.

Well, let me get some pita to go with the hummus. I think we're off to a good start, don't you? What would you like to drink? I've got wine—red and white—beer, and some liquor—scotch, bourbon, vodka, and gin.

What kind of white wine?

It's a Pinot Grigio and chilled.

That's the ticket for me. Bring on the wine.

I'll get some glasses, the wine, and pita. Be back in a moment.

While Ondine went into the kitchen for the wine and pita, Augusta looked around the living room and was impressed with the beautiful array of textiles hanging on the walls, draped over the furniture, and covering the floor. There were also handsome vases, small statues, and delicate glass ornaments. The room was softly lit by table lamps, and a scent of incense subtly infused the air. This was one of the most interesting apartments she had seen in Detroit and all the more surprising because—and she caught herself—it was Ondine's apartment. What did she expect of this woman whom she professed to see beyond mere appearance? Augusta realized she had unconsciously made a lot of negative judgments about Ondine because of the woman's very physical qualities that Augusta professed were attractive. She felt she had to confess her prejudices to Ondine. No. There might be a time for that but it was not now. Ondine returned, poured wine for both of them and sat in a chair opposite Augusta who was seated on the couch.

Augusta, a toast?

To what?

How about to Shellington Elementary?

To Shellington Elementary. Ondine, tell me, where have all of these beautiful things come from?

Really, Augusta, please call me Mud. I like the name.

I'll try but it still sounds like a slur. I just can't bring myself to call you Mud anymore. Ondine is such a beautiful name. It's really you, not Mud.

"Mud" is a slur but I embrace it. It reminds me constantly that I am who I am.

But, Ondine, there are less pejorative ways of identifying yourself.

For instance?

Ebony goddess. Onyx empress. Midnight maiden. Iron princess.

Uh-huh. Let's stick with Ondine if Mud doesn't work for you. Okay? Do you have a nickname?

Funny you should ask. Nobody ever called me by a nickname except my sister, Leona, and even she doesn't use it anymore.

What is it, Augusta?

It's kinda silly.

Okay, but what is it?

Caesar.

Caesar?

Yeah, like Caesar Augustus. Leona called me Caesar Augusta. She must have learned something about Roman Emperors in school. You know what? Roman names run in our family. There's my mother, Clemenza, and sister, Leona. My brothers who live in Hot Springs, Arkansas are Leander and Titus. That's kinda strange, isn't it?

Not so strange. I like Caesar. It fits you as principal.

Yeah, my little empire, Charles Shellington Elementary. So, Ondine, tell me where you acquired these beautiful things in your apartment?

It starts with my family. My father was Egyptian from Nubia in the south of the country where the dark-skinned people of Egypt lived. He managed to enter this country illegally in the 1930s. He knew a lot about cars so he came to Detroit and got some kind of job in an auto repair garage. My mother lived in the neighborhood of the garage and she passed it frequently to and from the apartment where she lived with her parents. Apparently, my father noticed her and, in his limited English, introduced himself as Omar Mahmoud. My mother ignored him at first but the more she saw him, the more interested she became. Her name was Samuella Dash and she was a Negro almost as dark as my father. Anyway, they talked a little because my father's English was very limited. I guess they fell in love, or fell in lust. They started living together, first in my father's rented room, then in a little apartment in a two story building in Black Bottom.

Do you mean near Hastings Street?

Yes, in the neighborhood near Hastings Street and Mack Avenue. You know Hastings was like Main Street for Negroes in Detroit. It had everything. It had grocery stores, shoe and clothing stores, little take-out barbecue and fried fish places, laundries and dry cleaners, storefront churches, movie theaters, hardware stores, car repair shops. It was almost a completely self-contained world for Negroes. Most of the buildings and businesses were owned by whites but Negroes owned or ran a few shops and businesses. I mean there were Negro lawyers and doctors and undertakers. Folks lived in apartments above the commercial shops and there were also rooming houses, whore houses, and some single family homes. When I was born, my parents lived above a law office in a two story building. We had to use a stair in the alley behind the building to enter our apartment. I was the first of their six children.

That's a lot of kids.

Yeah. We were crowded into two rooms.

Two rooms for eight people?

That's right. Our parents slept in the bedroom with the babies and toddlers. The older kids slept on mats in the living room. Girls to one side and boys on the other. We hung sheets between the two sides. My parents made our home seem like a palace. It was very organized, regimented, and clean. Everyone had to stick to my mother's schedule. We were all very disciplined because we learned to care for, and look out for, each other. There were no princesses or princes. And, my memory is

349

that we all accepted our home as a place of love and respect. I think one of the reasons everything worked so well was the fact that my parents never married because my father was an illegal. Everything legal was in my mother's name. She had the power and authority which she used like a queen. She was firm but gracious. She didn't tolerate dissent or abuse but she didn't use punishment to impose order. She used consensus. We had family discussions to define and maintain order and discipline.

So, Ondine, is that is another secret of how you operate your classes?

Correct. That's what I learned in my family and that's what I use with my students. We operate by rules that are enforced by consensus.

Wow. I'm impressed that it works.

Of course, it works, Augusta. Think about it. If you want to break the rules for some reason, no matter how valid your motivations are to you, consensus brings you back into line because the group prevails over the individual.

But the individual has to accept the power of the group. What if the individual defies the group, Ondine?

Then, that individual is given the choice of leaving the group or submitting to it.

I see. So, if an individual chooses to leave, the problem is solved but if the individual stays and only grudgingly accepts the group, what then?

It's not a perfect arrangement because humans are not perfectible beings. There's always some friction.

Okay. I like this. I wish some of your colleagues could learn from you.

Augusta, maybe some will. Maybe we could have a teacher workshop on classroom skills.

Great idea, Ondine. I'll work on it.

Well, how about some dinner now, Caesar Augusta?

My mouth has been watering ever since I entered your apartment. But, tell me something first. If your father never married your mother, how did you get his last name?

I changed my last name legally to honor my father after he died. Officially, I'm Ondine Dash-Mahmoud.

Amazing.

The women moved to the dining area on the other side of the living room near the kitchen, and Augusta took a seat. Ondine went into the galley kitchen and returned with a curious ceramic serving dish that was covered by what looked like a ceramic teepee. She placed it at the center of the table, returned with a tray of other dishes, then sat down opposite Augusta and removed the lid to the serving dish. The aroma of the food inside spread through the room like a perfume.

Augusta, this is called a *tagine*. It's a Middle Eastern dish, a kind of stew. This *tagine* is with lamb, onions, garlic, green olives, carrots and spices like cumin and saffron. It's served with couscous. I also made some sautéed okra as a side dish.

Ondine, this is wonderful. I've had different kinds of food but this is really different. Thank you.

Help yourself and let's see if you really like it.

Augusta served her own plate, sampling the *tagine*, couscous, and okra. Since she was an adventurous eater, she didn't hesitate to taste the various dishes. And, when the flavors and textures had a chance to work their magic, she sat back in her chair and exclaimed her utter delight. Ondine, who had fully expected her guest to enjoy the food was, nevertheless, pleased by her positive response. When the meal was completed and the table was cleared, the women returned to the living room seating and resumed their conversation.

Did you learn to cook from your father?

No, actually I learned from my mom. But she learned to make the dishes my father liked. She found recipes somewhere and cooked his favorite foods. I helped her and learned from working with her.

And how did you decide to become a teacher?

As the oldest of six kids in my family, I was often teaching my siblings practical as well as academic knowledge. You could say that at an early age I was already a teacher. I thought that would be a good fit for me professionally. I had to work in order to go to college because, by the time I graduated high school, my dad was dead and my mother was too old and tired to work. We lived on welfare and aid to dependent children. We were poor, really poor but we kids were focussed on making something of ourselves. I liked learning about how to educate and work with young kids, like I did with my siblings. It seemed the natural way to go. What about you?

Well, that's a story. Teaching was not my first interest. I wanted to be an artist, a painter in fact. I had a keen interest and talent when I was a child. My mother didn't know anything about art and didn't know how to encourage me. But, when I started school, my teachers saw I had an instinctive artistic ability. I had materials in school to make drawings and paintings. I guess what I made really impressed my teachers, and I enjoyed what I was doing. All through grade school and high school I was drawing and painting and sometimes trying sculpting and photography but painting was my real desire. When I decided to go to college, I wanted to study art but my mother told me that would not help me get a job. She was insistent I had to prepare myself to work and maybe support myself unless I got married. Well, marriage was not my chief concern. I just wanted to paint. So, when I began college, I did what my mother wanted and studied English. I got my degree and started substitute teaching in the public schools. My heart wasn't in it but that was what my mother wanted. I did that for about ten years. However, during that time, I decided to study art with the idea of starting a career as an artist. My mother was furious and told me I would end up on the streets whoring to stay alive.

Augusta, that was a fairly extreme reaction and conclusion.

"Fairly extreme reaction and conclusion" is an understatement. You would have to know my mother and her background. She was speaking from her own experience. She was afraid I would become what she had become. She yelled and screamed at me all the time. She cried and cried. I almost gave in to her. But I felt I had to do what I wanted and so I began night classes. It was liberating. I loved the classes and the teachers. I was learning so much about observing the world around me. And about studying the faces and bodies of people. And about understanding how artists through the ages represented their worlds in painting. I had one teacher, a white man actually, who really encouraged me. He pointed out things he thought were really exceptional in my work and things that didn't succeed as well. I felt his concern and honesty. I pushed myself hard and got into all of the student exhibitions and got lots of good responses. I thought I had made the right decision. I would become a professional artist.

Did you?

I tried. Really, I tried but I couldn't get into the art galleries in Detroit. No one was interested in a Negro woman artist not even Negro male artists. I wasn't one of the boys and I was a Negro. There was nothing in Detroit to encourage or support me. My mother couldn't stop telling me she told me what would happen. I was still determined to prove I could succeed and that she was wrong.

What happened then?

I went to New York for two years. It was difficult, very difficult. I had to find crappy jobs just to live. I had no real space to paint. I did what I could in my room in Harlem. I tried to find a gallery that would show my work. But, like Detroit, there was no interest. I couldn't even get into improvised exhibits that male Negro artists organized in Harlem. They didn't want a woman, at least not this woman. Nobody did. Quite simply, a Negro female was less than nothing in a male world, black or white.

At least, Augusta, you were probably considered attractive if not beautiful. I mean a fair-skinned woman with a good figure and lots of personality must have turned guys on.

Oh, yes. They thought I was attractive but my talent was useless.

Imagine not even being considered attractive and you have me, Miss Mud.

Ondine, I get it. I really get it.

So, what did you do?

I came back to Detroit and returned to the public schools as an English teacher. That's how I ended up at Shellington Elementary. It's a familiar story, right?

Too familiar.

But, you know what? I learned a lot from that experience. For one thing I learned about Negro women who had been artists in the past and some who are working even now. I also talked with a lot of Africans who came to this country. They told me things about Africa that I never learned about here. I began reading everything I could get my hands on. I discovered African cultures that were as important as any elsewhere in the world. This cultural history made me a better teacher. I wanted to be a teacher who could fill the void of knowledge of my Negro students about their African ancestry. I wanted to counter the negative messages they've received about themselves from their own biased and racist country.

Here's to knowing our place but doing something positive to change it.

The women finished their wine. It was now becoming late and Augusta mentioned she should be heading home. She thanked Ondine for a delicious meal and a chance to get to know her better. She hoped that next time Ondine would come to her apartment. She admitted she wasn't as good or creative a cook as Ondine but she would provide something tasty and filling and, of course, plenty to drink. The women said their goodbyes and parted. On her way home, Augusta thought about the delightful evening. She even realized Ondine was becoming, in her mind, more than the physical person she presented. She was a genuinely lovely young woman. For the first time in a long time, Augusta wanted to make a portrait—of Ondine. She decided she would ask Ondine to pose for her. She still had most of her painting equipment in a basement storeroom of her apartment building and could set up an area to paint in her living room if she put a drop cloth on her carpet. She hoped Ondine would be willing to pose. As she reached her apartment in Lafayette Park and thinking about resuming painting, her attention shifted from Ondine to her niece, Obra-Jean. Was Obra-Jean headed for the same disappointments Augusta had experienced? Were Leona's fears about her daughter's interest in architecture well founded? Was Augusta's encouragement of Obra-Jean a sentence to failure? As she approached the parking lot of her building, she remembered her niece's enthusiasm for the buildings in Europe, how passionately she observed and tried to understand architecture. Passion was a good thing, wasn't it?

Augusta wanted to make good on her promise to have Ondine to dinner at her apartment. She decided to make a party of it and realized that she could also celebrate Leona's birthday as well. So, in addition to Ondine and Leona, Augusta invited her mother, Clemenza, her nieces, Toby and Obra-Jean, and her nephew, E.J. Everyone accepted except E.J. who had a date with his girlfriend, Vergie. Toby asked if she could bring her roommate, Ronnie, who now preferred her given name, India. Augusta had already planned for six guests and welcomed India in place of E.J. She would prepare a buffet, and everyone could serve themselves. Since she was not, as she admitted, such a good cook, she decided to have dinner catered by her favorite soul food restaurant. There would be an array of Southern dishes, including fried chicken, fried fish and shrimp, collard greens, green beans, stewed cabbage, mashed potatoes, sweet potatoes, baked macaroni and cheese, biscuits, and a chocolate cake for dessert with strawberry ice cream. She was sure everyone would get their fill and folks could take the leftovers home. There wouldn't be a lot of work for Augusta so she could attend to serving drinks and actively participating in conversations.

The night of the party was an unusually cold Saturday evening in November. An early winter snowstorm the night before covered the city making car and foot travel treacherous. A ground crew had cleared the snow from the guest parking lot and shoveled the walkways leading to Augusta's building. Augusta's guests arrived with heavy coats, scarves, and hats that Augusta arrayed on her bed. She asked everyone to leave their boots in the building's hallway and place their birthday presents for Leona on the credenza next to the dining room table. Perhaps, because everyone except Ondine had been to Augusta's apartment previously, the family members arrived early. Leona drove her mother and younger daughter. Toby came with India who drove them both in her car. As everyone was getting settled and sampling the appetizers, Ondine rang the intercom. Augusta buzzed her in and a few minutes later Ondine knocked on the apartment door. Augusta welcomed her inside and introduced her to her family as she took Ondine's coat, hat, gloves, and scarf. Ondine recognized Toby at once and said she remembered her from their jobs in the university's administration building. Leona invited Ondine to join her on the couch where Obra-Jean also sat. Augusta finished taking orders for drinks, served them, and positioned herself in a chair that closed the circle of guests. Small conversational couples and groups formed. Leona and Ondine having introduced themselves to each other, Leona introduced her daughter to Ondine who turned to Obra-Jean.

I understand you're a student at Wayne State University now, Obra-Jean.

Yes, Ma'am.

Please call me Ondine or Mud which is a nickname some of my friends call me.

Mud?

Yes, I know, it sounds like an ugly name but I like it.

I'll call you Ondine. Okay?

Sure. No problem. What are you studying?

Right now I'm taking art classes my first year of college at Wayne but next year I hope to enter the University of Detroit School of Architecture.

Why didn't you start college at U of D instead of at Wayne?

Well, that's because of a couple of things. My mother is paying for my first year of college and she could only afford to send me to Wayne but Wayne doesn't have an architecture school. She was not happy about me taking art and she's really not happy about me studying architecture. But I've applied to U of D and asked for financial support. If I'm accepted and get a scholarship, I'll start architecture classes next year.

That's very interesting. A female architect. Good for you.

My mother isn't happy about my plans because she thinks I should study something that will guarantee me a future job. That's why in high school at Cass Tech I was in the science curriculum. But, I became interested in art as a way to better prepare for architecture.

Your mother may be right. It won't be easy for you to become something that hardly any Negro woman I know of has ever been. But, I have to say, I think all of us have to try and break barriers. I would encourage my students to do what they think they want to do only after they've considered the pluses and minuses. After all, we have to calculate the risks as well as the possible rewards. What do you think, Leona?

Obra-Jean knows I don't approve. She's smart and, I guess, she has talent but I would rather see someone else's daughter try what she wants to do. I want my daughter to have a good life and I don't believe architecture will do that for her.

Mom, I've thought about that but I know I can do well in architecture school. My college counselor advised me about preparatory courses. She told me there aren't very many women in architecture, white or Negro, but she agrees someone has to try and change that. Someone has to take that chance.

Obra-Jean, look at your Aunt Augusta. She thought she could be an artist and she had to give it up. Thank goodness, she found a practical career in teaching.

Well, Mom, if I can't succeed as an architect, I could always change later on and do something else too just like Aunt Augusta.

But look at all of the time and money your aunt wasted following an impossible dream. Why can't you learn from her?

If I may say so, Leona, impossible dreams are what keep some people going. Now, I was also taught to be practical. But, as you can see with your own eyes, my problem is that people see me in a certain way as one who doesn't fit in. Please excuse my fat butt on this couch. So, even though I followed a safe path, I had no guarantee I would succeed simply because I look a certain way. And, don't kid yourself or me, Leona. I know how I look and how people see me and I'm okay with it.

I'm happy for you, Ondine, because I guess I'm one of those people.

Forget about it, Leona. I know, in my own mind, I'm not how people see me. You don't have to feel bad that you feel the way you feel. You know, I knew your daughter Toby when we worked in the same university office. She's as beautiful as you are. I guess all of the women in your family are beautiful. And, I used to stare at her because I thought she was so pretty. But, at the time, I couldn't bring myself to try and be friends with her.

You never became friends, Ondine?

Uh, no. Not really. She tried to talk to me once at work but we never became friends. I've had to do a lot of work on myself. I had to realize some people can really like a person because they have the capacity to see more than just how they look.

Ondine, I'm flattered you think me and my girls are beautiful.

Don't you think that's so, Leona?

I guess men have always found me attractive.

And women too. Come on, Leona, you're kidding yourself and me again. Admit that you're beautiful. Why not?

Okay, I admit it.

And you like being beautiful, yes?

Yes, Ondine, I like the fact that men look at me but that's as far as it goes.

Well, we've crossed that bridge. Now, how about Obra-Jean? Shouldn't she go for architecture?

Ondine, you're a teacher. Tell me, why she should waste her life on something that very likely won't work out for her?

Leona, why is it a waste of her life if she's being who she is? What if I had said to myself I'll never succeed because I'm not beautiful? I would probably be dead by now.

Excuse me, Ondine, for saying so but you can't help how you look. Obra-Jean does have a choice about what she wants to be.

You're right, Leona. But Obra-Jean's choices come down to what she wants, not what you or someone else thinks she should want.

You remind me now of my late husband. He said the same thing to me about Obra-Jean.

So, maybe we're right, Leona?

I'm not there yet. I'm really afraid for my daughter. Do you hear that, Obra-Jean? I am afraid for you. I don't want you to be hurt, disappointed or crushed. That's what this world can do to you. Ondine knows that as well as me. Do you think you're strong enough for what the world has in store for you?

Yes, Mom. Don't be fooled. Your daughter is tough. I'm ready for the battle.

Spoken like someone, Obra-Jean, who doesn't know what this world can really be like.

Mom, this is 1961. We've got a new, young president who wants young people to try new things. I'm eighteen and not a child anymore. Let go of seeing me as a child. In case you haven't noticed, I know how to get around. I know how to take care of myself and take care of anybody who wants to mess with me. I'm aware of a lot more than you think. Someday I just might tell you a few things that could surprise you.

Leona looked at her daughter as if she were seeing a stranger. She had a unsettling feeling that this Obra-Jean was not the daughter she gave birth to and raised. This was someone else's daughter who just might walk right over you. In fact, if Leona could overcome her feelings, she would have realized that Obra-Jean was more like herself than she could ever admit.

While everyone was chatting, Augusta returned to the kitchen to bring out the serving dishes. Clemenza followed to offer her help. While both women were in the kitchen working silently—they both knew the routine—Augusta glanced at her mother. It was as if she were really seeing her for the first time. This small, plain, dark-skinned woman was her mother. She worked so assuredly and economically with no wasted motions. She worked as if this were her kitchen and she knew everything about it. When all was ready, she asked Augusta if she needed help taking the dishes to the dinner table. August leaned over to Clemenza and kissed her on the cheek. Clemenza leaned into Augusta's body and rested her head on Augusta. It was just a moment and it passed. Both women carried the dishes to the dinner table and Augusta then arranged everything along with silverware, napkins, and water glasses. Once the table was ready, Obra-Jean and Leona were first to fill their plates with food. Meanwhile, Ondine walked over to Toby and India who were still sitting and waiting their turn to fix their plates. India introduced herself. Toby expressed surprise to see Ondine again after four years. Ondine smiled and then, leaning close to Toby, mentioned that she would like to talk with her after the meal. Clemenza asked the women to help themselves and soon everyone had food. The conversation languished during the meal but resumed as everyone finished eating. Leona then invited India to join her and Obra-Jean on the couch. Ondine remained seated in a chair next to Toby. Clemenza returned to the kitchen to help Augusta with the dishes and to prepare packages of food for everyone to take home.

Toby, I hear you graduated from business school. It's an interesting choice.

You know, Mud, that's quite a story. I decided to study business when you and I were working in the university administration offices. It's something that never occurred to me. I didn't know any Negroes in business. Our supervisor suggested I might do well in it and now I'm working as an accountant at a company downtown.

Which one?

You probably never heard of it. Hawley, Smith, and Thompson, Associates. It's a low level position but I think I can work my way up to something better.

I'm sure you can.

You're teaching at Aunt Augusta's school?

363

That's right. She's a great principal.

And I hear you're a terrific teacher, Mud.

I'm not going to fake any modesty here. I am a great teacher but I've learned a lot from Augusta. For one thing, she's helped me to be more gracious and that's what I want to talk to you about. I owe you an apology.

For what? The fact that you used to stare at me?

Not that but I'm sorry, Toby, if I might have upset you. I thought you were so pretty.

I wanted to be friends with you. I thought we could get something going but it never worked out and I don't know why.

Toby, I couldn't believe someone as beautiful as you could be friends with me.

You embarrass me, Mud. Thank you for the compliment but I thought you were stunning.

Come on.

Really, Mud, I thought you knew. Everything you probably thought of negatively about yourself, I thought was spectacular. I guess I felt you pushed me away.

You make me laugh, Toby. Pushed you away? I thought I was out of your league.

I was powerfully attracted to you. I thought I could persuade you to be friends. You see, I thought it was my fault for being too pushy. But, listen, Mud, let's let that go. We're both different now and we can start from now with a different relationship.

Let's try it. How about we get together for lunch sometime?

That's good.

Do you want to include your roommate?

India? She's not my roommate. She's my girlfriend.

You're a couple?

Yes, we got together a little while after I met you.

Augusta never mentioned anything to me about your relationship.

Mud, I wouldn't be surprised. Nobody in this family talks about it. They would prefer to stick with the roommate story.

You can understand why they wouldn't talk about the two of you as a couple, can't you?

Of course, I understand but I don't like it. There's nothing wrong with being lesbians.

Most people don't see it that way.

Are you most people, Mud?

I'm a "live and let live" person. I don't have a hangup about a woman loving another woman or even a man loving another man.

Did you believe that when we first met?

Toby, I wasn't the person then that I am now. I've learned a few things since then. When you look like me, it's hard to believe that a beautiful woman could be interested in me. I guess we were both limited by our perceptions.

I guess we were. Talk about limitations. That has been the problem forever between me and my mother and between my mother and my sister. My mother's limitations make her a very disapproving parent.

I'm not surprised. I found out this evening she doesn't approve of a lot of things. But you know what? She's genuine. I don't know how she got to be the way she is but she's strong and loving. If she wasn't, she wouldn't care what you or your sister do. Love like hers can damage a child if they aren't strong in themselves. If they are strong, like you and your sister, they can avoid or overcome a lot of damage. But the absence of love is, in my opinion, more damaging than too much love, and probably irreversible. I see the effects in the kids I teach and I try to help them learn, of course, but also to heal. You and your sister are lucky. I don't know but I think that Leona was not as lucky as you.

Do you mean with her mother?

Yes, I do.

So you know the story?

Augusta told me about their mother and about Leona's relationship with her.

I feel really sorry for Grandma. My mother has never been nice to her.

Maybe you can do something about that.

How?

I don't know but think about it. By the way, I hear that your girlfriend is a lawyer.

Yeah. Now that's another interesting story. When India and I first got together, she was interested in art. I don't think she planned to be an artist. In fact, I don't think she had any kind of plan. But, while she was taking art classes, she also enrolled in a few art history courses and discovered she loved it. I mean she loved learning about different art periods and artists but then she became fascinated with researching history for her term papers. It was investigation and putting together facts to argue a point of view that made her think about legal work. Maybe at first she thought she might be an art historian. But she decided to use research and her ability to argue to help people, not teach or entertain them. I think her motivation came from her family and that's how she became a lawyer.

I'll bet she's a good lawyer.

She's fierce. You should talk to her sometime. Oh, here comes grandma. Grandma, come sit here with me and Ondine.

Hello, Missus Post. I was talking with Leona and your granddaughters. You have such a lovely family.

Thank you, Ondine. They're beautiful women. I don't know how so much beauty came from me.

Beauty is not just appearances, Missus Post. The Post and Moore women are beautiful inside.

That's nice for you to say but I don't feel beautiful inside or out.

I would love to talk to you about that, Missus Post. Could I come to visit you sometime? Maybe, we could go out for lunch or dinner?

You want to visit with an old lady?

To me you are more than an old lady. You're the head of a family. I no longer have a mother or father. There are some siblings but they have scattered all across the country. It's hard to keep in contact. I admire your family and you for having so much to do with who they are.

Ondine, I'm not sure all of my family would agree with you.

Maybe not, but that's how I feel and that's why I want to visit with you. So, can we make a date?

I would like that. It would be nice.

Augusta announced to her guests that it was time for the birthday cake after which Leona could open her presents. Clemenza brought the chocolate-frosted cake from the kitchen. To celebrate Leona's forty-fifth birthday, there were four big candles—one for each decade—and one small candle for five years. Clemenza placed the cake on the coffee table in front of Leona and lit the candles. Everyone joined in singing "Happy

368

Birthday." Leona made a wish and blew out the candles. Clemenza then removed the cake to the dining room table where she sliced and plated the wedges that were then served to the women. Augusta retrieved several gift-wrapped packages with envelopes that were on the credenza and placed them on the coffee table in front of Leona. Leona smiled and reached for the largest package. Carefully removing the gift wrapping and opening the attached envelope, she read out loud the birthday card inside. It contained one of those treacly greeting card messages but also a more personal handwritten expression of love from her sister. Inside the box was an expensive beige cashmere sweater that Leona oohed and aahed over. She thanked her sister repeatedly and accepted a kiss on the cheek. The next package was somewhat smaller and carried an envelope with a birthday card from Toby and India. Toby wrote a surprisingly frank statement of love for "a tough but caring mother." The gift was a turquoise silk blouse that caused Leona to wipe away tears. Both Toby and India kissed Leona on the cheek. Leona next picked up a small wrapped package. Inside the package was a black silk scarf with a card from Obra-Jean that simply said: "Thanks for everything, Mom." Leona kissed Obra-Jean who was sitting next to her. Obra-Jean did not return the kiss. The smallest box had no card. When Leona opened it, she found inside a note and a diamond pendant on a gold chain nested in cotton filler. The note and pendant were a gift from Clemenza. The note, which Leona read aloud in a halting voice, said: "For my dear daughter." Leona started to cry. When she finally regained her composure, she thanked her mother and clutched the pendant to her chest. Clemenza nodded the acknowledgement. Finally, one envelope remained. It was from Ondine and the card inside contained a check for one hundred dollars. Leona was stunned. The handwritten greeting read: "There is nothing like a loving mother." Ondine kissed Leona on the cheek while cupping her chin with her hand. With all of her gifts opened, Leona thanked everyone again.

It was getting late and Leona wanted to drive Obra-Jean back to her grandparents house before heading home herself with Clemenza. Toby and India also wanted to leave; there was a new jazz club they wanted to check out. Everyone retrieved their coats and accessories, said their goodbyes to Augusta and left the apartment. Ondine stayed behind.

Can I help you clean up, Augusta?

Sure. Bring the glasses into the kitchen. Well, what do you think of my family?

I think they're wonderful. All of you are very lucky.

How so?

These are strong women like you. The younger ones are going places and doing things. I think your sister is going to find a new life without her husband or daughters. She's a good mother and I'll bet she'll make someone a good partner.

You're more optimistic than I am. My sister can be a piece of work. I love her but she tests my limits.

How so?

She can be so rigid. She won't consider alternatives.

I sensed tonight she might come around about Obra-Jean wanting to be an architect.

She might. But that's not what bothers me. It's her attitude about our mother.

And about you?

Why do you add me?

She's jealous of you.

You've noticed. She admits it. It's crazy. I don't have anything more than she has. Less, in fact. I don't have a husband or children.

But you had the mother she didn't have. She believes you had love she never had. Haven't you noticed that?

Leona's been playing that tune for as long as I can remember. Now, I just ignore her. Our mother loves us both, in her own way. My Aunt Iris who raised Leona loved her as a daughter. Leona always seems to forget that important detail.

That's how it seems to you. Leona didn't feel that way when it probably mattered most her. She was young and left behind in Hot Springs.

But, Leona later came to Detroit and married Perry.

But she was left behind in Hot Springs. She felt abandoned.

She was with relatives. Loving relatives.

She felt abandoned by her mother.

Abandoned? Our mother didn't abandon her. She wrote her. We both wrote her.

Augusta, if you can't understand the feeling of abandonment, you will never understand her or why she treats your mother the way she does.

There's a lot more to it than love and abandonment. But, that's another story for another time.

Okay. Well, it is getting late and I should be on my way. Thank you for a wonderful evening. The food was delicious. The company was interesting. And I really appreciate how you've welcomed me into your family.

My pleasure. We'll do it again soon. Can I give you a little kiss goodbye?

You can give me a big kiss goodbye. And a hug?

A hug coming up. Umm. You are a good kisser.

So are you. How about another?

I thought you wouldn't ask.

The women embraced in a long, passionate kiss then stood silently facing one another but holding hands.

Uh. Ondine, this is a little awkward but would you consider spending the night? I know it messes with a lot of work stuff and rules and on and on but—pardon me for being so direct—I would love to take you to bed.

I thought you wouldn't ask.

Both started laughing to break the awkwardness of the moment but also in response to the rising anticipation. Augusta led Ondine to the bedroom but asked if she first wanted to use the bathroom. Ondine thought for a moment and decided she would. When she came out of the bathroom, she was wearing only her underwear—black panties and matching bra that seemed to disappear on her dark body. She carried her clothes and asked where she might put them. Augusta took her things and arranged them neatly on a chair in the bedroom. She then undressed while Ondine slipped off her undergarments. Augusta decided she needed to use the bathroom too and disappeared momentarily only to return to the bedroom and find Ondine in bed. She reminded Augusta of a Rubens's nude and a black French odalisque reclining sensuously on the white sheets. Augusta lay beside her and couldn't resist running her hand over Ondine's smooth, lustrous, ebony skin. Ondine reciprocated touching Augusta's supple flesh. The women embraced bringing their bodies together like a book closing flat. Augusta moved her hand lower on Ondine's body from her ample breasts and belly to the V formed by her legs and torso. She felt the soft patch of curly hair at Ondine's groin and then with her finger began rubbing her sex. She felt Ondine's body relax as if inviting Augusta to continue. Augusta moved her head slowly towards her finger as it penetrated Ondine. When she was looking directly at Ondine's crotch, she lowered her head and replaced her finger with her tongue. The effect was like an electric shock. Ondine shook and writhed. Augusta knew she had scored. After a short rest, Ondine reciprocated with Augusta until she murmured with pleasure. Afterwards, they both had a good night's sleep.

In the morning—it was Sunday—Augusta made breakfast for them—toast, eggs, and bacon. While they were eating, Augusta broached the subject of painting Ondine's portrait. Ondine smiled and asked if it was to be a nude portrait. Augusta considered the response and replied that the first portrait would be of Ondine's head and shoulders. Maybe, if the first try was successful, another full body nude would be necessary. The women continued talking about the birthday party, their school and, finally, their night of sexual pleasure.

Augusta, this clearly was not your first time. So, what's the story?

Well, it wasn't your first time either. So, I want to hear your story as well. But, here's mine. I guess I was always attracted to women but I thought that was because I never found a man who turned me on.

Do you mean to say that you ignored your attraction to women while waiting for the right man?

That's how I felt. I was sure if the right man came along, I wouldn't be attracted to women.

Okay, then what?

Well, New York City is what. I was living in Harlem trying to break into the art scene. I think I told you about that some time ago.

Yes, and when I suggested that men might be attracted to you, you said yes and didn't mention anything about women.

Right, Ondine, but let's be clear. You didn't ask about women being attracted to me.

Would you have told me, if I had asked?

Good question and I don't know the answer. It's not something that I've talked to many people about. In fact, I've never discussed it with my sister although she seems to suspect something perhaps because of Toby and India and the fact that I haven't had a boyfriend in decades.

What happened in New York, Augusta?

There was another gal about my age who was also an artist. She also lived in Harlem. We would see each other at different events in Harlem. We kinda circulated in the same crowd. She was a kind of bohemian very in tune with the Harlem art scene. I was very attracted to her, I thought, because of her somewhat eccentric character and appearance. She wore her hair natural. She dressed in jeans and work shirts and wore men's boots. One night we were at a party in some artist's apartment in Harlem. We were drinking and smoking marijuana—yes, I smoked—and I felt an urge to put my arm around her. She kind of snuggled up to me and something just went wild inside of me. I felt a rush of excitement and I knew it was sexual. Eventually, we got together and had sex and that was how it all started for me.

So, there were women after her?

Yes, in New York and here in Detroit. Oh, and a one night stand in Madrid. What about you?

I knew I was attracted only to women very early on. But, women didn't seem attracted to me. In fact, no one looked at me with what I would consider interest until I met your niece.

Toby?

Yes. We worked in the same office at Wayne. We sat near each other but never spoke. I stared at her because she was so damn beautiful. One day during a coffee break, she came over to me and introduced herself. After that, I kind of stalked her. Don't laugh. I did. I was waiting for an opportunity to talk to her alone without other people around. I invited her to coffee. We talked and something happened between us. We took a streetcar to Palmer Park and walked through the woods. When we thought we were alone, we kissed and hugged. That was it. I couldn't believe that this beautiful woman was attracted to me. I was upset so I told her we should leave the park. I stupidly decided not to see her again.

That was when Toby and India first got together?

I guess so. I didn't know about India at the time but it didn't matter. My head wasn't screwed on right.

What happened after Toby?

There were a couple of women but no real attraction or feeling, not until last night.

I'm glad you saved yourself for me. I really like you.

I like you too.

— The Story of Cairo —

Following their first intimate encounter, Augusta and Ondine regularly stayed the night in one another's apartment enjoying the warmth of intimacy. They didn't discuss their relationship with anyone else at school or in Augusta's family. Augusta was reluctant to tell her sister or her mother about the nature of her relationship. She told herself it was none of their business. Augusta and Ondine didn't, in fact, discuss their relationship with each other. They were lovers who enjoyed one another but had their separate lives partly out of discretion and partly to avoid discussing something that was still wrapped in taboos. There was never mention of living together. No one questioned them about their friendship because most folks were willing to believe that it was simply a close friendship of school colleagues. However, some had their suspicions.

Augusta had a list of countries she wanted to visit with Ondine including Japan, Turkey, Morocco, and Egypt. Since Ondine's late father was Egyptian, she asked Ondine if she had ever thought of visiting that country. To her surprise, Ondine replied that she had been to Egypt during the summer of 1958 following her graduation from Wayne and before she began working at Shellington Elementary. Her father's family had a small but prosperous export business in Cairo involving spices. Since his family had maintained contact with Ondine's mother after the death of her husband, they had a general idea of the state of Ondine's family. They were very proud that, despite the poverty of her family, Ondine was a university student who would soon graduate and become a teacher. They wanted to meet this illustrious daughter of their deceased relative and offered to pay for her visit to Cairo. Ondine needed no persuasion. She booked her flight to arrive in Cairo at the beginning of August. On the plane, she became anxious for the first time. What would these people be like? How would they react to her? How would they communicate? Would she have to dress like an Egyptian woman? When the plane landed at the Cairo airport in Heliopolis, Ondine's concerns doubled and tripled. She began to regret having agreed to this visit without considering all of these issues in advance. As she entered the airport's reception hall after retrieving her suitcase and passing through customs and immigration, she saw a small group of men and women looking expectantly in her direction. One man held a sign that said: "Mahmoud Fayez." She nearly cried. In fact, as she approached the group, she did cry because she recognized that these people looked just like her. They were big and black. The men stood at the front of the group. Several women in long robes and headscarves stood behind them.

The men bowed slightly to Ondine and stepped aside as three women rushed forward and embraced Ondine who couldn't understand anything that anybody said. However, the joy was real and needed no translation. In the hubbub of the moment, a man stepped forward to Ondine and introduced himself in English as Fahim. He had written the letters for the family although he was not a member of the family. He was a neighbor and friend. Fahim explained that they would take several taxis from the airport to a neighborhood near the center of the city. For the next week, she would live with the women of the family in their quarters. They would provide her the proper clothing. She should not wear Western dress in public. He would escort her for any visits they might make to the Great Pyramids or other sites she might like to visit. However, most of her stay would be with the women. Fortunately, one of the younger women, a daughter of one of her uncles, spoke some English and she would assist Ondine for most of her visit. All of Ondine's trepidations evaporated in an instant. She was with family. She didn't know any of these people but she knew that she belonged. She was not the outsider, the oddity, or the misfit. She was with people who saw her as one of them.

Ondine's uncle, Ashraf, and his two adult sons, Ramy and Maat, were the three men who met her at the airport. The three women were her aunt, Nawal, and two adult daughters, Nour and Jana. There were many things that surprised her but the first and biggest surprise was to learn that the family name was not "Mahmoud," as she had believed all of her life, but "Fayez." Fahim eventually explained to her that Ondine's father never used his family name but instead referred to himself as Omar Mahmoud, as if Mahmoud was his family name. Well, Ondine thought, she had wanted to name herself in honor of her father but it really didn't matter that she didn't know his actual family name. Mahmoud was good enough.

What Ondine could not, and in fact did not, imagine was her life in Cairo. Nothing was as she imagined it. Although the women observed the prayers and customs of their Muslim faith, they laughed and joked with Ondine even though she could only learn what amused them by translation. She worked side by side with them as they cleaned, shopped, and cooked. She watched food preparation very closely and tried her best to learn the names of the spices used in various dishes. The women wanted to know everything about her. They were fascinated that she attended a university since the female Caireens had only attended elementary school. When she explained that she would become a teacher and work side by side with men as well as with women, they were astonished. They wanted to know more about her family. What had happened to her father and mother? Where were her sisters and brother? Where did she live? They wanted to see the clothes she brought with her. With some embarrassment and amusement, they tried on Ondine's clothes. Ondine decided to let them keep most of what she brought with her and retain only what she needed for the return flight to Detroit.

Her excursions outside the walls of the family home in central Cairo were few. Fahim did take her to see the Pyramids of Giza, the Great Sphinx, and the Pyramid of Saqqara at Djoser. She did have the opportunity to visit markets with the women when they shopped for meals. Perhaps the most unexpected visits were again with the women, but accompanied by the men, to the local mosque for religious services. The segregation of the sexes after a few days seemed natural to her although she constantly checked her instinct to assert herself as a woman. She told herself she was in a different country with a different culture and customs, and this was her family. She needed to be respectful not assertive. She was not the Ondine of Detroit who used her appearance as a shield and weapon. She fit in here. No one saw her as different. The women were as black as she, as big, and, in a moment of pure revelation, as beautiful. She was looking into the mirror of her distant female relatives and she saw herself and them as perfectly marvelous. They were glorious sisters.

The week ended all too quickly for Ondine. She was on the plane returning home before she completely realized how extraordinary the week had been. Something quite fundamental had changed for her. While she had learned in her own family to be self-reliant and confident of her abilities, she had never been able to see herself as attractive because she had accepted as fact that beautiful was something she was not. She saw beautiful women all the time and they didn't look like herself or her siblings. During the past week in the cloistered home of her relatives among a group of women who looked like her and saw their own beauty, she could begin to fully and unapologetically accept herself. No one could judge her on any account because she was her own judge and she passed the test on all counts. She was ready to start a new life. This life now included Augusta and her family.

— Art & Nature —
Fall 1961 to Fall 1963

Augusta kept her word to Ondine and brought all of her painting gear out of her storage area in the basement of her apartment building. During one of Ondine's stay-overs, Augusta coaxed Ondine to sit for a portrait. Augusta had prepared a smallish canvas she placed on her easel. In order for Augusta to look directly ahead at Ondine, she posed Ondine on one of the stools from a counter separating the kitchen from the living room. She asked Ondine to relax and assume a pose she could easily return to for however long it took to complete the painting. Then, she explained that they would work in twenty minute bursts of activity followed by a ten minute break. Augusta would paint for perhaps three or four hours total. If the portrait seemed finished at that time, then they were done. If it needed more work, they would continue in another session at a later date. Ondine understood and assumed a pose that was relaxed but staring directly at Augusta. Augusta started the painting with a quick outline in black oil paint to determine the scale, shape, and positioning of the oval head and squarish shoulders on a rectangular canvas. Once she was satisfied with the proportions and composition, she began noting Ondine's facial features—her short nose with flaring nostrils, her small, full-lipped mouth, and sloping, cat-like eyes. These she defined by applying various colors to establish the skin tones and their relationship to the background of her subject. Augusta worked quickly but often stopped and simply stood back from the painting to observe its evolution. By the end of three hours, she had achieved a substantial representation of Ondine. However, she noticed several inaccuracies in the facial features and their proportions. She told Ondine they would have to continue another day to give the paint a chance to dry. The following weekend, the portrait sitting resumed. Augusta made many corrections according to her earlier analysis. Still something was amiss. The painting looked like Ondine but it didn't capture her liveliness or her true beauty. Again, Augusta stepped back and finally sat down and examined the painting and compared it in every way to Ondine who remained in pose. Augusta realized that analysis was not what was needed now but to give herself over to the painting by letting her unconscious actions direct the process. She picked up her brushes and painted without controlling the process. She simply let her impulses take over. This freedom from the mind's control transformed the painting into a less accurate representation of Ondine but captured a truer expression of her being. Augusta stopped and declared the work finished. Ondine took a look and kissed Augusta on the cheek. There would be more portraits later including full-body nudes.

During the next few years, Ondine and Augusta frequently met in the faculty lounge between their classes. Several other teachers were present. One was listening to music on a transistor radio. Whenever other faculty were present, Augusta addressed Ondine more formally. Ondine inquired of Obra-Jean's progress in the architecture school at the University of Detroit. It was now her third year of study and all reports were very positive. Augusta explained that Obra-Jean was at the top of her class and showed great promise as a designer. She had a inherent feeling for architecture and a passion for buildings that impressed her instructors.

Ondine, you know, I always had faith in my niece because I knew she would prosper once she had the chance to do things the way she wanted. I think I contributed in a way by taking her on her first trip to Europe. Now, she's receiving awards and commendations for her student work. She's gotten stipends to travel to see important buildings in other cities around the country. Already she's been to Boston and Chicago, Saint Louis and Los Angeles. She's filled a pile of sketchbooks with studies of buildings. She's taken, I think, hundreds of photos. And, her drawings are beautiful. They're very detailed and, yet, somehow, I don't know, poetic. You get a great feeling for the character of a building. Just between us, I think her fellow students are jealous that she's attracting so much attention. She's really the star of her school.

I can see why you're proud of her. I hope when she finishes school, she gets the same kind of encouragement in the real world.

Well, you know, I hate to admit but I worry about that. My sister is often wrong about her children but, in this case, I think she might be right that Obra-Jean is too far ahead of the times. Sure, someday, there will be Negro women everywhere but that doesn't seem to be true right now. I thought the Reverend King's march on Washington would change things. But change is slower than a snail with a boulder strapped to its back.

But it happens, slow as it is. By the way, I was thinking of inviting Clemenza to lunch. We haven't had a chance to talk and spend some time together in ages.

Clemenza would love to see you. She told me after your last visit together that she felt like she had rejoined the world. You know my sister is mellowing a little towards her. But, she just can't seem to bring herself to completely let the past be past. If only she could open her heart, I think she, more than our mother, would benefit. So, yes, I believe Clemenza would love to go to lunch again. It would be very kind of you to invite her. I . . . uh . . . um. Wait. Hold on a minute. What was that I heard on the radio? Ondine, did you just hear someone say they were interrupting the music for a special announcement?

Yes. Someone is talking on the radio.

What is he saying?

They shot the president.

Oh my god. No.

Lord help us.

— Ladies at Lunch —
Spring 1964

Ondine belatedly kept her word and invited Clemenza to Sunday brunch. The YWCA near the east-side of downtown had a large cafeteria where, in contrast to many of Detroit's more popular eateries, blacks felt welcomed. In addition, the food was fresh and delicious and there was a wide array of choices. Ondine drove to Leona's house, retrieved Clemenza, and headed to the "Y." After they made their food selections from the steam tables—Clemenza chose only a bowl of bean soup, a small tossed green salad, and a bowl of strawberry Jello—they found a table away from other customers.

I love your dress, Missus Post.

Baby, please call me Clemenza.

I keep forgetting. It's an old habit. Clemenza, that's a beautiful dress. Where did you get it?

It's so old, I don't remember. Maybe I bought it at Crowley's. They always had small size dresses that fit me. They weren't expensive but they looked nice. I've never been much of a fashion person. Leona is the one who really has the wardrobe.

Well, that dress is perfect for you. How's your soup?

It's good. They make good soup here. You know, I've been coming here for years. It's about the only place I ever ate at because our folks don't eat out much. I could always feel I got good food for just a little money. How's your pork chop?

It's good, real tender and tasty. And the mashed potatoes and peas are delicious.

I used to be a cook, you know. I worked for a lot of white families and a made some money. Since I've been living in Leona's house, I've cooked most of the meals for the family. I gave Leona a break from having to work at her job and take care of the meals. But, now it's just me, Leona, and E.J., Sometimes he invites his girlfriend, Vergie, to dinner. I help around the house with cleaning and such. But when Leona is home, I stay in my room most of the time and read. She never has much to say to me.

Don't you feel lonely?

Well, the kids used to come to see me sometimes, especially Toby. E.J. never talked with me much. Obra-Jean only started talking with me after she moved to her other grandmother's house. But, of course, I don't see her anymore now that she's in college.

Don't you have friends who could visit you or whom you could visit?

Honey, most of my friends are long dead. The few who are still alive don't feel welcome in Leona's house. I don't drive and the bus takes too long to visit somebody. So I don't see anybody else anymore. I could ask Leona to drive me but my child has so much on her mind.

You're like a prisoner.

Baby, I'm not a prisoner. It's more like I'm stranded on an island. I'm free to go but I can't go anywhere.

Clemenza, just between us I've been told that you don't have the best relationship with Leona.

Honey, Leona doesn't bother me. I know my family thinks Leona is hard on me because she ignores me all the time. But she isn't hard. Augusta and Toby think she doesn't love me but she does. You know something,

I've learned that love and hate are different sides of the same thing. To other people, Leona seems to hate me sometimes. But I know it's really love. If she didn't love me, she would be indifferent to me. She wouldn't be bothered with me. Instead, having me around and living in her home actually allows Leona to love me in her own way. Now, if she was indifferent, I wouldn't be in her home. I would have to find some other place to live.

You certainly are philosophical about your daughter. I would never have believed you could have such kind thoughts about her.

Honey, I wouldn't have lived this long with all that I've had to deal with in my life if I wasn't philosophical.

Well, we'll have more dates for lunch or even dinner. How about that?

You're very kind, Ondine.

That's terrible what happened to President Kennedy. Clemenza, I loved that man. He met with Reverend King before he was killed. It seemed like, finally, we Negroes were going to get our fair share.

I know. In my day, we had that kind of hope with President Roosevelt. We made some progress with him. With Reverend King and President Kennedy, we really started moving ahead. That march on Washington with all of those Negroes at the Lincoln Memorial speaking up for our people, that was a glorious day. And, there were white people too who stood side by side with us. I thought to myself, I lived this long to see our people really gain their freedom. All of those young people marching and sitting-in. And protesting. And being beaten by the police and sprayed with firehoses and attacked by dogs. It was horrible but inspiring. They were going to change things. In my day, we had lynchings. Negroes hanging from trees, sometimes burned alive and having their insides cut out. Women cut open like hogs and their unborn babies thrown to the ground. Men having their privates cut off. That was what it was like back then down south. When I came to Detroit, we had it hard here too. We were, and still are, treated badly. But, we also had opportunities we could never have dreamed of in the South. Negroes got real jobs. They could go to school. They could become doctors and lawyers and teachers, like you and Augusta. They could buy nice homes and live good lives. They could raise families and send their children safely to school. Detroit ain't heaven but it ain't the hell we lived in down south.

Clemenza, you've seen a lot of change in your life. We Negroes have a long way to go before we have true equality with white people.

I think lazy Negroes are holding us back as a people.

Yes, Clemenza, there are lazy Negroes. And, there are lazy white people too. But laziness is not what's holding us back. White racism is what holds us back. We were brought here from Africa, enslaved. White people created this country on the backs of our free labor. They maintained slave labor as a capitalistic enterprise until Emancipation. Then they created new forms of enslavement but called it by different names like Jim Crow and segregation of the races. The objective was the same. To keep us down, inferior, second class, subservient, dependent, and poor. We were at the bottom of society—the lowest of the lowest class—and that's where they want to keep us. They get their value from us and we get their leavings. That's how this country was planned and that's how it still operates. We have fought against this oppression from day one and slowly we've made progress to throw it off. Reverend King got President Kennedy on board to help us and we see he was cut down like an animal. But, you know what? We'll keep on keeping on. There will be other presidents who will see what's right. With Doctor King, they'll help us and help this country become a better place for all of us, black and white.

I see what you're saying. But if Negroes move too fast, the whites will cut us down like they did President Kennedy. That's why I tried to teach my children to go slow. Don't push too hard because they'll be hurt and disappointed. Leona learned that lesson. She's tried to teach it to her daughters. I think she did the right thing.

Clemenza, there was a time to go slow when we were powerless and had few allies. That time has passed. The young people today aren't going to wait until somebody decides to give them what they want and deserve. They're going to push hard. When they are pushed back, they'll push harder still. That's what's going on now. I believe it will intensify. People are going to die for our freedom. That, unfortunately, is what I see unless and until we can live like anyone else. We need to use our abilities, our intelligence, and our talents to become what we want. That's what your granddaughters are trying to do. That's what Toby has done and what Obra-Jean is doing. She's taking a chance pushing against all of the forces that want to hold her back and she's going to be an architect, a great architect.

I wish I was a young person with your faith, Ondine. Maybe I would have been someone different.

You would have, Clemenza. But, who you are helped to bring these wonderful women into the world. You're the matriarch of a line of strong, beautiful sisters. What was your mother like?

My mother. My mother was Astra Rose Bevin. She was little like me but pretty, and dark. All of the women in my family were dark except Augusta. My mother had long, straight, wavy hair like an Indian princess. She always said that there was Indian blood in our family. She used her looks and her body to attract men. My mother had lots of babies and she didn't care how she got them or what she would do with them once she had them. She only seemed to care about the men in her life, not us children. My mother wasn't a mother to me. I had my sisters, especially Iris, who was the only real mother to me. She was kind and smart. She tried to teach me things since I didn't have much schooling. I only stayed in school until the sixth grade. I was close to Iris and learned from her. But, then, like my birth mother, I got carried away with men once I figured out what they wanted from a woman. Iris warned me but I wouldn't listen. So, I paid the price. I became a mother and that wasn't what I wanted to be. I was lucky that I had two beautiful daughters and two handsome sons. But I wasn't a good mother to them. I don't know how they turned out to be so good. It wasn't because of me.

Clemenza, you're a good person. You may have done things you now regret but you've done good and these woman are the proof.

Bless you, Baby. I wish I could believe you.

Clemenza leaned over and gave Ondine a kiss on the cheek. Ondine hugged her and kissed her forehead.

X

Sisters and Brothers
The Moore Family

— One Helluva Picnic —
Summer 1964

Each year since the birth of Toby in 1937, Styll and Barry planned a Fourth of July picnic with their son, Perry, and his family, including his in-laws, Clemenza and Augusta. Styll's other sons, Carson and Mason, also attended. Their favorite picnic site for the nine family members was Belle Isle—an island park in the Detroit River—because the island was a short drive across a bridge from the city proper. The family could load up their cars with food, folding chairs, and all other items needed for a day's breezy outing in the middle of the Detroit River. Besides being a verdant and serene setting, Belle Isle provided a view of Detroit as well as of Windsor, Canada because the Detroit River is a waterway border between Canada and the USA. Most importantly, blacks felt at home in this park believing it belonged as much to them as to whites. However, blacks only claimed a few areas of the park for themselves that whites generally avoided and there was seldom any mixing of the races. Peace and harmony reigned until such times that it didn't.

By the time Obra-Jean began high school, a new, tri-county authority began creating a ring of metro-parks outside of, around, but distant from the city limits of Detroit. The Moore/Post extended family found one of these parks more congenial to their outing than Belle Isle although reaching it required a longer drive. Lower Huron Metropark lies southwest of Detroit in a bucolic setting on the Huron River as it meanders eastward towards Lake Erie. After exploring the park over the course of several years, members of the family determined that blacks, if not exactly welcomed by suburban whites, were not molested by them if they confined themselves to certain areas away from whites. The family settled on a secluded, wooded spot near a stream far away from other families where they could spread out, picnic, play games, catch baseballs, sleep, and be black people in complete tranquillity. This is the park the family chose for their annual Fourth of July picnic in 1964, the year following the assassination of President John F. Kennedy. It was a very hot, cloudless summer day, perfect for a park outing. The gathering lacked Perry, of course, who was long deceased, and Carson who had moved to Philadelphia. Otherwise, the entire extended family roused themselves to attend this ritual gathering. Leona tasked E.J. to take her car to arrive just after dawn at the park. E.J. picked up his long-time girlfriend, now fiancé, Vergie Thomason, along the way and together they commandeered the family's favorite picnic area long before many other visitors arrived. A little later, about eight, Augusta drove up with Leona and Clemenza. Then, Styll deposited herself, Barry, and Mason at the gathering. Finally, Toby accompanied by India and Obra-Jean made a dramatic but late entry with India's large and friendly female German Shepherd, Sidney. The only other non-family member was Ondine who was also late because she became confused by the road signs in the park and missed the correct turn ending up in the wrong area before backtracking and finding the correct location.

The family encampment resembled more a staging area for a longterm siege than a day's picnic setting. There were folding tables and chairs in addition to the park's huge wooden picnic table with benches. Baskets, hampers, coolers, umbrellas, portable grills, a small tent, blankets, table cloths, first-aid box, jackets, sweaters, sporting equipment, board games, playing cards, trash bags, pots, pans, covered dishes, dinnerware, silverware, and enough food for a large, starving village demarcated a new and seemingly permanent settlement near a stream. The various family sub-units marked off their space within the compound and set up folding tables and chairs. However, the consensus—actually Styll's decision—was that everyone would assemble and eat together at the large wooden park table for supper at four o'clock. Therefore, the table needed to be set for twelve people—five on a side and one at each end. Meanwhile, Styll with Clemenza's help took charge of organizing the dinner and serving tables and assigning tasks for the communal meal. In Styll's mind, her schedule allowed everyone plenty of time for recreation, games, conversation, and relaxation. And, after the meal, everyone could continue their activities until dusk then pack up and head home before twilight and heavy traffic returning to the city.

E.J. and Barry readied the grills with charcoal, sticks, and newspapers for cooking the hamburgers and hotdogs later in the afternoon. At their homes, Styll and Leona had prepared fried chicken, baked spare ribs, and honey-baked ham. They had also made several different salads—potato, egg, corn, macaroni, green bean, and lettuce and tomato. Clemenza provided sandwiches with ham, or salami, and cheese for folks who hadn't had time for breakfast. Augusta brought fresh fruit and pastries including several fruit pies and two peach cobblers. Toby set out an array of snacks—potato chips, pretzels, crackers, cheese, olives, sliced carrots, and celery sticks—and created a huge watermelon salad. Ondine unpacked a surprise: a Middle Eastern selection of hummus, baba ganoush, tabouli, and stuffed grape leaves with pita bread. With so much food, most grabbed a sandwich or snack and something to drink. Since everyone had brought their preferred drinks, there was plenty of beer, wine, soft drinks, fruit juice, coffee, tea, and ice water. Barry had secreted a bottle of bourbon in a picnic basket because, legally, alcohol—other than beer—was banned from the park. To work up an appetite for the picnic supper, the younger folks decided to set up a volley ball net and play a couple of sets. After several vigorous rounds during which the team of Toby, India, and Ondine was consistently victorious over Obra-Jean, E.J. and Vergie, the younger group decided to stroll over to the canoe rental and row on the Huron River for a couple of hours. Meanwhile, the older women had gathered in two groups around folding card tables to drink, snack, and chat. Leona and Augusta paired off as did Styll and Clemenza. Barry and Mason stretched out on blankets for a nap and then later went for a walk together. Styll and Clemenza focused on their gin rummy game. As the day continued to warm, they moved their table out of the sun to a shadier spot. When they had equaled one another in the number of games each won, they put their cards down and took in the beauty of the setting.

It really is a lovely day today, isn't it Clemenza?

Yes indeed. We sure are lucky this year, Styll. Remember last year it rained and rained. We sat in our cars hoping it would clear up and it didn't? So, we gave up and went back to the city.

Yes, Ma'am. All of that work and we had the picnic at my house. It wasn't as much fun as being in the park but that didn't keep this family from eating everything in sight. The weather is really cooperating this year. This is great July weather. I'm glad I've got my big straw hat to keep the sun out of my eyes. How about you? That baseball cap isn't doing you much good.

I could use a hat like yours.

Honey, I've got another one just for you. Here, in my bag. This will keep the sun out of your eyes. Sugar, you seem a little down today. What's going on?

Styll, I've been thinking. You have a husband. You two seem about as happy as people our age can be. We're getting old, Styll. You know I'm sixty-five now. Everyday something new is going wrong with my body. I've got heart trouble. My kidneys are acting up. I've got sugar diabetes. I can't see good with these cataracts.

You can see these damn cards all right.

Yeah, but I keep forgetting things. Misplacing things. There's all this good food here and I don't feel like eating anything. I have no appetite at all.

Believe me, Honey, I know what you're saying. When we were young and healthy, we didn't have all of these medical problems. If we had them, our families couldn't afford a doctor or hospital. Us Negroes probably couldn't have used them anyway. White folks didn't want us around them. Well, they did need us to take care of their homes and cook their food and take care of their children.

You got that right.

And spread our legs for the husbands and sons. The things we had to do just to stay alive. We did what we had to do.

Yes, we did. These young folks, they don't understand that. You know, I've always accepted my life as it is. I don't complain because, first of all, who's going to listen or care? I'm just glad to have what I have. But, now, I don't know. I feel like I just want to give up. You know what I mean? I don't have anyone, like you do, to keep me company. The kids are gone from the house. Leona has her own life. I don't go anywhere except a lunch sometimes with Augusta or Ondine. My few friends, they're too old to come to see me. I can't drive so I can't go to see them. I don't go anywhere unless somebody takes me. You know it takes forever to go anywhere in this city by bus. So, why am I living like this? Why am I living at all?

Because, Baby, this is our life. This is the only life we have. We didn't choose this for ourselves. We made do with what we got. If we wanted to live and have any life at all, we had to do what we had to do. See. Now listen to me. You've lived your life so you could be here for your daughters and your grandchildren.

Styll, that's just not true. That's not what I wanted for my life. I didn't care about my kids the way you cared about yours. I wanted them to do well so, when I got old, they could take care of me. I've got a good deal with Leona. That's why I put up with the way she's treated me all these years.

Honey, Leona never understood you. She never understood your life. Never. She only understands her own hurt when you did what you felt you had to do for yourself. I'm sorry she's not the forgiving kind. But, she isn't. That's Leona. She's got a lot of good qualities. You know I love her like she's my own daughter. I'm sorry you two haven't had what I've had with her. If I could change that, I would. I hope you know that.

I do know it, Styll. I'll tell you the truth. I didn't give much thought to Leona when I left her behind in Hot Springs. I thought she would be happy with my sister. My sister always loved her. But I guess Leona wasn't happy. So, I don't blame her for how she feels. What really bothers me is this. She carries her hurt inside her like it's a disease. She's let that disease infect her own daughters. It scares them, Styll. They avoid her. If I had loved and cared for Leona the way she wanted, maybe her own children would love her the way she wants.

Clemenza, that horse is out of the barn and down the road in the next county. It's too late to lock the barn.

I know. I know, Styll. I wish I had known then what I know now. I was a selfish mother who didn't care enough about her child. I didn't know better.

Honey, you did care about her but in your own way.

Oh, what's done is done, Styll. I can't change anything now. I can't change myself or my child.

Baby, there must be something you could do.

Like what?

I'm thinking on it right now. You know, I think a lot about my sons. But what can I do for them? Perry is dead. Carson left his family. He only talks to me when I call him in Philadelphia. And, Mason. Well, Mason is a lost child. I don't know what happened in my body to make him the way he is. He's a grown man but still a child without his own life. He's always gonna live with his parents in his parents' home. He not interested in anything. He doesn't have a future. What's gonna happen to him when me and my husband are gone? Maybe if Mason had got help when he was real young, he might be different. But there was nothing to help Negro boys. I tried doctors. I tried his school. I tried social services.

There was no help for us. I watched my beautiful child disappear inside himself.

We hurt them, Styll. It's our fault.

It's nobody's fault. It just is what it is. It ain't that bad. Baby. Look at Leona and Augusta. They both have their own homes. Leona's three children are making something of themselves. They've gone to school. They've got a good education. They're going to make it in this world. Leona did that. Now, Augusta's a principal. She's big time. She lives well. She might even get married someday and have her own children.

Oh, Styll, Augusta is too old for children now.

She's not too old to get married. She could still find a husband.

She could but I doubt she will.

What are saying?

She's not going to marry, Styll. Augusta doesn't need a husband. Besides, she seems happy with her life as it is.

Okay. So, she's happy. Anyway, your daughters are doing just fine. They're doing better than their mother. And Carson is doing better than his father. We'll leave Mason out of this. Think about it, Baby. We're making progress as a family. This Negro family is progressing. We're becoming something in this world. Our grandchildren will do even better than their parents. It's gonna happen, Clemenza. You can see it now with Toby and E.J. and Obra-Jean. Those kids are breaking loose. They're finding their way. Nothing is getting in their way. That's it, Clemenza.

They're the future. They carry us forward. We'll live on in them. We'll all be better because of them. Our people will be better because of them.

Styll, you're always so positive. You're more positive than I could ever be.

That's because I've got my faith, Baby. I've got faith in the lord. If you had faith, you might see things more positively too.

Styll, I wish that was true. Faith won't do much for me now. Besides, I try accepting the life I have. Sure, I wish my life was better. Who wouldn't? But, I've had my chance. What I want most of all now is to see Leona happy. At least as happy as I think her sister is. I want my daughter to lose that hurt. I want her to feel like she's a whole person. Not a person who feels she's lost so many things. I want her to feel like she can laugh and enjoy what life she has. How can I help her feel that way?

Have faith, Honey. You'll find a way. Stay focused on that. You'll find the answer. I promise you. Just have faith.

I want to believe you, Styll. I want to believe you.

That's what faith is, Clemenza. Believing.

While Styll and Clemenza chatted, the group of younger folks reached the canoe rental that was about half mile from their picnic encampment. As they passed through the park, they began seeing more visitors, in fact hundreds of people, mostly white. While most folks were busy setting up their own picnic areas, others had already begun playing ball games or stretching out on blankets in the sun. Children chased each other; one almost collided with the Moore group. Most whites ignored them. A few stared as they passed through the throngs spread out over the grassy areas of the park. When they reached the canoe rental, Toby and India got in line to rent a canoe together as did E.J. and Vergie. Ondine never intended to canoe because she didn't like being on the water. Instead, she and Obra-Jean watched the others board their canoes and paddle away from the dock. When the canoes were out of sight, Ondine and Obra-Jean took India's German Shepherd, Sidney, for a walk around the park.

The Huron is not a large or very deep river. It's tranquil enough for canoeing and many boaters were cruising back and forth. The canoes of Toby and India, and of E.J. and Vergie glided along the river with many canoes headed both downstream and upstream. There was some congestion on the river but given that the day was beautiful, the water tranquil, and everyone seemed to be in a festive mood, the canoeing was great fun. Although most people managed to steer their canoes without bumping into others, some were less than coordinated and contributed to the occasional traffic jam on the waterway. Almost inevitably there were a few boaters—young white males mostly—who, having too much to beer and feeling a rush of testosterone, recklessly paddled their canoes without consideration of their speed, course, or safety. They produced a certain amount of havoc as more responsible boaters attempted to avoid collisions with them. E.J. exchanged angry words with one particularly belligerent boater. A fight might have happened if it were not for the fact that everyone was in their own canoe and unable to assail people in another canoe. Soon, however, the reckless few moved on away from the other boaters. Meanwhile, Ondine and Obra-Jean with their canine companion, who sniffed and peed at every opportunity, explored the park.

There sure are a lot of people here, Ondine.

Practically all white, I see.

Most of us in Detroit still go to Belle Isle. I guess we can be ourselves there without white people always looking funny at us like we don't belong.

Well, they certainly seem to be noticing me.

Ondine, everybody notices you.

That's because, Obra-Jean, I'm a big, black, beautiful bitch and proud of it. I'm also a goddess. You, on the other hand, are just black and beautiful.

Thank you. Ondine, can I ask you a personal question?

Sweetie, how personal?

Well, people do notice you because of your size and color.

And, they think I'm ugly.

Well, that's what I want to ask you. How did you become so confident of yourself in spite of how people see and treat you? I mean, I was always confident of myself until the first time I was treated differently because I'm a Negro.

And, then, you lost some of your self-confidence?

Sort-of. I mean I've always been pretty confident but I know at any time some white person could treat me badly for no reason at all except that I'm a Negro.

Well, Honey, being treated badly is what I've lived with my whole life. And, I think, I've had it a lot worse than you.

So, how did you become so self-confident?

Ah, that's a story. When I graduated from college and before I started teaching, I was invited to visit Cairo. My dad was Egyptian and his family still lives in Cairo. They invited me to come and visit them. When I saw them waiting for me in the airport, I knew I belonged to people just like myself. These people, especially the women, looked like me. But, they were in their own country. Nobody was mistreating them because of who they were and what they looked like. In other words, there were no white people in charge of everything who looked down on them. Do you get what I'lm saying?

I think so. We Negroes in this country are a different class of people than white people. White people are in charge and so they can and do treat us any way they want. It's not that way in Egypt. Your people are in charge of themselves. You are one of those people.

I think that about says it. You catch on quick.

But now you're here. Your people are not in charge here.

Ah, Obra-Jean, that's the point. I am not in charge of anything or anybody but myself. And, I'm in complete charge of me. Nobody can make me feel bad no matter how they see me or how they treat me. Because I believe in myself, I can accept who I am.

So, what you're saying is I must believe in myself and accept myself. I don't have to feel bad if people don't like me. Is that it?

Absolutely, Obra-Jean. However, if people treat you badly, you don't have to accept that. You can stand up for yourself and let them know their behavior is wrong. That is what works for me. No one wants a big, black woman in their face. You're not big but you can act big. I think that should work for you too.

I get it, Ondine. Thank you.

Speaking of how other people see you, I think some of those young white boys are looking at you, Obra-Jean. I think they would like to get into your very tight Capri pants.

That's not gonna happen.

Don't those boys at your school give you the once over?

Are you kidding me? The boys at school? Architecture students think models of buildings are sexy. Drawings of buildings are beautiful. Blueprints are hot. They practically have an orgasm when they see photographs of Mies van der Rohe's buildings.

Mies who?

Ludwig Mies van der Rohe. He designed the apartment building where Aunt Augusta lives.

I've never heard of him. Who is he?

He's German but lives in this country now. He left Germany before the Nazis took over. He lives and works in Chicago. He's famous for his sleek glass and steel designs like Aunt Augusta's building. Originally, he was supposed to design most of the buildings in Lafayette Park. He designed those beautiful one- and two-story townhouses near Aunt Augusta's building that are so popular. I would love to live in one of those someday.

Obra-Jean, you sound like the boys you described.

To tell you the truth, the same things turn me on.

See what I mean?

You bet. Models of buildings are very sexy. I love buildings. It's all I've ever really loved since I was little. It's what I want to design and build. If I could be just a little bit as good as Mies, I would be in heaven.

Sweetie, if that what gets you going, you've got it made, orgasm and all. So, how is school?

I'm finishing my architectural degree next year at U of D. I've taken a lot of design classes and learned about structures and engineering. I love what I'm learning but . . .

But, what?

I've been the only girl in my architecture class and, actually, I'm the only Negro. It feels isolating.

Sweetie, you are isolated. They're treating you okay though, aren't they?

Well, it's a little hard to answer. As a girl, I stand out. The boys, they all stick together. Since there are no other Negroes, I don't even have a Negro boy for a friend. There's this one white boy. His name is Harvey Glass. He's been my teammate for a design project. He's a little shy and quiet but he's pretty smart and really talented. He's helped me to understand some things about designing with different building materials but we don't talk about anything personal. It's all architecture all the time.

Has anybody ever said anything about you being a woman or being a Negro?

Are you kidding? They may not say it to me directly but they always imply I'm different.

To them you are but are they mistreating you?

Not exactly. It's the way they sometimes look at me. Then, they turn away and talk to one of their classmates just like some people are doing here in the park. They look, then they turn away. You can tell what they're thinking. "What are 'they' doing here?"

Are your professors like that too?

They're hard on everybody. Really hard. Nothing pleases them. They're always very critical. They tear everything apart that we do. I guess, that's how we're supposed to learn and improve our designs. That's how we learn what makes a good design.

This is what you've learned?

Of course. I'll tell you, Ondine, and this will sound like I'm full of myself—as my mother would say. I'm the best student in my class. Maybe in the whole architecture school.

Whoa! You think you're that good? I mean I believe you're probably a good student and you'll likely be a good architect. But do you really think you're the best?

Okay, I know I've got a long way to go, Ondine. Even I'm not sure if I can get there or will even have a chance to get there. But I'm the best there is right now at U of D. Nobody's design work is as good as mine. That's what my favorite professor says. He's German and he's the most innovative architect in Detroit. Because of him, I'm giving it everything I've got. Nothing is going to stop me from trying.

But you said nothing pleases your professors. How is he different?

He's different because, after he criticizes my work, he tells me it's really good. He just wants it to be better and he always thinks I can make it better.

He sounds like a good man. Stick with him. You found your perfect mentor. You won't hear me question you again about how good you are.

I don't mind you questioning me. I trust you, Ondine. I hope you trust me too.

I think I do. Thank you, Sweetie. Hey, look over there. Let's see what's over there by that big shed before we head back to our picnic area. I'm getting a little hungry. How about you?

I could try some of those things you brought. What do you recommend?

Try the baba ganoush with pita and some stuffed grape leaves.

Okay.

Obra-Jean and Ondine continued their walk. They discovered that the big shed was a performance space and some musicians were setting up their instruments to play. The musicians were a small country music band that, once they began playing, attracted a crowd of curious listeners. Obra-Jean and Ondine joined a group who kept a little distance from them, apparently, because of the dog. Although the band was entertaining, the women realized it was not their kind of music and eased out of the crowd. They decided to return to their family's picnic area by completing a big loop around the park. Everywhere they went, there were dense clusters of picnickers. There were families and couples and groups of young college-age people who, apparently, came to the park together. Some lay on blankets on the grass. Others grilled hotdogs and hamburgers. Smoke from the grills rose in columns up into the trees. Many of the younger men had stripped off their shirts and sunned themselves. Ondine and Obra-Jean nudged each other at the sight of white people trying to tan their pale skin. Lobster red seemed to be the desired goal. Before long, they realized that they were nearing the Moore family picnic area. When they arrived, they noticed that Styll and Clemenza were sitting together apart from Leona and Augusta who were talking in close company. The also noticed the absence of Barry and Mason, E.J. and Vergie, and Toby and India.

I guess the gang's not back yet from canoeing. I wonder where Grandpapa and Mason are?

They probably took a walk somewhere. Poor Mason probably doesn't get out much.

He hasn't been anywhere as long as I've been staying with Grandmama and Grandpapa. He sits and looks at the TV a lot. Sometimes, he listens to rock and roll music on his radio. He lives in his own world. Anyway,

I'm going to try your food and go sit with my grandmothers. Before I go, can I ask you another personal question?

Sure, Sweetie.

You told me about your family in Egypt but what about your family here?

Oh, Obra-Jean, after my father died, my mother, my siblings and I were in a bad way financially. We were on Welfare and Aid to Dependent Children because my mother was too sick to work. As the oldest of six children, I had to work to stay in school. After I visited my relatives in Cairo and told them about my family in Detroit, they began to send money to my mother. That is how the family survived until she died last year. My five siblings all finished school and went to college. When they graduated, they got jobs in different parts of the country. Most of them are married now and have their own families. We keep in touch but I haven't seen them in a couple of years.

Is that why you've become close to our family?

Well, Honey, I feel I'm part of this family because of Augusta. She brought me into this family.

Ondine, I'm curious. Tell me about you and Aunt Augusta? What's going on there?

Do you mean, what is our relationship?

Oh, I know you work together but I believe there is something else?

I love Augusta and she loves me. Is that what you're asking?

Yes. But, isn't it more than love? Isn't it like Toby and India? I'm not trying to embarrass you. I just want to hear the truth from you.

Your aunt would prefer that we not make our true relationship known to the family.

What? Everybody knows your true relationship. What's not to know? We just don't talk about it.

I guess we should have known you can't hide yourself from this family.

No way, Ondine. So, you two are lovers?

Yes.

Okay. That's that. I just needed confirmation. I'm going to get some of your food now. See you later.

I guess I'll get something to eat too, then join Augusta and your mother. Thanks, Obra-Jean. You've given me something to think about.

After fixing a paper plate with pita, baba ganoush, and stuffed grape leaves, Obra-Jean approached her two grandmothers who were still seated at a folding table. She pulled up a chair and sat down with them while they continued their conversation. Styll, who finished her thought with Clemenza then turned to Obra-Jean.

Did you go canoeing, Baby?

No, Grandma. We just watched the others paddle down the river, then we continued walking through the park. The place is really crowded today.

About a mile away is a bandstand where some musicians were playing country music. We listened for a while until we had enough. Then started walking in a big circle until we arrived back here. Did you try this baba ganoush that Ondine brought?

Baba-what?

Baba ganoush. It's made from eggplants.

Egg-what? It doesn't look like any egg I've ever seen.

Grandma, It's not made from eggs. It's made from a vegetable called an eggplant. In French, it's an *aubergine*, like my name.

Your name? What are you talking about? Honey, nobody named you an eggplant.

Grandma, ask my mother how she came up with Obra-Jean. Listen to how I say it; it's sounds like "owe-bear-jeen."

Clemenza, did you ever hear of such a thing?

Styll, I know Leona had something on her mind when she was pregnant with Obra-Jean. I can't say what it was. When this child was born, her mother said her name would be Obra-Jean. Now, nobody in our family has a name like that. But, that's what Leona decided. You'll have to ask her where she got that name.

I think I'll do that right now. Excuse me ladies. I'm on a mission. Okay, Leona, here I come.

Styll left Obra-Jean with Clemenza and walked a little distance to where Augusta, Leona, and now, Ondine were seated in chairs at a folding table. She pulled up another chair, sat down, and interrupted their conversation.

Augusta, excuse me and you too, Ondine. I know I'm interrupting your conversation but I just heard something that I want to straighten out with Leona. Baby, I was just talking to your mother and daughter and we were wondering how you came up with the name "Obra-Jean."

I liked the name.

But where did it come from? How did you pick that name?

Mother, Obra-Jean was born twenty-one years ago and just now you want to know about her name?

I never thought about it before but now I'm curious. Your daughter thinks it's like some French word for eggplant or something. I never even knew about eggplants. Is she right?

Mother, you know Obra-Jean knows everything about everything, right?

She's smart. So, was she named for an eggplant?

Yes.

What? But why, Leona?

Because to me she looked like an eggplant. Does that answer your damn question?

Pardon me, Leona. I never knew you were so touchy about her name.

A name is just a goddam name. Let's drop the subject. Okay, Mother?

Styll, a bit unnerved by Leona's sharp response, returned to the table with Clemenza and Obra-Jean. She confirmed that Obra-Jean was correct. She couldn't quite get over Leona's tone. Although she heard her talk to other people like that, Leona never snapped at Styll and Styll was puzzled. She asked Obra-Jean and Clemenza if they knew what would set off Leona like that. As life-long objects of Leona's moods, they were not surprised. While they continued talking, the canoe gang—Toby and India, E.J., and Vergie—returned to the family picnic site. E.J. and Vergie looked through the picnic baskets for a snack. After stopping to speak to her mother, Toby with India joined E.J. and Vergie.

Toby, where are Grandpa and Mason?

Mother says they went for a walk, E.J.

How long have they been gone?

Mother didn't know much. She couldn't tell me more than that. They may have been gone while we were canoeing.

Where did they go?

I just told you Mother didn't have much information.

It's been hours. Shouldn't they be back by now?

E.J., why are you asking me all of these questions? They'll be back. Why wouldn't they be?

Because it's kinda strange, Toby. Grandpa doesn't walk too well, and Mason is not all there. So what could they be doing?

I guess we'll find out, E.J., when they return. Okay? Be cool, Little Brother.

Did anybody just hear a siren?

It's coming through the park, India. What's going on? I'll ask Grandma Moore if she knows anything about Grandpa and Mason. Oh, wait, here they come.

Barry and Mason approached the picnic area. Barry supported himself holding on to Mason's arm. Mason was agitated. They walked over to Styll. Barry sat down exhausted. Mason remained standing staring straight ahead at nothing in particular.

Barry, what's wrong with Mason?

Styll, he saw someone drown in the river.

Drown? How could anyone drown in that river?

Some white kids were acting a fool and one of their canoes turned over. One kid couldn't swim and there was no one who tried to save him. An ambulance just arrived. They must be getting the body from the water.

Barry, that's terrible.

Styll, some things are a lot worse.

413

Don't you think I know that?

Styll, I'm just saying.

Well, everybody's returned. Now we're all together here safe and sound. Let's relax before serving supper. Here, Barry, you stay in this chair. I'm gonna ask Leona and Augusta if they want to play some pinochle. I brought the cards. We can use one of these card tables and set up two more chairs. Mason. Mason, Baby. Mason, your Mama's talking to you. Sit down on the blanket and rest until we eat. Okay? that's a good boy.

After getting her husband and son situated, Styll went over to Leona and Augusta and suggested they play cards until time to get supper ready. Meanwhile, Toby and E.J. wanted another round of volley ball. They wrangled India, Vergie, and the reluctant Obra-Jean and Ondine to join them in a game. Between the card and volley ball game, the participants passed the time and worked up an appetite. It was now mid-afternoon. Styll asked E.J. to start the grills. She assembled all of the women to begin setting out the food and organizing its placement on the tables. When the meat was cooked and all was ready, everyone found a place to sit. Styll and Barry sat at the ends of the big wooden park table. Conversation during the meal was subdued. In part, this was simply because of the tremendous amount of food to sample but also the drowning squelched some of the enthusiasm the family and guests brought to the picnic. Styll was particularly quiet and everyone seemed sensitive to the absence of her usual ebullience. After everyone had eaten as much as they desired, there was a distinct impulse to scatter again into small groups but Styll wanted to change her own sour and sullen mood so that the rest of the day wouldn't be spoiled. She was about to make an announcement when a police car drove into their secluded area with its red light flashing. The car stopped a short distance from the family encampment and two white police officers exited the vehicle and approached the family's picnic table. Sidney started barking and snarling. India had to calm her down and restrain her.

Good afternoon, folks. Nice dog there. We're from the county sheriff's patrol. We're sorry to interrupt your meal but we would like to ask some questions.

Good afternoon, Officer. Your name is . . . ?

Officer Wisnewski and this is my partner, Officer Blatnik.

Welcome, Officers. I'm Missus Estyllene Moore and this is my family. What can we do for you?

Well, there's been a canoe accident on the river and we have information that you folks might know something about it.

Excuse me, Officer . . . Say your name again.

Wisnewski.

Yes. Officer Wisnewski, I'm just curious. Why do you think any of us in this big park over here in this out of the way spot would know anything about an accident on the river?

Uh, someone reported to us that, maybe, some of you might have had words with the victim who fell out of a canoe and drowned.

Some of us? Why us? There are a lot of people in this park.

Well, to be honest, Ma'am, the report said "some Negroes" and there aren't that many Negroes in this park.

415

As you already know, Officer, uh, Wisnewski, we are Negroes but, I believe, all of us have been here at this spot all day long. Nobody has left from here all day. I can swear to that on a stack of Bibles.

Well, Ma'am, we have eye-witnesses who said a very big Negro woman with a big dog, like this dog, was at the bandshell. A Negro man got into an argument with one of the victims in the canoe. And two Negro men witnessed the drowning. Now, I'm just asking, could that be any of you?

Officer, I think you said there are more Negroes in this park besides us. I'm telling you, as a good Christian lady, my family has been at this spot all day. No one has left it. That is the honest-to-god-truth. Do I look like a woman who would lie to police officers? In any case, you can ask anyone here any questions you like. Go ahead. Ask.

I'm sorry, Ma'am, we're only checking everybody out. If you say everybody was here all day, I guess everybody was here all day. But I would still like to ask some questions if you don't mind. We're just doing our duty, Ma'am.

Go ahead, Officer, uh, Wisnewski, ask away.

Thank you, Ma'am. You, Sir, it was reported that an elderly Negro man with a limp was near the site of the accident. Could that have been you?

Excuse me, Officer Wisnewski, for answering but the man you are questioning is my husband. He has a bad heart and a lot of other problems. He hasn't left this picnic area all day, did you Barry?

Well, yes, Honey, I did. While you were talking with Missus Post, Mason and me went for a long walk. You were busy and probably didn't see us leave or come back. Officer, we did see the accident. There were three canoes with a bunch of young white boys who were drinking beer and acting up. One canoe crashed into another one. One of those boys fell out of the canoe and drowned. He was drunk and couldn't swim. That's what I saw and my son, here, saw what happened too.

Is that true, Sir?

Mason, answer the officer.

Yes, Papa.

You'll have to excuse my son, Officer, he's a little slow, if you know what I mean.

I see. I'm sorry, Sir. I have to ask everyone who saw something. Okay. So you say it was all young men in the canoes. Nobody from here?

Yes, Sir, there were only young white boys, no Negro boys.

Well, maybe someone here did have an argument with those young men. Is that possible?

Grandma, Vergie and I went canoeing. You didn't notice we were gone because you and Grandma Post were talking and busy getting things ready for supper.

Oh, thank you, E.J. I was so busy running my mouth with your grandmother, Clemenza, that I didn't know you left or come back. It's my fault, Officers. An honest mistake. Now, you tell the officers exactly what you saw, E.J. Go ahead. Tell them everything. Don't leave anything out.

Yes, Ma'am. See, Officer, me and my girlfriend here were canoeing and these white guys in a couple of canoes were ramming into everybody else, including us. They had been drinking and thought what they were doing was funny. I told them to watch out and they gave me the finger. Then one of them said that niggers don't belong in their park. We ignored them and continued on our way. We didn't see them again. That's all that we know.

E.J. is it? Well, E.J., I'm very sorry that somebody spoke to you like that. But, I guess you cleared up that part of what happened. And, you say, you weren't present when the young man fell out of the canoe? Is that correct?

Yes, Officer. That is correct.

Which one of these women is your girlfriend?

I am, Officer. My name is Vergie and E.J. told you everything we both saw and heard. He told you the absolute truth.

Thank you, Vergie, for corroborating E.J.'s story. Now . . .

Excuse me, Officer Wisnewski, I'm the big woman with the dog. My name is Ondine Mahmoud and I was at the bandshell. I didn't see anything or talk to anybody except these folks here. I'm a guest of this family.

I see. Thank you, Ma'am. Just to be clear, you weren't at the river.

Correct.

You didn't witness the argument.

Correct.

You didn't see the canoe accident?

Correct again, Officer. I left the bandshell and came back here with this beautiful dog where I've been up until now.

Thank you again. Miss Mahmoud, is it?

Yes.

Officer Wisnewski, Sir, I do owe you an apology. Here I am telling you that my family was at this spot all day. Believe me, I thought they never left this spot. Now you know that some of them were where you say your eyewitnesses saw them. I hope you don't think I was lying to you. I wouldn't lie to a policeman on a stack of Bibles. But I could have sworn everyone was here all day. I was wrong. It's an old woman's mistake. You'll forgive an old lady, won't you? It was an honest mistake.

I understand, Ma'am. I'm sorry we had to disturb you folks and your meal but we needed to make this investigation. Please enjoy the rest of your stay.

Oh, Officer Wisnewski, before you leave, may I ask you a question?

Yes, Ma'am, Missus Moore.

Have you and Officer, uh, Blatnik, is it? Have you all had something to eat for supper?

No, Ma'am. We've been busy all day checking on accidents and fights in the park.

Well, let me fix a couple of plates of food for you both. As you can see, we have a lot to eat here and all of it is delicious. Now, how about some of this fried chicken and a hamburger with these salads? And, how about some hotdogs for a snack later. Wouldn't you like that? And some desserts?

Sure, I would, Ma'am. How about you, Blatnik?

Oh, yes. Me too, Ma'am.

Okay, Ladies, let's get these gentlemen some food. Let them see what we have and let's load up their plates with whatever they like. Officer Wisnewski, my granddaughter, Toby, say hello to the officer, Toby, yes, she will serve you your plate. Just tell her everything you would like. And, you, Officer Blatnik, my other granddaughter, Obra-Jean, say hello to the officer, Obra-Jean, she will serve you your plate. You just tell her what you like and she'll fix it for you. Now, Ladies, make sure that the officers also get some of these appetizers and desserts. Load up their plates and cover them. We can put everything in these shopping bags we brought with us so they can carry their food back to their car. I'm sure they've got some more investigating to do with those other Negroes in the park.

The two police officers were almost giddy with delight at the prospect of so much food being heaped on paper plates for their meal. Nearly everything they were offered they accepted. When Toby and Obra-Jean had finished preparing their plates and packing them into the shopping bags, the two officers thanked everyone several times, headed back to their patrol car, and departed the Moore encampment accompanied by

Sidney's barking. When their car was out of sight. Styll looked at her silent family and started laughing. Everyone joined in. After the laughter subsided, Styll asked everyone to be seated again at the big table.

Listen, everyone. What happened just now is one of the ways us Negroes must handle the police. We have to be respectful but not Uncle Toms. We must stand together or they will take us one by one. Barry and me, we know this routine. We've dealt with crackers all of our lives. They know they've got the power and they'll use it. So, we have to be soft and gentle but also clever. Tell them what they need to know and no more than that. Then, show them kindness. So when they come after the next group of Negroes for some bullshit thing, they might remember. Now that they're gone and we've safe here together, I've got something important to say:

This beautiful family is gathered here for another annual picnic and a fantastic meal prepared by all of these beautiful women. Oh, yes, E.J., you grilled the meat. Thank you, E.J. and thank you too, Vergie. As I was saying, we owe our thanks to the beautiful women of this family, the Moore and Post ladies and our adopted daughters, India, Ondine, and Vergie. What would men do without us? E.J., if you hadn't grilled the meat, us women would have taken care of that too and we wouldn't have overcooked it. Sorry, Baby, Grandma's only kidding but the meat was a little too done. Yes, women fill our bellies, keep our homes, raise our children, and take care of you men. Without women, what would men be? Well, for one thing, there wouldn't be any more men because, so far, they haven't figured out how to make babies between themselves. Lord, if Carson was here right now, he would have given me the evil eye. My beautiful son, Carson. Bless him. He went his own way when his mother and father didn't love him the way we should have. Barry, I blame myself as much as you. I should have stood up for Carson and told that child he had the right to be who he was. And, I say this because that is what I want every one of you to understand. Each of us has to be who we are. There are no good and no bad people here. There are just people who sometimes do good things and sometimes bad things. When we do good, we deserve praise and when we do bad, we need forgiveness. Forgiveness is what our lord teaches us. I want each of you now to think of someone here you need to forgive. Include yourselves first of all because we have to forgive ourselves. Then, I want you to go to someone at this table and ask their forgiveness. Don't be shy. This may be the only and possibly the last opportunity for us to ask forgiveness. We don't know how many days any of us have left on this planet. So, don't put off what you can do right now. Okay. Nobody's moving so let me be the first.

Styll got up from the table and walked over to Mason. She asked him to stand up and she gave him a long embrace and started to cry. She told him she wished she had been a better mother to him and could have helped make his life better. Mason seemed stunned. When she released him, Mason looked at his mother, and to everyone's astonishment, the thirty-eight year old man began to speak.

Mommy. I know you love me. I love you and Daddy. I'm happy. You take good care of me. Thank you.

He then turned towards Obra-Jean.

Gracias, Obra-Jean.

Everyone looked at Mason then Obra-Jean with astonishment. Obra-Jean sat still, then stood and faced Mason.

Muchas gracias, Uncle Mason. You've been a good friend to me while I've been living in your home.

Then she walked to where her mother was sitting and gave her a kiss on the cheek. Toby did the same. Leona stood and walked to Clemenza who had started to cry as she approached. Leona leaned over and gave her mother a light kiss on the cheek.

Ondine watched the Moore and Post women with a sense of satisfaction and amusement. Here was a family so unlike her own and, yet, these were people whom she loved and who loved her. She reached beside her and grasped Augusta's hand. She looked at Augusta intensely as if her look alone would communicate her thoughts. Augusta returned her gaze with puzzlement as if questioning Ondine's intentions. Ondine squeezed her hand and Augusta understood: Ondine planned to make an announcement. Augusta felt a wave of anxiety course through her body. Her eyes began to water. Augusta's tension passed to Ondine who took a deep breath, stood, letting go of Augusta's hand, and clapped her hands together to get everyone's attention. It didn't take much for folks to notice Ondine. She seemed to tower over the table and everyone seated there. Those folks who were standing sat down. It was apparent that Ondine was about to make a speech, probably a long speech.

Dear lord, we are so blessed to be here together today. We have three generations of families here. We hope that there will always be more of them to come. Our elders, Sister Clemenza, Sister Estyllene, and Brother Barry, are a bridge between us and all of those loved ones who have long since passed on. Those elders made it possible for us to be here together today to enjoy this bounteous meal. We honor them by remembering their names and their lives. We preserve them in our hearts and our minds. We give them eternal life by our deeds. We enable your divine plan by our community. We are all different but we have a common purpose. That purpose is to love one another. Our love nurtures each and every one of us. Our love lifts our spirits. Our love heals our hurts. Our love keeps us going when we want to give up. Our love forgives our mistakes, our misdeeds, our failings, and our wrongs. It helps us accept that we are, in fact, only human. We have the capacity to learn. We have the incentive to change. We have the ability to grow. We have the imperative to understand that our perspective is not the only perspective. We have the need to be humble in the face of so much that we cannot know.

We have here today the children of our elders, Sister Leona, Sister Augusta, and Brother Mason. These folks are the bridge between a past and a future. They have learned from their elders. They were nurtured by their elders. They have taken their lessons and tried to teach those who follow them, including their own children, Sister Toby, Brother Elgin James, and Sister Obra-Jean. We know that with each generation, and the three that are here today, the great passage from one to another is not easy, smooth, or even sometimes welcome. Each generation faces new challenges. Each must adapt to those challenges or be washed away in a flood of new ideas, innovations, and realities. She who refuses to adapt will be broken, She who denies realities will be crushed. Love cannot save a mind that is closed or unthinking. Love cannot save a mind that is unwilling, or unable to consider what is different from what has been received and considered as final. There is no final. There is no absolute. There is no one and only way. All of the folks here today testify to the many possibilities of life, love, and happiness. We must celebrate those possibilities because without them we are less than our potential suggests.

Look at those among us, including myself, who come from other families, Sister India and Sister Vergie, and who bring their lives, experiences, and histories to this community. I, Sister Ondine, offer myself to this loving family, to enrich it, to nurture it, to challenge it. Yes, challenge. Just as I want to learn from all of you and be graced by your love, I want to teach all of you and share the love with which I have been blessed. So, the best love is truth and truth is what I want to share today. The love of my life is sitting beside me, Augusta Post, daughter, sister, aunt, and my life companion. May we be a blessing to this family and may we feel the love of each and every one of you.

With that concluding statement, Ondine sat down next to August and, again, took her hand. Toby leaned over to India and whispered in her ear "Well, that cat is finally out of the bag." Later, after everyone had hugged Ondine and Augusta, the group settled into smaller clusters. Toby pulled her sister aside out of hearing range of the family and took a couple of folding chairs with her.

Obra-Jean, sit down. What was that all about between you and Mason? I mean, he thanked you in Spanish. I didn't even know he spoke English.

He thanked me for helping him learn to draw. I also taught him some words in different languages just like Aunt Augusta taught me. And we played different games. We're friends.

Different games? What kind of games? Friends? Listen, Sister, cut the bullshit. I've known you all of your life and I know when you're bullshitting and outright lying. You've done this since you were a kid and nobody seemed to catch on, except me. I know you. What's between you and Mason? Don't fuck with me.

What's with you? I told you the truth.

Obra-Jean, stop lying. I just want to know the truth. I don't care what the truth is. I just want to know it.

Okay, Sister, but this has to be between the two of us. Just you and me. Don't tell India or anybody else.

I don't like keeping secrets from India but, okay, just between us, I promise.

No judgment either. Okay?

What did you do? Fuck him?

Yes, I slept with Mason.

Really? Are you kidding or something? He's your goddam uncle.

I told you, no judgment. I know he's my uncle. I had sex with him, a couple of times, when I first moved to Grandma's house. That was it. Nothing since. He would come to my room and we would talk. I found out that he liked to draw. He seemed so sad. I asked him if he ever had a girlfriend. Of course, he never did. I thought, well, neither of us ever had sex so why not try it with him? Grandma Moore always said to me to try different things.

I'm sure that sex with your defective uncle is not what she meant. But, hold on, you say you never had sex before our uncle? I don't believe you. This sounds like more bullshit.

What do you want me to say?

The truth. Damn it. Do you even know what truth means?

Yes, I do. Okay, I did have sex before Mason, if you really want to know. And, just so we are clear, I've had sex with women and men. Alright? I like sex. It's no big deal. Can I continue now? So, I asked him if he wanted to do it and he was really shy and didn't reply. He may not have even known what I meant. One afternoon, however, when Grandma and Grandpa were away, we tried it. I showed him what to do and he liked it. So, we did it again and that was it. Then, he lost interest and so did I.

Sister, really? With Mason? Did you at least use protection, I hope?

It wasn't necessary. He never came. I don't think he's really completely functional down there or, maybe, it's his brain that doesn't function. He couldn't make it hard.

Sister, Mason is your uncle, our father's brother. That's some kind of incest.

Yeah, so what? There were no babies. Nobody got hurt.

Are you kidding me? It's not about babies. It's about having sex with a close relative, your father's brother. Do you know what, Sister, I'm not sure what to believe about any of this. This sounds like more bullshit. Why can't you just tell me the straight truth?

The straight truth? Why should I tell you something that's none of your business? So, don't ask me for the straight truth. My business is my business just like you with India, E.J. with Vergie, and Aunt Augusta with Ondine.

Oh, you knew about Augusta and Ondine?

Sister, I've learned to pay attention to other people, to listen and watch them carefully. You and everybody else think I'm this naive kid who only thinks about architecture.

I wonder why we think like that, Obra-Jean. I don't really know you. Who the hell are you, anyway?

Watch me. Maybe someday you'll find out.

Toby began walking back to the picnic table but she was intercepted by Ondine who stopped her, took her hand and said "Toby, I missed a great opportunity with you because I was so silly. I think you made a good choice with India."

Toby was briefly puzzled until she remembered the walk with Ondine in Palmer Park years ago. Yes, she thought, she and Ondine might have been a couple. Well, that was a long time ago. Toby had India, and Sidney. Life is good. The two women hugged and parted. Toby rejoined the grandmothers, her mother, her aunt, and India.

XI

Sisters and Brothers
The Post Family

— Some Interesting News —
Fall 1964

It was Saturday—house-cleaning day for Leona. With her children gone, there was actually little to clean and that was a good thing for Leona who was never much interested in cleaning house in the first place—a task she previously delegated to Clemenza and the kids. Nevertheless, she made a pass at the bathroom and kitchen and vacuumed the center of the new wall to wall carpeting. She was done and exhausted after two hours. As she sat in the kitchen sipping her third cup of coffee of the day, Clemenza came out of her room and circled the kitchen trying very hard to gauge Leona's mood. She had a mission and, as she circled, Leona noticed her. Clemenza stopped, turned towards Leona and in the most measured and monotone voice she could muster, posed a question to her daughter.

Leona, I have some bad news. Can I talk with you?

Relax, Clemenza. Of course you can talk with me. What is it?

I got a phone call from your brothers, Leander and Titus. My sister, Iris, in Hot Springs is dying. She wants me to come there to see her one last time.

She hasn't seen you since you left Hot Springs a hundred years ago. So, why, after all this time, does she want to see you one last time?

We've kept in touch all these years with letters. I've talked a few times with her on the phone. She's my only living sister, Leona, and I want to go. But I can't go there by myself. I'm too old for that.

What do you want me to do?

I hate to ask but can you come with me?

All the way to Hot Springs?

Yes. I'm afraid of airplanes and airports and everything that's involved. If you came with me, I think I could do it.

I don't know, Clemenza. Why can't you get someone else to go with you. Why me?

I want you to come too. You knew my sister. She was like a mother to you. She took care of you after I left Hot Springs. Your brothers live there too. You remember them, don't you? Well, they were still youngsters when you left Hot Springs. We could have a kind of family reunion before my sister leaves us.

I haven't seen those people in decades. Besides, why don't you ask Augusta?

430

Augusta can't leave her school now. And, she never really knew any of the Hot Springs family. She was too young, just a baby, when we left there. But I'm sure you remember them, don't you?

Of course I remember them but I haven't thought about any of them in years. They probably don't even remember me. They wouldn't even recognize me now.

Leander and Titus both asked about you. They remember you and they want to see you too.

Really? I don't know. That's a long trip to see people I barely remember.

They're your family, Leona. They're the family you've been missing all these years. They've missed you.

The person they miss doesn't exist anymore.

That's not how family works, Leona. Family is forever.

Clemenza, I've never heard you talk like that. You, of all people, talking about family. That's not how you lived your life.

You're right. Now I know how wrong I was. If I had a second chance, I could be a different person. A different mother.

Then, maybe I would be a different daughter. When were you thinking of going?

Right now as soon as possible. My sister says she can't hold out too long. We would have to go real soon. Please, Leona. I never ask you for anything. I know how you feel about me leaving you behind in Hot Springs. There's nothing more I can do to make that up to you except die and be forever out of your life. I know I don't have a right to ask you this favor but I'm asking. I'm hoping you'll agree to go with me. Maybe, if we both go back to Hot Springs, something will let us make peace with each other. I want that more than anything before I die. Please, Leona.

Leona had difficulty deciding what to say. Her immediate reaction was to say no simply because she didn't feel she owed her mother any favors. She also thought Augusta, not herself, should go with their mother. But something moved her about both of them returning together to Hot Springs — not to see Iris nor to reconnect with Leander and Titus. Somehow, having Clemenza all to herself suddenly pleased her even as she recognized the irony of having lived in hostile proximity to Clemenza for so many years. Now, for the first time in her life, she really didn't feel any more of the toxic resentment towards her mother. A spirit of goodwill took possession of Leona and she laughed to herself at the irony of it all.

I'll go with you, Clemenza. I'll take care of all of the arrangements. You won't have a single worry. E.J. can take care of the house and himself while we are away. He may even like being alone because he'll probably have Vergie stay with him while we're gone.

Thank you, Leona.

You contact your sons and find out if we can stay with them or if we need to get a hotel room. I'll see about ordering the airline tickets when everything is settled. Augusta can help me with that.

I already know we can stay at Leander's house. He has a spare bedroom.

Fine. I'll call now for the tickets.

The airline trip from Detroit to Hot Springs was a first flight for both women and they were nervous. There were three flights involved: one from Detroit to Saint Louis, another from Saint Louis to Little Rock, and the last from Little Rock to Hot Springs. While the first flight was on a jet, the second and third used small propeller planes that bucked and rolled in buffeting air currents. With each lurching movement of the planes, Leona clasped Clemenza's hand as much to calm herself as to assure her mother. Both were relieved when they finally reached Hot Springs but began dreading the return flights six days hence. Standing in the arrival hall of the terminal, Leona scanned the crowd for her brothers. She wasn't sure she would recognize them from pictures they sent to Clemenza but there they were, waving at them. She was immediately struck by how much they looked like their mother and how different they looked from herself. They were short, stocky, and very dark. Both were dressed in suits that made them look like undertakers or pallbearers at a funeral. Since Leona and Clemenza had not seen the brothers in decades, their initial greeting was a bit tentative and formal. Clemenza was never one to show much emotion and she performed to type in the terminal. Leona wanted to embrace her brothers but checked herself and allowed only one kiss each from her brothers on her cheek. Fortunately for all, as Leander steered the car towards the center of Hot Springs, the initial formality began to slip into a more familiar rush of questions and answers, laughter, and a few tears. The brothers were seeing their sister for the first time in over thirty years and their mother for more than forty years. Their joy increased with each passing moment. By the time they reached Leander's modest home, everyone seemed at ease. Leander was effusive. He wanted them to meet his wife, his children, and his grandchildren. His brother's family also awaited them and Leander listed all of Titus' family members they would meet as well. As driver and passengers exited the car and retrieved the luggage, a rush of folks descended from the front porch of the house and enveloped them in hugs, kisses, and garbled, hasty introductions. Leona was giddy. Although she knew none of these people, they were in one way or another her family. The years that had separated her from her place of birth and the people who lived there dissolved for her into a chaotic, overpowering feeling of belonging. It would be a while before she realized that what, as a young woman, she had given up in Hot Springs to be in Detroit near her mother, was a lost opportunity to have been nurtured in, and matured with, this loving community of relatives. It would be later still when she truly understood that she had abandoned her own Hot Springs family many decades ago. She did, in fact, exactly what she felt Clemenza had done to her.

Someone whisked Leona's and Clemenza's suitcases to their bedroom as everyone else squeezed into Leander's house and then into the backyard where tables and chairs were arranged to accommodate the large, raucous gathering. Leona and Clemenza were seated at separate tables—Leona with Leander, and Clemenza with Titus. Leander wanted to know details, first, about Leona's family. He had known that Perry died in an automobile accident but hadn't learned how Leona survived and provided for her children and mother. Leona questioned Leander in great detail about his life—his schooling, his family, his work but most importantly how growing up with his Aunt Iris affected him. Leander confessed he and Titus always considered Iris their mother. Clemenza was such a vague presence to them when she left for Detroit that they quickly forgot about her. Iris loved them. There was never any money to speak of in the household but, as children, they never went hungry. Somehow, Iris always fed them, encouraged them to attend school, kept them out of trouble, and coaxed them into marrying smart, decent girls. Iris' husband was not an influence in their life since he was seldom home and when he was, he ignored the boys. He had other women with whom he sired children who carried his blood line. When he died, his passing went unremarked. Iris was the sole center of their life. Both identical twins completed high school and found the kinds of jobs available to young black men in the hotels, baths, and casinos of Hot Springs. After they married—within a year of one another—their wives also worked between pregnancies which were frequent. Between the twins and their wives, they had a total of six children (two more had died at birth). Although each brother had his own home, the children were raised communally within a blended family. Iris was matriarch of this community and she was revered. Mother Iris, as everyone called her, now lay dying in a hospital as a result of kidney failure, congestive heart problems, and diabetes. She had never seen a doctor in her life until she recently collapsed at home and was helpless to prevent an ambulance from taking her from her home and family to a hospital. There was nothing the doctors could do for her except for palliative care to make her as comfortable as possible until the inevitable end. This was when she contacted her sister in Detroit.

While Leona spoke with Leander, Clemenza listened to similar stories from Titus but her attention drifted and it soon became apparent to her son that his mother was disturbed. He finally asked her what was wrong, and she replied she wanted to see her sister as soon as possible. This was the main reason she came to Hot Springs and she didn't want her sister to die while she was enjoying herself in her son's backyard talking about the past. Could she excuse herself now and be taken to the hospital? Titus immediately signaled his brother to prepare to leave and take Clemenza and Leona to see Iris. The drive re-introduced Clemenza and Leona to a much different cityscape than the one they left and remembered. The hospital itself was something of a shock because, when they lived in Hot Springs, the small community of black folks didn't have access to hospitals that only treated whites. Leander and Titus accompanied their mother and sister up to Iris' room which she shared with a elderly white woman. Tubes and sensors streamed from Iris' body to machines that hummed and beeped. An oxygen mask covered her nose and mouth and nearly obscured most of her face. Her eyes were closed when Clemenza approached her bed. Clemenza said softly, "Sister, I'm here." Iris opened her eyes and tried to focus. Clemenza took her hand, and Iris looked in her direction. Tears flowed from her eyes as she locked onto her sister's gaze. Clemenza then said, "Your niece, Leona, is with me. Here she is." Iris tried to re-focus on Leona who stepped forward to kiss her aunt's forehead and brush back her thin gray hair. Iris couldn't speak. A feeding tube was inserted down her nose into her stomach. Leander brought two chairs for Clemenza and Leona. They sat side by side next to Iris' bed. The brothers drifted in and out of the room while their mother and sister sat in silent vigil with Iris. After an hour or so, Iris violently vomited into her plastic face mask. Leona summoned a nurse who asked her and Clemenza to leave the room while she attended Iris. A doctor appeared and after examining Iris, informed the woman that the end was near and nothing more could be done. Iris was sleeping and everyone should leave. Leander and Titus had to support Clemenza to walk her to the elevator. When they finally arrived back at Leander's house, Clemenza went directly to bed. Leona sat with Leander and his wife, Parsetta; all of the other family members had long since returned to their own homes. Titus was the last to leave and he kissed his sister goodbye, promising to see her again during her stay in Hot Springs.

When quiet settled over the house, Leander asked Leona about Detroit. She started by saying the city had changed so much from the time she arrived there to today. White people were leaving the city in a panic since the riots of 1967. Businesses were also leaving the city for the suburbs. Fortunately, for her, the federal government kept its offices in downtown Detroit. Many of the automobile companies, including the one where Perry had worked, either went out of business or moved their factories to the South or out of the country. Detroit was becoming a desolate place with many abandoned and burned-out homes, empty commercial structures, and deserted, decaying factories. Detroit had become a majority black city with fewer resources and population. It was hard to find a supermarket or movie theater in the city. Everything seemed to have relocated to the suburbs. She remembered when she first arrived in the city, blacks owned businesses in Paradise Valley and Black Bottom. There were nightclubs and bars for blacks. Social life was exciting. She made many friends and, together, black folks created their own world in their own neighborhoods. All of that started to change when the city began building freeways through black neighborhoods and tearing down black folks' houses and businesses for urban renewal. Leona explained that she and her husband, like so many of their friends, started looking in white or integrating neighborhoods for new and better housing. The old close-knit social order began to fray as friends moved further and further away from their old neighborhoods and their friends. The new neighborhoods never quite developed the life found in the old, mostly destroyed districts. With three children, Leona focused on them and their lives and futures. Her family became her world. Leander could see that Leona was tiring from the travel, the hospital visit and, now, conversation so he suggested she go to bed. They had several days ahead of them to continue their talks. As Leona stood to go to her bedroom, the phone rang. Parsetta answered it. She called Leander to the phone; it was the hospital. "I see," said Leander as he listened to the voice on the phone. Iris had died.

Funeral arrangements for Iris had been prepared in anticipation of her death and a date of burial was set to coincide with the day before Clemenza and Leona were scheduled to return to Detroit. Meanwhile, Titus wanted to show his mother and sister around Hot Springs, including places they might remember as well as many new things around town. The first stop on their tour was Bathhouse Row, centerpiece of downtown with its fine hotels, casinos, and spas for tourists who flocked to Hot Springs for the reputedly healing waters. This key section of town had put Hot Springs on the national map as a leisure destination. The casinos were also a prelude to, and perhaps, an inspiration for the later rise of Las Vegas as a gambling wonderland. However, Hot Springs' isolation along the southeastern edge of the Oauchita Mountains in mostly rural Arkansas may have precluded the kind of sprawling development facilitated by the flat desert terrain of Nevada and its proximity to several major urban centers. As a quieter retreat than Las Vegas, Hot Springs remained a preferred destination for certain travelers less dazzled by nearly naked showgirls. While Clemenza and Leona had known of Bathhouse Row when they lived in Hot Springs, they had never paid it much mind because it was the preserve of white folks. The historic black section of the city was just southeast and in walking distance of Bathhouse Row but it might as well have been in Missouri or Kansas. Bathhouse Row did not touch upon black lives except as a place of menial, but critical, employment. Having seen this—the most central feature of Hot Springs—Clemenza and Leona were content to spend the rest of their time in town visiting relatives and attending the funeral service before returning home.

Both Leander and Titus had jobs, in fact, at one of the most elegant hotels in town, the Arlington Hotel at the north end of Bathhouse Row. Leander was a janitor and Titus was a cook in the hotel kitchen. They could not take time from work during the day to socialize with their mother and sister and, therefore, left it to their wives to entertain them. The wives, Parsetta and Glendie, were both local women who, because they had been friends from childhood, met their respective husbands at the same time in high school. Although the twins were identical, Parsetta took a fancy to Leander and, fortunately, Glendie immediately liked Titus. Both couples each had three children—two boys and a girl for Parsetta and two girls and a boy for Glendie. The children stayed together as if they were all siblings. It helped that their two residences were in the same block separated by only four intervening houses.

Although the wives also worked at the Arlington Hotel as maids, they were able to adjust their schedules so that one wife could always be with Clemenza and Leona during the day. Clemenza didn't have much to say so she simply listened to the other women converse. She was often lost in thought about her deceased sister and the fact that they had so little time together before Iris' death. She began to lament all of those years lost when she could have kept in closer touch with not only Iris but also her other two sisters, Gladiola and Concordia, both of whom had died years earlier. Why did she not visit Iris sooner? The thought turned over again and again in Clemenza's mind. The fact that Clemenza seemed distracted and not present did not bother Leona. She enjoyed talking with both wives about raising children, about husbands, and about work. That Leona was a secretary working for the federal government gave her enormous status with the two wives. They wanted to know every detail of her office, her boss, her co-workers, and her duties. No detail was uninteresting; in fact, the wives often asked Leona to repeat things she had already told them because they were so fascinated to know about her world that seemed so glamorous to them. There was also no small amount of jealousy. Leona dressed at a much more expensive and professional level than the wives in their plain, discount store dresses. She was well-groomed with beautiful, long polished nails and pressed, styled hair and she didn't look like she had birthed three children. Her figure was trim and shapely compared to the stout, meat-and-potatoes look of the wives.

Leona reveled in the wives interest—and jealousy. Here she was—a product of the same environment—a woman who had gone to the big city and become a professional female, albeit a secretary. She had the foresight to bring lots of photographs with her of her late husband, children, sister, friends, home, and office. If Leona had said she had come from Hollywood, she could not have made a bigger impression. The joy she felt being among more humble relations began to wane as she thought about who she would have been had she not left Hot Springs. Would she have been like these wives, a maid in a hotel fattened on too much pork? Then another thought completely unsettled her: What if Clemenza had never left Hot Springs? Would Leona, then, have left on her own, or remained? There would have been no reason for her to go to Detroit except for the fact her mother was there. But why did she even want to follow Clemenza when Iris was as much of a mother as anyone could want? Iris was her mother, a mother she, Leona, abandoned and to whom she never gave a second thought after leaving Hot Springs. She never kept in contact with Iris despite Iris' letters inquiring of her well-being. She never remembered her birthday or thought to wish her Merry Christmas and Happy New Year. She was so focused on Clemenza all those years that all of the other people she left behind in Hot Springs— her aunts, Iris, Gladiola, and Concordia, and her brothers, Leander and Titus—became irrelevant to her. That was what she did. She was as thoughtless and unconcerned about them as she accused her own mother of being about her. Who was more guilty?

Leona suddenly had the impulse to cook. Since the wives worked, she arranged to prepare all of the meals alternately for Parsetta's and Glendie's households. When she told Clemenza of her plan, her mother offered to help so that both households would have meals prepared for them each day. Leona and Clemenza made breakfast, prepared lunch bags for the women and men, and cooked dinners. This work, and it involved shopping, prepping, and cooking, was a joy for both. Leona felt none of the resentment that sometimes overtook her with her own family. Instead, she experienced pride in her skills and love in assuming the labor for her sisters-in-law. Clemenza's cooking reconnected her with her sons but more importantly created a bond with her daughters-in-law and softened the hurt she had endured all those years living in Detroit with her own daughter. The remaining days in Hot Springs passed quickly.

The day of the funeral service was hot and the small Baptist church was crowded with relatives and friends. Given the heat, the service was brief, intensely emotional, and ultimately a relief to the immediate family. After internment of Iris' remains at the local black cemetery, everyone was invited to Leander and Parsetta's home for a meal. Although Clemenza, Leona, Parsetta, and Glendie had prepared a bountiful table, guests brought pots of fried chicken, salads, pies, and cakes. There was also a fair amount of beer and liquor but these were kept out of sight in deference to the many tee-totaling church-goers. When the party finally dispersed in the early evening and the sun began to set, Parsetta and Glendie and their adult daughters begged Clemenza and Leona to rest and visit with Leander and Titus on their last night together before returning to Detroit. Mother, daughter, and sons remained in the backyard seated at a table. Clemenza now lamented that Augusta could not be with them on this occasion. Clemenza could have had all of her children together, maybe, for the last time in her life. The twins nodded in agreement. Clemenza started to cry. Leona offered her a handkerchief from her purse. Leander leaned over to his mother and spoke.

Mother Clemenza, why don't you stay here with us in Hot Springs instead of returning to Detroit? Leona took good care of you all these years. It's our turn now. We've got a room for you. We could look after you. You would have all of this family around you.

I agree with Leander, Mother Clemenza. Stay with us. We loved Aunt Iris as our adopted mother. But you're our birth mother. We need you now. Our children need you. Their children need you. You'd be the mother of this family. We would be a whole family for the first time.

Leander, Titus, that's so sweet. of you boys. You know I never guessed I'd have such a strong feeling about this place and about you after all of those years in Detroit. Leona and Augusta have been good daughters to me. I love my grandkids in Detroit. It's my home, really, a good home.

Mother . . .

Leona?

Mother, your sons are right. You belong here. This is where you really belong, with people who have nothing but love for you. Yes, I've taken care of you these past years. But I know I haven't given you love, not the kind of love you're getting from your sons and their wives. I wish I could feel like my brothers feel. I wish I hadn't let a hurt keep me from loving you all I could these many years. I'm sorry. Now, I know I can't undo what I've done. You can't undo what you did. Forgive me.

Leona, Baby, what you've just said now eases my mind. I was not a good mother to you. I was not a good mother. But here I am now with three of my children. All of you are the most precious things in my life. Leander, Titus, how could I choose now to leave my daughter again to be with you? Leona, how could I stay with you and miss the chance to be a mother now to these boys? What can I do?

Mother, stay with your sons. Augusta and I can come to visit. We will come to visit. I have a family in Detroit. I need to be a better mother to my own children. Stay here. It's best for you.

Leona had to dig out more handkerchiefs from her purse because everyone was crying including Leona. Although nothing had been decided, it was clear to all that a new arrangement was coming. After Clemenza and Leona returned to Detroit and mother and daughter continued to discuss the twins' proposal, both women saw clearly what would happen. They brought Augusta into the discussion as well, and she quickly agreed that Clemenza should do what she thought best for herself. Clemenza packed her clothes and other belongings with Leona's and Augusta's help, and shipped them to Hot Springs. She returned there nearly a month to the day of her most recent visit for her sister's funeral. She never left Hot Springs again.

— The Sisters Chat —
Early Summer 1964

When Clemenza moved to Hot Springs, Leona found her house painfully empty. There was no husband, no daughters, and her son was spending all of his time with his fiancé. Leona was alone. Very alone. As she had feared most of her life, she was alone, in this big house, with no one to talk to. No one to supervise. No one to complain about or complain to. She tried reading. She watched TV. She cleaned the house. She washed everything that could be washed. She gardened. She was miserable. She needed a dog. A dog would be a good friend and companion, and would show her all the love and affection she needed. Of course, she would have to walk it and feed it and take it to the vet and clean up after it. It would be like having a child again and she was certainly finished with that part of life. Instead of having a dog, she invited her sister over for dinner. At least they could have a good, long conversation over food and drinks. Augusta asked if she could bring Ondine. Leona replied a bit too quickly and sharply, "No." She just wanted to be with her sister. Maybe, another time she would entertain Augusta and Ondine but not right now. In fact, Leona wanted to unload. There were thoughts that had pressed on her mind ever since the reality of Clemenza's leaving Detroit settled on her. She had dreams and memories that had remained inside her too long. It was time to stop cleaning house and clean out her own mind.

The evening of their dinner, Augusta was cheerful as always and enjoyed her sister's beautifully prepared meal of baked ham with scalloped potatoes and collard greens as side dishes. Leona also made a lemon pound cake that she served with vanilla ice cream. After dinner, the sisters settled in the den with drinks and Leona got down to business. Leona rambled for a while about this and that when Augusta abruptly stopped her cold. She told Leona bluntly that she wasn't interested in chit-chat. She wanted to know why Leona reacted with annoyance at the Fourth of July picnic when Styll asked her why she was thinking of *aubergine* when she named her daughter's name. Leona's mind came in sharp focus.

Okay. This is what I really need to tell you but I didn't know where to start. Take another drink. You'll need it. I need it. Here we go. So, you know I was married in Hot Springs before I met Perry. Right?

Of course I knew that. You were divorced when you met Perry and were four years older than him. That's why Styll didn't want him to marry you. She said a divorced older woman would be a bad bet. She was wrong but that was then.

But, any man is a good bet, right? We all know that from experience. Well, maybe not you.

I know something, too, about men, Leona.

Yeah, sure you do. We can forget about that, Sister. So, my first husband was not as handsome as Perry. He was very dark-skinned with kinky hair not light-skinned with beautiful wavy hair like Perry. He was shorter in build than Perry and heavier. Maybe I fell in love with Perry because he was the opposite of Farrell. Farrell Broadstreet. Hell, I haven't said his name in years. Well, Farrell and me were still almost kids when we met.

He smelled bad because nobody taught him how to take care of himself and stay clean. He didn't grow up in a family. He seemed like some kind of orphan who lived where he could. He didn't have any people, no family. Maybe, that's why I took to him because I felt like an orphan too. Farrell made a little money doing odd jobs and he liked to party, and so did I. We were crazy kids but I thought we were so grown-up. He had smarts. He was strong. Nobody messed with him. Farrell was actually very sexy and he really knew how to make me happy in bed. He could go at it all night. Well, that's a different story. Hey, don't be surprised. I'm just being honest here.

I'm not surprised, Sister. I like sex too, you know. It's no big deal. Continue.

He was blessed, you might say, in the equipment department. I mean the man had a big one. This big. Yeah. Amazing, huh? I know it's not fair to compare husbands but between Farrell and Perry, it wouldn't be a contest. Farrell would win. Don't look so shocked. Perry wasn't lacking down there but Farrell had him beat by a yard or at least a couple of inches in every direction. Okay, you're laughing. It's funny, I know. Anyway, once I got him cleaned up what really got me about Farrell was his personality. Yes, his personality. He joked. He laughed. He played the fool. He was only serious about having a good time. I loved him for that because I wanted to have a good time too. He was a janitor and made a little money that we spent on having a good time. I was in my last year of high school when we got married. When I graduated, I got him to bring me to Detroit and we partied at clubs in Paradise Valley. We loved the music and dancing. We drank a lot and then came home to have our private party. Mister Farrell could get-it-on. I was in heaven until my life became a hell. There was another side to Farrell's personality. He would, without warning, turn angry and vicious. I think he had been mistreated when he was younger and, not having parents to raise him, he never got over that. Sometimes, he would just start yelling and throwing things. I tried to calm him down but he would turn his anger on me. He would call me names and accuse me of doing things I didn't do. He would go from zero to a hundred in seconds and it would always catch me off guard. I could never tell when he would go off or what would send him into a fit of anger. He would come out of it as quickly as he went into it. After a while, I tried to stay out of his way but he took that as me ignoring him. It only made his fits worse. More often than not, he directed his anger at me. Then he began pushing and hitting me. I told him to stop or I would leave him. I guess my threats made him try to control himself. So, for a while, everything was okay.

Leona, what about *aubergine*? Get to the eggplant.

I'm coming to that, Sister. Okay? You wanted to hear a story so relax. I'm getting there but there's stuff you need to know first. There's a lot to tell. Where was I? Oh, okay. I went to the Eastern Market one day because I wanted to fix Farrell a really nice dinner. Afterwards, we could go out to a club and come home for a good time together. As I was walking around the market and looking at the produce, I noticed something I had never seen before at a vegetable stand. I asked the man in charge of the stand what it was and he said it was an *aubergine*. I said: "It's a what?" He said an *aubergine* is an eggplant and explained it as a vegetable. Now, since I had never had an eggplant, I never noticed one of these before. I suddenly had the thought that this dark purple *aubergine* reminded me of Farrell, you know, his equipment. Alright, his dick. Don't laugh. Really, the man was huge and his dick was very dark like an *aubergine*. Come on, stop laughing. It's funny, I know, but you haven't heard everything yet. Stay with me here. So, this *aubergine* stuck in my mind. When Obra-Jean was born, she was very dark like an *aubergine*. As I thought about my newborn, I thought about that eggplant.

Leona, you lost me somewhere. Obra-Jean was not Farrell's child. She's Perry's child, and you just said that Perry's "equipment" was different from Farrell's.

I'm glad you're paying close attention, Sister. That's right. Now, you're gonna know something about Farrell and Perry that I've never told anybody. It's been my secret. Maybe you'll understand why. Don't look so puzzled. We're getting there. Let's back up to Farrell. One night in one of his rages, Farrell raped me. Yes, rape. I told him "No" but he forced me to have sex. Afterwards, of course, he felt sorry and apologized. But, that's why I kicked his sorry ass out of our apartment. When I knew I was pregnant, I found a woman who gave me an abortion. Now, that's two pieces of news for you, right? Let's move on. Soon after Farrell was out of my life, I met and then married Perry. After we had Toby and E.J., I didn't want any more children and I didn't really feel like having sex. It wasn't satisfying to me anymore. You know what? I don't think I ever enjoyed sex with Perry like I did with Farrell. In a few moments, you'll know why. Anyway, Perry got mad at me for depriving him of his satisfaction. I thought he then started having sex with other women which was okay with me. Then, one night when he had too much to drink and, yes, Sister, your brother-in-law drank too much, he raped me just like Farrell did. It started like this. We were living in our little shitty apartment. The kids were staying with Styll and Barry, for the weekend. It was Saturday night and a nice, cool evening in the fall. I made us dinner. I think it was a meatloaf with mashed potatoes. That was one of Perry's favorite meals. I thought, well, we have the weekend together without the kids and we can have a special evening. After we finished dinner and I cleaned up the kitchen, I came into the living room where Perry was sitting in his favorite chair drinking his beer. I think he had about three beers that night and he was smiling at me when I sat down on the couch. He had that look on his face like "I'm feeling no pain and I'm looking for a good time." Perry started in with me with bullshit. "Baby, you know you're the only woman in the world I love." When he had too much to drink, he always got so sweet and lovey-dovey. But I told him what I told him before. "Perry, I don't care if I'm the only woman you love. I don't enjoy sex anymore. Not with you, not with anybody so don't push me." And he was so "Oh, come on, Honey, you know how it used to be with us. You always enjoyed a good time. You always liked doin' it. I want to hear you scream and holler. I want to feel my love come down." I just looked at him like he was the crazy drunk which he was. He got up from his chair and came over to the couch and sat close to me. I could smell the beer on his breath. He tried kissing me and I turned away. He said: "What's the matter, Baby? Don't I turn you on anymore?" I said to him again that I wasn't interested in sex with him. I would never have sex with him again and that was that. That's when he turned. He grabbed me by the shoulders and pulled me to the floor and lay on top of me so I couldn't move. He started kissing me and pulling up my skirt. I could tell he was unzipping his pants. The next thing I knew he was forcing himself inside of me. He was so heavy on me I couldn't push him off but I kept saying to him to stop. When he came, he rolled over onto the floor and fell asleep. At that moment, I wanted to go into the kitchen and get a knife and cut off his fucking dick. But, I thought to myself, this must be my fault. I caused him to do this. If I had just had sex with him, he wouldn't have raped me. That's when I thought that I was in this situation because of Clemenza. It was her fault because she didn't teach me right about men. She left me to grow up on my own. I hated Perry for what he did but I couldn't get rid of him like I did Farrell because of my children. So, when I became pregnant, as revenge on Perry and as a reminder of what had happened to me, I named the baby Obra-Jean after Farrell's dick. That's the story.

Jesus, Leona. Farrell raped you and you had an abortion. Perry raped you and you named his child after your first husband's dick. Why have you been keeping all of this a secret?

Why? You don't broadcast this shit. I was ashamed of myself, of Perry, of Clemenza, of my life.

Leona, rape is rape. It doesn't matter if it's your husband who does it. You're not to blame. Your husbands are to blame.

Sister, I only understand that now. I've lived my forty-eight years with these memories in my mind and body of two husbands violating me. I've had dreams and nightmares about the rapes. Obra-Jean is the proof of those violations. I had to blame someone, so I blamed myself and Clemenza.

.But you do understand now that you're not to blame?

I think so.

And what about Clemenza?

Poor thing. After all of these years of blaming her for everything I didn't like in my life, I know it wasn't her fault. And even if it was her fault, my punishing her all of these years was just mean and didn't solve anything anyway. I thought I would feel better if she suffered but I was wrong. We were both unhappy. And because I was unhappy, I made my children unhappy. I thought I was being a good mother but I was worse than Clemenza. I thought I was protecting my daughters but I only pushed them away from me. I only wanted them to have what I didn't have. But, I had a mother. She was Iris. I didn't appreciate her. I abandoned her.

Leona, you are a good mother. You haven't pushed your daughters so far away. They love you. They're living their lives and, as far as I can see, they are living quite well. You can take some credit for that. And you helped Clemenza to be with her sons. These are good things, Leona. Really good things. Let go of the past and live in the present. You'll see it's a lot nicer than you've thought.

I know you're right. I admit it, you're right.

Okay, let's have another drink.

But there's one more thing.

Oh, lord. You're kidding? Something else, Leona? Now what?

It's about Perry. There's more about Perry, about his drinking, and raping me.

This is the other shoe?

Right. Size twelve. So, you know how his brother Carson is.

What do you mean?

That he likes men.

Okay. I guess he's always been that way.

Well, he wasn't the only one who was that way.

Leona, you are not about to say what I think you're about to say?

Perry was like Carson but he hid it from me. He hid it from you. He hid it from almost everyone.

Leona, you've just told me that the father of your three children raped you. Now, you're saying he really liked men?

I'm not just saying it. I have proof.

Proof? What proof?

The man he loved told me.

Oh, shit. The man he loved? What man is that?

His best friend and buddy, Henry Hatcher, was also his lover. This is a bitch. You see, I always thought Perry was having affairs with other women. But, in fact, if I had really paid attention to what he said, I would have realized that it wasn't women he wanted. He spent as much time as he could with Henry. He told me so but I thought it was a cover story for whoring around with women. But it wasn't a cover story. He was fucking Henry. Henry told me they had been in love.

Why would Henry tell you that? How do you know what he said was true?

I got a telephone call last spring from a woman who said she was his sister. She said she knew that Henry and Perry were good friends and she wanted me to know that Henry was in the hospital. He was terminally ill but he wanted to talk to me before he died. I said sure and went to the hospital on the Sunday Clemenza went to brunch with you and Ondine. When I arrived, Henry was in a hospital bed. He looked like he was already dead. I called his name and he opened his eyes. It seemed like he was trying to figure out who I was so I told him. When he recognized me, he started to smile but then he began crying. I sat down in a chair next to his bed. I held his hand. He had trouble speaking but he finally said that he missed Perry who was his good and longtime friend. He sort of got himself together and said in a very low voice that he loved Perry. At first, I assumed he meant that they were just very close friends. Then, he told me a story.

Perry and Henry met when both of them were teenagers working at DeSoto. When Perry told Henry that he had met me and we were in love, he warned Henry that we would get married and have a family. Henry asked Perry what about the two of them. They were having sex with each other. It had started when they were drinking and fooling around. Then it got serious. Perry told Henry he didn't want to be like his brother, Carson. Perry understood Carson and tried to protect him. But he hid his own feelings. So, when Perry met me, he thought that would end his affair with Henry. But it didn't. He also wanted to be with Henry and Henry wanted to be with him. Perry thought that having sex with Henry wouldn't affect his love for me or our children. I asked Henry how long their affair lasted. He said they were lovers until Perry died.

I let go of Henry's hand. I wanted to smother him with a pillow. I was angry and hurt and trying to disbelieve Henry but I knew in my heart he was telling the truth. So, I asked him why he decided to tell me this shit now. Why didn't he just die and keep his secret? Henry said he had to let me know how much he loved and missed Perry because no one else knew about his love. He felt he lost the love of his life when Perry died. He said he hadn't been the same since. He said Perry made him feel happy. He felt that he made Perry happy. And because Perry was happy, he could love his wife and children. When he finished, I felt I knew what I had always known. Perry had always kept something from me, and I denied what it was. I believe Perry did what he thought he had to do by being married. When he couldn't control his feelings and be happy, he drank. When he drank too much, he really lost control. I think he raped me because he really wanted to fuck Henry. He shouldn't have punished me for his feelings. I can't forgive him for that. I wish he could have been honest about himself. I wish Perry would have chosen one of us to be with instead of trying to be with both of us. But, who knows if I could have lived with him if I knew he loved another man? Hell, I was willing to live with him when I believed he loved other women. Why not a man? I wasn't having sex with him so what difference would it have made?

Perry was good in his heart and a loving father. We had a pretty good life together. I know I didn't kill Perry but I'm glad he died. Somehow, the way things turned out makes sense to me. Sister, I know this is too much to put on you. It was too much for me but now all of this is out of me. You know the truth. I know the truth. Perry is dead but we're still here. All of these years I've blamed Clemenza for every mistake I've made and for everything bad that has happened to me. I know now it wasn't her fault. I made my own decisions, my own bad decisions, and, I guess, it's finally time I took responsibility for them. I've stopped blaming her. That woman in Hot Springs has suffered too much from my anger. As you, my own sister, has said to me over and over again for many, many years, let it go, Leona, and move on. That's what I'm trying to do.

That's a hell of a story, Leona. Give me time to take this all in. Meanwhile, I do have one more question. Years ago, you told me that you found out about women that Perry was seeing. Who were those women?

The truth is those women were only acquaintances from the bar that Perry and Henry frequented. The woman who called and asked for Alexander was a barmaid. She knew Perry by the name "Alexander" because that is how Henry affectionately called Perry.

What a world. What a crazy world.

XII

Aubergine Perry Curtis

— Speaking of Plans —
Late Spring 1965

The campus of the University of Detroit is located on the city's northwest side surrounded by residential neighborhoods of mostly middle income families. Unlike Wayne State University—a public institution in Detroit's midtown district—U of D is a private Catholic university. It has the only architectural study program at university-level within Detroit. Obra-Jean wanted to attend the University of Michigan, a public university with a prestigious architectural study program in nearby Ann Arbor, but she was offered a scholarship to U of D and not to U of M. Therefore, her expenses would be considerably less since she planned to continue living with her grandparents until she finished her degree. As the years progressed, she felt more assured that her knowledge and skills were improving to the point she could confidently pass a State licensing exam and apply for a position as a junior architect in one of the city's large architectural firms. She favored Hill, Reedsworth and Kohl— called simply HR&K—because over many decades the company had designed major buildings in Detroit that Obra-Jean admired. In fact, she thought their designs were far more distinctive than those of their competitors. Academically, she was in the top tier of her class and assumed she would have good credentials to be hired by HR&K. Her fellow students constantly discussed their post-graduation plans. Some wanted to create their own private practices. Others talked of joining offices of nationally and internationally famous architectural firms, like SOM (Skidmore, Owings, and Merrill), and Minoru Yamasaki, Associates. There were a few students who imagined working with the most innovative architects in the world like Le Corbusier and Louis Kahn. Obra-Jean thought she would start close to home and gain experience before moving on to a prestige firm or even starting her own office. She believed she should dream big and work hard to realize her dreams.

During her last semester at U of D, Obra-Jean, like all of the other senior students, was given a semester-long final project to design. The requirements were simple: Choose a neighborhood in the Greater Detroit area with an eyesore building that would benefit from redevelopment, and create a plan for that redevelopment. This senior project would test all that students had learned during their years of study in the architectural program. Obra-Jean liked the challenge however she wasn't sure what area of the city she felt would benefit from redevelopment. Detroit, like many USA cities, had jumped into urban renewal after the Second World War. Many, if not all, of the renewal projects were aimed at old, often deemed rundown neighborhoods that, not coincidentally, housed blacks and other minorities. Together with freeway construction, these projects did not renew but, instead obliterated entire neighborhoods, displacing their residents and destroying communities bound together by common social, cultural, and political interests. The displaced populations fanned out into adjacent areas and often failed to bond with their new communities creating discord and tensions among neighbors. In light of the failures of urban renewal, Obra-Jean quickly concluded that her project would build upon existing elements of a community instead of obliterating them. Since she had limited knowledge of Detroit's neighborhoods, she asked her classmate, Harvey Glass—the only male student with whom she had developed a friendship and who, importantly, had a car—if he could drive her around the city so they both could examine possible project areas. With some hesitation because of his shyness, Harvey finally agreed, and the two classmates planned an itinerary for their survey.

After visiting, mapping, and photographing several potential subject areas of the city, Obra-Jean selected a far east-side neighborhood bordered by the Detroit River. Called Jefferson-Chalmers for two of the main streets, the area consisted of both substantial and substandard homes and a large industrial district comprising portions of a Chrysler Assembly Plant and the Conners Creek Power Plant. Once she began work, Obra-Jean literally began living in the classroom for architecture seniors on the third floor of the old Engineering Building where the School of Architecture was housed. Like the other senior students, Obra-Jean had her own drafting board and desk where she kept all of her notes, drawings, books, supplies, and equipment. The overhead fluorescent lights burned day and night for students who were hard-pressed for time to complete their work by the deadline at the end of the semester. Often, Obra-Jean was the only student working in the room, a fact that did not go unnoticed by the faculty or the cleaning staff who had to work around her each night to complete their tasks. She frequently skipped meals or brought sandwiches from home made by her Aunt Estyllene who was desperate to keep her granddaughter fed while she worked day after day and sometimes all night. As Obra-Jean's project began to take shape in her mind and, ultimately, in her sketches, drawings, and text, she allowed herself to be pleased with how she was able to use everything she had learned from her teachers and from her own experiences and observations. As a capstone to her project, she built a desktop model of her proposal for a redeveloped neighborhood. When the day arrived for the critique by the faculty, Obra-Jean was confident in her project. She listened to her fellow students as they explained their work and paid close attention to the criticisms of her instructors. She noticed her instructors would encourage some students and discourage others from continuing in the field of architecture. The instructors encouraged Obra-Jean. After the critiqued concluded, her favorite instructor, Professor Rainer Lotz, asked her to stop by his office after her last class of the day. He would be working until late and wanted to discuss something with her. When he and everyone else left the classroom, Obra-Jean walked over to her model, leaned over, put both hands on it as if to caress it, and air-kissed it. At four-thirty, she knocked on Professor Lotz's office door and was invited to enter. She closed the door behind her.

Good afternoon, Miss Moore. Please take a seat. How are you after the critique today?

Very well, Professor Lotz. Thank you. I'm pleased with my work.

Good. As you know, I have followed your progress here very closely. I have always admired your creativity and your dedication to your work. I feel you have justified my advocacy for your entry into this architectural studies program and for the financial support we've provided you.

Thank you again.

You see, when you applied three years ago, my colleagues were reluctant to grant you admission despite the fact you had superior grades and showed as much potential, if not more, than any of the other students in your cohort. I was very impressed with your sketchbooks and drawings you submitted with your portfolio. Your depictions of buildings in Europe and America were intelligently observed and beautifully rendered. I particularly liked the ink line drawings. They showed a remarkable sensitively to form, volume, and the importance of light and shadow in architecture. For instance, you captured the immensity of space in the interior of Saint Peter's Basilica and the way light illuminates that space and casts deep shadows. Your sensitivity to the architectural forms and details was very impressive. Even more than that —which was sufficiently persuasive to me—were your own designs. Even before beginning your architectural training, you had an innate sense of composition and form. I would have fought my colleagues to the end for your admission to our program because they would have overlooked an important talent, and that is you.

Thank you, Professor Lotz. I don't know what else to say. I know you've been very supportive of me.

Well, I'm sure you have noticed none of my colleagues have shown you the kind of enthusiasm for your work that I have.

I thought they treated me as fairly as they treated the other students. We've all been heavily criticized for our work. I thought that was the purpose of the program.

Well, yes and no. You see, we do critique students' projects to push our students to excellence. However, you've received more criticism and, in my opinion, more undeserved criticism than your fellow students. You know, Miss Moore, I am not a native of this country. You may or may not know I am a German but now an American citizen. Although I was very young during the Nazi era in Germany, I was aware of the injustices and cruelties my fellow Germans perpetrated upon the Jewish people and others they disrespected and despised. When I had the opportunity, I left Germany to come here. I married an American woman of Jewish descent and that marriage allowed me to stay here and become a citizen. In coming here I did not really know how black people were treated by white people. Although conditions here are not presently like those in Nazi Germany, this country's history is full of examples of injustice and cruelty toward black people that certainly match the atrocities of my native country. It is because of this history that I recognized your unique status in our program. It is why I insisted you be admitted to this school. Of equal importance is the fact that you are a woman and, as you have no doubt noticed, there aren't any other women in our program. Your sex has been a factor in your treatment here as well as your race. I can't say which of the two has worked more adversely to your prospects. You have not been treated fairly on either account but, despite that fact, you have excelled and that is proof you belonged here. You have somehow been untouched by the slights of your fellow students and the dismissive attitudes towards you of some of your instructors. I think a less strong or determined student would have abandoned this school and profession long ago. You are the best student I have had the privilege to teach in all of my years at this university.

Professor Lotz, excuse me. I certainly appreciate what you're saying. I thank you for believing in me and for helping me. It was my family that taught me and my siblings to work hard, to make something of ourselves, and not to be distracted by other people and what they think or do. My family has made me strong.

Well, you have been taught well, better probably than you could ever have learned from me or anyone else at this school. We've had many conversations these past years but I've never heard you talk about your family. May I ask you to tell me something about them?

Of course. My father, Perry Moore, died in a car accident many years ago while our family was returning from vacation in New York and the East coast. Although he worked in an automobile factory, he was very smart and very loving to me. He wanted me to follow my instincts. He always encouraged me and never criticized me. My mother, Leona Moore, well, she worried about us kids, especially me because she didn't think architecture was a practical choice for a Negro girl. She's a secretary and wanted me and my siblings to enter professions that accepted Negroes and women. It's funny to me now that you're pointing out she was right. Architecture wasn't a practical choice but, then, my father was right too when he encouraged me. I had to follow my instincts.

That is very well said, Miss Moore.

I have an older sister, Toby, who is an accountant. She lives with her girlfriend who is a lawyer. My older brother, Elgin James, who is married and starting a family, is a high school math teacher. Our mother, Leona, lives alone in Detroit. My mother's mother, Grandma Post, once lived with my parents but now is in Arkansas with her sons. My father's parents, Grandma and Grandpa Moore, are the people with whom I now live. Augusta, my mother's sister, studied to be an artists. She helped me to decide to study architecture. She took me on my first trip to Europe where I saw many of the great buildings of history and where I made many of my drawings.

Did you visit Germany?

No, but maybe one day I will.

You will see many great buildings there too.

I'm sure I will. There is so much in the world to see. So, I've told you about most of my family. They are all good people who have helped me and helped one another. I guess that's how Negroes survived for generations in this country despite the kind of cruelties and injustice you mentioned.

You are very lucky, Miss Moore. As you know, there are no other women and no other black people in this school. You have beaten the odds.

Thank you, again, Professor Lotz.

But, now, we have to get really serious because the next step is going to be even more difficult than your schooling.

What do you mean?

I have done a lot of checking and I'm sorry to report that no one will hire a black woman architect. I have inquired discreetly just to, you know, test the waters. I have talked to colleagues and friends in architectural offices all over this country. There are not very many women in architecture and I am unaware of any black women at all anywhere in major architectural offices. There may be some but I've not been able to locate any.

My aunt told me there have been some Negro women architects. Not many, of course but a few. Why is that?

I'm sure you know the answer. Most white men do not want to work with black people.

But, you're a white man.

Yes, in this country I'm white. But I am a native German. I didn't grow up here in this environment. I have my prejudices, for sure, but they do not include black people. I am on your side if you want to know the truth. I want to see you succeed because I know you can. You have talent, intelligence, and personality. You only need opportunity.

Are you saying I can't get a job anywhere in this country?

Not likely in a major office. Not, that is, without my help.

How can you help me if no one will hire me?

I think I have convinced someone just as I have persuaded my colleagues to accept you in this program.

But who is this "someone" and where?

Well, right here in Detroit. You have told me previously you are interested in HR&K. Is that correct?

Yes.

Well, the "K" of HR&K is a German like me. He is an older man but a German or, I should say, German-American, because his family came here in the late nineteenth century. But he's more German than American especially when it comes to race. By that I don't mean he is trying to hire black architects or engineers but he is not opposed to hiring someone who is well-qualified, and that would be you. I have talked to him. I have told him all about you. He is willing to take a chance and hire you as soon as you finish your degree. You can apply for your license after you begin work.

This is amazing. It's unbelievable. I can work at HR&K?

That is what my friend tells me. He will do this as a favor to me because he wants me to do some consulting work for him. He will see that you are placed in the design department where you can learn the company's design philosophy and procedures.

That's wonderful and I appreciate you making this contact but I'm not sure, now, given everything you've said, that I'm ready for such a big company. You don't know this but my mother has always warned me about overreaching. I thought she was silly and too cautious but could she be right? Am I a person who could do this? Professor, you've had a lot of students but none like me. Do you think this is really possible for me?

Of course I think it is possible. You are a strong young woman. I am very happy to help you because I believe you will do well. The only difference between you and my other talented students is your color and sex. These are handicaps but they haven't been crippling to your abilities thus far. Why should they be a handicap in the future?

Now I'm not so sure about the future. I'm sorry I just suddenly felt my confidence leave me.

Don't worry too much. We all have doubts about ourselves. I certainly have all the time. Uncertainly means we are being realistic. Only a fool lacks self-doubt. But, I have to ask you to promise me one thing. Do not mention this opportunity to your fellow students or to your other instructors. In fact, please do not tell anyone else in this school. I do not want anyone to try and block your hire.

I think I understand. I promise.

There is one more matter.

Really? What's that?

The architecture school has organized a two week overseas trip this summer for a small, select group of students to visit Morocco. A gift by an anonymous donor to the university will pay all expenses, except for personal purchases. The visit will include several cities, including Tangier, Rabat, Casablanca, Marrakech, Quarzazate, and Fes. If you are interested, I will nominate you as one of the participants.

Oh, my gosh. That would be wonderful but why Morocco?

You would be immersed in an entirely different culture from the ones you have experienced in this country and in Europe. I also think there will be types of architecture that might inspire you and, being among people who look more like you, might give you a different and more positive idea of your place in this world.

May I ask why would you do this for me?

Because I like you. I admire you. You are going to be very good, if not great, architect. Now, do you want to go? I need to know now to inform the committee handling this project.

Can I let you know tomorrow? I need to talk with a family friend first.

Of course. But, please, no later than tomorrow.

I promise, Professor Lotz.

Then, I will see you in class tomorrow and you can tell me your decision.

Goodbye, Professor Lotz, and thank you so much.

Before you go, I have a little present for you. This is a book about the history of architecture in Germany. I know you've been collecting books on architecture for a while. I would honored for you to add this to your collection. It was a gift to me from a dear friend but I have another copy. So I want to give this one to you.

Thank you. I'll keep it forever.

Okay. Goodbye, Miss Moore, and good luck. If ever I can be of help to you, please just ask.

Obra-Jean wanted to talk with Ondine, whom she knew had been to North Africa. She called and received no answer. So she called her Aunt Augusta only to discover that Ondine was at her aunt's apartment. Augusta passed the phone to Ondine. Obra-Jean quickly explained the proposition offered by her professor to visit Morocco. She outlined the scope of the trip and concerns about being the only woman and a black woman with a group of white men in a Muslim country. Ondine noticed the excitement in Obra-Jean's voice but also the apprehension. She assured Obra-Jean that given her success in architecture school among white men, she would have not trouble with a few men on a trip to a foreign country populated by non-white people. As for the Moroccans, to Ondine's knowledge they were among the most progressive and liberal people of the Arab-speaking world. Obra-Jean would not be the one who didn't fit in. On the contrary, she would blend in only too well although she would always be seen as a foreigner. Obra-Jean wondered if she would need to dress like a Moroccan woman. Ondine assured her that, as long as she dressed modestly covering her arms and legs, she would not offend Moroccan sensibilities. Finally, Ondine reiterated what Obra-Jean had heard from Lotz: This was a great opportunity and would only expand Obra-Jean's knowledge of the world and further develop her skills as an architect. Their conversation finished, Ondine passed the phone back to Augusta who congratulated her niece on the opportunity and urged her to show the same zeal of study in Morocco as she had shown in Europe.

— A Different Vacation —
Summer 1965

Morocco was hot. It was summer and the sun heat-blasted everything exposed to its rays. The sunlight was also intense, much more so than Obra-Jean had ever experienced. But, she loved it, with sunglasses—for the first time in her life. As the only woman and only black with three white male students, their Moroccan tour guide, and their Moroccan van driver, she thought she would stand out in Morocco as she had since beginning architecture school. However, she quickly realized she blended in with Moroccans because of her color and, therefore, it was her classmates who stood out. It was an odd realization but it gave her an even greater strength and confidence in herself than she had previously possessed. She became leader of the group.

It didn't take long for her to observe how Moroccan cities differed from those in Europe and the USA. And, yet, there were buildings and neighborhoods that were not so different. These, she understood, had been influenced by European architecture and were probably built by or for Europeans. Although Obra-Jean enjoyed seeing the several cities included in the tour, when the group came to Fes and entered the old walled town, called a *medina*, she was transfixed. The narrow, twisting, turning streets were barely wide enough for wheeled-carts, people, and produce on display all sharing the same paths. Shops selling everything imaginable—and unimaginable—from clothing to household goods to food jammed together along the lanes. Obra-Jean found it difficult to maintain a sense of direction and, in a moment of insight, she decided direction was unimportant. She allowed herself to simply let the *medina* work its magic on her and follow the winding streets to wherever they took her. While her attention was drawn to the endless rows of shops with merchandise spilling into the lane, she noticed that the upper stories of buildings were mostly residential. Realizing that it was impossible to sketch in this setting, as she had done in other cities, she took dozens of photographs of everything that caught her eye. Here, in this nearly claustrophobic urban setting, all manner of human activity was jumbled together and, yet, because it was human activity, it all made sense. Everything complimented everything else. The architecture was simply a framework—a human-built hive—for human life in all of its variety, complexity, and excessiveness. It was architecture built by humans for humans not to be admired for its own sake but for how it met and satisfied human needs. That was its only reason for being. Obra-Jean questioned if she had learned this rationale for architecture in her studies at school. Had her studies taught her to be an architect who would simply solve problems or to be an architect who would create monuments to her own ego? Or, was there a third possibility? Had her studies taught her to be an architect who could create livable, flexible spaces in which humans could be completely human? All of these thoughts did not come to Obra-Jean at once. However, one past experience pressed itself on her thinking. She remembered the Old Streets of Detroit exhibit at the Detroit Historical Museum. It was something about the intimacy of that re-creation that she related to the streets of Fes. What she enjoyed about that exhibit years ago was what she now discovered in an actual city. It was days, months, and years before she could fully assimilate her experience in Fes. She hoped someday she would be able to realize her ideals by designing buildings that delighted people.

A more immediate realization was along the lines suggested by Professor Lotz. In Morocco, Obra-Jean was among a majority of people who looked like her. Even as a woman in a Muslim society dominated by men, she felt judged only by her gender not her color. Her skin color was irrelevant and that was a revelation to her. She felt a kinship with Moroccan women as she had experienced in her own family. That kinship was not subject to the whims of another, more dominant and powerful group. Ever since grade school at Saint Catherine, she was made aware of her status as an outsider because she was black. This feeling was reinforced at architecture school. Now, upon graduation, she was, as Professor Lotz predicted, more aware of her place in the world of people more like her. Her awareness amplified a sense of self that no longer contemplated, feared, or accepted subordination to a majority simply because of who she was and how she appeared. Now she understood the secret power of Ondine.

— The Office —
Summer 1965

Obra-Jean graduated with honors from the architectural program at the University of Detroit and, after returning from Morocco, interviewed at Hill, Reedsworth, and Kohl, Architects, Incorporated for a position in the design department. She had become accustomed to being in an all-male and all-white environment in school so HR&K was no surprise. There were, in fact, a few more women—all white—who worked as secretaries and clerks but not as architects. The stares she received when she walked through the front door of the office building alerted her to the fact that she was an oddity in her new place of employment. At the lobby reception desk, she informed the female receptionist she had an appointment with Mister Gustav Kohl. The receptionist dialed a number, spoke to someone, and announced Miss Moore was in the lobby awaiting her appointment with Mister Kohl. The receptionist said thank you, hung up the phone, and told Obra-Jean to take an elevator to the fourth floor, turn right, and knock on the door marked G. Kohl, Partner. Obra-Jean did as told and was beckoned into the office which turned out to be a secretary's office. An older woman asked Obra-Jean to take a seat and told her that Mister Kohl would see her momentarily. Obra-Jean looked at photographs on the office wall and recognized many of the buildings in Detroit the company had designed. There were also drawings and sketches for buildings she didn't know. While she was looking, a door opened and an elderly man with white hair in a very stylishly-tailored, dark grey suit with crisp white shirt and solid purple bowtie stepped into the secretary's office and invited Obra-Jean to join him in his office.

Mister Kohl's office was spacious but sparely furnished in a modern style. Various art works hung on the wall including more drawings of buildings. Kohl indicated that Obra-Jean should sit in one of the two metal frame chairs to one side of the office. He then sat near her in the other chair.

Welcome to Hill, Reedsworth and Kohl, Miss Moore. Of course I have heard a lot about you from Professor Rainer Lotz. I believe he was your advisor, mentor, and principal instructor.

Yes, Sir, he taught me a great deal about architecture and he was very patient with me.

Patient. Yes. Professor Lotz is a good man and an excellent architect. I wish he would come to work for me. You had one of the best mentors in this city. I am assuming you know his buildings in and around Detroit.

Yes, Sir, I've visited all of them and we've discussed them in detail because I wanted to understand how he approached each design.

If you understand his design philosophy, you will have learned a lot about modern architectural concepts and the practical issues facing today's architects. I hope you will use what you have learned from him in your work here.

I hope so too, Sir.

Now, Miss Moore, having met you I can see why you are a favorite of Professor Lotz. Let me assure you we will hire you. However, there is a matter about which we must come to an understanding.

Yes. What is that, Sir?

You are both a woman and black. I am not telling you anything you do not already know, of course. We have never had a black male architect in this firm and frankly we have never had a woman architect, white or black. I suppose it is our fault but, understand, men have made architecture for centuries and in this country it has been white men who have created architecture. Now, Professor Lotz has convinced me you have the talent and temperament to work in this environment. Is that the case?

Professor Lotz has warned me regarding what I will probably encounter here.

Really? Dear man. I wonder if he has truly prepared you for what this place is really like or anywhere else in our profession. Many of the men here will not believe in your talent and may not give you the opportunity to use it. That is beyond even my control. I cannot dictate to my employees how they should feel about you, and my employees make the decisions about how this architectural practice functions. As a partner, I, generally, do not intervene in the operation of the company. I hope that does not surprise you. You see, I have a lot of power and authority about the direction of our company but not about how it functions on a day-to-day basis. That means you will be at the mercy of men, white men, who make this company function. I would not be able to keep the kind of design talent I have here if I did not give my subordinates and employees complete freedom to do the day-to-day work the way they see fit. This company does its best work when our designers and department heads can make all of the parts of this operation synchronize smoothly. Do you understand what I am saying?

I do, Sir, but what you're saying is I could be treated very badly by the other employees and you would not intervene.

Yes. I am afraid so and I cannot do anything about that. Well, let me amend that statement. No one can physically abuse you. That is against the law. But no one is obliged to be polite or even helpful to you. However, if your treatment by someone endangers the work of this company, that is a different matter and I, or my subordinates, would have to intervene. On the other hand, if there is someone here like Professor Lotz to act as a kind of guardian angel, then you are in luck. If not, then your life here could be quite unpleasant and you may not want to stay. But, I think, there are one or two men here like Professor Lotz, and my responsibility is to make your introduction to them. As I said, the reason I am hiring you is because Professor Lotz has convinced me you can function in this work environment. After what I've said, do you still want to try?

I would like to try but I have to be completely honest with you, Mister Kohl. Although I feel I'm pretty tough and know how to defend myself, I'm just one black woman with, what, a hundred white men?

Yes, and men who have never had someone like you in their midst and may not want you in their midst. Furthermore, they may want you out of their midst and will do anything short of physical violence to see you gone. Think of yourself as a foreign and unwelcome body in an exclusive club.

I think I am pretty realistic about things but am I being foolish to try this? Please be honest with me.

Foolish, yes, but let me say this. It may take a fool to work in this office and only by working here can changes begin to take place. Even if you do not succeed, another fool will eventually follow you and then another until one day all of what I've described changes. So, be a fool and give it a try. At this point, what have you got to lose? Okay? Now, I'm going to call one of my designers up here, a man I think who can work closely with you. I have prepared him for your presence and I hope he can find a way to ease you into your new job.

Thank you, Sir.

Obra-Jean's confidence in herself was thoroughly shaken by Kohl's blunt assessment. She had become so accustomed to the gentle support of Rainer Lotz that she had mistakenly imagined a job wouldn't be any worse than school. She now realized she was completely and, maybe, fatally wrong. A job could be a lot worse. Kohl had asked her to take a seat again in his secretary's office until Henry Vapoorgian arrived. Vapoorgian was a senior designer in the firm and a longtime employee. If anyone could situate this young black woman in the design department, it was Vapoorgian. Obra-Jean didn't have long to wait because Vapoorgian entered the office without knocking. He was not an image of a senior architectural designer Obra-Jean had imagined. Wearing a rumpled, ill-fitting brown suit with tie askew, he had a wild ringlet of uncombed and untamable wiry gray hair on his otherwise very bald and shiny head. Extending his hand, he introduced himself and almost pulled Obra-Jean out of her seat in order to lead her out of the office to an elevator. He talked non-stop about how busy he was and how he didn't have a lot of time to spend with her. She would be shown to a cubicle on the third floor and assigned to a lead designer. She would be his assistant and do whatever work he gave her. When they reached the third floor and its open-plan workspace, every man in the room turned to follow Obra-Jean's progress across the floor to her cubicle where she was told to sit and wait.

The stares were unnerving to Obra-Jean. Sure, she had been stared at in school but never as intensely or seemingly with such open disdain as here. She was almost inclined to get up and leave, admitting that all of this was a mistake and that her mother had been right all along. As she gathered her composure to bolt for an elevator, a tall middle-aged man wearing black slacks and a black vest over his blue dress shirt and yellow bowtie stood in the opening of the cubicle.

Miss Moore, I believe. I'm Ernst Whitty. I understand you are to be my assistant.

I think so, Sir. That's what Mister Varpoorgian said.

Why don't you come to my office and we can chat on the way? By the way, please call me Ernst and shall I call you Obra-Jean? That's a very interesting name. You must tell me about it sometime. As you can see, this space is the main design floor where the architects and engineers work out the basic schemes for buildings. On the lower floors are the drafting rooms where another set of architects and engineers create the working drawings for blueprints. On the top floor are the administrative offices, conference rooms, and a gallery for the display of models and sketches of buildings we've planned or are under construction. Here is my office. Let's go in and, if you will excuse me, I'll close the door for our privacy. Please have a seat at the work table. Henry Vapoorgian already alerted me to your coming here. I would not be honest with you if I said I'm pleased you're to be my assistant. I've been told you are very good, maybe one of the best students from your school. So, it's not your color that troubles me but your sex. I'm something of a misogynist, that is I don't get along very well with women. Let's hope that you prove to be an exception. You'll have to be a very good architect to work with me because I won't accept anything less than the best and I won't cater to your sensitivities as a woman. Now, let's get started on my project.

Whitty moved his chair next to Obra-Jean at the work table that was piled with drawings, photographs, and printed documents. Whitty outlined the project for an office building that had been under development for more than a year. The client wanted a six story building that would be free-standing on a newly cleared site near downtown Detroit. Whitty reviewed the client's requirements for the allocation of the space to the functions that were to occupy each space. He organized and gave form to these requirements then he consulted with engineers who determined the structural and mechanical features. Once the basics were established, estimators assessed the expected cost of construction of the project. Although the plans had been in development for over a year, the client wasn't satisfied with earlier iterations of the building or with the projected budget. Whitty continued redesigning the project to contain costs and, yet, preserve both spatial and functional requirements. Whitty told Obra-Jean her immediate task was to learn all of the plans and planning documents and know every detail of the project by next week. He provided her copies of the material then excused her to return to her own cubicle.

Obra-Jean was excited and shaken. Although she had coursework in school touching on all of these matters, she had never been confronted by an actual building in process of being developed for construction. She made up her mind to burrow into the papers and drawings to learn everything she could and, what she couldn't figure out, she would ask Whitty for help. Already, she thought he had been polite to her and seemed willing to accept her as long as she didn't somehow behave as a woman. But, then, the work he gave her was a test and should she fail, she would be out the door without a goodbye. After settling into her cubicle, she began scanning the drawings. The proposed building was not complex. It was fairly simple and straightforward. Dull, is what she thought, but utilitarian. When she had an overview of the design, she turned to the printed documents that contained the client's requirements, expected budget, and legal contracts. It would take more time, maybe a lot of time, to digest this material but she would be ready by the following week.

Around noon, she noticed the activity in the office ceased and many of the men left the floor presumably to go to lunch. Others were in their cubicles with sandwiches and paper cups of coffee. No one had told her if she could go to lunch so she went to Whitty and inquired. He told her there was an hour lunch break and there was a delicatessen across the street where she could buy a sandwich and beverage to bring back to the office if she desired. The food was okay at the deli. A lot of the men went there. Obra-Jean asked if she could bring him something and he replied he had his lunch and would be eating at his desk. Obra-Jean left the building, found the delicatessen, and ordered a salami and Swiss cheese sandwich and a coffee to go. While she was waiting near the counter, a couple of young white men who were waiting for their order came over to her.

Well, you must be the new person, right?

Do you mean at HR&K?

Yeah, at HR&K.

I'm new, yes. I recently graduated from the University of Detroit.

How did "you" get a job in "our office?"

Excuse me? What do you mean by "you" and "our office?" Who are "you?" I know you're not Mister Kohl because I've already met him. He hired me. Are you Mister Hill and Mister Reedsworth? I believe that's impossible since they're both dead.

Hey, Tom, this is a smart one. Look, Jemima, we're both real architects not some inexperienced lowlife just out of school. We actually design buildings for the company.

You know, whoever you are, my name is not Jemima. If you need to know, although it's really none of your business, Mister Kohl hired me on the recommendation of my professor because of my design skills.

Who was your professor?

Rainer Lotz.

Lotz? You studied with Lotz?

Yes, I did, Tom. Why does that surprise you?

He's probably the best architect in the city, not that the architects at HR&K aren't good too. But, he's an innovator. Why did he let you study with him?

Why did he let me? He didn't let me. He asked me to study with him because I was the best student in my class. He liked my work and I liked his. He's shown me all of his buildings as well as his designs for some that aren't built yet.

You're a Negro and a woman.

You are very observant, Tom. Now, since I already know who and what I am, I don't need you in order to refresh my memory.

Blaine, Tell her there aren't any other Negroes in our office.

I'm standing right here, Tom, and I heard you. Again, that word "our." Do you know what? I know I'm the only Negro and I know I'm a woman. And, it's "my office" now as well as "our office."

I wouldn't get too comfortable, if I were you, because you might not be in "our office" for very long. Besides, have you noticed there aren't any women architects either?

Tom, you really do notice things, don't you? However, did you notice there's a restroom for women? So women do belong in "our office." I don't have to piss at a urinal in the men's restroom while you boys watch. I think I'll be comfortable enough.

You really have a nasty mouth to talk to us like that. You won't be making many friends at HR&K. So, why are you here?

I thought you were so observant, Tom. Can't you see I'm buying a sandwich? Oh, you don't mean "here" in this deli, you mean "here" at "our office?" What do you think I'm doing "here" at "our office?" The truth is I'm an architect who happens to be a Negro and a woman. I'm also smart and sometimes I have a nasty mouth.

So, you think you're smart. You'll have to be more than just smart around here. You'll have to work hard. You'll have to be as good as us but I don't expect it's possible for you to be anywhere near as good as us.

I won't be working for your expectations, Tom, or your approval of me personally. I have a boss, Mister Whitty. He'll be the judge of me and my work, not you.

You'll never fit in. Negroes can't design buildings. Women don't design buildings.

I did fit in at architecture school, Blaine, and I was the only Negro and the only woman. And, I did design buildings that met the approval of my professors so I think I'll fit in at HR&K. Besides, I don't need you two in order to do my work.

Probably, the only reason you did well in school was because you slept with Lotz.

If I did, Blaine, you're probably jealous because you missed the chance to sleep with him.

Are you calling me a homo?

No, I'm calling you a whore.

Jemima bitch, this isn't architecture school. This is the real world, and I could fuck you silly.

Even if you had a chance, which you don't, you would have to, first, find your little dick.

Listen, you black cunt, we make the rules here not your professors. We keep people like you out. We don't want any women and certainly no Negroes in our company. You can't possibly do anything decent for HR&K so you shouldn't even be here.

Guess what, Tom? For now, I am here and I plan to stay because I'll do everything I can to stay. Let me be clear, I don't give a shit what you think or what rules you have or your beliefs about women and Negroes. Right now I'm here to stay. So, fuck off, assholes.

We'll see your black ass is put out on the street.

Let me tell you now. Don't fuck with this sister. If anybody puts my black ass out on the street, it will be me. Now, thanks, boys. This has been a lot of fun. I've enjoyed your very welcoming and informative conversation. Unfortunately, I've got to take my lunch and get back to "my work." See you around "our office."

Excuse me, Miss Moore. I believe that's your name, correct?

Yes, and, you are . . .?

My name is Etienne Savarin. I'm the division head of commercial projects. These two gentlemen you've been talking to actually work for me. Could you excuse us a moment? I need to talk with them privately

480

and then I would like to talk with you if you could wait a few minutes until I return. We'll step over here out of your way for a moment.

Mister Savarin, excuse me, what's up?

Tom, Blaine, come with me over by the window. I have something I need to say to you both.

Is there a problem, Mister Savarin?

There won't be a problem, Tom, after I tell you something. It's this. Don't ever talk to Miss Moore like that again either at the office or out of the office if you want to keep your jobs.

But, Mister Savarin, she was rude to us and she doesn't belong in our company.

Yes, she was rude, Blaine, but you insulted her first. I heard the whole conversation. Your behavior was reprehensible. She is a new employee. The company made a deliberate decision with her hire. She came highly recommended and she obviously has a lot of potential. The fact that she is a Negro and a woman is something all of us will have to get used to. Her hire was not some odd decision. She may be the first but there will be more after her. It may take a while but our world is going to change and we have to change with it. This may be hard for you and others to accept but change is coming. You can fight it if you want but you're not going to win, not at HR&K. So, you are on notice. Don't jeopardize your jobs by making your own rules for our company. You and she have to follow the same rules. Do you understand what I'm saying?

Yes, sir.

Yes, sir.

Okay. Let this be the last time I have to speak about this. I'll see you back in the office.

— Moore about the Office —
1965 to 1966

The first few weeks were difficult for Obra-Jean, not because of the work, which was hard enough, but because she was silently ostracized by her fellow employees in the design department with the exception of Whitty. She stayed as close to him as possible and tried to ignore the slights and rudeness of other men. Other than Whitty and Vapoorgian, there was no one else in the building whom she encountered who attempted any show of friendliness. It was as if everyone had decided she really didn't belong there and they couldn't wait until she was gone. Obra-Jean focused on her work—actually Whitty's work—because he didn't provide her any assignments other than to familiarize herself with the drawings and documents for his project. She began to wonder if she would ever be an architect who actually designed buildings within this company. However, her paychecks began to give her some hope. She reasoned if she wasn't doing some kind of useful work, she wouldn't be paid. As the checks accumulated, she opened her first bank account then decided to rent her first apartment. She asked Toby to help her find a studio apartment in the Wayne State University district. The apartment she rented certainly wasn't as nice as the apartment where Toby and India lived, but it would do for the time being. Obra-Jean tried to emulate the spare, modernist style she saw in Kohl's office but quickly discovered such spareness and style were expensive to achieve. She opted instead for furniture she found in second-hand stores and junk shops. When her place was reasonably furnished, she made a date with Toby and India to come for dinner.

At the office, Whitty gave some documents to Obra-Jean to take to the department of commercial projects. When Obra-Jean reached the office of the department head, she remembered she had met Etienne Savarin at the neighborhood deli during her first day of work. She spoke with his secretary who then escorted her into Savarin's office. He rose from his desk and extended his hand to Obra-Jean and invited her to take a seat in front of his desk. He then came around and sat in a chair beside her. She explained the purpose of her visit which Savarin already knew. He took her documents and placed them on his desk. He slouched in his chair as if he were settling in to get comfortable for a long chat. In fact, it was a long chat. He wanted to know about her—literally everything about her. Feeling at ease, she told the story of her family and her mother's opposition to her desire to become an architect. She talked about her schooling and the experiences at the University of Detroit with Professor Lotz. She mentioned how kind Mister Whitty had been to her but alluded to the coldness which she felt came from almost all of the other male, and many of the female, employees. Savarin laughed. He told her what he had said to the two men in the deli the day he interrupted their conversation with her. She was startled at the news and wondered aloud if the two men had not, in fact, poisoned the minds of other employees. He assured her that was not the case. He kept an open ear of rumors in the office and he had heard nothing spoken of outright hostility toward Obra-Jean. Mostly, the men were annoyed that their bastion of testosterone was somehow violated. They'll get over it, he promised.

Meanwhile, he wondered, what she was planning in her private life? She explained that she had rented a so-so apartment in the university district. She was focused exclusively on her work and didn't have much of a social life beyond occasional events with her family. Savarin then sat up straight in his chair, looked directly at Obra-Jean and asked if she might like to join him for dinner some night. He knew a fabulous restaurant that was quiet with excellent food and they might have an extended conversation together. Obra-Jean paused for a beat and responded that she would love to have dinner with him anytime. Savarin sat back in his chair and said how about this weekend? Saturday evening, perhaps? Obra-Jean agreed, they continued talking about the office, and then Obra-Jean announced that she really had to return to work, thanked Savarin, shook his hand and, as she was preparing to leave, he stood, moved close to her, and put his arms around her shoulders. There was a moment's hesitation, as she tensed, and, then, he kissed her. Obra-Jean made no effort to stop him. In fact, she pressed into him and held him around his waist. After a few moments, Savarin said, "Until Saturday." Obra-Jean nodded, released him, and walked to the door, opened it and left, closing the door behind her. She smiled as she headed back to her cubicle.

Toby and India arrived at Obra-Jean's apartment on the designated evening for a dinner they both thought would be, at best, a disaster. However, Toby wanted to be supportive and decided to avoid being critical in any way of Obra-Jean's apartment or attempt at cooking. India laughed and said, "Good luck with that."

Sister, you've done wonders with this place.

Oh, sure. Toby, I know this apartment looks like a junk shop.

But you have a good eye for nice things. Don't you think so, India?

Come on, Toby. It's junk. Obra-Jean knows it's junk. Who are we kidding? Obra-Jean, I would have done the same thing if I didn't have much money and I was furnishing my first apartment. I must say Toby does have a point though. This place actually has a kind of charm, old and dusty but charming nonetheless.

Thanks, India. I get shit from the office and now I'm getting shit from my sister and her partner in my own home.

Sis, I didn't know you had accumulated so many books. They look like they're all about architecture.

Thanks to you, Sister Toby, who gave me my first architecture book, I've been buying a few books here and there mostly on the cheap from old book shops. I look at them from time to time to remind me what I would like to do someday. I've also found in the junk shops a couple of old prints and drawings of buildings that I will eventually have framed to hang on walls.

It's impressive. India, what do you think? Should we get the architecture lady a proper bookcase as a house-warming present?

It looks like she could use one or two, or three.

Okay, done deal. Enough "Better Homes and Gardens." Little sister, how did Styll take the news you were moving out?

She was encouraging, as always. Grandma Moore can't be anything but positive. However, she couldn't disguise her disappointment. She feels all alone now in that house since Grandpa's stroke. And Mason, as we all know, is not a conversationalist.

Your buddy, Mason? What's he going to do without his niece to keep him company?

You know it's been a long time since I was pals with Mason.

Pals, that's how you call it now?

Toby, don't make me regret I ever told you something personal.

Everybody in this room knows my sister is not the innocent she's always wanted folks to believe she is. Oh, no, Sister, Dear. Let's finally be honest with each other. In the past, you've had a very flexible idea of the truth. And, don't excuse yourself again by saying I've never been interested in you or your life. Tell us, what was your relationship to Mason?

I know what it is to be honest, Toby. Alright? I did attempt to sleep with Mason a couple of times but, as I said, he never really functioned sexually. On the other hand, I have slept with other men who did function sexually. I happen to like men unlike you, Sister, who only likes women.

One woman.

One woman now but, what? You never told India about the women before her?

You make it sound like there were a lot of women.

Well?

Only one. Just one.

And who was that, Sister, as if I didn't know?

Who *was* that, Toby? You made me believe I was your first.

India, you were my first but . . .

But what?

It was Ondine. We kind of got together but we never had sex like you and I had.

Why didn't you tell me this way back when?

India, I really didn't think it was anything serious and it was never a relationship.

But, Toby, I've told you everything about my love life before I met you.

I know. I'm sorry. I should have told you.

You're damn right. All of these years Ondine has been part of your family and you didn't say anything about an intimate relationship with her?

I did tell you I was fascinated with her but I was stupid not to tell all. I should have been completely honest. I didn't want to say anything that might spoil our relationship.

I thought our relationship was based on honesty.

I made a mistake, Honey. I'm sorry.

It's a good thing I'm not a jealous person or a person who holds resentments.

India, darling, you are and have been the only woman in my life.

Well, I hope I'm the only woman in your life with whom you've had sex.

Oh, my, what have I started here? Toby, I didn't mean to stir up this mess.

There you go again with the innocent sister act, Obra-Jean. Now I have to thank you for helping me to become a completely honest woman.

No shit, Sweetie. If you want me to be honest, set a good example, Big Sister.

Okay, I got it, Obra-Jean. Thanks. Let's get back to Styll. I wish she and our mother could live together someday. Now that mother is home alone. Well, she's does have that dog. I don't know why she got a German Shepherd. Anyway, instead of living alone, she and Styll could keep each other company.

Yeah, Toby, two old woman, one crippled old man, one mentally defective man, and a dog. That could be a very happy home.

Listen, you two. You're not the only sisters in the world with family issues.

India, dearest, what family issues could you possibly have?

Okay. My folks make a great couple, right? They're well off. They travel. They have a beautiful home in Chicago's Hyde Park. But, I'm sure you've noticed they've never been here to visit us.

I know you invited them. I thought your mother finally accepted the fact you were living below your class.

Honey, they always say they might come here to visit someday when they're not so busy.

Well, India, we've visited them. So it's not like they don't approve of us living together after all of these years.

True. They've made their peace with having a lesbian daughter. But they are still snobs.

Snobs?

Yes, snobs, Obra-Jean. They don't like Detroit and they don't like their daughter living, in their opinion, with the help.

What do they think? That our family is lowlife?

It's always been a class thing with them, Obra-Jean. They see themselves, especially my mother, as belonging to a much higher social class. On my mother's part, I think it's because she married a white man and that gives her the protective cloak of whiteness. She really thinks she's better than other blacks.

Well, isn't that a kick in the ass? Families. Who can live with them or without them? It's too bad Toby and I are so ghetto.

My parent's attitudes are their attitudes, Obra-Jean, not mine. I wouldn't be here in the first place if I thought like them. Toby, Sweetie, we'll go home after dinner and I'll soothe your feelings.

Does that mean what I think it means?

Yes, Ma'am.

See, Obra-Jean, this is the advantage of having a partner. Maybe you should think about being with someone you care for as much as you think about your job and career. You might be happier.

Gee, Sis, you sound like our mother. How interesting. You've been converted.

In a way, yes. I see she wanted us to have a good life. She was wrong to criticize us for following our dreams. How can we have a good life without our dreams? What do you think, India?

I think Obra-Jean will follow her dream and also find someone she wants to be with. But, it has to happen the way she sees it, not the way you or your mother see it.

So, Leona was wrong?

So far, yes, Toby. Obra-Jean is doing what she's wanted. How happy could she be if she hadn't become an architect? All of us are trying to be who we want to be. We may not follow our parents' dreams for us but their guidance helps us. To me, that's what is important.

The three women continued their conversation over drinks then sat at the table Obra-Jean had prepared for their dinner. Toby and India exchanged amused glances at the simplicity of Obra-Jean's meal—spaghetti with meat balls the size of golf balls, and canned tomato sauce. They joked with Obra-Jean that they would buy her a cookbook to help her prepare meals. Apparently, she hadn't had much practice, inspiration or progress fixing meals since living on her own. Obra-Jean acknowledged she was not a cook but she had a lot of other things on her mind.

I want to do some real architecture work and I'm not being given a chance. I don't know what to do?

Can't you ask your boss to give you more responsibility?

Toby, I've asked him when he thought I might have my own project and he says it's too soon.

Maybe, it is too soon, Sis.

Some of the other new guys who came in after me already have their own projects.

Maybe they have more experience than you.

No. They're just out of school like I was.

Toby, I think your sister is being treated unfairly but in her field or in that office, she may not have a choice. You, in your office, are moving up the ladder but you've been at your job for several years. It's the same for me at my law office. We've both been at it for some time and we were treated at first like Obra-Jean is being treated now. But at our offices, there were other women and a few other black people. Obra-Jean's office is completely different. She's all on her own as a black female. That's a big rock to push. White folks aren't willing to let us blacks get ahead even if we are well qualified. We either have to work on our own, like my parents, or work in places where we have jobs white people don't want. Obra-Jean has known from the get-go she wasn't going to have it easy. I don't fault her for trying but she must be realistic. If she's going to move ahead, it will be slow if at all.

India, you surprise me. You, who've had so many advantages are telling my sister she has to settle for what is? She's out in front for black women pushing boundaries. We should be telling her to push harder. We should be working on strategies for her to shake things up.

Toby, you know as well as I do your sister has practically no allies and no support in her office. One person on her own can't change a system of discrimination.

Then, India, we have to work with her to bring about that change. That's what Doctor King and Malcolm X and other black leaders have been telling us. Isn't that what the Civil Rights movement is about? This is a collective fight.

Okay, it's a collective fight, Toby, but it's taken how long to get to where we are now? Two hundred, three hundred years in this country? Only recently have we gotten some laws that supposedly protect our rights. We've got rights but white folks don't care. They get what they want and they don't want us to get what we want. They have the power to keep things their way.

So, you've saying Obra-Jean and the rest of us will have to wait? Until when?

Until change comes.

We may all be dead.

Maybe so.

The conversation continued into the night. Obra-Jean felt discouraged. She was beginning to realize she had come this far only to face what her mother had warned her about from the beginning. Her path might be a dead end.

— Rebellion —
1967 to 1975

Month after month, as several years passed, Obra-Jean asked Whitty for more responsibility and work. Gradually and grudgingly he gave her additional tasks. She became liaison with project managers and the draftsmen who took Whitty's designs and converted them into working drawings for blueprints. Obra-Jean developed a reputation for being well-informed, thorough, and precise but also demanding and uncompromising. She expected professional work of managers and draftsmen all the time, every time. Although she didn't become one of the boys, she was, at least, treated more civilly. In fact, the men began to see her as a fixture in the drafting office where the real work of creating a functional building took place. One draftsman, Orin Calumet, who was about Obra-Jean's age (she was twenty-four in 1967), was often assigned to prepare working drawings for Whitty's designs and he, therefore, worked more closely and consistently with Obra-Jean. Their conversations were always about their projects and about work. Obra-Jean could not help but notice that Orin did not wear a wedding ring and thought to ask him about his marital status. He was single and lived alone on the far west-side of Detroit in a rented house. It was not an area of Detroit known to Obra-Jean since she never had a reason to visit it.

Why did you choose to live in that neighborhood?

I was born on the far west-side. My parents still have a house there so I decided to stay in the neighborhood. It's mostly single family homes. It's very working-class. Quiet. You know, a typical Detroit neighborhood.

Yeah, it sounds like the neighborhood where my mother lives on the east-side.

I've never been to the east-side. What's it like?

Nothing special. Just homes, some stores, a few small apartment buildings. You know, the kind of stuff you find all over Detroit. The neighborhood now is mostly black people. What about your neighborhood?

Wow. Mine, I guess, is all white people. I've never seen any black people in my neighborhood. To tell you the truth, I don't think they would be welcome, I'm sorry to say. I've heard my parents and their neighbors talk about what they would do if black people moved in.

What is that?

They would move to the suburbs.

That's what happened on the east-side in my neighborhood. Nearly all the white people moved out after blacks started moving in. My best friend from grade school was a white girl. Her family moved when we started high school, and we lost contact with each other.

That's Detroit for you.

Yeah. Well, I'd better get back to my office and check and see if Whitty has any updates for me. If he does, I'll be back to give them to you.

Okay. Maybe I'll see you later.

There were no further updates that day and Obra-Jean left the office at the end of the work day and headed to her apartment. She called her sister to see if she and India wanted to go out to eat and see a movie. Toby told her that she and India already had plans to visit with friends. Obra-Jean warmed herself a can of beef vegetable soup and made a small lettuce and tomato salad. After eating, she looked through the *Detroit Free Press* to catch up on the news. Later, she turned on the TV to see if there was a favorite show to watch. Although there was nothing of interest for her, she left the TV on as a background distraction while she resumed reading the newspaper. She thought she heard the sound of sirens but that wasn't unusual. However, there were more sirens and then the TV broadcast was interrupted by a reporter who announced, somewhat frantically, that rioting and fires had erupted on the near west-side on Twelfth Street. Shops and homes were burning. There was looting. Police were on the scene as were fire trucks and TV crews. Shots could be heard. Some people may have been injured or killed. Obra-Jean's attention now was fixed on the TV. This was serious. Nothing like this had happened in Detroit in her lifetime although her parents and family had talked about a race riot in Detroit in the early 1940s. What was happening now and why? It was days and weeks before the full story became clear. What became known as the 1967 Riot, and much later the '67 Rebellion, was about to change Detroit.

The area of the initial uprising was devastated. Whole blocks of buildings were destroyed by fire. People lost their homes. Businesses were in ruins. Flare-ups in other parts of the city did comparable but not as extensive damage. The losses, however, were similar. Displacement, grief, and anger. And fear. As if someone said, "Let's get out of here," entire neighborhoods of whites picked up and left the city selling their homes and businesses to whoever had some cash. There weren't as many takers as sellers and, therefore, many buildings were effectively abandoned. In slow motion, but within a relatively short period of time much of Detroit became a different kind of city. It began to hollow out as its population declined and became increasingly black.

At HR&K, the workforce returned to their jobs when some semblance of order was restored to the city by police and National Guard soldiers. The mood in the office was somber with whispered conversations. Out of a sense of safety some employees had decided to seek work elsewhere outside of the city. Others wondered if the disorder would resume and engulf their office building. Obra-Jean noticed she was attracting attention again but people drew a kind of cordon around her. When she came to the drafting room with notes for Orin, he was wary and silent.

What's wrong? Why are you and everyone else so quiet?

Are you kidding? The city has been burned. We're all scared.

I'm scared too but why is everyone avoiding me?

You're black. People don't know if they can trust you.

What? I haven't been burning buildings or looting.

We don't know that.

Are you kidding me? Do I look like I would riot?

I don't know. I don't know anything about you.

You've worked with me for several years. How is it you don't know me?

I don't know who you are or how you feel about us white people.

I'm just another person who works here.

Listen, just tell me what I need to know about the project. I can't talk about this anymore. It's too confusing and upsetting.

I'm sorry. I thought we were friends.

Well, I guess we're not.

Obra-Jean gave Orin notes from Whitty and returned to her office. She wondered if she should discuss her conversation with Whitty and decided to go to his office. He was at his desk.

Mister Whitty, I just had a conversation with a draftsman on your job and he told me that people here are afraid of me.

I think you can see why some people might be upset and see you as part of why they are upset.

No, I can't see what I have to do with the riot because I had nothing to do with what is going on in this city.

But your people do.

My people?

Yes, black people are destroying this city.

Some black people are rioting not all black people.

Who knows what's going on with black people?

Do I look like someone who would riot?

I guess not but this is confusing. I don't understand it. I don't know why people are behaving this way.

Well, I'm sorry you think just because I'm black that I'm guilty of something. I love this city and I'm sorry about its destruction but I didn't cause it. I'm not responsible for what is happening. And I don't know anyone who has rioted. I'm just as confused and upset as you and everyone else here.

Maybe, we should all just get back to work.

Fine.

Obra-Jean returned to her office and nearly cried. What was happening? Over the next weeks, she talked constantly with her sister, with India, with her mother and family, and other friends. They all felt sorry for people who lost their homes and businesses. The damage to the city hurt them all but none of them had taken part in its destruction. However, they could name many injustices that fed the flames and believed that whites, not blacks, had created conditions that sparked the rioting. Whites were unwilling to allow blacks an equal chance at life in the city, had held them back and held them down, and blacks had finally responded in fury. It was a long time coming but here it was. Payback.

Within months, something new happened at HR&K. Several black women and a few black men were hired. The women got jobs as clerks and secretaries. The men became draftsmen. All had the requisite skills and training but, until being hired, they had few opportunities to demonstrate their abilities. Obra-Jean was surprised but her fellow white employees were stunned. Black faces in what had been an almost completely white office were so unfamiliar to whites as to confirm in a new way the recent upheaval in Detroit. One of the new draftsmen was Tyrone Curtis who replaced Orin Calumet on Whitty's projects. Orin left HR&K abruptly and, according to some draftsmen, found a job at an architectural firm in a suburb. Obra-Jean's task, in working with Tyrone, was to bring him up to speed on the working drawings that Orin left incomplete. Tyrone was a plain-looking fellow a few years older than Obra-Jean. He was gentle, respectful, and seemingly delighted to be working with her. As she soon discovered, he was also a talented draftsman and quick to understand the project drawings. He had not attended college but learned drafting in a public high school. For the first time since she began work at HR&K, Obra-Jean felt she had a comrade. They began having lunch together near the office and talked about their lives. Tyrone, eventually, asked Obra-Jean on a date for dinner and a movie. She accepted.

Obra-Jean never had a steady boyfriend although she did date boys in high school and college. She never discussed or revealed her private life to anyone in her family. She had not been particularly interested in black men since she had mostly been around white boys and white men from grade school until she began work. Etienne Savarin played an interesting role in her life. They frequently dined together and she spent the night at his home in Grosse Pointe, one of Detroit's richest and most exclusive suburbs. Theirs was not a romance but a friendship, of sorts, with sexual benefits. Neither expected or received anything more from the other. Therefore, when Tyrone joined the office, he appealed to her perhaps because he was so deferential to her and her position in the company. He also made no secret of the fact that he liked her, and she liked him because he was, as she called him "cute." Dark skinned like Obra-Jean, stocky, and muscular, Tyrone did not stand out from the crowd. He was the "chocolate" equivalent of "vanilla." However, he dressed simply but neatly in dark slacks and crisp white shirts. He liked Obra-Jean immediately, and their common interest in their work fostered a bond that Obra-Jean understood, or wanted to believe, was love. To her family's surprise, within a year they were engaged and married in 1969. Obra-Jean wanted to move out of her small apartment and buy a house. Since she earned far more money than Tyrone, she made a decision and bought a house in the Sherwood Forest neighborhood near her alma mater, the University of Detroit. She made another decision upon marrying; she officially changed her name from Obra-Jean Moore to Aubergine Perry Curtis—Perry, obviously, was in honor of her father. Within three years, she and her husband had two children, both boys. Aubergine worked during both of her pregnancies and took a leave only before giving birth but returning to work two months following birth. Her maternity leaves were shortened by persuading her mother to move into Aubergine's four bedroom home. Leona would attend the babies while the parents were at work. Leona sold her own house for a loss because, with so many homes on the market in Detroit and a shortage of people who were interested in them or could afford to purchase a home, market prices fell sharply. Besides, she no longer felt safe in her own neighborhood because so many houses were abandoned and the type of people moving into the neighborhood were a type not to Leona's taste. They were black, mostly young, under-educated, and without steady employment. Her neighborhood had become noisy, unkept, and rife with petty and some serious crime. Her house had avoided being burglarized because her German Shepherd frightened away potential intruders, but her car was vandalized, and she felt unsafe walking to and from her bus stop. She and her dog settled into her daughter's house.

At her own home, Aubergine installed a burglar alarm, ornamental bars on the first floor windows, and security lights for the side drive and back yard. These were necessary measures, she felt, in post-riot Detroit. Toby and India also sensed a personal threat in their neighborhood and decided to move to an elegant apartment in a gated enclave on the riverfront. On the east-side of Detroit along the river were a cluster of older multi-story apartment buildings originally built for Detroit's elite. These spacious apartments reminded India of many such apartments along Chicago's Gold Coast that had long been denied as housing to blacks. She and Toby rented a four bedroom river-facing apartment on an upper floor. There was an expectation that someday the apartments might become condominiums and the women wanted to be first in line to purchase what would become a luxurious and stunning home. If they were able to purchase, they wanted Aubergine to design a remodeling. If this came to pass, their home might be Aubergine's first private commission.

HR&K made a momentous decision. It would design a new headquarters for itself downtown by completely gutting an old but solid five-story concrete frame building, redesigning its interior, and completing a new all-glass exterior. When finished, the company would move from its old building in the New Center area and show the company's testament of faith in Detroit by remaining and investing in the city. It was a risky and solitary move because HR&K's competitors were moving out of the city as quickly as they could find new, sufficient office space in the suburbs. With the shift downtown and the steady increase in the number of black faces in the office, Aubergine hoped that, at last, she would be given design work of her own. Soon after moving to the new building, the senior designer, Henry Vapoorgian, called Aubergine into his office.

Please have a seat, Missus Curtis. How are you? It's been a long time since we talked. You've been here, what, ten years, I think? That's what they tell me. Anyway, the reason I asked you to see me is that Mister Whitty is retiring soon. Actually, he is retiring early because of health issues. I've been thinking about who could replace him. There are, of course, many men who have a lot of experience with us and with other companies but I was thinking of you and I'll tell you, honestly, why. Would you like a coffee? I'll ask my secretary to bring you one. Let's see, just a moment while I call her. Yes, please bring two coffees with sugar and cream separate. Yes, immediately. Now, Missus Curtis, as you know a lot is changing in this city and our firm is committed to being here because we believe in Detroit and we think there is a lot of opportunity to build and rebuild this city. We wouldn't have invested in this expensive renovation if we didn't have faith. You understand that, I'm sure. Well, we want to do a lot of this rebuilding work in Detroit but, you see, we have a problem. Are you following me? Well, of course, you are. This city is becoming more black. We have more blacks in the city government. We even have a black mayor, the first in the city's history and, I believe, that is a good thing. However, in order to do business in this changing city, we need to show the people in power we understand what kind of city this is. You understand me. Right? Sure you do. So, here you are, a black person and a woman, the first if I remember correctly, in our company. The only one, I think. Yes, of course. Anyway, we want you to be prominent in our company and work with the city administration so that we all remain friends and can keep this company in the city and continue to hire more people like yourself. Do you see what I'm saying? Oh, here is the coffee. Thank you, Miss Williams. Do you two know each other? This is Missus Curtis from our design department. She's a longtime employee. Very good. Very professional and very talented. She's one of our best employees. Well, I'm sure the two of you will have a lot to talk about sometime, another time. Thank you, Miss Williams. Now, Missus Curtis, do we understand each other? I think you will continue to advance in this company, in time. You can prove your worth to this company by helping us stay at the top in getting city projects for our firm. What do you say? You are onboard, right?

I do understand what you're saying, Mister Vapoorgian. You want me to be your black liaison to the black city. Do I understand you correctly?

Yes. Yes. Liaison. Yes. That would be quite a feather in your cap.

Well, I don't wear a cap and I certainly wouldn't put a feather in it.

It's a figure of speech, Missus Curtis.

I know that. My question for you is this. What do I get out of this arrangement?

What do you get? You will be an important person in this firm who interacts with the community.

What will I be designing?

Designing? You will be a liaison and doing here what you've been doing.

What I've been doing is being a go-between for Mister Whitty and the drafting room. I've not really done any designing which is what I've always wanted to do and what I hoped I would be doing here ten years ago when I was hired in 1965.

Well, designing . . . I didn't have that in mind. Men seem to be the best designers, don't you think?

Really? How can you make such a comparison when there haven't been any women designers here who actually design buildings?

Missus Curtis, through the ages, men have always been the architects.

That's because men haven't given women a chance to design. Certainly, not here, at least.

Why would you want to design when you would have this important liaison position?

Because design is what I studied to do. I've always wanted to be is a designer.

Well, I don't know. How do we trust you with a design project when you've never designed anything?

That's a circular argument. How could I design something if I never had the chance? You trust men all the time who have much less practical experience than me.

But, men are natural designers. It's history. Men have always designed buildings. What have women designed?

We don't know because we haven't had the chance. Now, I'll tell you something. Give me a chance to design and I'll be your liaison too. I have lots of energy and experience.

No. No. No. I can't do that.

Yes, you can, Mister Vapoorgian.

No, I can't. I really can't.

Give me a small project to design and I'll show you.

No. That's impossible.

Then I can't be your liaison.

Then you don't have a job.

You would fire me, the only black woman architect here or anywhere in a major firm in this city? You better think about that, Mister Vapoorgian. Firing me wouldn't look good to folks in this city and they would find out. Just give me a small job, a chance to show what I can do and you'll get your liaison.

I would have to discuss this with my superiors.

Okay. But let them know the situation. This city burned because black people have been excluded by the very reasoning you use.

But, I'm not prejudiced against black people.

Really? How about women?

Missus Curtis, I need to be completely frank with you. There have certainly been issues about your race and gender over the years but, I'm afraid, that is not the complete story. Architectural practice, in case you haven't noticed, is also based on class. Unfortunately, you originate from the working-class in our society. Am I correct? Your associations are with working-class people. Whereas our clients prefer to work with architects of a higher class and that, frankly, excludes you.

So, talent, ability, dedication, industriousness, and loyalty, these qualities don't matter.

Oh, yes, they matter but class rules over all else in our profession.

Pardon me for asking, Mister Vapoorgian, but what class, exactly, do you belong to?

In truth, Missus Curtis, I come from a very humble family.

So, how did you manage to rise to your position in this company?

I would rather not discuss that. I will talk with my superiors about your request. I make no promises, Missus Curtis. I see now that you are far more savvy than I or my colleagues have given you credit. We'll see what can be done. Now, thank you for your time. We'll talk later. I have a lot of work to do now. Goodbye, Missus Curtis.

XIII

Aubergine and The Seven Sisters

— A Transformation of Sorts —
1975 to 1990s

Aubergine got her wish. Sort of. The company made what must have been a difficult decision fostered by the evolving politics of an increasingly black city ruled by a black mayor. The company's administration decided to perform a little Kabuki theater. They would create a show of change without really changing anything. Aubergine got design work but of the most inconsequential kind. She was assigned small design jobs that no other designer wanted. For her, it was something. It was at least designing. The projects all had small budgets, tight schedules, and no architectural statement. They were the equivalent of plain brown packaging without fancy, eye-catching appeal. However, these projects made lots of money for the company because they could be fast-tracked, and Aubergine got to design a lot of them. Over time, she arrived at a decision. This was to be her professional life. She could either accept it or leave it. She accepted it. Since her income increased with her design responsibilities, she encouraged her husband, Tyrone, to begin college and obtain his degree with night classes.

She made another decision as well. She wanted to enlarge their house with a two story addition to the rear. Aubergine had long wanted a proper library for the collection of books she had acquired since college, and she needed a home office. The library and office would occupy the first floor of the extension. On the second floor would be the master bedroom with its own bath and walk-in closets. In considering the exterior design of the addition, Aubergine decided to respect the faux-Tudor style of the original house so that the new blended seamlessly with the old. Aubergine wondered what her mentor, Professor Lotz, would think of her decision. She thought he would approve because the integrity of the appearance of the whole building was more important than an egotistic, out-of-context statement by the architect.

As their sons, Leon and Brice, grew from childhood to adolescence, the boys attended private non-sectarian schools because their parents disliked both public and parochial schools. Both sons matured into intelligent, attractive young men who were encouraged to plan professional careers for themselves. Their great-grandmother, Clemenza, died when they were pre-teens, and they never really had a chance of knowing her because she had long ago relocated to Hot Springs. Their grandmother, Leona, was a dominating presence in their lives and in their home. Although Leona always referenced her own growing-up experience to her grandsons, she completely changed her attitude with regard to their futures. While she had tried to restrain the ambitions of her own children especially the girls, with no small amount of irony she encouraged her grandsons to become whatever they wished. Aubergine had conflicting feelings about her mother's role in her sons' lives. She recognized her sons were receiving consistent messages from all members of their family. However, she was resentful her own mother could not have been both supporting, as well as cautionary, to her own daughter. The conflicted nature of Aubergine's feelings were not lost to her. She reasoned that, given her mother's life and the times in which she lived, her mother could not have been anything but what she was. This insight allowed Aubergine to accept her mother and to appreciate her presence in her home and in her life and that of her children. Leon and Brice both attended college out of state but returned to Detroit to begin their work careers. The brothers shared an apartment in the suburb of Southfield.

Aubergine's brother, E.J., and his wife, Vergie, who married in 1966, moved to Atlanta in 1968 where E.J. taught high school. There, they raised their three children, two boys and a girl. The boys were born early in their marriage but the girl came much later much to her parents' surprise. She was the result of an unplanned and completely unexpected pregnancy in 1980 when both of her parents were turning forty. The child, Serena, more familiarly called Scoot because she scooted across the floor on her behind before she learned to walk, showed an early interest in buildings much like her Aunt Aubergine. When E.J. conveyed his daughter's interest to Aubergine, Aubergine decided to mentor her niece. With her brother's consent, Scoot came to spend the summer of her seventeenth year, in 1997, with her aunt in Detroit.

— A Visitor —
Summer 1997

After retrieving her niece at the airport, Aubergine and Serena headed into Detroit in the family car driven by Tyrone. Along the freeway, Aubergine enumerated many of the region's landmarks, most of which were not actually visible from the freeway. She noted the Ford empire, including The Henry Ford Museum, Henry Ford's beloved Greenfield Village, and the massive River Rouge automotive complex. As the car approached the central city, Aubergine commented on the extensive devastation of neighborhoods abandoned by their residents. Empty lots and burnt-out houses stretched for miles along the route. Serena caught a glimpse in the distance of the towers in downtown as Tyrone changed freeways to head to their home in Sherwood Forest. After all of the desolate cityscape, Serena was surprised by the orderly, tree-lined streets with sturdy well-planned brick houses in Sherwood Forest. Her aunt and uncle's house was one of the most handsome on their block. With its wide and deep front lawn and spacious lot, the house was a welcome sight that relieved some of the anxieties she felt during the ride from the airport. Once inside, she noted modern furniture, subdued color scheme, varied textures, and accents of large, vibrant figural paintings. Serena was going to enjoy this visit.

On hand to greet her were Leona, who gave her granddaughter a bear hug and kiss, and Augusta, who followed her sister's example. Aubergine's adult sons, Leon and Brice, who were visiting for the occasion, said a brief hello and excused themselves to play pool in the basement recreation room. Tyrone took Serena's suitcases upstairs to her room. Everyone was talking at once, asking questions, not waiting for answers, changing topics, and having a raucous time. Dinner time was approaching. Leona and Augusta planned and prepared the meal. Augusta provided appetizers. When Tyrone returned from upstairs, he interrupted the conversation and offered to serve everyone drinks. When he left, Leona turned to Serena.

Scoot, tell us all about Atlanta. You know I've always wanted to visit that city. Your father has invited me year after year but, you know, I'm getting too old for such travel.

My sister is not too old to travel. She's just too lazy.

Hush, Augusta. Tell me all about Atlanta, Baby.

Oh, Grandmama, I think it's a great city. We live in a nice area southwest of downtown. The homes there are very nice. They are much newer and bigger than the houses in this neighborhood. But, they are also a little more boring. Mostly black people live in our neighborhood. We like it that way.

Baby, is your school nearby?

No, Aunt Augusta. My dad drives me to my school which is about a half hour away. It's a all-girl private high school. Very preppy and about half black and half white.

Scoot, I understand that Atlanta, like Detroit, has a black mayor.

Yes, Grandmama. Most of Atlanta is run by blacks.

But I hope it isn't in the same sad shape as Detroit. This city is depressed and very depressing. This is one of the few neighborhoods that still has some white folks.

Grandmama, Atlanta has a lot of whites but they live in their own neighborhoods. Black people in Atlanta want to live in their own neighborhoods too and run their own businesses. They don't care what the white people are doing. And, Atlanta has those great black schools like Spelman and Moorehouse. A lot of black people are doing quite well in Atlanta.

Well, Detroit isn't anything like that. We've got a lot of poor, uneducated black folks here. Their lives are really sad. The schools are falling apart.

The city can't seem to repair the streets or pick up the garbage. It's a shame.

Come on, Leona, Detroit's not all bad.

You can say that, Augusta, because you live in lily-white Lafayette Park.

Leona, you know Lafayette Park isn't lily-white. Lots of blacks live there.

Listen, Mother, Auntie, we can continue this conversation all summer long while Serena is here. By the way, do you prefer to be called Serena or Scoot? To me, Scoot sounds a little out of place for a young lady.

Please call me Serena, Aunt Aubergine.

Okay, Serena, let's sit down to this dinner my mother and aunt have prepared for us. Tyrone, please call your sons up from downstairs.

Sure, Honey. I'm on it.

Dinner was simple but delicious. Leona prepared a stew of chicken and dumplings with a side dish of sautéed spinach. Instead of baking a dessert, she purchased a deep dish cherry pie that she served with vanilla ice cream. After dinner, Aubergine wanted to show Serena her library and home office. They excused themselves from the rest of the family, went into the library, and closed the door. Serena was astonished by the room. The library was a long rectangular space—spanning the width of the house—with a window in the center of each of the short walls. Along both long walls and one short wall were floor to ceiling bookshelves. The shelves were filled with books, models of buildings, and ornamental architectural fragments retrieved from demolished buildings. The fourth wall on a narrow end of the room had a long, deep cabinet for storing drawings and papers. Displayed above it on the wall were framed photographs and prints of buildings as well as framed newspaper articles. In the middle of the room was a large Oriental rug. On it stood a grand wooden desk stacked with papers, drawings, and blueprints. A metal desk chair, table lamp, and overhead light fixture completed the furnishings. Serena wandered around the library glancing at the titles of the books nearly all of which concerned architecture, cities, or art. Aubergine encouraged her to remove any book that interested her and examine it. Serena pulled several from the shelves and flipped through the pages. She asked Aubergine about the models and architectural fragments. She took a close view of the framed photographs and prints. She wanted to know everything about everything. Aubergine smiled and explained that she could spend as much time as she wanted in the library during her visit to Detroit. Any questions she had, Aubergine would answer. They would be spending a lot of time together and everything that Serena wanted to know would be part of her visit. Aubergine was so delighted by her niece's interest that she decided then and there that Serena would be her protégé. She wanted Serena to know everything she could teach her. And thus the visit began.

— An Office Visit —

Aubergine brought Serena to work with her soon after she settled into the Curtis household. She wanted Serena to see the company's building and become familiar with the kind of work that Aubergine did. She introduced her niece first to the women at the reception desk then proceeded to the executive offices on the top floor where the upper administration was housed. In particular, she wanted her niece to meet the new design chief, Armand Assouf, who replaced Henry Vapoorgian when he retired. Assouf was a naturalized American citizen from France.

His family originated in Algeria but migrated to Paris and settled there before Algerian independence. Assouf was gracious to Serena and complimented Aubergine for her excellent work in the firm. He gave a general explanation of the company's history, its design philosophy, and the scope of its work in Detroit, the USA, and overseas. Like many large architectural offices, HR&K had to have an international reach to compete for the most lucrative commissions. Since he had limited time to talk before he excused himself, he suggested that Aubergine could provide more detailed information during Serena's visit.

Aubergine then took Serena to the drafting floor and introduced her to some of the draftsmen who discussed the working drawings they were preparing. Tyrone still worked on this floor but was promoted from draftsman to job captain. He took over conducting the visit while Aubergine went to her own office to check on her projects. Tyrone explained the process of turning the designing architect's sketches and schematics into drawings for blueprints. More work now was being done with computers so the drafting skills of former times, when Tyrone first began work, were transformed into computer programming. Tyrone admitted he was not as adept with the new methods as he was with the old but design work had to adapt to the new age. Serena remained with Tyrone in the drafting room until lunchtime when she, Tyrone, and Aubergine went to lunch at a nearby restaurant. Following lunch, all three returned to HR&K and Serena accompanied Aubergine to her office while Tyrone headed to the drafting room.

What do you think of this place so far?

Oh, Aunt Aubergine, I love this office. It's not at all what I expected. It's so big and there are so many people working on so many projects all at the same time. I had no idea of the amount of work one office could handle. I thought maybe one or two projects but there are dozens of projects being worked on all at once.

This is a big operation, Serena. Sometimes, I'm a bit amazed by the complexity of it all but everyone seems to know their part in it and most do their work very well.

Aunt Aubergine, do you think that, while I am visiting Detroit, we could see some of the buildings you designed?

Of course, Serena, but my buildings are all small projects and not very interesting. They are mostly utilitarian buildings, not spectacular or noteworthy architecture.

I don't care. I just want to see what you've done. I know it's been difficult for you to design anything. Whatever you've done would be interesting to me.

I'll go you one better and take you on a tour of Detroit. I'll show you some of my buildings and some of the other buildings in this city that are my favorites.

Wow. That would be very cool.

Most of these buildings are older and not well known outside of Detroit and Michigan but they are great buildings in my opinion. You might not find them in the architectural magazines or books about architecture. But, you'll see they are solid buildings that give Detroit its particular character. I would say these older buildings really define Detroit more than most modern buildings do.

So, its like going to Europe and seeing the old buildings there?

A little bit like that. You've been to Europe already, right?

With my parents about two years ago.

Many years ago, I went to Europe for the first time with my Aunt Augusta. That trip changed my life. I knew I would do anything to be an architect after that visit.

That's funny because after my trip to Europe, I decided I wanted to be architect. I had thought about it before the trip because Daddy talked so much about you, the architect. He's really proud of you and talks about you all the time. That's why I wanted to come to Detroit and visit you and the rest of our family.

Talk about funny. When we were kids, your father did nothing but criticize me. I guess that's what siblings do. But, he seemed really down on me and I have to admit I sometimes believed what he said about me. On the other hand, his criticism somehow pushed me to do better and work harder.

Since my brothers are so much older than me, I never had much to do with them. They weren't really interested in me. It was my daddy who encouraged me and pushed me.

Parents. My father also encouraged me while I thought my mother tried to hold me back from doing what I wanted to do.

My momma is a lot like your mother. She's always been a housewife. That's been her job and I don't think she thought a girl could do the kind of work men do.

Well, here you are and here we are. Listen, I need to go to a meeting now and then another after that. If you just want to wander around the building or visit with your uncle in the drafting room, do so. We'll all leave for home at five. So, be back here just before five.

Thanks, Auntie.

— It's About Family —

Aubergine decided to have a family gathering and dinner so that Serena could meet everyone. As usual, Leona offered to plan and prepare the meal because Aubergine, frankly, never became a good cook. She didn't have the time or enthusiasm or talent. Leona asked Augusta to make appetizers and told Toby and India to bring dessert. Since Ondine had long become a de facto family member, she volunteered to provide a special salad. Aubergine designated Tyrone as bartender, and Aubergine with Serena's help straightened up the house and set the dinner table. Aubergine's housekeeper did the actual cleaning. Leon and Brice helped with grocery shopping at the Eastern Market, an open-air farmers' market near downtown. The cooperative effort was years in the making as everyone, except Serena, had done their tasks many times as part of family gatherings. Aubergine missed having her grandmothers, Clemenza and Estyllene, present. Since their deaths, Clemenza in 1986 and Estyllene in 1990, the generational cohesion of the sisterhood was evolving. It no longer benefitted from the stories and experiences of an elder generation reaching back into the late nineteenth- and early twentieth-century. The elder generation was gone but now a younger generation brought a fresh outlook and renewed hope for the future.

Aubergine scheduled an early dinner for four o'clock in the afternoon on a Sunday. Augusta had arrived early in the morning so that she and

Leona could begin preparations. Leona wanted roast beef with mashed potatoes and gravy, roasted carrots, and steamed string-beans. She took care of the roast and gravy while Augusta prepared the vegetables and appetizers.

Mother was still alive, I think, the last time we did this menu for a family gathering.

Oh, my god, Augusta, was it that long ago?

I think so . . . eleven years ago, Leona. Don't you miss her?

Of course, I do. I'm glad you and me had a chance to visit her in Hot Springs before she died.

I'm glad you finally let go of feeling abandoned and forgave Clemenza.

What I really did, Sister, was to forgive myself.

So, here we are, two sisters in your daughter's, my niece's, home making dinner for the family. That's a good thing, Sister. Let's enjoy it. Did you hear the doorbell?

I did. Obra-Jean, are you answering the door?

Yes, Mother. My god. We're stilling yelling to each other in this house just like we did in my mother's house. By the way, did you hear what my mother called me, Serena? My mother still refuses to call me Aubergine. It will be Obra-Jean until she dies or until I die, whichever comes first.

My mother still calls me Scoot. So, I guess I'll be Scoot to her forever too.

Some things never change. I've got the door. Hello, Sister. Hello, India. Come on in. This is Serena, our niece. Serena, this is my sister, Toby, and her partner, India.

Hi, I'm so glad to meet more of my family at last. This is so great. Boy, you two look beautiful. There are so many beautiful sisters in our family.

And, you're one of them. Isn't she adorable, India.

She is beautiful, indeed. There are nothing but gorgeous sisters here.

Toby, take the dessert into the kitchen. Mother and Aunt Augusta are in there cooking up a storm.

Come on, India, let's go greet the grande dames.

Gee, Aunt Aubergine, I'm so excited. I didn't expect to feel a part of group of women. It never really occurred to me there were this many women in our family. See, I grew up with my brothers and they and my father dominated our house. My mother and I weren't really that close. We get along okay but I always kind of felt alone. Maybe because I was so interested in architecture, I just didn't connect with my mother. She was just there giving orders and taking care of our house which, by the way, is huge. I guess I was an architecture nerd. It seemed to me my mother wasn't interested in what I was doing.

Well, while you're here, we'll talk about nothing but architecture. Maybe Tyrone will join us. Oh, there's the doorbell again. It's okay, Mother, I've got it. Hi, Ondine. Come on in. This is my niece, Serena. Serena, this is Ondine Mahmoud. She and my Aunt Augusta worked together at the same school. Ondine is now a school principal at Cass Technical High

School where I graduated long ago. Come on in, Ondine. Make yourself comfortable.

I'm pleased to meet you, Miss Mahmoud.

Honey, call me Ondine or Mud. Mud is my old nickname. I think you have one too.

My family called me Scoot but I don't like that name. So I tell everyone to call me Serena.

Well, Serena it is. Your Aunt Aubergine tells me you want to be an architect.

That's right. Auntie Aubergine took me to her office and I had a chance to see inside a big architecture company. I also saw some of Auntie's office work. We're going to visit some of her buildings and other buildings in Detroit. I'm very excited. This is what I've been dreaming about since I was invited to Detroit.

You know, Serena, I wish we had more students like you at Cass. Our kids are already so beaten down by poverty, absent parents, and lack of inspiring role models that, by the time they get to high school, they've lost interest in their own futures. They can't even imagine a different life for themselves. I'm afraid we've failed as teachers to rekindle that spark of life in them.

Teachers can't substitute for parents, Ondine. I always thought my mother tried to turn me away from my dream of being an architect. Now I realize it was her concern for my future, not her opposition to my dream, that really mattered. Serena has it all. Her parents support her.

She has role models. And she has a better opportunity to succeed, certainly, than I had.

Oh, Aunt Aubergine, you are my hero. You're a big success. You work for a big company. You've got a good position there and you get to be an architect.

All true but you're going to be even more successful than me. I'm sure of it. Let's go see where everyone is. I know Leona and Augusta are in the kitchen. Oh, I see Toby, India, and Tyrone in the family room.

Hey, everyone, Ondine is here.

Come give me a hug, you sweet thing. Don't you look sharp today. Is that a new dress?

It's special for this occasion, Toby. How are you? And, you too, India? Hugs for everybody. Even you, Tyrone. You're a brave man to be here with all of us women.

I've gotten use to it, Ondine. I have enough of the boys at work and our two sons are always here for a free meal. It's nice to be with you ladies. I love being the only man, well, one of three men.

Tell me, Tyrone, after all of these years that you and Aubergine have been together, I don't think I've ever heard anything about your family.

There's not that much to tell, really. I grew up in Detroit. My mom, Mildred Curtis, was a single mother. She was a beautician and had her own shop. Mom's deceased now. I never knew my father but I have a brother, Horace, who lives in Denver. He's married and has five kids. We keep in touch but it's not a close relationship. When I met Aubergine and we started working together, I fell for her right away but I didn't think she would be interested in me.

Why not?

She's so together. Sharp, tough, educated, and bodaciously beautiful. She scared the shit out of all of those guys in the drafting room including me. They knew they had to be completely on top of things with her. No bullshit. No nothing but the facts and clean, precise, and accurate drawings. I was kinda surprised she was into black men since there were practically nothing but white guys in our office. But, she worked with me. She was business-like and courteous. I took a chance and asked her to lunch one day which she accepted. We got to know each other little by little then we realized we wanted to be together. And, that was that. I didn't think she wanted a family but as you know, we have two sons.

Aren't your sons here too.

Yes. Those human garbage cans are downstairs in the recreation room waiting for the dinner bell. They'll come up for dinner, eat, and disappear again. I'm afraid they're only interested in the food and, maybe, are a little intimidated by all of this sisterhood.

I guess young men aren't interested in us old women.

Ondine, they're not interested in anything but food and young women. They both finished college and have good jobs in administration with Chrysler. But I wish they had more ambition like Serena for their futures besides getting laid.

I know what you mean. The hormones at my school are raging.

Hey, Ondine, come and have a seat with us and tell us about those raging hormones.

Is there room on that sofa for my big butt?

India and I will always make room for your big butt. Actually, Girl, haven't you lost weight? You seem positively skinny and, look, no ass.

Those kids at Cass are like animals in heat. They are working me to death. I've practically stopped eating because I'm always running, running to staff meetings, faculty meetings, disciplinary hearings, more meetings, paperwork piled up to the ceiling, conference calls, administrative conferences, and more meetings. It just doesn't quit but, I have to admit, I love it.

Well, we'll have to feed you an extra helping of everything today so you can restore that butt.

That's okay. I can afford to lose weight. It means I can move faster to outrun those kids.

Excuse me, ladies, my job is to get everyone's drinks. Let me take your orders and I'll get to work.

After Tyrone noted everyone's drink choice and disappeared into the kitchen where a bar had been set up, all attention focused on Serena who was bombarded by questions about her school, her future plans, her family, and Atlanta. She was pleased to be the center of attention, something she lacked in her own family. She realized all of these women were professionals and appreciated her because of her ambition. She felt a sisterhood. Before long, Leona emerged from the kitchen to announce that dinner was ready and everyone should be seated at the table. The long, rectangular dining room table, when extended, was large enough to seat ten people, four to a side. Aubergine and Tyrone sat opposite one another at each end of the table. On Aubergine's right, sat Serena, Leona, Toby, and Leon. On her left were Ondine, Augusta, India, and Brice. As Serena surveyed the table, she realized that there were seven women and three men. The seven women, including herself, were a sisterhood she never imagined could exist, and here it was in her family. They were not all blood relatives but they were a family nonetheless. Seven black sisters. And, three black brothers.

— The Seven Sisters —

Aubergine made sure Serena had opportunities to visit many tourist attractions in Detroit and its suburbs, including the Neo-Classical gem, the Detroit Institute of Arts in midtown; the sprawling complex of the Henry Ford Museum and adjacent Greenfield Village in Dearborn; and the Detroit Zoo in Royal Oak. For these visits, Augusta and Ondine were the usual guides. Aubergine took time off from work to show her niece the architecturally significant buildings she thought would interest Serena. Because the buildings were dispersed over the sprawling metropolitan area and because Aubergine wanted to spend sufficient time with each building to discuss all of the information she had acquired, their excursions were spread out over the entire summer. The highlights included: In the New Center—Albert Kahn's elegant Fisher Building and the massive General Motors Building—masterworks that expressed the one-time automotive power of Detroit. Downtown, there was the Guardian Building—an art deco skyscraper masterpiece by Wirt C. Rowland—and John Portman's Renaissance Center, a cluster of four office towers surrounding a hotel, the tallest building in Detroit. On Wayne State University's campus in midtown, Minoru Yamasaki's elegant McGregor Memorial Conference Center sits like a faceted jewel of glass and white marble among more utilitarian academic buildings. In suburban Bloomfield Hills—Eliel Saarinen's serene and sublime art school campus, the Cranbrook Academy, sits among an expansive, bucolic landscape. Finally, in Palmer Woods, near Aubergine's own home, is the only building in Detroit designed by Frank Lloyd Wright, the Dorothy G. Turkel House built in Wright's Usonian style. Aubergine and Serena talked long and analytically about each of these buildings and many others. Serena was truly impressed by the range of architectural styles and the powerful images these buildings created but Serena began to wonder when they would visit her aunt's buildings. Finally, she spoke up.

Aunt Aubergine, I love everything I've seen so far and I've learned so much but I really want to see something you designed next. Why haven't we seen any of your buildings yet?

Serena, Honey, I'm a little embarrassed to show you what I've designed after you've seen some of the greatest and most wonderful buildings in this city.

But you designed them. I want to see what you've done.

They really are insignificant buildings. They aren't worth looking at.

But, you promised me, Auntie. Please, I really want to see them.

Okay. I'll show you the best one. It's nearby.

Aubergine drove onto the freeway and exited within view of downtown but in a somewhat forlorn neighborhood of scattered and battered houses and derelict industrial buildings. Vacant lots with weeds and trash were more prominent than any buildings. Aubergine stopped the car on one such street and parked across from a very modest three story modern office building. In contrast to the neighborhood, this building showed that, at one time, it must have shined like an onyx gift box with its dark tinted glass amidst so much detritus. The building was unoccupied but not, apparently, abandoned by the city government that once housed business offices here. Its dark glass facade was intact. Crisp vertical and horizontal black steel mullions outlined individual panes of glass and set up a steady rhythm across the boxy three story structure.

Well, this is it. This is the most interesting design job I've had at HR&K and it's lost here in this neighborhood. It's my abandoned child.

But, Auntie, it's beautiful even here in this condition. I'm not disappointed. I'm only sad nobody else can see it and appreciate it. You did a good job and you could have done even better if you were given the chance.

I know but that's how it is.

Can we get out of the car and take a closer look?

Sure, but keep your eyes open. This is not a safe neighborhood. When we're done here, I want to take you to see something else and tell you a story.

Aubergine explained the origins of her building project. The city wanted a new facility to house the department of transportation's administrative staff. All of the department's scattered offices would be consolidated in one structure. While the upper two floors contained offices, the main floor consisted of a lobby and open reception area. Mechanical services were in the basement and enclosed in a penthouse on the roof. The structure was steel encased in fire-proofing supporting concrete floors.

Tinted glass held by black mullions surrounded all three floors. Elevators, stairwells, and all utilities were concentrated in the central part of the building with offices and meeting rooms on the periphery. The inspiration for the exterior design was the work of Ludwig Mies van der Rohe who designed the most prominent buildings in Lafayette Park. Aubergine expected her niece to be disappointed by such a subdued and minor building but, of course, Serena was delighted that this building existed at all and proud that her own aunt designed it. She lavishly praised it.

After spending an hour looking at and discussing Aubergine's building, the women walked around the desolate neighborhood while keeping a watchful eye for any dangers. The area consisted mostly of vacant lots with overgrown weeds and discarded objects like old, broken furniture and rusted car bodies. Aubergine would not have been surprised to find a body or two among the debris. Here and there, among several burned-out houses, were a few intact homes that, apparently, were still occupied. Amid all of this abandonment, there was still life. As the women were discussing the state of the neighborhood, they noticed an old black woman on the sidewalk in front of one of the few occupied houses. She stared intently at Aubergine and crossed the street heading towards her. At first, Aubergine was apprehensive and prepared herself for she didn't know what. But the old woman was smiling and waving her arms as in a greeting. She extended her arms toward Aubergine as if to embrace her but stopped short a few feet away from the women, raised her hands to her face, and said to Aubergine: "You have the aura." Then, she turned and walked away across the street and disappeared behind her house. Serena looked at Aubergine as if to say: What was that about? Aubergine suggested they return immediately to the car and proceed to the next stop.

Aubergine drove the car along several residential streets. Soon they came to a boulevard lined with large homes that were once grand but now mostly battered or mutilated by inappropriate changes and awkward additions. The boulevard terminated at the riverfront but a roadway continued across a bridge to an island in the Detroit River. Aubergine drove around most of the island, then stopped and parked on the side of the island facing the city. They got out of the car and walked towards the water where Aubergine suggested that they sit on its grassy, sloping bank. Aubergine began her story.

Serena, this island is called Belle Isle. You know "Belle Isle" is a kind of bastard French for "beautiful island." As I told you driving here, it is a large island in the Detroit River. Now, what we Detroiters call a river isn't actually a river at all but a strait connecting Lake Saint Clair, which you can see over there on our right, to Lake Erie, which is out of sight on our left beyond downtown and a bend of the river. French explorers chose this spot on the strait for their community. Of course, there were already indigenous people living here who, being peaceful inhabitants, didn't oppose the French intruders. The French decided to call this location, in their own language, *d'étroit* meaning "the strait." *D'étroit* became Detroit, a much less melodious name in English. The city rose to power at the beginning of this century by becoming the automobile capital of the world. You saw some of that at Ford's River Rouge complex that you visited. However, even before that, Detroiters chose this island in the river as a place for relaxation and recreation. They eventually connected the island to the city with a bridge that we crossed over there, you see on your left, appropriately called the Belle Isle Bridge. This graceful span provided the only auto and pedestrian link to the city proper. Our family used to come here for picnics every Fourth of July. It's always been a favorite and welcoming place for black people in Detroit.

Like its name, Belle Isle became a beautiful island park in the late nineteenth century. That was when it was designed as a park by the famous landscape architect, Frederick Law Olmsted, who also designed Central Park in New York City. Over the years, this island park acquired the gorgeous Scott Fountain at its western end that we saw during our drive, as well as various pavilions. There is a bandstand, some museums, and lots of athletic fields. There are also picnic areas and a golf course. Let's see, there's also an aquarium, a botanic conservatory, a beach, and private boating clubs. All of that on this island. The ring road we drove allows auto traffic an easy, if slow, cruise around the island. The north side of the island, where we're seated, provides views of the Detroit shoreline that we're facing. While the south side, behind us, parallels Canada and the shoreline of the city of Windsor, Ontario. Yes, Canada is to the south of Belle Isle because of the peculiar geography of the Canadian peninsula. The landmass on which Windsor is situated tucks under Detroit and Michigan so that the Detroit River flows nearly from east, at the south end of Lake Saint Clair, to the west, at the northern corner of Lake Erie. Visitors to Detroit are always confused by this geographical configuration. It's hard, in fact, to imagine what I'm describing without looking at a map. They say, "What do you mean Canada is south of Detroit?" But at *d'étroit*, it is.

On your right, at the eastern end of the island is a wooded, marshy area with a view of Lake Saint Clair. One can also see the eastern shoreline of Detroit with its array of apartment buildings, houses, and boat facilities. Your Aunt Toby and India live in that apartment building there in front of you on the left. But for many decades the massive Conners Creek Power Plant dominated the shoreline over there on the right where, someday, there will be a park. It consisted of a huge, elongated, multi-story brick structure with another taller but narrower, multi-story building trailing behind it. Seven gigantic smokestacks rose above and out of the larger structure. Two additional smokestacks stood on the taller but narrower trailing building. The group of seven stacks was so impressive they became affectionately known as The Seven Sisters. The two additional stacks were called, of course, The Two Brothers. Together they formed a river landmark that defined the shoreline second only to the towers clustered in the city's downtown district downriver to the west. The Seven Sisters symbolized Detroit's industrial prowess and focused attention on the city's position on this system of waterways, called the Saint Lawrence Seaway. The Seaway begins on the west at Chicago on Lake Michigan and at Minnesota on Lake Superior. It stretches to the east at Toronto on Lake Ontario and Montreal on the Saint Lawrence River. Finally, it terminates at the Atlantic Ocean near Nova Scotia.

As you can see by the big empty space, The Seven Sisters are gone, demolished last year because they were no longer needed to provide electricity to the city. And, their stacks were conduits of pollution. Detroit is no longer the automotive capital of the USA in this age of the globalization of industry. The city's demands for electric energy to power its industries have dramatically decreased. Giant smoking chimneys are no longer a sign of progress or of a healthy environment, quite the contrary. The city, after a painful decline, has lost half of its population, mostly white people, but also many affluent blacks. It's also lost much of its industry and too much of its wealth. It is greatly diminished in nearly every way except for its inhabitants who are determined to keep this city alive and to reinvent it for a very different future era. Belle Isle is being restored after decades of neglect and decay. The city skyline is changing with a few new buildings. The shoreline is being reclaimed from its industrial past for future parkland. The Seven Sisters no longer dominate this picture. They are but a memory . . . A lot has changed in Detroit but I miss The Seven Sisters most of all.

Now, I'll tell you why this once great symbol means so much to me. It's not just nostalgia for a lost landmark. Nor is it regret for the destruction of so much that once symbolized the prominence and might of Detroit. No. I had a personal connection with The Seven Sisters because I designed a project, when I was in my last semester of architecture school. My professor's assignment concerned redeveloping neglected neighborhoods and repurposing massive, derelict landmarks that somehow spoiled the cityscape. At that time, even though The Seven Sisters were still an active power plant, most people thought it was an eyesore and wanted it removed. People also disliked the concrete storage silos that once dominated the river near downtown and the massive abandoned tire factory near the entrance to the Belle Isle Bridge. All of these reminders of Detroit's old, but defunct, industries were deemed blight. Auto factories disappeared such as DeSoto, Cadillac, Dodge, Packard, and American Motors. Warehouses became abandoned hulks. Several department stores disappeared, including Crowley's, Kern's, and Hudson's. It seemed that no one missed them. Folks wanted the blight gone because it reminded them of a lost past. But once they were gone, nothing took their place. Detroit became a cityscape of emptiness. And with the industry and people gone, whole neighborhoods disintegrated into rubble like the one we visited today. Detroit regressed to something less than a city. And, yet, the people who remained had hope, a kind of crazy, unrealistic hope, that the city would revive. That's what I felt and I wanted to show how The Seven Sisters could have a new and even exciting life on the river.

When I went to Europe with my aunt and we stayed in Rome for a few days, we saw many amazing buildings. The most amazing, for me, was the Basilica of Saint Peter. But, we also saw many ruins of ancient buildings, just fragments of what were once incredible structures, like the Colosseum. And, of these ruins, the one that astonished my young mind and that I could not forget was the Basilica of Maxentius and Constantine in the Roman Forum. Only about a third of the original building survives and when I tried to imagine the whole, intact building, the ruins seemed even more impressive. I asked my Aunt Augusta, who accompanied me, if she could leave me while I made drawings of the ruins in my sketchbook. I found a good spot to sit, away from all of the other tourists, where I could view the huge concrete vaults that were raised several stories above the ground on thick walls of Roman concrete. The great volumes of space enclosed by this masonry seemed grander and more vast because of the way the intense Roman sun cast deep, deep shadows that emphasized the massiveness and volume of the ruins. I later learned these ruins had existed for centuries and thousands upon thousands of visitors had seen what I was seeing. One such visitor was the first architect of the Basilica of Saint Peter, Donato Bramante. These ruins inspired his conception of Saint Peter's Basilica and, although he didn't complete the building, the architects who did, including Antonio da Sangallo and Michelangelo, followed his conception.

I was thinking about my sketches of the Basilica of Maxentius and Constantine in my design class and how it inspired Bramante for the design of Saint Peter's Basilica. As I thought about The Seven Sisters, I wanted to repurpose these buildings by capitalizing on their industrial grandeur. For my project, I designed new buildings at the front and back of the power plant suggesting that the entire complex was an enormous ocean liner with giant smoke stacks above the decks. The new building facing the city was the ship's stern and the building facing Belle Isle was its bow. I did a lot of research on The Seven Sisters' neighborhood and learned there were no recreational facilities in the area. Therefore, I conceived of the two new buildings as an amphitheater for performances in the bow and a swimming pool, gym, and ballgame courts for the stern. If the power plant itself was decommissioned, its interiors could be transformed into space for shopping, theaters, and other recreational facilities lacking in the neighborhood. The entire complex was quite an image with the smokestacks soaring above the body of a ship. I envisioned new housing and apartments for the neighborhood surrounding The Seven Sisters. I interspersed parkland and ballfields among the buildings to create a kind of self-contained village. My instructor loved the project and congratulated me. Of course, it seemed an impossible and impractical dream but it was stunning. Now that The Seven Sisters are gone, so is my dream. It was my dream to be an architect. It was nearly impossible to make it become a reality. Nobody then wanted a woman as an architect, certainly not a black woman. Nevertheless, I thought I would succeed. I was talented. I had prepared in school. I got excellent grades. My teachers encouraged me. But, that door was not open. I was willing to take any job. Finally, there was an opportunity. HR&K hired me on the recommendation of my mentor and advisor but I wasn't given any design work. There were always reasons. They wanted someone with more experience. My student work was not suited to their projects. There were no other women in the office except secretaries. I thought about freelancing but no one I knew had design work or money to hire me as an architect. I settled for what I could get at HR&K, got married to Tyrone, and had my boys, Leon and Brice. Finally, I got small jobs like the one we saw. That's what happened to my ambition. Now I hope you can do better. You've got a better chance to be what you want to be. Black women have more opportunities now. You'll have to work hard. Push hard. But you can make it happen, Serena. Maybe, if I had someone pushing me, I could have gone on. You've got people to support you. Help you. Take advantage of that. Set your goals and keep pushing. Don't give up. Maybe, I didn't push hard enough. Maybe I didn't have the confidence. I didn't see other black women doing what I wanted to do. I wanted to be a first. It wasn't my time. But it's your time. You can do it. Work for it and don't quit. Be a proud sister.

Aunt Aubergine, I have one question.

What's that, Serena?

Do you still have your drawings and sketches?

Yes, of course I do.

Could I see them?

I'll have to look in my library but I know where I keep those things. I would be delighted to show them to you and, if you want, you can keep them.

Wow. I do want them. Thank you, so much for everything.

Let's head home now. You'll be returning to Atlanta soon. I hope you know I'll miss you.

— An Invitation —
Fall 1997

Aubergine was sitting in her office at HR&K working on still another minor project when the phone rang.

Aubergine Curtis speaking. How may I help you?

Uh, is it Missus or Miss Curtis?

Missus Curtis.

Oh, okay. Missus Curtis, my name is Gwendolyn Magrew. Please call me Gwendolyn.

You're with the city planning department, right, Gwendolyn?

Yes, we've met before but there was no reason for you to remember me. I was always just one of the people in the background.

No, no. I certainly remember you, Gwendolyn. You're a young sister, in your thirties, I would guess.

Yes, I'm thirty-four.

I'm a lot older than you, as you probably know. I'm fifty-four, twenty years older than you.

You look a lot younger.

Well, thank you, but believe me, I feel my age.

Missus Curtis . . . .

Call me Aubergine.

Alright. Aubergine, I'm calling you first of all because you're liaison between your company and the city planning department. But, I've been asked by the head of city planning to call you for another reason.

Yes, what is that?

We would like to meet with you here in our conference room next Monday at ten o'clock to discuss a project we are considering.

What is the project?

535

We would like to wait about mentioning that until you're here. We want as few people as possible to know about this meeting at this time. Could you attend the meeting?

I'll put it on my schedule but I'll have to postpone a meeting here in order to attend. If I can't attend, I'll call you to let you know. If I can, I'll see you at ten on Monday in the city planning conference room. Is that okay?

Sure. Thank you, Aubergine.

At lunch time, Aubergine and Tyrone had sandwiches together as usual at a soul food restaurant near their office. Aubergine waited until they had settled at a table and ordered their food before she mentioned the earlier conversation with Gwendolyn. She emphasized that it was unusual for city planning not to explain the purpose of a meeting. The secrecy was puzzling. In any case, she was able to reschedule her HR&K meeting and would attend the city planning meeting. Tyrone suggested the secrecy indicated something big was up, and he was very excited for Aubergine. She gave her husband a kiss to thank him for being her number one supporter. That next Monday at ten Aubergine arrived at the city planning conference room. Only a few members of the staff were present including Gwendolyn Magrew and Lenny DeCollette, head of city planning.

Welcome, Missus Curtis or may I call you Aubergine?

Of course, you may. It's good to see you again, Lenny. Hello, Gwendolyn. Where should I sit?

Why don't you sit here at the head of the table.

All right, Lenny. Thank you.

Excuse the hush-hush of inviting you to this meeting but we want our plans to be very closely held until we're ready to make a public announcement.

Does that mean you want me to keep what we discuss here a secret from my office?

For the time being, yes, it would be preferable if you could. Let's just keep it between us family members.

That would be very unusual. I mean I can certainly accept your conditions but can you explain why the secrecy is necessary?

We are going to discuss an important new and large project which, in itself, is not a secret.

Then, what is the secret?

We want you to design the master plan for it.

Me? You want me to design your project? I don't understand. Usually, you present projects to the head of our design department and to the senior members of the company. I'm assuming you haven't done that. Is that correct?

Yes, that is correct.

I can't recall, as long as I've been with HR&K, that a client chose a specific architect for a project without approaching the senior staff first.

And, it is especially unusual to request an architect who hasn't designed very much or, really, hasn't designed any significant buildings.

But that's not true. You have designed a building that will be at the center of our new project.

What building is that?

The building is our city office in the Russell Avenue neighborhood.

That building is not even occupied and the neighborhood is practically deserted. I just visited the site a few weeks ago with my niece who plans to be an architect.

Aubergine, we know all of your professional work and your qualifications perfectly well. We consulted with your mentor, Rainer Lotz, whom we respect above all others. He thought you were the most creative student he's every had. He told us about your proposal for The Seven Sisters and commented that it was the most original and exciting student project he ever saw. That's why we are proposing a project that will involve you as its lead architect.

I'm listening but I'm concerned about how my company will react.

We'll come to that eventually. First of all, our black mayor, Dennis Archer, wants to begin a pilot program aimed at reviving our depopulated and derelict neighborhoods. Revitalization is, all of us believe, essential to the future of this city and the well-being of its majority black inhabitants. We want new housing and amenities that will attract middle income families but that will also serve the needs of our poorest citizens. The Russell neighborhood will have this new housing anchored by your office building which will be re-purposed and enlarged as a community center within a multi-purpose shopping complex and village square. We are calling the project Russell Commons. It will begin with the entire block where your office building stands and expand east and north into neighboring blocks until we have an area that might house up to a thousand or more residents. If it proves successful, we will scale up the project into an even larger area still further east and north to hold a population of several thousand. It's an ideal location because of access to the freeways and major surface streets. The medical center is only blocks away as is the cultural center, Wayne State University, and Eastern Market. Redeveloping the area would link together these other centers and would demonstrate that the city is interested in the well-being of all of its neighborhoods and all of its residents.

That's a very ambitious, in fact, overwhelming but promising idea. Obviously, such a project would be an extraordinary opportunity for an architect. But, why me, Lenny? There hasn't been anything remotely created like this in Detroit since Lafayette Park.

Gwen, why don't you jump in here.

Sure. Aubergine, simply put, we in city planning and the mayor want a sister for this project. You are that sister. You have behind you one of the leading and most important architectural offices in this city and state. If HR&K wants this job in a majority black city, they will have to place you in charge as lead architect.

If I said I didn't want to do this, Gwen, I would be lying. It's an incredible opportunity. It's something I've wanted to do my whole career. But, I must say that the big boys at HR&K are going to blow a gasket. They are not going to be happy.

Let them blow a gasket. Let them be unhappy. We can't win for ourselves if we aren't willing to play the game they have played forever. You are who we want and no one else. Either you are the architect or they don't get the project. Our next choice would be a small black architectural firm but we want a black woman and a big office to support this project. Will you do it?

Of course I'll do it. I'm shocked that you have this kind of faith in me. Really, Lenny, are you onboard with this?

Listen, if you could survive at HR&K all these years, that's good enough for me. Let's get down to business.

— Russell Commons —
1998-2000

Aubergine was correct, at least about the big boys. Assouf blew several gaskets just short of a stroke when informed of the city's decision. He fumed and raged as he faced Aubergine and her legal counsel, India Rhonda Sykes.

Absolutely not. HR&K will not allow a client to determine who will be a project lead architect. That is not our policy. I assure you, we cannot do that. I assign our architects to projects based on their experience and talent. A massive and ambitious project like this requires a more experienced architect than you. Your talent is really thus far untested, certainly not in a class required by a project of this scale, complexity, and cost. It's an absurd demand.

That's because in all of the years I've been in this company, Mister Assouf, I've only been given minor projects or industrial projects that no one else wanted.

That's not the case, Missus Curtis. We've given you a lot of work and much of it is essential to this company's prominence and finances.

Yes, but, with few exceptions, none of the work has been challenging for my design abilities.

That's the business you're in and you know the rules. All buildings have to be designed, even minor ones. That's where we've employed your talents. However, this project is an increase in scale by several powers that are far beyond anything you've done. You are completely unproven for this task and, under no circumstances, would I even consider your for this project. Now, you'll have to tell the city planning department you cannot and will not be assigned by this firm to Russell Commons as lead architect. That is final.

Mister Assouf, I have to be very direct here. I won't tell them that because they have already said, if I am not the architect, HR&K won't get this project. They are emphatic, and the mayor backs them up.

The mayor?

Yes, the mayor. He wants me and only me and if it is not me, then HR&K loses out to a small black firm. He wants a black woman and a big company. I am that black woman and I work for one of the biggest firms in this city. Now, what do you say?

We'll have to talk to the mayor and explain that what he wants is impossible. It's not how we operate.

The mayor wants what he wants. It seems that you, not the mayor, will have to change his mind.

This is ridiculous. I don't even know how I can discuss such a preposterous idea with the senior partners. This is unprecedented.

Excuse me, Mister Assouf, but what is requested here is neither preposterous nor unprecedented. As counsel for my client, Missus Aubergine Perry Curtis, I can name ten jobs by your company where the client specified the company architect. I don't think the mayor would like to know, when it comes to my client and the city of Detroit, that you suddenly have an ironclad rule that excludes her and the mayor's wishes.

Councillor Sykes, where did you get your information about our assignment of architects? I assure you it is not correct.

My information comes from your company records which I have obtained. I know what I say is correct.

Obtained how, may I ask?

That is my business. If you would like to see them, I have copies here.

You could only have obtained those records illegally. By theft.

How I obtained these records is not the issue. The issue is the information they contain and which, if we cannot agree on the assignment of my client to the Russell Commons project, will be forwarded to the city planning commission and to the mayor. I assure you, if I am forced to do that, the damage to the reputation of your company in this city will be considerable and of much more consequence than how this information was obtained. We are all adults here. You have your rules and the city has its rules. Who do you think will win this contest of rules? And, why, if your company only stands to benefit in prestige and in remuneration, would you object to the mayor's condition?

Mister Assouf, please listen to my counsel. No one is trying to make trouble for the company. The city, in case you haven't noticed, is being run by black people. They want black people to have an active part in creating this city. This is a new era for me and for you. I assume you don't like the pressure that is being put on you and on the company but this is a matter decided by the planning department and mayor not me. If I'm assigned to the Russell Commons project and I'm not doing a good job, I'll acknowledge such and you can replace me. However, I know I can do the work and do it well.

Mister Assouf, as legal counsel to my client, I ask that we be reasonable and keep this matter between ourselves. We don't want to make a public fuss or cause harm to your company. Missus Curtis is a well-trained and experienced architect. She has performed her assigned duties over the years without a single complaint or reprimand. Her record speaks for itself. Apparently, your company has enough faith in her to have kept her employed in her design capacity for many years. The city of Detroit, based on her record, has faith that she can deliver the kind of project they want for Russell Commons. Let's agree to the city's endorsement and desire, and move on.

It's not my decision alone.

With all due respect, Mister Assouf, I know that it is your decision alone. But, if you want to discuss it with your colleagues, go ahead. We will expect a decision by next week that Missus Curtis is the lead architect for the project.

The following week for Aubergine at the office was tense. She encountered Mister Assouf in the elevator and he was stonily silent. She imagined he was quite angry for being caught in a lie but, she reasoned, that was his problem not hers. The following week, he called her into his office and gave her the company's decision which, in fact, was his decision.

Hi, India, it's Aubergine.

Hi, Honey. Any news?

I should say there is. HR&K assigned me as lead architect to Russell Commons. I'll have three associate architects as well as several engineers assigned to the project. The company really wants this project to succeed. You did it. You persuaded Mister Assouf.

Thanks, Aubergine, but I think you, backed by the power of the mayor and city planning department, won your own case. I only reminded Assouf of the hypocrisy of his defense. And, you need to thank your friend, Miss Williams for digging out those memos.

India, I have to clarify something. I didn't tell you the whole story about those documents. There's a slightly personal and embarrassing part to all of this. You see, Miss Williams didn't actually give me the documents. She only located them and told me where they were filed. I asked someone else in the office to retrieve them so that she was not implicated in their removal. He's a department head. His name is Etienne Savarin. He's the one who actually got the documents and gave them to me.

Why did he do that?

I'm embarrassed to say. The truth is he's been my lover.

Shit. Whoa. Aubergine, you're full of surprises. I guess Tyrone doesn't know about this Etienne, is that correct?

Right.

Whew. Okay. Who am I to judge? Client confidentiality, Aubergine. This is just between us.

Just between us. Not between us and Toby. Thank you

As I said, "client confidentiality." I was also about to say, it's always nice to have documentation to wave in their faces. We accomplished our mission. Now, have you thought about how you are going to design Russell Commons?

Yes, it's all I can think about. When I have my preliminary sketches ready, I'll have you and Toby over for dinner and we can discuss it.

That's great. Give my love to your family. Thank Etienne. Talk to you later.

For the next weeks, Aubergine worked constantly on Russell Commons. Before making any sketches or even considering a design, she obtained maps and plans from the city's records office including street right-of-ways, utility lines including electrical, gas, water, and sewer. She also requested copies of current property ownership of each parcel of land within the eventual boundaries of Russell Commons. Then, she went to the neighborhood and took pictures and made detailed drawings of the entire site. She photographed every standing building including her own vacant office building. She talked to every person she encountered who still lived within the project's future borders. She checked for archival photographs at the Burton Historical Collection of the Detroit Public Library. As the documentation accumulated in her office, she closely examined every piece of information. She also obtained several books about the city that included passages referring to the history of the neighborhood. She tried to be as thorough as possible in her research so that she understood the site as well as she knew her own body. It was a lot of work but she loved it. It was what she had dreamed of doing since beginning architecture school. It was what she learned from her teachers, in particular from Professor Rainer Lotz. Be thorough, he insisted. Don't start with some grand idea of the design. Start with knowledge of the place where your design will take shape. Know the site. Know its history. Know what the people on the site or near the site know. Know everything you can reasonably know before you pick up your pencils to draw. And don't start drawing dreams but, instead, begin by visualizing the needs of the future inhabitants.

As Aubergine began synthesizing her research, she again consulted the planning department's requirements for the site. They wanted housing for middle and low income people. They wanted five hundred units of studio, one-, two-, and three-bedroom homes to house an anticipated population of around one thousand people—single individuals, couples, and couples with children and/or older adults. They wanted off-street parking for three hundred cars, space for dozens of specialty shops including a supermarket, and an indoor and outdoor recreation area. They wanted a school campus for kindergarten through intermediate grades. And, they wanted all of this within a projected construction budget of four hundred million dollars to be funded by sale of municipal bonds. It seemed a generous budget at eight hundred thousand dollars per unit but that unit cost also included all of the site amenities and improvements. After weeks of study, she sat down with her husband and reviewed what she had learned and what she thought she needed to do.

Ty, I don't want to scare myself into thinking I've taken on more than I can handle.

Babe, you've got this. This is you. This is why you're on this planet. The universe has opened a door for you. You'll walk right through it to the other side with a project that will blow their fucking minds. Don't doubt yourself now for a moment. Look at all of the shit work you've already done and done well on budget. This is just a job that taps all of your skills that, until now, have been waiting for this opportunity. You've got the mojo. You've got the credentials. Baby, you're the man. Okay, you're the woman but just do it. And, whatever I can do to support you, you know I'm there for you.

Will you be completely honest with me and, if you see me doing something you think is a problem, will you tell me? And, if I won't listen, will you ask me to sit down and take a break, chill for while and clear my mind? I really need you to do this for me because I trust your judgment. I trust your knowledge. And, I love you.

I love you too, Baby, and I'm doing this for me as much as for you. I want to be married to the greatest black female architect ever.

I don't want to be the greatest anything, Ty. I just want to be really, really good.

No problem. That you can do.

When Aubergine began her first sketches, really little more than doodles, she started with the facts on the ground. This was not a virgin suburban site covered with trees, or former farmland. This had once been a vibrant residential city neighborhood. There was an existing street pattern, a rectangular grid of east-west and north-south residential streets, major arteries, including a freeway and a defunct railroad right-of-way, bordering the site. There were a number of occupied houses, as well as abandoned ones, tied to the grid. How could Russell Commons respect these realities but not be limited by them? After much experimentation, Aubergine realized that the grid could be maintained with the existing buildings but new construction was not limited by the grid. Instead, it could be tied into the grid's above-ground and underground infrastructure but sited in a new, more flexible pattern. No one would be forced out of their homes. Instead new homes, on and off the grid, would compliment the existing ones that were salvageable.

As Aubergine delved into incorporating more of the requirements of the planning department's program into her sketches, she experimented with various types of multiple dwellings, attached single family homes, low-rise apartments, and high-rise apartments. This approach to mixed housing was nothing original, however, it was distinguished by having shopping, a school campus, and other non-residential activities integrated into the housing at street level. What Aubergine began to feel was that it should be done with the pedestrian uppermost in mind while respecting the fact that automobiles also had to be accommodated. As she worked through possibilities, she thought about communities in other countries she had visited, including those with Tyrone and their sons. West Africa, North Africa, particularly Morocco, and the Middle East all provided ideas for a pedestrian-based solution but didn't solve the necessity of the automobile's omni-presence in Detroit. Parking garages and large surface lots were standard features of many planned communities. Garages attached to individual homes were convenient for occupants but necessitated an extensive road system for access. Underground garages connected by their own system of streets could eliminate the need for above ground roads and provide sheltered, surveilled parking but it was expensive because of excavation. It occurred to her that all of that excavated soil, instead of being trucked away to landfill, could be reused to create a landscaped greenway of gentle hills on Detroit's flat terrain, in a series of common areas interconnected by walkways throughout the new neighborhood. Therefore, above ground, pedestrians had priority. Below ground automobiles and service vehicles on circulating streets dominated. It was a hybrid solution that could separate pedestrians from automotive traffic and, yet, make cars convenient to their owners if it could be done within the projected budget.

She discussed her preliminary sketches with her team of architects and engineers and they offered several astute observations and suggestions, all of which Aubergine acknowledged improved the concept. She wanted to know from them if all of the structures could be built of modern materials, such as steel and reinforced concrete, and older materials like brick, concrete block, and stone. She did not want to use wood for structural supports, only for interior finishes. They responded that what she wanted could be done but construction costs would rise, perhaps, well beyond the budget. She wanted to proceed on her assumptions and begin designing schematics for the project. Then, the estimators could analyze the plans and produce a projected cost. As her plans crystalized in her mind, for the first time, she began to fear she might be dooming the success of her own project with practical but overly expensive solutions.

Ty, I'm worried. I'm not sure I'm being realistic about this project. It may cost much more than is budgeted. Besides, what I'm designing is usually built for wealthier people not for the kind of people intended as residents of Russell Commons.

So, lower income people shouldn't have nice places to live?

You know that's not what I believe but it is a reality.

Yes, and the reality is that a black woman shouldn't be in charge of a project like this. But, she is. You are. So why not create a beautifully designed community for people at the lower end of the income scale? Detroit is full of such folks. Are we gonna wait for wealthier white folks to move back to Detroit or are we gonna provide for the people who actually do, or want, or need to live here?

If it were my decision, you know what I would want. But it's not up to me. I can only propose.

Then propose and then we'll convince the deciders what the right thing is to do.

Ty, I want this project to succeed and be built. I don't know that I can say, "Take it or leave it."

Okay. How about this? Propose your plan. Make it so good they won't want anything else. They can find the money if they want what you give them. Make them want it. Do your best, Honey. Do your best.

Aubergine worked through many stages of her design. In consultation with her team, she refined both her concept and her design solutions. After many tries, she devised a design that both satisfied the program and presented a handsome community of homes. It was still expensive, more so than the budget, but she felt proud and committed to fighting for her design. The senior partners balked and refused to endorse her plans. City planning and the mayor loved her design. The presentation drawings were stunning. A huge, detailed model of Russell Commons allowed all to see the project three-dimensionally. It was exciting. The price, however, left them in shock. It would be difficult to raise the initial budget. It was impossible to find funds for the estimated costs. The design had to be scaled back to fit within the budget. The result was what Aubergine had always been required to do for her previous work with HR&K, an undistinguished but functional design on budget. But, the project didn't move forward because the city could never arrange any financing through sale of bonds. As the city continued to decline in populations and resources, its fiscal position became increasingly unstable. As a result of all of her work, Aubergine was left with only her plans and a model. In her life, she had tried many things but of all of those things, this is the only thing she really loved.

— News —
Fall 2000

Aubergine's office was piled with sketches, plans, documents, and models. She loved living with this material because it so vividly represented this major part of her life. Her home and family were certainly another significant part but when she was really honest with herself, it was her work that was most important to her. While she was going over estimates for a new industrial building, her phone rang.

Aubergine Curtis, here.

Hey, Sister Curtis, this is Toby.

Hi, Sis. How are you? I'm so sorry I've been busy and haven't called you lately. What's new?

Little Sister, I've got some bad news. I hate to drop it on you like this but I have pancreatic cancer.

Toby, no. No. No. Pancreatic cancer? Shit. When did you find out?

I was feeling seriously sick a while ago and went to see my doctor. He did a lot of tests. A few weeks later he called me in for a consultation and told me my condition was terminal. Just like that. I could undergo radiation and chemotherapy. They can't cure me and treatment will only give me a few more months with a lot of pain. That's not what I want.

Toby, this is horrible. First, Mother, now you. Her stroke left her like a vegetable. She was unconscious for weeks in that hospital until we decided to end it all for her and let her go in peace. Now, my only sister? Toby, I don't want to see you suffer.

I won't. It will be quick because I'm not going to prolong my life. Don't ask because I don't want you to know. So here's the deal. I want you to become a real sister to India. She'll need family through all of this. And, I want to ask you a favor. I want you to be with me as much as you can. Don't quit your job. Just kidding. I know you wouldn't do that. But, really, whenever you can spare the time, stay with me. Hold my hand. Tell me dirty jokes. Read me poetry. Cook your spaghetti and meatballs. I will try to eat as much of it as I can even if it makes me puke. And, when I'm gone, remember that I loved you even when I didn't like you. You are a good sister and I'm proud of you for pursuing your dream.

When Toby ended the call, Aubergine closed the door to her office and cried. Her only sister was dying. Somehow, Aubergine had never considered life without her sister. Her mother and both grandmothers were all dead. The circle of women in her immediate family was diminishing to one, herself. With effort she reminded herself of the women who still lived. There was her Aunt Augusta, Serena, her niece, Ondine, and India. She promised herself to become closer to all of them.

She would honor her sister's wish, and reach out to India. If anyone needed support now, it would be she.

Toby died within four months of her announcement, her life shortened, Aubergine believed, because she couldn't bear the pain of the effects of the cancer even with medication. Toby was buried with her parents and grandparents in a cemetery chosen by Estyllene years before as the final resting place for the Moore family. Aubergine did observe her sister's wish and spent more time with India. She frequently invited India to her home for family dinners, and India arranged for the two of them to have meals together at India's apartment and at restaurants. They often talked about Aubergine's niece, Serena, and her plans to become an architect. Both women recognized that Serena needed to break the class, race, and gender barriers that had hindered Aubergine's success. Serena needed something that intelligence, talent, and academic study would not alone provide her. In order to move beyond her middle class upbringing, which would serve her in most professions, she would require direct and sustained familiarity with other cultures in order to navigate the more rarified and snobbish circles of potential wealthy clients. She should travel the world to know firsthand the habits, customs, histories, and environments of other peoples. Aubergine and India would finance a year of travel and study abroad for Serena. She could choose the countries she thought to be most important to her future but Aubergine and India would stress the need to visit countries on all of the continents, perhaps with the exception of Antartica unless Serena was interested in snow, ice, and penguins. Aubergine explained the scheme to Serena by recalling Eliza Doolittle in *My Fair Lady*. Aubergine and India were acting the roles of Professor Higgins and Colonel Pickering in transforming the lowly flower-seller, Eliza, into a woman who could associate with the aristocracy of Europe. This was Aubergine's and India's plan for Serena. When this opportunity was explained to Serena, she was overwhelmed and grateful. She immediately began planning and, with additional support from India, spent two years abroad. After returning to the USA, Serena quickly set her mind on becoming an exceptional and successful architect.

Before Serena left on her two year sojourn abroad, Aubergine tried to refocus her attention on her work at HR&K. She received more significant projects to design than the very humble buildings she was given prior to Russell Commons. Nothing, however, engaged her as much as that aborted project. Nevertheless, she did her best work, as always. While she was discussing a new project with Tyrone in her office, her phone rang and she answered. The voice on the other end of the line was that of a woman and it was unfamiliar. The woman asked to speak to "Obra-Jean Moore." Aubergine explained that was her former name. The woman replied she knew it was her former name but it was the name she knew her by many decades ago. The woman introduced herself as Janette Redmond. Aubergine knew her as Janette Fulgenzi when they were students at Saint Catherine.

Janette, what a complete surprise to hear from you. Excuse me a moment. I was discussing business with my husband. I'll ask him to come back later.

Ty, I need to take this call. Can you come back in about an hour?

Sure, Honey.

Okay. Janette, I'm back. My goodness, how did you know how to contact me and why have you called after all of these years?

It's a long story but I read about you and your big project in the paper some months back but it took me a while to put together your old and new names. When I figured out you were "Obra-Jean," I made up my mind to call you.

Wow.

Aubergine, I've never forgot about you. You were the best friend I ever had. I learned so much from you. I just wish I had known my own mind as well as you knew yours. I wish I could have done what I wanted to do instead of what my parents wanted. You were right to stick to what you wanted. Look where you are now.

Gee, Janette, I did become an architect and do have a pretty good job here at HR&K but my ambition was unrealistic. There have been so many barriers here because I'm a woman and black and working-class. It's been a fight from day one and I don't know if the battle was worth it.

But you did design the amazing project that I read about. That's a success for you even if it's not built yet.

Janette, I doubt it will ever be built.

But there's all of your other work. I read about that too.

I know but that work isn't much to celebrate. It's pretty routine.

Listen, Aubergine, you've accomplished a lot. You stuck with it. You've made a name for yourself. I'm very proud of you.

Thank you, Janette. What about you? You have a new name.

Yes. I'm married. Well, I'm separated from my husband. See, I went to that small Catholic college in Indiana like my parents wanted. But, I met this young black guy there. It's funny, somehow he reminded me of you. He was sure of himself too and smart and he was really nice. His name is Reginald Redmond and he's from Saint Louis. We got married. My parents disowned me. Reggie's parents practically disowned him. We felt all alone together. We had one girl. She's grown now and has her own family. I'm a grandmother, three times. You know, I didn't graduate from college. I dropped out when I got married and got pregnant and started having a family. We moved to Saint Louis when Reggie graduated and that's where I'm living now. Reggie pays me support so I get by. I have the house we bought. I'm doing okay.

Janette, why did you stop calling me when we were kids and never answered my calls?

I was afraid of my parents and my family. They really hated black people. I didn't know what else to do.

But you married a black man. You must have known how they would react to that.

I was in Indiana. I thought I was far enough away from them so they couldn't do anything to me. And, Reggie really loved me.

Why are you separated?

Aubergine, it's not easy being white and married to a black man. Our child is mixed race and she's had a terrible time trying to figure out who she is and where she belongs. She didn't have a big family for support like you had with grandparents and aunts and uncles. She only had her parents. Reggie and I just weren't realistic about what our lives together would be like. The hatred around us became too much. A black man has a hard time protecting his family and himself from that kind of hatred. We still love each other but we can't be together.

I'm sorry, Janette. I hope someday you two can find a way to be couple again.

Maybe, Aubergine. Maybe. Meanwhile, I would love to see you if you ever come to Saint Louis. You know you were more than a friend to me. I felt you were like a sister.

— A New Old Plan —
2010

Aubergine worked at HR&K until she retired at sixty-five in 2008. Tyrone retired the year after her. Together, they planned more trips to countries they always wanted to visit. They would also have more time to visit their sons, Leon in Los Angeles and Brice in Boston, their wives, and grandchildren. Aubergine remained in close contact with Serena, her brother's only daughter. She had followed her aunt's lead and became an architect, a very successful one at an architectural firm in Atlanta. She was not the only female architect nor the only black female architect. But she was very talented, smart, and assertive so much so that she decided to create her own architectural practice. On a trip to Detroit to consult on a possible project there, she visited her aunt and uncle. In addition to a tour of Detroit, she accompanied Aubergine to the cemetery where members of her family were buried. Located almost an hour's drive from downtown, the cemetery was very much like a park with flat stone grave markers flush with the ground instead of a forest of vertical stone monuments. It was a beautiful, sunny Sunday afternoon in spring.

Why is everyone buried way out here so far from the city?

My grandmother, Estyllene, thought it would be a good idea for the family to invest in this cemetery back in the 1950s when this farmland was first transformed into burial ground. The owners marketed it to black folks because they knew it was difficult for us to be buried at that time in a lot of the white cemeteries in the city. So, one by one, members of our family were planted here. My dad, Perry, was the first to go. That's his grave there. His father, Barry, is next to him, and then there are the graves of Estyllene, Carson, and Mason. On the other side of my father's grave is my mother, Leona, and my sister, Toby. She died much too young from pancreatic cancer at age sixty-four. So, there are still plots for your father and me. This is where we are supposed to end up.

What about your husband and my mother? And what about us children?

I don't think Estyllene thought through this project to later generations. Besides, who knows if any of the rest of family even wants to be buried here.

Do you visit here often?

Not really, Serena. It's a long drive and I don't need to see their graves to remember them. In fact, I wish they all had been cremated and the urns placed in a columbarium in a cemetery within the city. I would prefer having my ashes scattered.

You'll have a long wait.

Maybe.

Auntie, I want to thank you again for recommending me to your city planning department.

Who else but my own niece could do the job?

It's ironic though isn't it that a project you designed over a decade ago might be revived?

I thought Russell Commons was dead but it looks like it may still have life. Certainly the need to rebuild and revive this city still exists, more now than ever before. The time may be right.

Be assured, Auntie, if it goes forward I will do my best to realize your original vision for it.

Don't do that, Honey. Make it your own vision, Serena. Lots of things have changed in ten years. The project needs to be seen with new eyes for new circumstances. You have to make Russell Commons your child. My project will always be my child in my mind. That's good enough for me.

We're not going to bury your project here. You had great ideas and they're still valid. I want to build on your framework.

Well, we'll see. Whether or not the project ever really happens with you, well, we'll go on. We sisters keep trying. We do what we can do.

— This is the End —
Fall 2011

An early and heavy fall rain poured from low, dark clouds completely blotting out the sunlight. The windshield wipers on the car struggled furiously to clear the sheets of water that obscured views of the road ahead. Even driving slowly with headlights on, Aubergine could barely see more than a car's length ahead of her car. Why, she wondered, had they not paid closer attention to the weather forecast and chosen a different day to celebrate Augusta's ninetieth birthday. If they managed to reach their destination without an accident, they might not be able to get out of the car because of the downpour. Maybe, they should just turn around and head back home. She looked at her Aunt Augusta sitting in the passenger seat beside her who had nodded off. How could the woman sleep at a time like this, she wondered? Ondine and India in the back seat were chattering away as if certain annihilation were not imminent. The trip was long-planned. It was difficult to arrange schedules so that all four women could spend the day together and make the journey. It seemed to Aubergine that it might be wiser now to give up their plan and try again another day. Just as she was about to say something, there was a brilliant flash of lightning and a terrifying crash of thunder. Ondine and India stopped talking. Well, that got their attention, Aubergine chuckled to herself. It was, as if for the first time, the women in the back seat noticed the weather conditions.

Aubergine, where the hell are we? I can't see thing out of these windows.

Well, Ondine, now you know what I've known for the past ten minutes. But, in answer to your question, we are about halfway to the restaurant. I'm thinking we should turn around and go back home.

If we're halfway, why not continue? There's nothing to be gained by going back.

I can't see a thing. I'm not even sure where we are because I can't any buildings. Can you see anything, India?

I just saw something I recognized. I think we're almost there. Aubergine, turn right at the next traffic light. There's a gas station there where we can pull under a canopy and wait till this rain eases up.

Okay, here's the light. I see the gas station. I'll pull under the canopy . . . There, we made it. Whew! Thanks, India. I feel safer waiting here a bit until this storm passes. What were you and Ondine talking about? I could hear bits of your conversation but I couldn't concentrate because I was so pre-occupied driving in this rain.

We were talking about Toby and how we both met her. It's been ten years since she died. She went so fast. I never imagined that pancreatic cancer could bring her down so quickly. I'm glad you agreed with me not to use heroic measures and to let her die in peace.

India, I know you loved Toby and didn't want to let her go. But, you and I both knew Toby would not want to live in constant, unbearable pain.

She was a sister to us all.

Amen, Ondine. Although she was my blood sister, you've been a sister to me too.

And, to me. When Toby died, I felt my world collapse. You were there for me, Ondine, and you too, Aubergine.

I feel lucky to be part of this family, as I know you have, India. Being Augusta's partner all these years has made me feel I had all of you as sisters.

Speaking of the devil, look who's waking up. Welcome to the world, Aunt Augusta.

It's raining? Where are we?

We're waiting in a gas station until the rain lets up. It's beginning to look like the clouds are clearing. It's a lot brighter now than it was when we pulled into this gas station and there's a lot less rain.

I fell asleep.

We know. How are you feeling?

Old, Baby, old. Ondine, how old am I?

Ninety, Sweetheart. We're celebrating your birthday today.

Jesus. Ninety. Ladies, I don't recommend this for anybody. Being old is a bitch. Did you say we are in a gas station. I've got to pee. Where's the restroom?

I'll take you inside. Ondine, please hand me that umbrella. Thanks. Auntie, I'll come around and help you out of the car and walk you to the restroom. Don't forget your cane. Ladies, we'll see you in a bit. Don't drive off without us now.

We won't. India, it looks like the rain is stopping.

Yes. I guess that was the worst of it today. Ondine, there's something I've wanted to talk to you about for a long time now.

What's that?

You and I are possibly as different as two women could be and, yet, here we are together, in effect, in the same adopted family. We've known each other in this family for what, about fifty years or so?

That's about right.

Why did we choose this family, these people, with whom to share our lives?

I can't answer for you, India, but for me I found acceptance, support, and comfort in their love. They're imperfect human beings, as we all are, but their imperfections only remind me that human failings are what make us human. We sisters understand that, and that's what makes us sisters.

And, we both are two women who really love women. You know, I fell in love with Toby when we were in a calculus class together. She always thought I was the smart one but she was really smart. I don't think she really recognized her own talents, intelligence, and beauty. When we went to visit my parents in Chicago way back when for their wedding anniversary, it was Toby who tried to stop me from walking out on my snooty parents. She understood better than I did the importance of family. Now, I know Leona was a difficult mother but she was a good mother in the sense that she did everything she could do to protect her children. She wanted her girls especially to be prepared for a world that she knew would not completely accept or encourage them. Now, Leona couldn't foresee that her daughters were exceptional and would exceed the limitations of their gender, race, and class. I believe that they did succeed because Leona was their first and, perhaps, most difficult hurdle. She made it possible for them to stand up to people with far more power than Leona had but not with nearly as much force of her personality. Leona was aptly named. She was a lioness who roared.

You know what, India? I always thought that Leona was a sweetie. She cared not only for her daughters but also for her mother and mother-in-law and she didn't do badly by her son, either. And, Augusta loved Leona. There was a bond that was unbreakable between those two despite the fact that they were such different people with very different and strong opinions. I always thought there was a lot of love in my family but I've seen love in the Moore and Post women that is truly remarkable. They brought us together.

Sister, Ondine.

Sister India.

And then there's Aubergine. Who could have guessed that someone as single-minded and focused on architecture, architecture, architecture, someone who only seemed to pay lip-service to family, would become the sister to us all?

Well, she did, god bless her.

Here they come now. Sister Aubergine and Sister Augusta.

Okay, y'all. We're back. Auntie, let's get you back into the front seat. Come around this way. Let me get the door. There. Okay. Is everybody ready to eat? I can't hear you. Okay, that's better. Let's see. The sun's shining and we're going to have a beautiful day. We're almost at that new upscale soul food restaurant. Girls, are we ready for some haute cuisine fried chicken and barbecued ribs? I thought so. You know, Augusta's sorority sister owns that restaurant in, of all places, Bloomfield Hills. The white folks must be beside themselves thinking of all of us black folks invading their lily-white community. Well, I say, let the invasion begin. Stop giggling. Ladies, now before we get there, I want to tell you something. I'll make this short and sweet. First of all, I'm grateful we are still here together on this planet when so many of our loved ones have departed. And, I'm proud that my niece has taken over the Russell Commons project and made it even better than I could. And, it's going to be built with private financing, finally, after all these years. I'm really proud of her. She's the daughter I never had but always wanted. She's an associate at HR&K now, that's the power of black people in Detroit. But, seeing where she is now and where we are now reminds me of when I was a kid and dreamed my dreams. I wanted so much from life, more than life could ever give me. And Leona, God bless her, warned me. Over and over, again and again and again. But, you know what? I'm glad I tried and I'm blessed for what I got. I have a husband, two beautiful sons, grandchildren, all of you, and a niece who may become the greatest black female architect yet. I wasn't the greatest architect in Detroit but I was good when I had a chance. I did my best. Sometimes, we don't realize our dreams the way we want but that doesn't mean we shouldn't dream. Hey. Have all you women fallen asleep? What the hell? Here I am talking to myself. Oh, well. Mom, I wish you were here.

Baby, I am here . . .

And I'll always be here for you . . .

As long as you want or need me, I'll be here

Thanks

Early one morning in June 2021—4 am. to be exact—I awoke and felt thirsty. Our apartment was completely dark and silent. I went to the kitchen for a glass of water—all in the dark—and sat on the sofa gazing into the darkness outside the window/glass door onto our brownstone rooftop terrace. The morning was so still and dark that the only sound came from humming air-conditioners of neighboring buildings. As I drank my glass of water and pondered the darkness, I remembered a dinner party of the previous night at a restaurant on the upper east-side. A good friend whom I had not seen since before Covid, was celebrating her birthday with a party organized by her two young daughters and attended by eight friends including Harold and me. There were seven women and four men at the dinner party. We all sat at a long table, several of us in a restaurant for the first time since the start of the pandemic. My seat mate was a woman whom I've known from other celebratory occasions to which we had been invited by our birthday friend. In the course of our chit chat, we discussed what we had done during lockdown and quarantine and how our lives had changed during the entire year of 2020. I mentioned that I had written a manuscript for a new novel. My seat mate expressed some surprise and asked me the title. I replied "Aubergine and the Seven Sisters" to which she expressed curiosity. She wanted to know when it would be published and I explained my plan. As I recalled this mention of the title while I was sitting on the sofa drinking my glass of water, I thought—for the first time—that title reminded me of "Snow White and the Seven Dwarfs." Although my story had no relationship to the Grimm Fairy Tale or the Disney movie version of the story—indeed, I hadn't even considered "Snow White" while composing my manuscript—there was this unmistakable parallel between the titles. While musing over the titles and noticing the darkness slowly, imperceptibly abating, I thought of other titles built on the number seven—Akira Kurasawa's *The Seven Samurai* and John Sturges' USA knockoff, *The Magnificent Seven*. I even remembered *Seven Brides for Seven* Brothers. Morning was arriving. The birds had begun chirping. It was time to return to bed.

I did not consciously derive the title *Aubergine and the Seven Sisters* from any earlier source but, clearly "seven" had imbedded itself in my brain. As this story evolved, I was searching for a proper title to embrace a growing list of black women who became its principal protagonists. In addition and, perhaps, most importantly, I wanted a title that would also relate to the thinking and experience of the individual whom I intended to become the main character—Obra-Jean Moore (Aubergine Perry Curtis). Literally, in a flash of remembrance, I recalled a conversation decades ago with a dear friend and Detroit architect, Charles Merz. Charlie and I first met in the late 1960s as draftsmen in an architectural firm not unlike the fictional HR&K, Architects. As our friendship developed, we shared more and more of our histories, and Charlie, at some point, discussed a project he designed as a graduate student for a class at the Cranbrook Academy of Art. His wonderful project (for Professor Daniel Libeskind) was an ambitious and comprehensive urban plan for an entire neighborhood that included as its centerpiece the Detroit Edison Conner Creek Power Plant—known affectionately as The Seven Sisters. While I was preparing this manuscript, Charlie provided me an electronic version of his original thesis with drawings and documentation. His work was the inspiration for Aubergine's imagined design which is critical to Aubergine's story. At an earlier stage in writing, the name, The Seven Sisters, seemed right for the title of the story. However, I eventually realized I wanted to place Aubergine at the center of this story, and her name completed the book's title. For Charlie's gracious permission to use his brilliant creation and for details he provided of his schooling, I am deeply and forever indebted. Charlie, who revels in his German ancestry, is a true mensch.

Another architect who worked with Charlie and me at that HR&K-like firm was Ernst Reeh, a German émigré and dear friend, with whom for many hours over many years I discussed both art and architecture. Ernst was the project architect for the actual office building described as designed by Aubergine. He is also the inspiration for Obra-Jean's professor, Rainer Lotz. To date, Ernst's building is still standing in the neighborhood I called Russell Commons. Sadly, it may demolished for a new redevelopment project.

After completing the manuscript, I discovered an article by Kate Reggev ("That [Most] Exceptional One": Early Black Female Architects) that lists and discusses several black women architects. The lives and careers of these women underscore the enormous challenges actual black women faced in pursuing their talent and dreams. While Aubergine Curtis is a fictional character, real black women proved that the "impossible dream" is possible.

Made in the USA
Monee, IL
09 December 2021